The Philanthropist's Danse

A Novel

Paul Wornham

Edition: June 2012

Set in Georgia 10/11 Font

Book Design by Paul Wornham

Cover art by Judy Bullard www.customebookcovers.com

Acknowledgements

This book would not have been possible without the unwavering support of my wife Lesley, who never doubted for a moment that there was a book inside me, just waiting to be written.

My duo of beta-readers, Maureen and Terrie, offered good advice and caught many mistakes. Any remaining errors in the work belong to me, not them.

This is my first book, but it was the last one my father read. I'm glad he got to see it, even if it was only the rough first draft.

I think he enjoyed it, I hope you will too.

About the Author

Paul was born in England and raised in the picturesque city of Bath. He lived and worked across the South of England and in London.

He moved to Canada in 1996 and lives in Ontario with his wife Lesley.

The Philanthropist's Danse is Paul's first novel.

Visit Paul at www.paulwornham.com

Twitter: @paulwornham

Facebook: facebook.com/AuthorPaul

For Lesley

Chapter One

"It's time, sir. The first car is just a few minutes out."

William Bird nodded. "Thanks Jeremy. Are we ready?"

"Yes, we're ready. Their timing is fortunate indeed. Another hour of this snow and we'd be cut off until this storm is over." Both men had worried their careful preparations would be undone by upstate New York's unpredictable January weather.

Jeremy saw a flicker of light through the trees and pointed. "Here they come." A line of headlights appeared from the side road as a convoy of twelve luxury sedans made the final turn on to the long driveway. The cars slowed to a halt, and the drivers waited for directions from the valets.

Jeremy took his leave. "I'll go and supervise the arrival. Good luck, Mr. Bird, with everything."

As the last car was unloaded, Bird was relieved to see all twelve of his guests were accounted for. His abiding fear had been that one or more might change their mind about making the journey, but his employer's name was a powerful motivator. He need not have been concerned. Bird absently smoothed his graying hair, a habit his wife would recognize as a sign of nerves.

Jeremy, the great mansion's major-domo, stepped back into the room. "We're all set. Your guests are accounted for and are waiting in their suites. A few were quite distressed by the deception, of course, but they have been told to wait for your call. Will there be anything else for the time being, sir?"

"Not now Jeremy, let's give them a few minutes to settle." The major-domo tilted his head in acknowledgement and left, silently closing the door behind him.

William didn't need to give his guests time to settle, the delay was for his own state of mind. He was desperately tired after a frantic week of locating twelve people and organizing logistics around the globe to ensure each person's attendance on time tonight. Each guest had been promised a private meeting with his client, the famous philanthropist Johnston C. Thurwell. He could imagine their anger now they discovered the invitation was not as promised.

Bird checked his reflection in the window, brushed invisible creases from his tailored suit and made an unnecessary adjustment to his already perfect tie. Satisfied he at least looked ready, William stepped briskly into the lobby where Jeremy's efficient staff swept the entrance clean of detritus that had blown in with the guests.

The house felt different now others were here, and he was no longer the staff's sole charge. He looked up at the sweeping gallery and the long hallways that led to the guest suites. The people waiting up there would demand explanations from him, but would be far from happy when they got them.

There was no more time for organization, everything was as ready as it could be. Any further delay would only be procrastination. It was time for the *Danse* to begin. He reached for the telephone and issued the order to bring his guests to him.

* * *

Bird did not wait for more than a few minutes before Jeremy led the first person down, a short blond man in his late thirties dressed in an elegantly tailored suit and tie. Johnston Thurwell III, or Junior as he was more commonly known, strode into his father's conference room and looked around slowly before deigning to notice the lawyer.

"William, you better have a bloody good reason for bringing me here under false pretences." Junior's sneer was condescending, but Bird ignored his casual rudeness and forced a smile.

"Good Evening, Junior. I apologize for the deceit in your invitation, but I assure you that there is a good reason for it that I'll explain very soon." Bird gestured toward the large conference table. "Seating is assigned. You may take your place when you're ready."

Junior took a walk around the table, inspecting the place cards. "I know some of these names Bird, but what are they doing here?" There was an edge to Junior's voice, but the lawyer pretended not to hear it, there was no point antagonizing the philanthropist's mercurial son. Not yet.

"Junior, I'd prefer to explain just once, when everyone is present, so please, a little patience?"

Junior glowered. He was used to getting what he wanted immediately, but saw the logic in the lawyer's request and let it go. He'd find out soon enough what his father was up to. He took a position with his back to the vast fireplace and started rocking on his heels, forward and back, heel to toe. The lawyer watched with concealed amusement. Junior thought the rocking disguised his short stature, something he was sensitive of. No one had dared tell him that it didn't work.

* * *

William turned away and smiled broadly as Jeremy arrived with his next guest, a tall, graceful woman. Bethany Thurwell, the philanthropist's daughter, approached the lawyer with a soft smile. Her deep brown eyes were friendly and playful.

"William, it's been ages since I've seen you." She delivered deft air kisses near the lawyer's face. "But I do wish you had told me others were coming..." She shot a sharp glance at her brother and her voice took on a frosty tone. "Junior, I see you're here first, as usual."

Her brother sneered back. "Sister, it's so nice to see you too, darling."

Bethany grimaced and returned her attention to the lawyer as she combed an errant strand of dark blonde hair from her face. "So, what is all this about William? It's very mysterious for you to call me away from the City when you know Father has that simply enormous benefit next month. I'm a very busy girl, you know."

She looked directly into his eyes as she spoke, making him feel like he was the only person in her world at this moment. Bethany was hugely persuasive, but the lawyer was immune to her charm, having known her all her life. He tried to smile, but foreknowledge of his impending cruelty to her made the expression difficult.

"Bethany, my dear, I'll explain soon, take your seat if you'd like."

She smiled, defeated. She enjoyed teasing Bird but had learned to respect his stoic immunity to her devastating charm offensives. "Okay William, but it better be good." A smile danced on her lips as she walked gracefully to the table and performed a full circle to review the place cards, as her brother had done moments before. Choosing not to sit, she walked to the window and stared out into the night, apparently content to wait.

* * *

A shout alerted Bird to the philanthropist's youngest son's arrival. Philip Thurwell burst in to the conference room as he entered every room, with too much noise and motion. He was a good-looking man in his late twenties with long hair worn in a surfer style. He dressed like a poor art student, but his t-shirt was a designer brand and a Greenwich Village artisan had tailored his jeans.

He bounced past the lawyer with a dismissive wave and scurried to scoop his sister up in a hug. "Hi Sis!" Bethany pretended to be annoyed as he planted her back down, but was unable to disguise the amusement in her eyes as he pouted. "Miss me?"

She rolled her eyes, and her nose wrinkled in horror as she looked at her younger brother. "Philip, what are you wearing, exactly?" Bethany had quarreled with her brother about his fashion sense from the day she opened her first fashion magazine, but she had never won an argument over his apparel, not once.

Philip grinned and winked at her as he strode over to greet his scowling brother. "Junior, nice to see you're here too." He extended his hand, which was given a dutiful shake before being dropped, quickly. If Philip was upset with Junior, he didn't show it. Instead, he turned away and approached the lawyer with open arms and a fake grin. "If it isn't my old friend and nemesis Billy Bird, the turd."

He stopped a single step in front of the lawyer, deliberately invading Bird's personal space. "So, Bill. You dragged me up here on a false promise. Tell me why. How did I piss off the Old Man this time?"

The lawyer offered Philip a tired smile. "This isn't about you Phil, it's not another intervention. I promise. Find your seat and I'll explain soon."

Philip leaned forward, and his eyes became menacing slits as he opened his mouth to deliver some well-distilled bile, but Bethany called him off. "Philip, that's enough. William has promised to explain everything. I think it's all rather exciting, don't you? Now come here and tell me exactly where you've been."

Philip walked backward a few paces and maintained eye contact with the lawyer before he returned to his sister. The lawyer exhaled slowly. He had become afraid of Philip since the last time he was required to intervene in his life. Something had changed in him. A dangerous edge had appeared where a simple rebellious streak had once been.

William silently thanked Bethany for his reprieve when he caught movement in the corner of his eye and turned to meet his next guests. Jeremy delivered two people, a couple. Dennis and Janice Elliot entered the unfamiliar room nervously, but smiled when they recognized their employer's lawyer.

Janice immediately took charge. "Mr. Bird, sir, we've come as you instructed, but we haven't been given any duties and the staff have provided us with a guest suite."

Dennis waited for his wife to pause until he dared speak. "I haven't seen Mr. Thurwell yet and was wondering if he'll need me tonight, or will his man here see to him?" He trailed off as his wife gave him a sharp look before she turned back to Bird and encouraged him to answer her original question.

"Janice, you and Dennis are here as guests. The call for you to come and assist was a necessary deception, I'm afraid. There is no need to be concerned about duties as the mansion is fully staffed. You'll find places ready at the table, why don't you take your seats?"

The couple looked at each other. They were confused by the turn of events but walked to the table under the scrutiny of the three members of the Thurwell family. They were surprised to find they were not seated together, but after a whispered argument during which Janice repeatedly poked her husband in the chest, they took their seats at opposite ends of the table. They were self-conscious of the curious looks directed at them by their employer's family and kept their eyes downcast.

Bird caught a look from Junior who raised an eyebrow in unspoken question. The lawyer knew Junior was wondering why the hired help was seated at his father's conference table. It was a predictable reaction from Junior, but the lawyer put it out of his mind. He needed

Junior to be true to his nature tonight. In fact, he was counting on it.

* * *

Jeremy appeared again, this time escorting an elderly guest. She had traveled the farthest of all his guests and was utterly bemused by the whirlwind of events that had plucked her from an English farmhouse and dropped her into a luxurious mansion in America. Bird stepped forward and took the elderly woman's hand. "Mrs. Tremethick, I'm so pleased to meet you at last, ma'am. I hope your journey was comfortable?"

The old lady looked up, and her sharp blue eyes met his without flinching. "So you're Mr. Bird? Well let me tell you, I don't like this much at all, pulling me out of my own home with no proper explanation. Now where is this fellow that wants to meet me so badly?"

Her complaints were loud, and everyone watched the scene as the lawyer folded the woman's arm through his and walked her to a seat as he reassured her. The old lady grumbled but sat and greeted her neighbor, Janice Elliot. Janice smiled, but the smile never touched her eyes as she contemplated the old woman. Once Bird assured himself of the relative comfort of his aged guest, he returned to his place at the door.

* * *

A striking, petite young woman with a mass of thick black hair arrived on Jeremy's arm. She wore simple wool pants and a cashmere sweater, but she oozed feminine allure. She smoked a dark cigarette and a swirl of blue smoke framed her unblemished face and traced vaporous tendrils through her hair.

The young woman offered her hand. "Monsieur Bird, how nice it is to see you again." She spoke with a European accent that to Bethany's well-traveled ear sounded

Parisian French. The lawyer took the woman's offered hand and, conscious of the many eyes on them, shook it rather than delivering the kiss the newcomer had expected. She raised an eyebrow in a perfect arch and her black eyes smoldered with mischief as she exclaimed, too loudly. "So formal today, William? Pour quoi?"

He squirmed at her brazen goading, all too aware Bethany was watching. He gestured to the table at the center of the room. "Miss Jolivet, please be seated, we'll start in a few moments."

She noted his discomfort at her flirty entrance and turned slowly, making sure to deliver a good view of her shapely profile to the leering young man by the window. She walked to the table like a cat, fully aware that all eyes were on her. She circled the table slowly and ran a finger lightly along the back of each chair until she found her seat. She sat delicately and made deliberate eye contact with every person as she took a long drag of her cigarette.

"Do you have to smoke in here?" Everyone looked at Bethany as she issued the challenge. The newcomer's dark eyes rose to appraise Bethany as she mentally filed information about her challenger's clothes, nails and hair along with the million other details an attractive woman makes when she encounters a rival. She took another long drag on her cigarette and held it for a moment.

"Non, I do not have to smoke." She paused to take another drag, finishing her thought as she exhaled. "I choose to smoke." She leaned back in her chair with one arm draped over the back and watched Bethany for a reaction but was disappointed as Bethany was distracted by the next arrival.

A tall man with silver hair and a booming voice greeted the lawyer with a heavy clap on the shoulder as he called his greetings to the Thurwell family. Lawrence MacLean was familiar to the Thurwells as their father's oldest friend. Bethany instantly forgot the irritating French woman and embraced him warmly.

"Uncle Larry, I've missed you. I thought you were going to be in the Caribbean until March?" Bethany held MacLean's hand as Philip stepped forward to greet the old man with a smile and handshake. The three of them wandered back to the corner by the window, leaving the lawyer alone again.

William saw Junior frown at the warmth between his siblings and Larry MacLean. Recent history between the two men had been problematic, but Bird did not know why. He assumed Larry reached his limit of how much of Junior's attitude he could take. It happened routinely to people who knew Junior.

* * *

The lawyer turned to meet his next guest as Jeremy escorted her into the room. Caroline Smith extended her hand, which he took as he struggled to raise a genuine smile. She greeted him coldly, irritated by the lies he had told about her meeting. It gave her one more reason to despise William Bird.

Smith realized on the drive north from the City that her limousine had become one in a larger convoy, and had immediately become suspicious of what lay ahead. She had spent the rest of the journey imagining scenarios in preparation for whatever lay ahead. She, along with the others would soon be shocked by how little she knew.

She saw Junior standing alone, quickly assessed that he was the senior Thurwell in the room and took a position at his side. He was annoyed at having to share his commanding position at the fireplace, but she ignored his coolness. Smith was pleased that she had chosen to wear flat shoes. She would not have dared to stand next to Junior if she had appeared taller than him. He did not forgive such slights.

15

She studied the people in the room, paying particular attention to two unfamiliar faces, a ruddy-faced old lady and a dark beauty smoking a heavily scented cigarette. Strangers bothered Smith. They were unknowns, perhaps even threats. Her eyes flicked to the door as another guest arrived, yet another stranger. This time the doorway filled with the huge frame of a tall black man.

* * *

William Bird greeted Judge Ronald Freeman and tried not to show his feelings as they met face to face for the second time. The Judge stood six inches taller than Bird, and his voice filled the room with a deep, southern baritone. "Mr. Bird. I'm happy to see you under better circumstances, sir."

The lawyer regretted the Judge's lack of discretion but politely asked him to take his place at the table. Freeman agreed without fuss. He had an excited idea about the reason for his invitation to the famous philanthropist's home, though a cold finger of doubt nagged at him when he saw a room full of people who clearly had no idea who he was.

A hiss from Bethany made everyone look toward the door where William Bird greeted a short, neat woman. Freeman could tell she was familiar to the lawyer, they held hands long after the formality of their handshake. William chatted easily with Betty Freah as they exchanged pleasantries, but she was nervous. "Bill, this is awkward. I was never to be around JT's family."

The lawyer squeezed her hand and tried to reassure her. "You're here because he wants you here Betty, that's all I can say."

She looked skeptical, but released his hand and walked to the table, conscious of Bethany's unfriendly eyes. She found her seat and was relieved to discover she would be next to Dennis Elliot, a familiar face. She smiled warmly, but he flinched and looked away. Betty knew the reason for his reaction and nodded at Janice, who stared back with open hostility.

* * *

William waited for his final guest with increasing nervousness. The atmosphere in the conference room had become charged by Betty's appearance. Every woman that had loved or desired the philanthropist universally loathed Betty Freah. The last guest would have a similar effect on those who cared about Johnston Thurwell's business affairs.

Jeremy led a tall and obviously powerful man into the room. Bird greeted Freddie Hagood warmly but heard cries of surprise from the others. Junior and Caroline Smith exchanged words in a busy whisper as they saw who had arrived in their midst.

Freddie Hagood ignored the others and greeted the lawyer as if they were old golf partners. Hagood was Johnston Thurwell's greatest rival and controlled a personal fortune estimated to be near equal to the great philanthropist. "I don't know what Johnston's up to, but I see he's ruffled some feathers." Bird smiled at Hagood's pronunciation of feathers as 'fevvers'. Freddie had never lost the London accent of his childhood but wore it as a badge of honor of his humble beginnings.

Bird ushered Freddie into the room and walked him to the large table, seating the billionaire between Camille Jolivet and Bethany. The lawyer gave a nod to Jeremy to signal he was ready. The major-domo gave the lawyer a solemn smile as he left the room and closed the doors behind him.

Chapter Two

The guests moved to their seats, and Bird waited for them to settle. He reached for his prepared notes. He did not normally use reminders, but he had to cover specific points in this first meeting and did not want to forget anything. The *Danse* would begin with what he would say in the next moments, so he had prepared carefully and was grateful for his own foresight.

"Ladies and Gentlemen, welcome. Thank you for accepting my invitation and for your cooperation at the regrettable short notice." He took three measured breaths until he felt his rising anxiety subside. "Most of you know me, but for the others, my name is William Bird and I'm Mr. Johnston C. Thurwell's attorney. It is my duty to oversee the business that has brought you here, until its conclusion.

"Before I explain why you are here-"

Junior shot to his feet. "Goddamn it Bird! Get to the fucking point. Explain why you lied to get me here. I expected to meet my father privately and find instead that you've assembled a goddamned circus. My time is money, Bird, so enough bullshit. Tell me what the fuck is going on."

William raised his hand. "Please, Junior. Take your seat. I will explain, but first-"

"Do NOT interrupt me Bird, you goddamn shyster!" Junior's face turned from red to deep scarlet, a danger sign his siblings recognized. They readied themselves for the fury to be unleashed. "YOU take your orders from MY father. Now what the fuck is HE thinking, dragging ME up to his godforsaken country house? Where is he anyway, I demand to see-"

"Junior, shut the fuck up. Now."

William did not raise his voice, but the effect of his admonishment was as if he had physically slapped Junior, who stopped talking mid-sentence and stared at the lawyer, stunned. His mouth worked, but no sound came. The others stared in turn at Bird, then at Junior. Shock was registered on every face. William let the group absorb what had happened for another second and then continued. His voice was firm but calm.

"Junior, sit down and shut up. Or I will eject you from this meeting and you'll learn about what happened here in the newspapers."

Johnston Thurwell and his lawyer had realized early in planning the *Danse* that Junior could be a thorn in William's side if he was not controlled. The philanthropist had decided how to handle his eldest son and assured his lawyer that a sharp, public attack would send Junior an unmistakable message about who was in charge.

The lawyer had to admit that, despite his misgivings about confronting Junior, the Old Man had been right. Junior sank into his seat without a word, but his eyes were dangerous as he glared at Bird.

Bethany leaned forward, her pretty face had lost its pallor. "William, perhaps you had better continue... please." Her eyes were wide, and Bird could see she was forming an idea in the back of her mind too terrible to contemplate. She desperately needed to hear that she was wrong.

William did not answer her but made a point of returning Junior's stare until the furious son dropped his eyes, defeated. As soon as victory over Junior was assured, he continued immediately. "As I was saying, I must cover the formalities before we begin." The room was silent. He had achieved complete control over the group.

"Each of you was told you would be Mr. Thurwell's sole guest, so I understand you are unhappy to find this is not the case. However, you all agreed to identical conditions for your visit, and I must remind you of those conditions.

"First, you agreed to be here for up to one week but no less than two days. Second, you agreed to surrender your mobile phones, blackberries, laptops and other communications devices. There is to be no contact with the outside world. If you break this rule, you will be removed without discussion or appeal. Emergency communications are available through me, in the event they are needed.

"Third, you understand this meeting is extraordinary to the normal business of the Thurwell Foundation and Thurwell Industries, Inc.

Finally, I must clarify my role. I am operating under instructions that allow strictly limited discretion. You should understand that whatever occurs, I am bound foremost by oath and contract to my employer, Johnston C. Thurwell II."

* * *

Bird finished reading from his notes and looked at the faces staring back at him. Junior was still furious, but curiosity had overridden his anger for now. Camille Jolivet lit another cigarette and ignored her neighbor's disapproval of the smoke.

William looked at Bethany as she absently bit her knuckle. Her eyes were wide with growing fear. He hated what came next and had argued bitterly with his employer about this moment, but had failed to sway the Old Man's resolve. "Since you are all bound in this agreement, it's time to reveal the purpose of your invitation."

He took a deep breath and spoke the words that changed their lives forever. "Your task is to decide who among you is to inherit the late Johnston Thurwell's fortune."

* * *

Junior paled to a parchment color as he absorbed the news of his father's death. Bethany rocked in her chair, hugging herself and shaking her head. Tears streaked her cheeks as she realized she would never see or speak with her father again. Philip was uncertain what to do. His eyes darted between his brother and sister, but he sat frozen in his chair.

Larry MacLean held his head in his hands and ran his fingers through his silver hair. Only the elderly Mrs. Tremethick showed no reaction. William saw his guests trying to absorb the news, but his instructions allowed them no time to grieve. His client had insisted that he be merciless.

He raised his hand to signal for silence and was rewarded with immediate compliance, save for muted sobs. "Johnston Thurwell died one week ago, here in *Litore*, his country mansion. His death remains a secret that until now has been shared only by a few. There has been no announcement, and there will be none until your business is concluded.

"Mr. Thurwell had time to make arrangements before he died and this meeting is the culmination of his plan. In a moment, I'll leave you to your thoughts, but first you must understand what is expected of you tomorrow."

William checked to see everyone was paying attention as he dropped the hammer. "Mr. Thurwell's fortune is to be shared among the twelve of you. Your task is to determine who gets a share, if any, and how much.

"You begin tomorrow morning at 9.00 a.m. If you have not reached an agreement by midnight, the fortune will be reduced by twenty percent. The penalty will be repeated each midnight until you either reach an agreement or the entire fortune is transferred to the Thurwell Foundation. I will see you tomorrow, good night." He gathered up his notes and laptop and had left the room before his guests fully comprehended the implication of everything he had told them.

Chapter Three

Junior walked to the window and rocked on his heels as he stood with his back to the group with his fists balled tightly in his pockets. A casual observer might have seen that Junior trembled, but what the observer may not have guessed was that Junior Thurwell was furious, not grieving.

He was angry at William Bird for humiliating him. He was angry the family had learned of his father's passing in a room filled with strangers and servants. But what made Junior tremble with rage was his father's decision to force his own flesh and blood to compete for their rightful inheritance.

* * *

Larry MacLean was devastated by the loss of his closest friend. He wanted to know what extraordinary circumstances made his friend choose to die without saying a word of goodbye to his friends and family. MacLean could have understood if it were only he who had been excluded, but what the lawyer told them made no sense. He looked across the table and realized Bethany and her brothers had been informed of their father's death in the coldest imaginable manner.

MacLean could not reconcile the callous act with the man he had known since college. He knew Johnston was tough. A man needed a brutal edge to build an empire as vast as Thurwell had in one lifetime. Yet Johnston Thurwell had also been a dedicated family man, which made the rejection of his children jarring.

Larry tried to put himself in his friend's shoes to understand what might have made him leave his children out of his life at its end, but it was too hard for him to think as a person he'd never been. Thurwell loved family, whereas Larry had preferred to live free of permanent ties. He had never possessed the patience for the emotional debris families inevitably delivered into the lives of their founders.

He looked for his friend's family. Junior was alone at the window but appeared more controlled than when Bird had confronted him. Philip was comforting his sister, and the sight of Bethany's grief broke Larry's heart. The beautiful, accomplished daughter and her wayward brother were MacLean's particular favorites. He had enjoyed being their 'Uncle' from the day they had been introduced to him as warm, pink babies. He had been a part of their extended family as much as his travel and natural aversion to family ties allowed. He would offer his condolences, but first he wanted to greet the man whose presence confounded him. He wanted to speak to Freddie Hagood.

* * *

Hagood felt a hand on his shoulder and saw Larry MacLean. "Freddie, it's good to see you again, but what is going on? Why are you here? You and Johnston hated each other." Freddie shrugged, and the sumptuous silk of his jacket fell naturally into perfect folds, leaving his suit as unruffled by the gesture as he seemed unmoved by the news of his rivals death.

"I can't explain it, Larry, because I don't have a clue. I don't need Thurwell's money. I've got more than enough of my own. I can't profit from an early jump on the news of his death because I'm unable to call my people, which means I won't be able to take commercial advantage of the-" His face screwed into a frown as a thought crossed his mind and Larry knew what he had thought.

23

"I know what just occurred to you Freddie, but I think you're wrong. The news about Johnston will become public after we leave, if Bird is telling the truth. So there is no loss to you for being sequestered, right? The news will still be fresh to the outside world a week from now, so you'll still profit by it."

Hagood considered the truth of the statement and shrugged. "Then I can't explain it. I guess we'll have to figure out his reasons tomorrow." The two men chatted easily for a few minutes. There was no animosity between them because Larry was too relaxed to let his oldest friend's sour relationship with Hagood spoil his own enjoyment of a fellow wealthy maverick.

MacLean took his leave of Freddie to join Bethany and Philip. He sat next to Bethany and held her hand and whispered comforting words. Hagood watched until he saw a tear roll down Larry's tanned cheek and then looked around for someone to talk to. A tall black figure standing alone caught his attention, and Freddie moved to introduce himself.

* * *

Judge Freeman saw the media magnate's approach and extended his hand. "Mr. Hagood, I recognize you from the business networks. I'm Ron Freeman, US District Judge from Georgia. I'm pleased to meet you, though I could wish for happier circumstances."

Hagood had trouble getting his hand around Freeman's huge paw to shake it firmly. The billionaire was a tall man and unaccustomed to looking up at anyone, yet the Judge stood taller than he. "A judge? How interesting." Freddie was genuinely surprised. He had figured the large man was a retired football player. "How did you come to be invited to this gathering, Judge?"

Hagood saw a flicker of uncertainty on the Judge's face. "I'm not certain, to be honest. I had some occasion to be involved with Mr. Thurwell's Foundation. Perhaps that's it?" Freddie raised an eyebrow. "Judge, forgive my skepticism, but thousands of people are involved in one way or another with the Thurwell Foundation. I don't see any others invited to share in his fortune. Do you?"

Freeman looked to see if anyone paid attention to their conversation, and dropped his voice to a whisper. "Honestly, I don't know why I'm here. I'm as confused as you. I had suspected Mr. Thurwell invited me here to offer support for my Gubernatorial campaign."

Hagood's eyes widened as he remembered where he had heard of Ron Freeman before today. He had become a Judge at a staggering young age and had since made a name for himself as a gifted jurist. Freeman had been in the news for hearing the corruption investigation that resulted in the current Governor not seeking a second term.

"Well, Johnston's no longer in any position to offer you or anyone else any support. So I wonder. What are you really doing here?"

Freeman was uncomfortable under Hagood's scrutiny and had no desire to reveal his real connection to the philanthropist. He decided to escape. "Excuse me, I must offer my condolences to the family."

* * *

Camille Jolivet's emotions ran up and down like a roller coaster. She soared on elated hope one moment and plunged into desperate despair the next. Her future had seemed so bright until she discovered she was not the philanthropist's only guest. She looked at Bethany and watched with detached interest as the dead man's daughter sobbed on her brother's shoulder.

She was surprised by the American girl's lack of composure, but also remembered how protective her father had been of her. The man's fierce defense of Bethany was one of only two times she had been afraid of Johnston Thurwell. At his insistence, she had agreed never to communicate with Bethany. Yet now they were in the same room, and Thurwell had made it happen.

Her benefactor was dead, but she had understood the lawyer's words well enough. The people in this room would share the man's fortune. Camille stood to become richer than even she had dared dream. A smile crept unbidden onto her face, but she quickly realized what her expression might look like and quickly erased it. Her eyes darted around to see if anyone had seen her. She met the old woman's eyes and knew immediately she had been caught.

* * *

Mrs. Tremethick had seen the secret smile and the guilty look when the French girl tried to cover it. She wondered what was going on in the girl's mind that gave her reason to smile amid so much grief. Winnie Tremethick was confused because she'd been told she was in New York, yet it looked nothing like it did on her television shows. There were no towering buildings or busy streets outside the house, so she imagined they had lied when they told her where she was. She had no idea New York was an entire state, not just the famous metropolis.

She hadn't known whom to trust since she caught a couple of men peeking through her farmhouse windows a few weeks before. The next day she had seen them again, parked in the lane, taking pictures of her house. She had hurried to confront them, but they had driven away before she reached them. She had forgotten about the incident until a week later when a well-mannered gentleman from London arrived to explain that a wealthy American wanted to meet her, but was too ill to travel. He had offered her an all-expenses paid trip to New York for her to assuage the curiosity of a dying man.

Mrs. Tremethick had called her daughter in Scotland who had been instantly intrigued and encouraged her mother to accept the invitation. So she packed her only suitcase with a broken latch and was whisked across the Atlantic in a private airplane. Now Winnie sat alone and wondered how her trip had turned from visiting an ailing stranger into sharing in a fortune. The new turn of events worried her. Someone had made a terrible mistake, and she was afraid it might have been her.

Winnie caught a movement in the corner of her eye and looked at the woman next to her whose sharp features were focused on a man at the far end of the table. She was making gestures with her head, as if to summon him. "Excuse me miss, do you know that man?"

The woman looked at Winnie, surprised by the question. "That man is my husband, and he's too afraid to come over here and talk to his wife." She jerked her head again to summon the hapless fellow and Winnie watched indecision play on his face until he arrived at the realization he was likely to suffer more if he stayed put than if he moved. He reluctantly joined his angry spouse and stood shuffling from one foot to the other as he looked from the chair next to her to Junior who stood at the window.

"Sit down Dennis!" Dennis Elliot whispered something to his wife that Winnie could not hear, though she heard Janice's sharp reply. "If Junior wanted the seat, he'd be in it. Just sit down." With one more nervous glance toward Junior, Dennis sat next to his wife and they began whispering heatedly.

Winnie was unable to hear anything they said, and they paid her no more attention so she sat with her arms crossed and wondered what to do. She was exhausted and jetlagged after her first and only Atlantic crossing. She looked at the French girl and leaned over. "Are we supposed to stay here? I don't know what to do."

The French woman shrugged and reached for her Gauloise cigarettes. She felt a little sympathy for the old woman, who looked completely out of place. "I think you can leave, if you want."

The idea of a soft bed was attractive, and Winnie stood to leave. The whispering couple looked up at her and then away. They were talking about her. They were probably talking about everyone in the room. *I might too, if I knew anyone to gossip with*, she thought.

Winnie ached from too much sitting. She needed a walk to get some fresh air, but the falling snow outside was a problem, she had brought no suitable shoes. She walked to the door, but it was opened before she reached it and the man who had escorted Winnie earlier entered the room at a brisk pace. His attentive eyes scanned the room as he assessed the situation.

* * *

Everyone looked at Jeremy, and their conversations died. The major-domo spoke in a voice that carried throughout the large room. "Ladies and gentlemen, we have a selection of hot and cold food for you. The dining room and library are available, or you may dine in your suite. Please let me know your wishes, and I will see to them immediately."

The guests looked at each other and tried to decide if it would be acceptable to eat after receiving such tragic news. Some had no appetite at all and could barely tolerate the idea of food. Jeremy gently took Mrs. Tremethick's arm.

"Would you like something to eat ma'am?" Winnie shook her head and said she wanted to go to her suite. Jeremy signaled a waiting staffer who instantly took his place at her side. "This gentleman will escort you to your suite." The major-domo looked at his man. "See that Mrs. Tremethick has everything she needs."

She smiled gratefully and leaned on the strong arm as she was led to her room, away from the strangers and the confusion of the long hours since she had left England.

Chapter Four

Three men strode from the conference room into the dining room, where Jeremy found them after seeing to his other guests. Junior Thurwell, Larry MacLean and Freddie Hagood were arguing when the major-domo entered the room. Junior's voice was raised. "Larry, this is insane. You knew my father, why would he do this? To cut me out of a proper will is bad enough, but he did it to Phil and Beth too. And she was his fucking favorite."

Larry muttered a response, but Junior was in no mood to be interrupted. "As for you, Freddie, what the fuck are you doing here? Dad hated you, and you returned the sentiment. It's no secret the two of you would do anything to best the other, yet here you are, among the chosen few who'll share his wealth. It's bullshit. Whatever killed him must have taken his wits first."

"Junior, your father was my oldest friend, if you talk about him that way, I'll put you on your ass."

Larry's voice was thick with anger and grief as he growled at Junior, and the younger man became quiet. Jeremy took advantage of the awkward silence and stepped into view.

Junior flared at the servant. "What do you want?"

"Would the gentlemen care for some refreshments?" Jeremy kept his tone neutral, though he was faintly amused by Junior's overdone outrage.

MacLean and Hagood ordered scotch and sandwiches, but Junior waved the major-domo away and refused to continue his conversation until Jeremy had left. As soon as the servant had departed, he approached MacLean with his eyes full of dark rage. "Don't think you can talk to me like that, Larry, ever. My father might have tolerated your ignorance, but I won't."

He glared at MacLean and raised himself as tall as his stacked heels allowed, but Larry snorted. "Junior, you're full of shit. You're the biggest disappointment my poor friend ever suffered in his life. Don't threaten me, son. You're not man enough to back it up."

Junior flushed deep scarlet and stared at MacLean for a long second before he turned and left the room with the rebuke ringing in his ears. He walked fast, looking neither right nor left until he reached his suite and slammed the door shut. He didn't stop moving until he had circled the suite several times and felt his rage begin to ebb. His eyes were hot and wet. He hated that they welled with tears when he was enraged, it made him look weak.

Junior clawed off his expensive silk tie and poured a large slug of vodka into a glass with one hand as the other unsnapped his collar. He took an aggressive gulp and felt the satisfying burn of the liquor travel through his body. It warmed his body to his toes, but did not touch the cold heart that beat inside his chest.

Junior felt his calm return as a pleasant thought came to him. *I'm not Junior anymore. The Old Man is gone. I'm head of the family now. I'll get what's mine, and Larry MacLean can go to hell.* Junior looked at his reflection and tilted his head back. He believed that he looked taller in the pose. He would use the pose tomorrow. His self-confidence returned as he realized he would no longer have to live in his father's shadow. A cold smile appeared on his face. Junior Thurwell hummed a happy tune, and danced slowly around the room in celebration of his father's death.

* * *

Larry and Freddie sat in contemplative silence. The only acknowledgement of Junior's sudden departure had been Freddie's raised eyebrow. They faced each other in a couple of overstuffed wing chairs, neither willing to break the silence.

Jeremy returned with drinks and sandwiches and broke the mood. They exchanged small talk as they loaded their plates with food and enjoyed their host's choice whisky. Eventually Freddie looked at MacLean and asked the question that vexed him. "What was Thurwell thinking that made him do this to his family? Why make them compete for his money? I can't figure it out."

Larry understood Hagood's bewilderment. "I don't know. It's not what I'd have expected of Johnston." His voice cracked as he mentioned his friend's name. He was hurt that Thurwell had chosen to die alone. "I could have been here, if he'd just said something. You know, at the end. It's bad enough for me, but Bethany? How must she feel?"

MacLean felt old, his friend was gone and yet here he was in the library drinking with Johnston's arch-rival. Nothing made sense. Larry even felt some small sympathy for Junior. He had never warmed to the oldest son as much as he had to Bethany and her younger brother. He suddenly regretted his angry words with Junior and resolved to apologize when he next saw him.

Freddie Hagood was in a state of shock himself. He was well-used to meeting his rival at the mansion, though few people knew about their bi-annual rendezvous. In the City, they traveled in the same social circles and were both generous donors to charitable causes. Their well-publicized and bitter rivalry had appeared to the world as a blood sport, but, in fact, there was much that united the two magnates.

When William Bird had called last November to delay their scheduled year-end meeting, Freddie had thought nothing of it. When Bird called with the new invitation a week ago, Hagood assumed it was for the delayed meeting except Thurwell wanted up to a week of his time rather than the usual two days. Freddie had not expected to see a crowd when he arrived at the mansion and, like the others, had no idea his foremost rival was dead.

Something else, something personal, bothered Hagood and there was only one person he could discuss it with, Thurwell's lawyer. Hagood would have to wait until he could get William Bird alone before he could find out how much danger he was in.

He looked at MacLean, who was deep in his own thoughts, and they exchanged glances. Hagood wondered if Larry had anything to fear from the tragic turn of events as he did, or was he simply grieving the unexpected loss of his beloved friend?

* * *

The conference room hummed with low conversation, but no one spoke at normal volume. It seemed appropriate to use hushed voices in the shadow of the dark news.

Caroline Smith had been transfixed since William Bird delivered the news that her boss was dead. By the time she realized what the news meant, Bird had left and most of the others were scattered throughout the mansion. Smith cursed, and looked for Junior, she should offer her condolences. He was likely to ascend to rule his father's empire, and become her new boss. She saw him leave with two men, one of whom she recognized as Freddie Hagood. She calculated it would appear unseemly to chase after them. She'd have to wait and find Junior later.

Smith turned to an attractive older woman to her right who was dabbing her eyes with a tissue. They exchanged greetings, and Caroline tried to remember where she had heard the name Betty Freah before. She recalled Bethany's loud disapproval at Betty's appearance and her mind clicked facts and memories into place one by one until she found her answer.

Betty Freah had been the Old Man's lover. Thurwell had not married a third time, he figured that two failed marriages were plenty enough emotional and financial pain for one man to endure. He was aware that his fortune was more attractive to women than he was, so Smith assumed he made an arrangement with Betty where she could never expect marriage.

Smith introduced herself, putting the usual emphasis on her title, Chief Executive Officer of the Thurwell Foundation. She never used the CEO abbreviation. She enjoyed the sound of her full title and the power it conveyed. She was taken aback when Betty Freah said simply. "I know who you are."

Thoughts whirled through Smith's mind. What did this woman know? Had Thurwell mentioned her in private moments? Had he been positive or negative? Smith had no way of knowing what the other woman knew about her from the expressionless face in front of her. Not knowing bothered Caroline Smith more than she cared to admit.

* * *

Betty Freah felt as if something had broken inside her when she heard William announce JT was gone. She had arrived at the mansion looking forward to some time with him but now she felt guilty about her selfishness. JT had promised he'd take care of her. He'd paid her handsomely for her services, and given her many expensive gifts over the past ten years.

William Bird had said that she and the others stood to gain a share in JT's fortune, so he had kept his promise to take care of her. She regretted not having an opportunity to say goodbye, she had known him for more years than she had known any man. She had grown fond of her most loyal customer and the cruelty of his passing without a word to her stung. She had been comforting herself with private memories when Caroline Smith interrupted.

Thurwell had related stories to Betty about the crushingly ambitious Caroline Smith. He had not cared for Smith's naked ambition, but he had appreciated her willingness to do whatever was necessary to run his Foundation. Betty had no use for women like Smith who never hesitated to judge her, so she made excuses and left.

Smith was not surprised when Freah took her leave, but she was wrong about the reason. In her own mind, Caroline Smith was simply too accomplished for other women to accept, they always felt threatened by her. She supposed that was why she got along better with men than women. They judged her on her abilities. In truth, if she had been able to read the minds of the men she credited with admiring her, she'd have been sorely disappointed.

Caroline saw Bethany and Philip in mutual consolation at one end of the table and the Elliots in a whispered conversation at the other. Smith didn't like either option for company and instead walked to the window to see who would approach her first. Ten minutes later, she realized an uncomfortable truth and retired to her suite, angry at the ingrates who snubbed her.

* * *

Camille Jolivet watched Caroline leave. She had apparently been waiting for someone, yet no one had joined her. She was angry, but angry at whom? Camille filed the information away, even the smallest tidbit about a rival could prove useful at the right time. She considered another Gauloise, but decided instead to interrupt the odd couple opposite her. She smoothed her expensive clothes over her figure and noticed Philip take an interested peek. She smiled and moved over to the couple, exaggerating her walk to sway her shapely hips.

Janice Elliot ended her verbal assault on her husband as she saw the French woman approach them. "Not a word out of you, not one word. Until we know more, I don't want to hear a goddamn peep, you understand?"

She turned away from her husband to greet the French girl, her tight expression breaking into a thin, unconvincing smile. "Hello. I'm Janice Elliot, Mr. Thurwell's housekeeper from his Manhattan home."

Camille sat next to Janice, noting that she made no attempt to bring the man into the conversation. They're married, she realized. They had to be married. There was no mistaking the routine dismissal of her husband. Camille wondered why some men accepted being subjugated by their spouses, but since she despised weak men, she thought little of it as she introduced herself to Janice.

"How did you know Mr. Thurwell, Camille?" Janice was eager to discover why this foreign woman was included in the group. She was disappointed when Camille refused to say, even when pressed.

"I cannot say how I knew Monsieur Thurwell." Camille refused to be drawn by questions, and while Janice knew the French girl was hiding everything about her relationship with Thurwell, she had no solution to Camille's dogged refusal to answer. She changed the topic to discuss the other people in the room, a tactic designed to find out whom the girl may know or might admit to knowing. Her scheme was thwarted as it became clear that, with the sole exception of William Bird, Camille Jolivet had no prior acquaintances in the mansion.

Camille enjoyed the thrust and parry of the conversation. She sensed Janice's curiosity and it pleased her to frustrate it. William Bird had always insisted she remain tight lipped about her real relationship with the philanthropist. Eventually, Camille grew tired of the questions and asked Janice a question of her own. "Do you know the quiet gentlemen beside you?"

Janice flushed. She had totally forgotten Dennis and hurriedly introduced him. "This is my husband, Dennis. He's Mr. Thurwell's manservant in the city." He offered a hand as they greeted each other. Camille had briefly considered flirting with Dennis to annoy Janice, but his clammy hand made her shudder and turned her off the idea.

The two women engaged in a subtle conversational duel as they tried to figure each other out. Dennis was included in the conversation just frequently enough that he was forced to pay attention, but he preferred to drift into a comfortable numbness where he could contemplate his bleak future.

Dennis Elliot had not heard anything after the lawyer announced Mr. Thurwell had died. He was in shock. He had not understood what was to happen tomorrow, all he knew was that his boss was dead, and he was out of work. Right before the annual bonus was to be paid.

Dennis had been counting on his bonus, because he'd already spent it. Now he worried there may not even be a next paycheck and the thought terrified him. It would be much later in the evening before he learned from his wife that they would share in the Old Man's wealth. For now, Dennis moped as he listened to his wife talk nonsense with a pretty French girl.

* * *

William locked away his laptop in the office safe. He had nothing else to do until morning. His guests would be dealing with the news of Thurwell's death and the opportunity it presented them. He regretted that more guests would be interested in how much the Old Man had been worth than would grieve for his employer.

The lawyer could relax until the next session, or try to. While he felt some relief at having broken the news of the Old Man's passing, it was overshadowed by the daunting task of steering the group through the *Danse* as they decided how to carve up the fortune. He feared the outcome would be messy and unpleasant. By the time it was over, William would be shocked at how optimistic even this gloomy prediction had been.

He checked everything was secure and switched off his lights. He would get an early night. If the others were wise, they would do the same. Tomorrow promised to be a long day.

Chapter Five

The sun rose at 6.18 a.m., but the dawn sun could only lighten the sky to a pale gray to distinguish the transition from night to day. The mansion's windows looked out on heavy snow that had not abated all night. All the guests were awake. A few had slept well and some only a little. One had not slept at all.

Bethany hugged herself as she stood by her open window with a light shawl draped over her slender shoulders. She shivered as she stared out into the woods and relentless thoughts of her father spun through her mind. She had been at the window a long time, and her bare toes were bone white and bloodless, but Bethany felt nothing. She had been numb inside and out since William Bird announced her father's death. Philip had brought her up to her room around midnight. He offered to stay with her, but she wanted to be alone, so he had left in search of someone to share a drink with.

Bethany felt no eagerness to see the strangers gathered like vultures over her father's body, she had no stomach for it. She wanted to curl up in a ball and cry the pain away, to allow painful catharsis to envelop her. She recalled William's instructions about today and knew instead that she had to move and get ready for the day.

She had opened the window to let the chill morning air snap her out of her grief, but it had not moved her. Instead, she recalled a happy moment when her father took a twelve-year old Bethany skating on the frozen lake. Both of them had laughed like children as they enjoyed sharp cold on their cheeks and the sound of the ice under their skates.

That morning her father took a break to watch her skate and moved to the tree line on the shore. She had not noticed his absence at first, caught up in the pleasure of the moment. When she looked up and found him gone, she had panicked, fearing the ice had cracked, and he had gone under. He saw her panic and stepped forward, calling her name. She had berated him all the way back to the mansion for leaving her alone on the ice and giving her a scare.

Now, years later, her tears flowed as she recalled making him promise never to leave her again. He had broken his promise and this time he had left her forever. In his place was an open wound in her soul because he hadn't wanted her with him at the end.

A flicker of anger sparked in Bethany, she felt the heat of it in her frozen breast. He had rejected her and left her to discover his passing in a hurtful, humiliating and public manner. She loved her father deeply, but he could be a monstrous prick at times. Her anger grew at his rejection, and her hurt welled up. She snapped into focus, suddenly aware of the freezing cold in her room. She reached to close the window but felt hot gorge rise in her throat, and she leaned out quickly. Hot bile burned her throat as she voided herself into the fresh white morning.

* * *

Camille Jolivet woke from a deep sleep when the telephone rang at six a.m. She had requested a wake-up call from Jeremy, and it was his voice she heard on the telephone now. She smiled as she replaced the receiver. It had been a long time since the man she'd spoken to last thing at night was the same man to greet her the next morning. She remembered that she liked it.

Camille reached for her cigarettes and lighter from the nightstand, propped herself up on her plush pillows and lit the first cigarette of the day, drawing deeply with her eyes closed, savoring the rush as the nicotine worked its magic. She exhaled joyously and lay in her bed, truly happy.

She reviewed the events of the night before. Her first face-to-face meeting with her secret half-sister, the shock that her father was dead, and the realization she would be rich. Wealthy. Loaded. *Riche*. She rolled the words around in her mind, savoring them as she savored her cigarette.

Camille felt no grief at her father's death. She had barely known him and had never felt the lack of a father figure in her life. She had crossed the Atlantic Ocean because she wanted the man's money, not his love. She had suffered in life, but no one needed to know about her past. It was better they didn't. All they needed to see was the elegant French girl grieving for her father even as she staked her claim to his money.

She would soon have everything she had ever wanted. She could endure a few more days of faking a daughter's love, and after it was done she would be free forever. Camille listed the places she'd travel and the clothes she would buy and the jewels she desired. She stubbed her cigarette out in a heavy crystal ashtray on the nightstand, swung her legs out of bed and enjoyed the feel of the thick carpet between her toes as she padded to the shower, humming a happy tune.

* * *

Winnie Tremethick had not slept well. She had woken at 2am and been unable to return to sleep. Her routine at home was to wake for chores at seven, and her old body refused to accept the notion she was anywhere other than in Cornwall. She lay in bed for long hours until the dark sky turned lighter, signaling dawn's arrival.

She wanted a hot drink, but the idea of calling someone else to bring her a pot of tea seemed scandalous, so she went without. She drew a bath and picked out her best dress while it filled. The lawyer, Mr. Bird, had made it clear that today was important, and she wanted to dress appropriately. She picked out her favorite brooch, a gold oak leaf, and laid it on the bed next to her clothes before returning to the sparkling marble and gold bathtub.

Winnie was confused about why she was in America. The lawyer had asked her how she had known the famous philanthropist, but she had not been able to answer. She hadn't known Thurwell. She had never met an American in her life. Not many would have reason to visit her village and Winnie had never traveled. Her answer had clearly troubled Mr. Bird and she was sorry for causing him concern, he seemed like a nice fellow. She had promised to think on it overnight, and though she had been doing little else for the past five hours, no answers came.

She lay in the hot water, and the warmth eased her joints and gave some little relief to her arthritic fingers. She closed her eyes and wondered where and when she might have met a rich American that wanted her to share his fortune. As she pondered the stubborn question, she drifted back to sleep.

* * *

Caroline Smith was showered and dressed in a smart business suit at 6.10am. She stood in front of the mirror as she applied her make-up, practicing a sad expression she could use when she met Junior and his siblings. She added some darker shades under her eyes to make it look like she had not slept well, though the truth was she had slept soundly despite her growing excitement at how large her share of Thurwell's money might be.

She teased her hair one last time and stood straight, turning a quarter turn to the left to admire her tailored suit. She looked just right, businesslike and professional but with an air of mourning about her, attractive but not glamorous. Smith stepped out of the room, closed her door quietly and stood still for a moment.

A few soft coughs, water running and a flushing toilet were the noises of morning she heard. The mansion, for all its luxury, was like any hotel. She walked toward the grand staircase, looking forward to a healthy breakfast. Only at the last moment did she remember to suppress the spring in her step.

* * *

Dennis Elliot looked outside and watched the snow. Janice was still sleeping, but he had been awake for over an hour. He knew he should wake her, but figured a few more moments of peace wouldn't hurt, so he sat on the window ledge with his head against the cool glass and stared into the storm. He drew meaningless shapes with his fingertip in the fog his breath made on the glass. He was sad that Mr. Thurwell was dead. He had known the Old Man for a long time. He had been a good boss. He was more than relieved to know he and Janice would share some money.

Mr. Thurwell had always promised he'd take care of Dennis, and he had kept that promise, though the manservant was surprised to be included with the family. His wife stirred in the bed, and he sighed. She'd soon be telling him what to do, what to say and what to think. Jeremy had offered them separate rooms, but Janice had insisted they occupy only one, much to Dennis's annoyance. *She won't let me out of her sight for one Goddamn minute,* he thought.

There had been no love in their marriage for a long time. After the wedding, Janice had quickly taken control of Dennis and never eased her grip. She had killed what small independence he had possessed with the sole exception of his Tuesdays off. He had begged Mr. Thurwell not to give his servants a common day off, which had been granted with some disapproval from the Old Man and great rancor by Janice. However, it gave Dennis one whole day to himself and Tuesdays became the only respite he could look forward to.

He had taken to spending his day off at the track in the summer, or the OTB in the winter, betting on any tracks that offered a card. The habit had cost him most of his savings, but his problem in recent weeks had been increased pressure to pay off his bookie. Dennis owed an unforgiving man too much money and was uncertain what to do because his diminished savings didn't cover what he owed. It was convenient timing to come into money. Not that he meant Mr. Thurwell any ill will, but his death was well timed to solve Dennis' troubles.

He looked up and saw his wife's accusing eye appraising him from across the room. Her mouth opened for the day's first volley of invective. *Perhaps I can even afford a divorce,* he thought, as he stood and offered his wife a thin, beaten smile.

* * *

Philip Thurwell jumped out of bed and began restlessly pacing his room. He hated being cooped up inside the mansion. At 6.30, he climbed into a pair of shorts and a t-shirt and jogged to the gymnasium, one floor below. He was surprised to find the gym occupied. Larry MacLean pounded the rolling road, the sheen of sweat on his body suggested he had been running for a while. Philip nodded a greeting to his 'uncle' but said nothing. He liked his father's friend well enough, but they had exchanged some angry words at their last meeting and Philip was still sore about it.

Larry nodded his own greeting and maintained the easy pace of an experienced runner. It was his habit to run every morning, although he preferred actual roads to indoor machines. The weather made running outside impossible, so he closed his mind to the suffocating walls and drifted into his routine, concerned only with the rhythm of his strides and the evenness of his breathing.

Philip watched MacLean run. He had excellent form for an old guy. Larry kept in shape because it helped him keep up with the younger women he loved to love. Thurwell's youngest son grabbed a towel from the corner rack and began stretching. His back was to MacLean, but he was able to watch him reflected in the mirror that covered an entire wall of the gym. Philip ran through his warm-up, hopped on the bike and accelerated to a comfortable speed. He and MacLean faced each other as they exercised.

"Why'd he do it, Larry? Why die alone and not call us?" It was the question that bothered Philip most. He couldn't imagine his father not wanting his family around him when he was dying. It was out of character. Philip might have understood if his father had only called Bethany and left his sons out, but he hadn't even called for her.

"Son, the same question bothers me. I knew your father all his life, and for him to die without a word just seems wrong."

Philip nodded, wrong was the right word. It was all wrong. "This meeting, getting us all here at the mansion, does that seem normal to you? I don't know half the people we saw last night." Philip's legs pumped as the bike's program simulated a hill and he started to sweat.

MacLean looked at Philip with sympathy. The boy reminded him of himself in younger, wilder days. "Philip, I wish I had answers for you. But face it, we're in the dark here, only Bill Bird has the answers, and I'm not sure even he has all of them."

He saw a shadow cross Philip's face at the mention of Bird. Philip was silent as he rode the bike hard, and sweat rolled freely down his face. Larry looked more closely and saw there was more than just sweat on Philip's face. He was crying with his eyes clamped tight shut.

MacLean slowed his run to a walk and wiped his face with a towel. He stepped off the machine and drew an icy drink from the water cooler. He walked to the bike and put his hand on Philip's back. "It's alright, I understand."

"Fuck you Larry, it's not alright. It's not even close to being alright, and you know it." Larry stood next to Philip as the young man slowed his pace and racking sobs escaped him. He crumpled, and his forehead rested on the handlebars as his shoulders shook. "Be a sport and fuck off Larry. I'd like to think you weren't seeing this."

MacLean patted Philip on the back and left, he understood the anger in the boy was not meant for him, but his dead father. Larry looked back, Philip was still slumped on the bike but the thick glass suppressed the heart-rending sound of his sobs. MacLean headed upstairs and almost bumped into a large black figure coming down. They stopped, each surprised by the other.

"Good Morning, Mr.?"

"MacLean, Larry MacLean. You're the Judge, if I recall correctly?" The two men shook hands. "You were headed for the gym, Judge?"

"Yes, I like to keep my routine if I can. I thought it was this way?" Larry didn't like the idea of Philip being discovered in his grief. "Yeah, it is, but it'd be better if you skipped this morning." Larry put his hand on the large man's shoulder conspiratorially. "One of Mr. Thurwell's sons is in there, and he needs some... time." He looked into the Judge's eyes and tried to convey his meaning but needn't have worried, the man caught his intent.

"I guess I can skip this morning, maybe eat one fewer pieces of toast at breakfast." He smiled and turned to head up the stairs with Larry, who was grateful for the Judge's gentlemanly acceptance of his request. "So, Larry, how did you know Mr. Thurwell?"

MacLean stopped in his tracks. Philip was right, there were some strangers at the mansion, and the Judge was one of them. He sighed and felt the loss of his friend as he answered. "Johnston and I were college buddies and he was the best friend a man could have wished for." He looked at his shoes as he spoke, then up at the face of his companion, who reached down and placed a massive hand on MacLean's shoulder.

"Then I am sorry for your loss Larry, truly sorry." Larry nodded, the Judge seemed sincere, and there was richness to his voice he found comforting.

"How about you, Ron, how did you know Johnston?" The Judge paused and Larry though he saw a flicker of annoyance, or embarrassment.

"I had business with Mr. Thurwell in Georgia." His deep baritone contained a quaver Larry had not noticed before. He waited for the rest of the story, but none came.

"That's it? You did a little business with Johnston, but you get to share his fortune? Hell, half the country did business with him, and they're not here." Larry's voice had an edge to it, he was irritated. Who the hell does this guy think he's holding out on, damned 'business in Georgia.' What the hell does that mean?

The Judge looked at Larry and shook his head. "I don't know what else I can say, I'm sorry. I think we had better not say anything else until the meeting starts. There might be some ground rules about what we can say, or not." It was a weak excuse, and Freeman knew it.

Larry was angry, he thought the other man was stalling, but there might be something in what he'd said, so he let it go. "Maybe. I guess I'll take a shower and see you later."

The two men walked in uncomfortable silence until the Judge reached his room and disappeared. MacLean arrived at his own room and closed the door too hard. The slam broke his angry funk. It was time to get ready, so he started the shower and stepped into the stream of water, cursing as it scalded his back. He adjusted the temperature and angrily scrubbed himself. *We'll all need answers soon,* he thought, *or this meeting is going nowhere.*

* * *

William entered the dining room precisely at 7.45am dressed immaculately in a dark suit with a subtle pin stripe. He wore a fresh white shirt but his cufflinks were the same as yesterday, they were the lucky set his wife had bought him the first day he addressed a jury as a young lawyer.

He felt rested even though he had woken at 4.30 with nerves jangling and his stomach a mess of flutters. He had control of his emotions now as he looked around and saw Caroline Smith reading the New York Times.

He took a warm plate from the rack and nodded a good morning to Jeremy who stood to the side of the long buffet table. He assembled a breakfast of scrambled eggs and toast, hash browns and a small dish of fresh fruit and carried it to Smith's table. "Good morning, Caroline. I hope you were able to rest?"

Smith looked up from her paper, the only evidence she had already eaten were a few crumbs on the table, but she had a fresh coffee in her hand. "William, good morning. I guess I got some sleep, but not much. It's all so, well, sudden. For the rest of us." She made certain William caught the slight that he was not considered one of the mourners. He took a seat opposite her, and she returned to her newspaper, leaving him to eat without her company.

As Bird began his eggs, Betty Freah entered the dining room. She looked unsure what to do, but the attentive Jeremy expertly guided her to the buffet. He plated a meal for her and led her to sit with the others.

Caroline had remembered everything about Betty in her room last night. She recalled Bethany's reaction when Betty first appeared and realized the rumors that Thurwell kept a hooker on the payroll were true. She smiled but returned to her coffee and newspaper to let the whore and the lawyer chat. She hoped to curry favor with Bethany by attacking Betty, but would save her outrage for a larger audience when it would do her more good.

As more guests arrived, the dining room filled with the soft murmur of conversation and the clinks of heavy cutlery on fine china. The guests had spread out over the available tables. Philip and Junior sat together but had nothing to say to each other while Larry MacLean and Freddie Hagood enjoyed a quiet conversation across the room.

Only Bethany was absent when William walked to the center of the room. "Good morning, we'll start promptly at nine in the conference room, I'll see you shortly." He left to collect his laptop. He was ready, even if his guests looked far from it.

Chapter Six

William Bird entered the conference room and was surprised to see Bethany already waiting. *She looks like hell*, he thought, as he set up his workspace. His laptop stayed closed, it was only needed to record the group's votes. Everything else was on note cards or committed to memory.

Once he was ready, he looked at Bethany who looked back through red-rimmed eyes. "How are you, Beth?" She said nothing. Her eyes left his and returned to contemplate the table in front of her. "Do you want me to get you a coffee, or something to eat?" She made no indication of having heard him, so he let it go.

He walked to the window and waited for the others. Over three feet of snow had fallen overnight, but the groundskeepers had cleared the drive for the delivery truck that brought the day's fresh supplies, mail and newspapers. The drive was already covered again, the storm was relentless. It was going to be a long day for everyone, whether they were in the conference room or working at keeping its occupants comfortable.

He heard others arrive and noticed how their conversations dried up when they saw Bethany. Camille Jolivet saw her half-sister's disheveled grief with a wicked satisfaction. The guests found their places without needing nameplates to guide them, they all remembered their places. Jeremy's staff brought fresh coffee and stoked the fire, adding a couple of huge logs that would take hours to burn.

William stood behind his chair, his hands on the high back and waited for the group to settle. "Good Morning and thank you for being on time," he realized he sounded formal but continued, hoping the occasion might benefit from a little formality. "Let me recap the purpose of this meeting so there can be no misunderstanding your purpose."

No-one interrupted him today, even Junior just listened. "Mr. Thurwell has chosen you to share his fortune. There is no Will other than his instructions for the week. The decisions you make will be respected as Mr. Thurwell's last wishes." He paused and looked at Junior and Philip. "In the event of any legal contest to these arrangements, all disbursements will be voided, and the entire fortune will be seized and donated to the Thurwell Foundation."

Junior's eyes flashed in anger. William could tell the thought of contesting the process had already occurred to the eldest son. He scowled at the lawyer but said nothing. Bird was a pawn, his father had set up this humiliation, but for what purpose Junior had no idea.

Bird continued, relieved that Junior held his tongue. "As I told you last night, you have little time to complete your task. At midnight tonight, the fortune will be reduced by twenty percent. That penalty will be repeated each midnight until you reach a decision or there is no fortune left for you to share. The money you forfeit goes to the Thurwell Foundation."

He looked around the table where the guests exchanged glances that might have carried meaning, or not. "My role is to ensure Mr. Thurwell's last instructions are respected and to record the decisions you make. I can make no recommendations, nor can I change the terms of this gathering. If you successfully agree a person's share, that person may be excused from further deliberations but must remain at the mansion until all business is concluded. If you prefer to take no part in the discussions, you are free to do so but will forfeit your share and have no right of return."

"All decisions must be decided by a vote. Anyone may propose a motion, but it must be seconded. Votes will be cast orally, there are no secret ballots. Every vote requires a super-majority of no less than seventy-five percent. I will record your votes and will guide you on their validity. There is no limit on the time you have for debate, but the stroke of midnight will trigger the penalty, whether or not you are in session."

He paused while the few that were writing notes caught up. "Are there any questions?"

There was a pause while the group absorbed the information, before Freddie Hagood broke the silence. "William, what's to stop us from voting for a simple twelve-way split?"

Bird opened his mouth to answer, but Junior got there first. "What? Why the hell should you get the same as me, or Phil and Beth? We're his family for Christ's sake. We will take the largest share."

Hagood let Junior finish before quietly responding. "Your father didn't seem to share that idea, did he?"

Junior flushed red as his mouth worked and he tried to get words out through his rising fury, but William interrupted to regain control. "Let me stop you both. First, Freddie asked a good question to which there is a simple answer. There is nothing to prevent any outcome that has super-majority support. Second, as you can see Freddie, Mr. Thurwell's son objects to the equal distribution of the fortune. Now you can see the magnitude of the challenge before you."

Bird looked around the table and saw many questions, but none was given voice, so he began. "Good. Then I bring you to order and your deliberations may begin at once."

* * *

An uncomfortable silence fell over the room, punctuated only by the sounds of shuffling papers and the clink of cups. Larry MacLean broke the awkwardness. "If I may speak for a moment, it seems we have been issued an extraordinary challenge, one that would be difficult enough without the loss of our friend, parent, colleague and employer."

His eyes landed on people that fell into each category as he spoke and a few heads nodded. "I know some of you, others I have never met before yesterday. I think it is true that none of us knows enough about the others to decide anything. I suggest we take time for introductions, so we might better understand why each of us was chosen to be here."

Caroline Smith leaned forward. "I agree, it's impossible to decide anything if we have no context for each other's relationship with Mr. Thurwell." She smiled at Larry and he nodded at her, grateful for the support.

Junior acknowledged the sense in what Larry MacLean proposed, but not entirely. "Fine, let's hear the introductions, but I want to make it absolutely clear that the family will take the largest share." He had tried to sound statesmanlike, but had come off as petulant, and he knew it. He reddened as he tried to justify his position. "After all, we are his flesh and blood, and we deserve our inheritance." He made his point, but badly.

William saw Camille Jolivet look at him with a question in her dark eyes he was unable to answer. He knew what the revelation of her relationship to Thurwell would do to Bethany. He also knew it was inevitable. He suspected Camille would enjoy the moment, and regretted it. He looked from the French girl to the Judge. Ron Freeman was outwardly calm, but Bird guessed he was desperately trying to think up a story. He would not willingly share the details of his real connection with the philanthropist.

Larry took the lead. "Perhaps we should practice voting? I propose we each introduce ourselves, can I get a second?" Caroline gave her support, and MacLean called the vote. "All in favor of introductions say 'Aye', those opposed vote 'Nay'. William, do you need to record this?"

The lawyer nodded and flipped open his laptop to access a spreadsheet with twelve names listed. He entered a summary of the proposal and nodded at MacLean. "Ready when you are, Larry." MacLean nodded. "I'll start, I vote

"Aye." He looked to his right, to Caroline Smith who raised her hand and voted Aye, as did every person.

William leaned back in his chair as the vote passed him, unconsciously getting out of its way. He recorded the unanimous vote and looked at MacLean. "You have a successful motion, please proceed."

"Thanks, Bill. Now we have the first vote out of the way, do we have a volunteer to start?" MacLean looked to see who would offer to go first, but most of them had suddenly found a mark on the table or floor to look at.

Everyone was surprised to hear Bethany's quiet voice. "I'll go first. I don't have much to say. My name is Bethany Thurwell. I'm Johnston Thurwell's daughter and an executive at Thurwell Industries. Last night, my father broke my heart. He's dead and didn't give me a chance to say goodbye. I don't understand why we are being put through this, it's so cruel." She stopped as a tear rolled down her cheek.

There was a pause as Larry waited to make sure Bethany had finished. Only when he was sure she had said all she meant to say did he thank her and ask for the next volunteer. He was not kept waiting.

"My name is Philip Thurwell, and I'm the youngest in my father's family. I don't like this set-up any better than Beth, and I agree with Junior that the family should get the largest share."

He glared in defiance at the faces around the table, especially at Freddie Hagood. As Philip finished, MacLean didn't need to wait for people to volunteer, each person simply took a turn. Freddie Hagood introduced himself as a businessman, rival and admirer of Thurwell for more than 25 years. Janice Elliot introduced both herself and Dennis, emphasizing Dennis's long service. She felt his loyalty to the Old Man was their best shot at a share of the fortune.

Smith then volunteered. "My name is Caroline Smith, and I am the Chief Executive Officer of the Thurwell Foundation." She sounded imperious and important, as she felt. "I worked closely with Mr. Thurwell over many years and directly benefited his legacy with my tireless work. I recognize the importance of family, but I also recognize that, in the end, Mr. Thurwell chose to place us on an equal footing. We need to remember that as we move forward."

Her speech prompted Junior to speak up. "I'm Johnston Thurwell the third, my father's oldest son and heir, and I assert the rights of the family over you outsiders. Let me make it clear, I will not tolerate my inheritance being stolen from me by a bunch of strangers and sycophants." His eyes blazed as he hissed his last sentence, he made no attempt to hide his rising anger.

Freddie smiled, but said nothing. Larry MacLean decided it was time he took his turn and introduced himself, hoping to defuse a potential flashpoint. He sounded sad as he told of his long history with his friend and assured the group he would act only to preserve the good name of their absent host.

The people still to speak looked at each other, each unwilling to go next, until eventually the old lady spoke. "My name is Winifred Tremethick, but everyone calls me Winnie. I'm from Cornwall, in England, and I'm afraid I don't know why I'm here. I think there has been a mistake." She looked directly at Bethany, her eyes full of sympathy for the young woman. "I never met your father, miss, and I'd rather just go home. No offence, but I don't want to be here."

Bethany looked up, surprised to have been singled out, but smiled, not wishing to be rude. Junior had no such inhibition. "Perfect, then we can scratch one off the list. There's no point in keeping someone that doesn't want to be here, right Bird?"

The lawyer shrugged and tried to hide his irritation. "You should finish the introductions first. If you still want to send Mrs. Tremethick home, you can propose a motion." Junior sat back in triumph at the notion of easily dismissing one of the rivals for his fortune.

Larry looked at the old woman. "Are you sure you never met Johnston? You must have been invited for a reason." She shook her head, and Larry sat back, confused but determined to discover the old woman's connection to his friend.

Betty Freah was nervous. She had no regrets about her long relationship with JT, but she did not like to admit the truth publicly, especially to her client's family. She saw MacLean smiling at her and reluctantly accepted his cue. "My name is Elizabeth Freah, but Mr. Thurwell knew me as Betty. I was his... intimate companion."

Bethany closed her eyes and tried to shut out the reality of Betty Freah. She had known about her, but preferred not to think about her father being sexually active with a whore. Camille's eyes widened as she realized what she had heard, she'd had no idea there was another woman that could cause a scandal as great as her own.

Janice Elliot and Caroline Smith glared at Betty with open hostility. Both had offered themselves to the Old Man and had been rebuffed, or worse, ignored. They blamed Betty Freah for their failure. Each woman believed they were irresistible, if only Johnston Thurwell had been lonelier.

Betty sat back in her chair and tried to ignore the eyes on her. Betty could handle men, she knew how to disarm them with her abundant charm, but she often found herself defenseless against a woman's judging eyes.

Larry looked at Ron Freeman. He was dissatisfied with the Judge's first explanation about his relationship to Johnston and was curious to know the truth. The Judge saw his turn had come and took a deep breath. "I am

Judge Ronald Freeman of Macon, Georgia. I did not have the pleasure of knowing Mr. Thurwell personally as a friend or colleague. I surmised I had been invited to a meeting with Mr. Thurwell because he had expressed an interest in supporting my candidacy for Governor. I am as surprised to have been included in this group as some of you are to see me here."

Freeman looked at Larry as he finished, but he should have been concerned with Philip. The youngest Thurwell looked up with a sly expression. "Did you say Macon, Georgia?"

The Judge grimaced, and his eyes flicked nervously from Philip to William Bird, and back. Philip looked at the lawyer. "William, you and the Judge have met before, haven't you?"

Bird remained impassive. "I cannot confirm or deny a prior relationship with the Judge. That is for him to say. Or not." Tension thickened as Junior leaned forward on his elbows, interested in the unfolding story.

"What are you saying, Phil? What do you know about Georgia that makes you think Bill and the Judge have met before?"

Philip looked at his older brother and smiled the guilty smile he always used when he was caught. "I got busted in Georgia, and Dad sent Billy Bird to get me out. I never asked how he did it, but it sure seems like a coincidence that a Judge from the town I was busted in is here looking for a share of Dad's cash. What do you say, Judge? You got a dirty little secret?"

Judge Freeman closed his eyes and recalled the exact moment he had ignored his inner voice that advised him to throw the slick New York lawyer and his sordid offer out on the street. Instead, he had accepted the man's terms and had since convinced himself that the rich young man was a probably a decent kid and the life he'd live was worth more than one he'd taken. As the Judge looked at

Philip's mocking face, he no longer felt sure of his assumption.

He might be able to survive the fallout, but if his political career was wrecked, at least he could secure some of the philanthropist's wealth as compensation. The judge sighed and looked directly at Philip. "I have met William Bird before. He flew down from New York to represent you, following your arrest. Mr. Bird showed me evidence that compromised the legitimacy of your arrest, and I saw to it that the case against you was dismissed. I can hardly believe your father considered my intervention on your behalf deserved a great reward, yet who am I to argue?"

He was pleased with his response, it sounded reasonable. Bird would not contradict his story so all he needed to do was remain plausible. Philip stared at the Judge with hostile eyes, but he had no desire for the group to know the details of his crime, so he let it drop.

Junior did not share his brother's concern and jabbed a finger at the Judge as he interrupted. "What was my idiot brother charged with, Judge?"

"That information is privileged, I'm afraid. I can't comment. You'll need to ask your brother."

Junior glared coldly at the Judge but turned to his youngest sibling. "Well, Phil, what did you do?" Philip decided to simplify the story. "I crashed the 911, bro. No biggie."

Junior looked at the Judge and then back at Philip as his face registered incredulity. "So this Judge gets to steal our inheritance because you totaled your Porsche? Jesus, Phil!" Junior threw his head back in disgust. "The Old Man lost it, I knew it. I always knew he couldn't tell up from down when it came to you Phil. You're an idle fucking loser, but he forgave you everything. Well, little brother, if this fucking hick town Judge gets any of our money it's coming out of your share."

Freeman wanted to snap Junior's neck, but he remained still and pushed his trembling hands against the table top to stop them from shaking. Philip smiled at his older brother and casually lifted his hand in a fist before popping up his middle finger. "Yeah? Fuck you Junior, I don't think it works that way, right Billy?"

The lawyer regretted the brothers were already making things difficult. "All monies will be paid from Mr. Thurwell's fortune. The best you could do to Philip is to reduce his share. You can't insist he pays anyone else's." Philip gave Junior a victorious glance and Junior returned the look with one of pure malice. Before he could erupt again, Larry MacLean interrupted. "I'm not buying it Judge, I don't believe you've told us everything, not at all, and I want to hear more about it. But for now, let's finish our introductions before this family feud gets out of control."

MacLean nodded at the French girl, the last of them to make her introduction. The irony of using her to defuse tension would not be lost on him a few minutes later. Camille admired how Larry had naturally taken charge, and thought he was attractive, for an older man. She offered him a sly smile that made him look twice.

She saw everyone waiting expectantly and paused dramatically and reached for her cigarettes. "Certainment." She lit her cigarette and waved a hand in front of her face to dispel the first bloom of smoke. "My name is Camille Jolivet. I was born in Paris and came to America three years ago to meet my father for the first time."

She paused and saw Bethany's posture stiffen. "Monsieur Thurwell was mon pere, my father. I did not know this until three years ago, but there is no doubt. I am his daughter, his famille." She leaned back and pulled luxuriously on her cigarette as she watched MacLean, who turned ashen.

"That's not true, you're a liar. William, stop this woman, I won't have my father's reputation attacked by every whore in the room." Bethany gave Bird a pleading look mixed with fear. William took a deep breath and smelled the pungent cigarette as its smoke wafted over him.

He tried to hold Bethany's pleading gaze as he broke her heart for the second time in as many days. "I'm afraid it's true, Beth. Camille Jolivet is your father's daughter, your half-sister. We have DNA confirmation and your father admitted to an affair with Camille's mother. He didn't tell you because he didn't know how."

Bethany turned white and she uttered a single sob before hiding her face behind her hands. Junior sat in silence. He was shocked by the unexpected news that his father had sired another daughter. He was instantly trapped by his own insistence that the family deserved a larger share than the others. He had not expected the family to grow in number.

Philip stared at Camille and felt ill. He had decided to seduce the French girl after she had smiled across the dining room at breakfast with a look he now realized he had badly misinterpreted. MacLean was the first to recover. "How is it that you only found out about Johnston, your father, so recently?"

Camille relaxed now the secret had been revealed, and she was careful to find the right tone. She related her tale to the group, how her mother had kept her father's identity a close secret until she lay on her deathbed. How she had come to America in search of the only remaining family she had, and how she had been welcomed by her father. She told of her devastation that she had lost him so soon after finding him. She embellished the story with well-timed tears, and told of her yearning to meet her sister, but that their father had forbidden it.

Camille looked at Bethany and twisted the knife. "Dear sister, let us share our grief, we both loved him so much."

She stood, aware of everyone's eyes on her and walked to Bethany. Camille planted a light kiss on her sister's cheeks, then went to Philip and Junior in turn and repeated the gesture. She stood behind Junior's chair, and looked over the group, aware of her dramatic pose with her head defiantly tossed back. She finished her cigarette, dropped the butt into Junior's water glass, walked back to her seat and pretended to wipe a tear from her eye with a tissue.

Freddie Hagood exhaled loudly. "William, I think we need a break to let people collect their thoughts. Is there any objection?" The lawyer, who had known what might happen at the revelation but was shocked anyway, readily called a recess.

Chapter Seven

Freddie had suggested the break but stayed in the conference room and waited until the only person left sitting at the table was Winnie Tremethick. He asked if he could join her and while surprised he would want to sit with her, she agreed. Winnie was happy to see a friendly face, she had been nervous since she arrived at the mansion, but was upset now the business had taken an unpleasant turn.

Freddie offered her a coffee, which she accepted. She would have preferred tea, but the tepid brew she had received at breakfast had tasted so awful, she was afraid to ask for another. "I'm Freddie, and I was a rival of Mr. Thurwell." His reintroduction irritated Winnie, as if she wouldn't remember his name only minutes after learning it. She wondered what he wanted and wished he'd get to the point.

"You must realize if Johnston Thurwell wanted you to be here, there has to be a connection. He was too thorough to make a mistake about who you are." She looked into

Freddie's eyes, which had seemed friendly at first, but she could tell there was an edge under his polite civility. She sipped her coffee. It was hot and better than the tea.

"I understand you'd expect he'd have invited me for a reason. I don't blame you, or Mr. Bird, for thinking so. However, I am quite sure I never met poor Mr. Thurwell. I think I'd remember a rich American showing up in Cornwall, but it never happened. I never even met an American before I arrived here."

He smiled and leaned forward, but it was only for show, in case anyone was watching. "I don't know what secret you think you're protecting, but I'll find it, lady. So just tell me what it is and I'll help you get out of here." She shuddered, his menacing tone frightened her. Winnie pushed back in her chair to try and escape Freddie's closeness. "I don't know him, I never did. And if he knew me, I don't know how."

Winnie was afraid of this imposing man, but she was tougher than she looked, a long life on a struggling farm had provided depths of courage she rarely explored. As Hagood leaned in again to whisper, she loudly exclaimed. "I think you'd better go Mr. Hagood, I've nothing else to tell you."

He stopped, surprised by her outburst and looked around quickly. A few people were within earshot and turned to see what was happening. Dennis Elliot was one of the witnesses. For once he had found a moment to himself while Janice had gone to fawn over Bethany's grief. Dennis walked to the old lady and cast a suspicious eye over Hagood before he took the seat on the other side of the old woman and put a hand gently on hers. "Is there trouble here ma'am?"

Winnie turned to look at Dennis and saw a man who might have looked intimidating had he not possessed a defeated air. "There's no problem. Mr. Hagood was just leaving. And call me Winnie, dear. If you go around calling me ma'am I'm apt to go thinking the Queen's standing behind me."

She smiled with a twinkle in her sharp blue eyes and saw Dennis relax. He looked at Freddie again, aware something had happened, but Hagood was already walking away. Winnie was glad to be free of him, she would do her best to avoid being alone with Freddie Hagood, just to be safe.

Winnie and Dennis exchanged small talk. He told of his long service as Mr. Thurwell's manservant, and how he felt like an impostor to be included in a group he would usually be serving. Winnie nodded. She did not belong in the middle of a family battle over the fortune of a man she had never met. She felt Dennis's attention shift and his eyes flicked nervously over her shoulder.

Winnie knew the cause of his sudden nervousness. She was old but far from blind, so she was not surprised when she heard Janice's voice behind her. Dennis stood and introduced his wife to Winnie, who quickly reminded him that they had already met. The two women exchanged polite smiles before Janice looked at her husband and demanded why he was wasting time in idle chat with a confused old woman when he should be talking to William Bird or Junior, working to ensure they would be treated right.

She shook her head with a loud sigh as he offered no reply and grabbed his arm and marched toward the door. He looked like a schoolboy who'd been caught stealing candy from a dime store, and he gave Winnie a baleful smile as he was led from the room.

* * *

Bethany, Philip and Junior retreated to a corner of the library for a private discussion. Bethany was still in shock, her face was white as parchment. Philip was stunned, but

Junior was furious. "That stupid philandering old man, I can't believe he fell for that French slut's bullshit." His voice quivered with anger, and his hands shook with fury. "What are we going to do? It looks as if Bird is supporting her claim to a blood relationship."

"He's probably fucking her, and they'll split the cash she gets when this is over." Philip said it in a low voice. He too was shaken by Camille's revelation, but had fewer doubts his father might have sired an illegitimate child. Junior looked at his brother, surprised. "You might be right Phil, something's wrong with this whole scenario. Why would the Old Man die without calling for us, why set up this fucking circus?"

Bethany uttered an exasperated sigh. "Stop cussing, Junior. We're not going to swear our way out of this mess." He looked at his sister with open disdain. "So, Daddy's favorite girl has decided to get involved. Welcome to the party Beth, it's about time you woke up. We're getting royally screwed here, sister. If you don't get your pretty little head out of your ass, you might find your half-sister is shopping with your inheritance by the end of the week."

Bethany stared at her brother, stung by his blunt cruelty. She wanted to slap him, but something in his words rang true. She looked at Philip who just watched them fight, something he had enjoyed before he was even old enough to understand their words.

"What do you think, Phil? Do you have any wisdom to share other than that William might be sleeping with this French girl?"

Philip considered for a moment, sat forward in his chair and the others copied his movement until they sat in a tight circle, their heads almost touching. "All I know is, none of this adds up. I could understand if the Old Man

62

gave up on me, or Junior, but not you Beth, you were his favorite. What did you ever do to him?"

Her lips trembled at their mention of her close relationship to their father. Bethany's eyes filled with tears, but she fought them back. She drew on the flicker of anger inside her gut for strength. "We have to take control. If we don't take it, someone like Freddie Hagood will. And then, dear brothers, we'll be well and truly fucked."

She looked at Junior with a faint smile. "We need 75% to get a motion passed. There are twelve people in the room, so we need nine votes. We can count on Larry to join us, it won't cost much, he doesn't need any of father's money." Junior and Philip listened closely as Bethany continued. "I'm sure we can get the Elliot's support. Dennis will surely back our claim and Janice will too, for a fair price. That gives us six votes. So, who else can we recruit?"

She discounted Hagood and the French girl and shuddered as she forced herself to consider an awful choice. "We could get the whore. It would be cheaper to bring her in than have her working against us, don't you agree?" The brothers shrugged, they had less of a problem with Betty than their sister did. They agreed Betty could be number seven. Junior nodded as their plan came together. "Seven is a good number, but we're still two short."

Bethany's mind cleared as the act of dealing with their problem pushed her grief from being foremost in her thoughts. "With seven people voting our way, there's a good chance we can persuade two more to get on board, if we play this right. We should try to get rid of someone and see who joins us. I say we give that old woman what she wants and send her home. No one knows her, she'll go quietly."

Junior interrupted. "So when we get the group down to eleven people we'll only need eight for the next vote, assuming that Bird rounds down." He sounded excited, and Bethany picked up the thought. "That means we only need to convince one more person to join us, and we can get rid of another person. But who should we target next?"

Philip had anticipated her question. "Freddie Hagood or the Judge should be next. Either is capable of organizing against us, so we need to remove them fast. Also, it will be a lot easier to deal with Frenchie once we have all the power."

Bethany turned to her younger brother in surprise. "Phil, you're as scheming as we are."

"I'm not stupid Beth, just uneducated." He smiled his most charming smile and she felt a wave of affection wash over her. She could become extremely frustrated with Philip, but then he'd do something unexpected and flash that smile, and she'd fall helplessly in love with him again. Junior broke into their tender moment. "Okay. I like the plan, now let's figure out how we're going to get it done." Their heads lowered into a tight circle again as they quietly plotted.

* * *

Larry MacLean chatted with Caroline Smith in the lobby. She was a woman he admired for her achievements, but could not bring himself to like. Smith was full of barely concealed excitement at the exposure of Thurwell's illegitimate daughter and of the Georgia Judge's questionable intervention in a case against Philip. Her gossipy exuberance was unattractive and surprised MacLean, who had never seen her so animated. He realized she was thinking only in terms of her share of the money.

MacLean looked for a way out of the conversation and saw his chance as Betty Freah arrived beside him. She brushed his arm lightly and smiled as he greeted her. Caroline glowered, she was unhappy at the interruption. MacLean made a grand show of introducing Betty and the two women greeted each other politely but did not exchange handshakes. Betty looked up at MacLean. "How are you, Larry? It must be hard for you, losing Johnston so unexpectedly."

She had always liked Larry, it was he who had introduced her to JT and therefore, he'd been in large part responsible for her change in fortunes. He'd been a terrific lover too. She'd enjoyed their times together before JT insisted she drop her other clients. Thurwell's demand had upset Larry, and he'd argued with his friend about his possessiveness. Betty had provided a subtle solution by persuading a friend of hers to cross paths with Larry at a party, after which he didn't seem to mind losing Betty quite as much. MacLean had learned about her scheme not long after and laughed at her skillful manipulation of his wandering eye.

He smiled at her genuine concern for his feelings. He knew she had developed a bond with his friend, even if she was strict about keeping it businesslike. Caroline was angry at the interruption. "What do you care what Larry feels? It's a bit early to be looking for a new client, don't you think?"

The disgust in her voice was palpable, and Larry turned sharply, but Betty put her hand on his arm and shook her head. "Let it go, Larry, she's not worth it."

Betty turned away from Smith and looked at MacLean, who was torn between honoring her request and defending her anyway. Caroline made any decision irrelevant when she turned on her heel and left, muttering about the 'cheap whore' as she strode away. Betty winked. "That went well." Larry laughed, took her by the arm, and they went in search of fresh coffee.

* * *

Judge Freeman sat alone in a corner of the dining room, chewing on a bran muffin as he mentally reviewed what had been said during the session. He hoped he'd avoided implicating himself in anything illegal. Though he knew his actions must appear suspicious, he hadn't given any facts that could be used to condemn him. He considered how a campaign manager might spin the story if it leaked, and thought with luck he might still have a realistic shot at a political career.

He became aware of being observed and found Freddie Hagood watching him with interest. Freeman, like many others at the mansion, had been unable to fathom why Thurwell would invite his lifelong rival to share in his fortune.

Freeman raised an eyebrow that Hagood took as an invitation to join him. "Macon's a nice part of the world, Judge." Hagood spoke slowly, his manner was relaxed. "I've heard your name before. Some influential people think you have a pretty good shot at getting into the Governor's office."

Freddie smiled, but Freeman's guard was up, his courtroom instincts warned him there was danger close. "I thank you for saying so, Mr. Hagood. I certainly hope to serve the people of Georgia in whatever capacity they see fit to bestow upon me." He smiled his 1000-watt smile, the one he had flashed on the college football field after a win or on the courthouse steps after a successful case. Hagood stirred his coffee, carefully placed his spoon on a folded linen napkin and watched for a moment as a dark stain grew on the pristine white material.

"I think we both know your political career is already over, even before it's started. You're dirty. You didn't admit it in there, but you said enough for a man with my resources to find the truth. You took money from Thurwell to let his son go. I'm not buying it was a simple vehicle accident either. I'll find out your story, you can be sure of that."

Freeman's mind whirled. He had recognized Freddie Hagood when he first saw him arrive. Everyone knew HBN, his business network. Information was the man's stock-in-trade and Freeman knew Hagood could make good on his threat. He had given enough away for a man with Hagood's resources and determination to uncover everything.

In Macon, at William Bird's behest, Freeman had manipulated a young prosecutor until he dropped the charges against Philip Thurwell. But there had still been a body in the morgue. The community held a public funeral and later there had been some media fuss about an unexpected but large life insurance payout. While Freeman was sure it would be hard to track the money back to Thurwell, he had no doubt a man like Hagood could do it.

Freeman's large frame appeared to deflate in front of Hagood's eyes. "I suppose a man like you could find something unsavory about anyone he chose."

Hagood smiled, an expression that reminded the Judge of a snake eyeing its next meal. The businessman sipped his coffee to give Freeman more time to squirm. "Sometimes you need to dig deeper than others, but there is always something in a man's past that they'd rather keep secret." Freeman felt the full weight of Hagood's accusing stare and could not hold his gaze.

Freddie shifted in his seat. "Judge, your problem is you're basically an honest man. You're not used to having to act innocently, I think most of the time you *are* innocent. But you did something to earn yourself a place at this table. Johnston Thurwell brought you here to share in his fortune. When I see a random act of generosity like that, I get curious. I've seen smaller sums of money turn up a body or two before now. Is there a body in your story Judge?"

Freeman said nothing as his dreams of a future in politics dissipated like smoke in the wind. "What do you want, Hagood? What do I have that you want?" He sounded bitter, and he felt that way, his dream of becoming Georgia's first black Governor was over because of a spoiled, rich white boy. He knew if Hagood followed up on his story he would be found to have acted inappropriately, at best. Freeman had few options, but he might still be able to walk away from the mansion with a small fortune as consolation for his lost future.

"Why, Judge, I want what you want." Hagood warmed to his subject, he had overpowered the large man with only a mere suspicion of wrongdoing. "A man like me appreciates the long-term benefit of a loyal friendship with a successful politician, especially an untainted man like you."

Freeman saw that the way out of his troubles would be at the cost of being indebted to a ruthless businessman. He looked at Freddie, and a spark of hope rose in his chest. He might yet become Governor, and later, if he could find a way to negate Hagood's power over him, he would reclaim his independence. "I suppose that's true. I could see where you might derive a benefit from such an arrangement."

Freddie smiled broadly clearly enjoying himself. "Oh, there's more to it than that, Freeman. I need your cooperation here and now, at this meeting." Freeman was made to wait as Freddie finished his coffee before continuing. "I expect the Thurwells to deal with the problem presented to them by their father's unorthodox method of determining their inheritance. They will do their best to eliminate troublesome members of the group. People like me. People like you, perhaps. So it will be good for me and good for your future if we support each other."

Freeman thought about it and saw that Hagood made sense. The Thurwell family might try to eject him with a tiny slice of the fortune, or worse, nothing. They would eject anyone they considered a threat to their rightful inheritance. Hagood owned a business empire and a vast fortune. He did not need more money. If the Judge was thrown out, he'd have no money, and would still face Hagood's threat to dig into events in Macon.

Freeman weighed his limited choices and saw the inevitable path. It was better to leave this place with a share of the fortune than with no money and no future. He swallowed his anger and ignored his conscience for only the second time in his life as he reluctantly agreed to Hagood's terms.

Jeremy stood at the coffee bar and watched the two men part. He wondered what had been discussed. Whatever it was, it had been one-sided. Freddie Hagood walked away from the Judge looking like a contented cat while Ron Freeman slumped in his seat and resembled the remains of an unfortunate canary.

Chapter Eight

The Thurwell's agreed Bethany should represent the family to recruit Larry to their cause. She waited in the library, alone with her thoughts. Her grief seemed manageable now she was following a course of action. Philip had gone to find Larry to send his father's old friend to Bethany, so they could talk in the privacy of the library. Junior had agreed to mingle to lessen any suspicion of a brewing plot.

Philip found Larry in the lobby with Betty and noticed how close they stood to each other. He approached them with a friendly smile. He liked Betty and thought his Old Man had deserved the time he spent with her. She saw Philip nearing and muttered something that made Larry turn. "Phil, how are you holding up, son? This day becomes more bizarre by the hour."

"I'm fine, Uncle Larry, but Beth's hurting. Could you talk to her? She's in the library. Perhaps you could take a shot comforting her?"

Philip saw MacLean's immediate concern. He would do anything for Bethany, so persuading him to visit her was an easy sell. Larry excused himself to Betty, thanked Philip for keeping her company, and walked with quick strides to the library. Philip and Betty strolled around the perimeter of the lobby and chatted easily, pausing only when they reached the doors to watch the raging storm outside. Another ten inches of fresh snow had wedged into the corners of the entrance, and the day was eerily dark for the mid-morning hour.

* * *

Larry entered the library and felt the hush of the quiet room envelope him. He saw Bethany with her back to the door, her arms hugged tightly around her body. His heart ached for her grief, and he was only too happy to try and ease her pain. He approached and stroked her hair gently before he took the seat opposite her.

He was surprised to find her eyes clear of tears and a determined set to her jaw. He immediately knew something was up. "Philip said you needed comforting, but you look well, Beth. Especially after the shock of the French girl's claim."

The corners of her mouth fluttered. She was struggling to maintain a stoic facade. "Thanks for saying so, Uncle Larry, but I'm a wreck inside." She took a deep breath and collected her thoughts. "Philip, Junior and I have agreed that we must act quickly to save our inheritance. I can grieve later. First we have to take care of ourselves."

Her voice was firm, but MacLean could still hear the frayed edges of Bethany's pain. He started to speak, but she hushed him with a raised finger. "Let me finish, Uncle Larry, and then we can talk." He listened as she outlined their plan to form a voting bloc to protect their inheritance from their father's bizarre scheme.

Larry was pleased to hear they were acting together. "So who have you in mind to join your bloc?"

He smiled, and Bethany knew he would not disappoint her. "We think the Elliots will be cooperative and Betty Freah too."

Larry looked at Bethany, surprised to hear her speak Betty's name. She had never approved of her father's relationship with a prostitute. "What arrangements do you have in mind for the people that join you, Beth? And who are you planning to eliminate first?"

Bethany was pleased her father's friend got right to the details, but there was something in the question that surprised her. "What do you mean arrangements?"

"I mean, what's in it for them? Or what's in it for me, I guess, since you want me to help you."

She was irritated that he wanted her to spell it out. "Money, of course. We agree that, in return for supporting us, you'll be guaranteed a share of my father's money."

MacLean nodded, thinking. "I see, but how can anyone be sure your offer will beat what they might get by remaining independent? Or maybe a rival group might offer more?" He was thinking about Janice Elliot, she was one person who would quickly figure out how to sell her vote for the most gain.

Bethany relaxed, Larry was testing the details, not the strategy. "We think we can get the Elliots cheaply, Freah may cost a little more."

She was thinking aloud and was surprised when MacLean interrupted. "And how much am I worth?"

Her eyes searched his face to see if he were joking, but she did not see the usual crinkles around his eyes that often betrayed his teasing. She stumbled as she looked for words she had not thought would be needed. "Well of course you'd get something Uncle Larry, but how much do

71

you really need? You're already very wealthy." She spoke lightly, but there was tension in her voice. Things were not going as she had planned.

"Actually Beth, I'm not wealthy. Not anymore. Your father's been supporting me for a while. So I'm afraid I'm going to insist on a fair share of his money." Larry felt the burden of his dark secret lift a little, the humiliating truth was out at last. He felt no embarrassment. It was not his fault the family trust fund was broke. Larry had never taken much interest in the family fortune. He received monthly payments that supported his playboy life, and that was all that mattered to him. Until the day the checks stopped arriving.

Bethany turned pale and regarded Larry with disbelief. "How can you not have money? Your family has had money forever."

She was skeptical, which irritated him. "Nothing lasts forever, Beth. Not with a crook running the trust. Not after the IRS demanded back-taxes and we found the vault full of dust but no money."

She understood suddenly. MacLean's brother had managed their family trust, making the looting of his wealth a double betrayal. "I had no idea, I'm sorry. Of course, we can make sure you get enough.... I... we, just assumed..."

MacLean placed a leathery hand over hers. "I'm sorry I have to ask, but will your brothers agree? I'm sure you expected me to help for pretty much nothing, right?"

"We did think that, yes. But I think they'll agree it's better to give you a fair share than give any at all to Freddie Hagood."

Larry sighed and sat back, feeling the overstuffed leather soft against his tense shoulders. He had not thought about his financial troubles since arriving at the mansion. The news of his friend's demise had filled him with sadness, not a lust for money. He understood the

Thurwell's plan and admired their ability to come up with a strategy to handle the challenge left them by their father. What MacLean could not understand, was why. Why had Thurwell turned on his friends and family at the end of his life? The scheme he had concocted was a cruelty MacLean never suspected his friend capable of. He wished he could put the money aside and get to the reasons behind the bizarre method of allocating Johnston's fortune, but he needed to secure his own future first. And for that, he needed money.

"I want fifteen per cent. If you split the fortune equally between twelve people, I could expect a little over eight percent. But you're going to eliminate some people with less than that, perhaps even nothing. So, there's plenty for the rest of us."

Bethany's eyes widened with shock. "That's a big number, Larry." He noticed she no longer called him Uncle.

"I'm worth it Beth and I can guarantee you'll get Betty's vote." She paused. He was right, but Philip might be able to recruit Betty, so perhaps he wasn't as valuable as he thought. "Ten percent. I can get the boys to agree to ten, fifteen is too much." She already knew Junior would be furious when he heard about Larry's demand.

"Beth, I can't afford less than fifteen percent. Your father's support was keeping my entire family above water and I need to consider them as much as you." He spoke the truth, but if necessary his family would survive with the sale of a few homes and pieces of art. Larry needed to secure his own future and pushed Bethany harder. "I'm guessing Freddie Hagood would offer me what I want."

She was incredulous. You wouldn't Larry, not Freddie." She was almost speechless, and he regretted the words as soon as he uttered them, yet remained steadfast. He needed what he needed, and if he had to play hardball to get it, so be it. Bethany shook her head. "You'd sell us out to Freddie Hagood?"

"Not willingly. I'm sorry Beth, but you know Hagood will pay me what I need."

It took all of Larry's courage to remain impassive in the face of Bethany's obvious disappointment in him. She nodded. Freddie Hagood would do anything to secure a portion of her father's fortune. It was well known only money drove Hagood, he boasted about it. "Twelve percent. Anymore and I'll never get Junior to agree." She was calm again. "There's a good chance my father's fortune is larger than you think Larry, so twelve percent is probably more money than you expect now at fifteen."

He smiled, she had raised the question he was certain was on everyone's mind. Just how large was Johnston Thurwell's fortune? "Do you know how much it is?" Bethany shook her head. "No, but I think it's more than any of us realize."

Larry wanted to help Bethany and her brothers. He didn't hate Hagood, but it would be easier for him to sleep at night if he stood by his friend's family. "Okay, twelve percent then. Deal?" He offered his hand. Bethany had to take the chance her brothers would agree to the deal, but she needed Larry on her side before the meeting resumed. She took a deep breath and extended her hand, and they shook on the deal. Larry closed his left hand over their clasped hands and whispered. "I'm sorry, Beth."

She released his hand and let him go from her heart as well as from her company.

* * *

MacLean stood to leave and saw Caroline Smith watching them. He whispered a warning to Bethany and left, nodding at Smith as he passed. Her eyes showed considerable interest in what he and Bethany might have been discussing. Bethany was alone, and Caroline might not get another chance to speak with her. She sat in the chair Larry MacLean had vacated moments before. Bethany looked at her coolly. The two women had no friendship, but were professional enough to be polite. "I'm sorry for your loss." Caroline said the line she'd practiced in front of the mirror last night to make sure it would sound sincere.

Bethany thanked her, and Caroline noticed her demeanor had changed. Her eyes were clear and focused, the emotional wreck she had been last night was gone. Smith became more curious to know what had just been discussed with MacLean, but that could wait. "Bethany, I hope you know how much your father meant to me-"

Smith's voice was calm, but her stomach fluttered with excitement. She was certain she could secure a large share of the Old Man's fortune. All she had to do was ensure they understood she was a valuable asset, loyal to their cause. Bethany raised a skeptical brow, but indicated the other woman to continue. Smith leaned forward to deliver her pitch, but saw Bethany's eyes look over her shoulder. Someone was behind her. She turned in her seat and was surprised to see William Bird. Where had he come from? She cursed her luck. She did not want Bird to hear her making a deal with Bethany.

The lawyer smiled at the two women. "It's time to resume."

Bethany looked at Smith. "I'm sorry, but whatever you have to say will have to wait." Smith nodded. "We can chat later, if you agree?" Bethany promised to find time later, and they walked to the conference room together.

Bethany saw Philip hurrying toward her, and she moved away from Smith to allow him a chance to speak without being overheard. "Did you get him, is Larry with us?" She nodded, and he grinned. "Good girl, well done. But we didn't have time to plan how it will work. Will he take his cues from you?" Bethany whispered hurriedly as the others were already seated.

"I got Larry, and he promised us Betty, too. He will vote with us, but he didn't have time to get Betty on board. We need to stall. There can be no further votes until we have our alliance locked down, okay?"

Philip understood. He wanted to tell Bethany he had been close to recruiting Betty himself, but there was no time. He offered his sister his arm, and she smiled at her little brother's gallant gesture, folded her arm into his, and they walked into the room with their hearts full of hope.

Chapter Nine

William looked around the table and saw an assortment of worried faces and poker faces. He knew that deal-making and maneuvering had begun, it was inevitable. He hoped the Thurwells had allied with each other. If not, the whole thing might be over before they even realized what was going on.

Freddie Hagood looked unconcerned as he observed the group, much as Bird was doing. *Have you made a move, Freddie?* Bird wondered. Time would tell, but now he had to call them back to business. "Ladies and Gentlemen, we'll resume now. Your introductions are complete, so I return the meeting to you."

Junior attracted people's attention with a wave of his hand. He intended to chair the meeting.

"Alright, now know who we all are, even if it is unclear *why* some of you are here." He threw a dismissive look at Hagood and continued, feeling the thrill of power as everyone listened to his every word. "We must settle this business before the end of the day to avoid the ridiculous penalty. Everyone must realize that a smaller share today will be worth more than a larger share tomorrow."

Freddie interrupted. "I agree with Mr. Thurwell, we should settle this quickly. So let's vote on equal shares, and then we can all go home equally rewarded."

Junior was startled to hear himself referred to as Mr. Thurwell, a title he associated with his father. He was more concerned that a large number of people were in agreement with Hagood. Everyone looked back to Junior. He silently cursed Hagood who was trying to paint him into a corner as the impediment to a quick agreement.

Freddie appeared perfectly calm, which worried Junior. "Freddie, my siblings and I believe we are entitled to a much larger share than you others." He realized his slip, but it was too late to take it back.

"Well said brother. It is only correct that family comes first, non?" Camille was pleased Junior had made it so easy for her to remind everyone that she, too, was a Thurwell. Junior was furious. He reddened and wanted to scream to shut her up, but restrained his base instincts and forced a thin smile for the French girl. "Yes, of course, family first. If we can agree the family is entitled to seventy-five percent, we'll distribute the rest equally and will all be home for dinner." He suggested it without hope but was still taken aback at the force of the rejection.

Everyone except his siblings and Larry seemed to be shouting at him. Junior looked around in panic. He saw Freddie's face twisted into an ugly visage of greed and Janice Elliot openly mocked his proposal. Junior was only saved when Larry MacLean hammered his hand on the table and called the group to order.

When everyone quieted, Larry spoke. "Now listen, what Junior suggested is fair, if you accept that the family deserves most of their father's money." There were murmurs of discontent, but everyone listened. "But my friend Johnston didn't seem to think family was most important when he gave us each an equal vote, so what are we to think? If he wanted to give his children a large inheritance, why not just do it and leave them out of this farce? The fact is, we're all here as equals, and we'll have to agree a deal from that foundation."

Junior assumed Bethany had failed to recruit MacLean and darted an accusing glance in her direction. Her eyes were calm, and she gave him a barely perceptible shake of the head, a signal that MacLean was on board. Junior's mind raced. *Then what was Larry's purpose with this speech?*

"My oldest friend in the world is dead, and for some reason, he saw fit to call the twelve of us here to share in his fortune. I, for one, would like to understand why each of us was invited. I think that is at least as important as who we are." Bird watched MacLean with admiration. He'd managed to get everyone to calm down and think about why they had been invited here. Only Hagood seemed unmoved.

Bethany added her voice to MacLean's. The tearful girl had been replaced by the businesslike vice-president her father had depended on. "Larry is right. I want to know what each of you meant to my father before we make any decision about how to distribute his money. We all know why Larry is here, and myself and my family is obvious, even our... sister, is understandable." She did not see the French girl's self-satisfied smirk, but kept her eyes straight ahead. "I'm surprised my father invited Dennis and Janice, but I think I understand it.

I can even understand why Betty is here. All of us had close connections to my father." She paused, and the people she mentioned visibly relaxed, but they all stared intently at the remaining four.

Junior recovered from his slip to pick up the thread. "Yes, well said, both of you. We should know why our father invited you here. Caroline, with all due respect, you were just another manager in father's empire. He could have invited any number of his executives, but he didn't.

You run the Foundation yet were singled out to be here. I'm curious about that."

She opened her mouth to speak, but he held up his hand. "Let me finish. Then we have Freddie, father's greatest rival. Why are you here, Freddie? I'm interested to know why he wanted you here." Freddie shrugged. He was content to listen but not offer Junior an answer.

Junior continued, pointing now at Ron Freeman. "Judge, there are questions about you that I'd like answered. Your membership in this group is a puzzle to me." Freeman glared but didn't respond. He didn't dare. Everyone turned to look at the one person still to be addressed.

Junior looked at the old lady. "Mrs. Tremethick. You are, by far, the greatest mystery. You claim to have never known my father and, considering the geography, I'd have to agree a connection is unlikely. Yet here you are, in my father's mansion with an equal vote in how to divide his fortune. I want to know who you are, what you meant to my father and why you have no idea of the reason for your invitation."

Winnie regarded Junior with sad, tired eyes. She lowered her eyes and tried to ignore the eleven curious people staring at her.

* * *

Freddie Hagood looked calm on the outside, but he had not expected this turn of events. He had hoped for an easy vote to eject the old woman and then lobby more recruits to his alliance. Now he may have to explain his presence, and that was dangerous. The others could not discover his secret, or he would be at their mercy. He had to think, he'd had no time to prepare a cover for this eventuality. He cursed Johnston Thurwell. *What had he been thinking?*

Larry looked at the lawyer. "William, do you know why these people are here?"

"Larry, I can't tell you. I can't tell you anything unless my instructions permit it. My job was to get you all here, explain the situation and monitor your deliberations. Once you start voting, it's my job to record the outcome of the votes and make the proper payments at the conclusion of your business. That's all. I can't chair the group, I can't answer your question, and I can only offer limited advice. Is that clear?"

Larry nodded. Bird had the trust of the group. He was the only common link between them, having arranged to get each of them to the mansion. Even the lies he had told had been forgiven. Each of them stood to be rich, what was the point of being angry with the man that brought them that opportunity?

Freddie spoke before the others could continue. "I acknowledge I'm in a minority, but I disagree that investigating the reasons we're here is more important than the fact there is a heavy penalty if we don't reach an agreement before midnight."

He looked at Bethany, Philip and Junior. "How much money are you willing to sacrifice to find out why your father invited me? Or the Judge? Or this old lady?" He saw he had hit a nerve with Janice the housekeeper and perhaps Camille Jolivet too. "Mrs. Tremethick says she wants to go home. I say we give her what she wants."

Winnie looked at Hagood and wondered if he was being kind and looking out for her wishes, or if he just wanted one less rival to share the money with. Bethany shook her head. "No Freddie, not so fast. I want to know why she is here, and while I agree with Junior that the family should take the most money, I'm unwilling to send anyone away with nothing. Father invited everyone for a reason, even if we don't know what it is."

Hagood had assumed Bethany would want a fast end to the chaos, but realized she had become curious about the people. She wanted to understand her father's last actions.

She needed closure. Freddie went all in. He expected to lose but decided to push the issue and see who might be vulnerable under pressure. "I want to propose a vote anyway. All in favor of sending Mrs. Tremethick home raise your hands."

Junior and Larry shouted protests, but William brought the group to order. "Anyone can propose a vote. Freddie has the same rights you all have and proposing a vote is one of those rights. But you must follow the rules, Freddie. Every proposal must have a second. Do we have a second for Freddie's motion?" Judge Freeman seconded Hagood's motion, carefully avoiding the eyes of any family member.

Junior glared at the Judge then moved his malevolent gaze to the lawyer, but Bird stared him down and opened his laptop. "The motion is to remove Mrs. Tremethick without a share in Mr. Thurwell's fortune. When I call your name, cast your vote."

"Mr. MacLean?"

"Nay."

"Mr. MacLean votes nay."

"Mr. Johnston C. Thurwell III?"

"No."

"Mr. Thurwell votes nay."

"Ms. Bethany Thurwell?"

"No."

"Ms. Thurwell votes nay."

"Mr. Philip Thurwell?"

"No."

"Mr. Thurwell votes nay."

"Ms. Camille Jolivet?" Camille paused for a moment, avoided a sharp look from Bethany and cast her vote. "Oui."

"Ms. Jolivet votes aye."

"Mrs. Janice Elliot?"

Janice didn't care why the old lady had been invited. Her only interest was increasing her own share. "Yes."

"Mrs. Elliot votes aye."

"Mr. Dennis Elliot?"

Janice stared down the length of the table at her husband, willing him to copy her vote, but Dennis refused to look at her. He looked at the old woman in the corner with curiosity. He too wanted to know why she was here. He sighed when he saw his wife glaring at him. He knew what she wanted him to do, and he lowered his eyes so he would not witness his wife's fury. "No."

"Mr. Elliot votes Nay."

"Mrs. Caroline Smith?"

"Aye."

"Mrs. Smith votes Aye."

"Judge Ronald Freeman?"

"Aye."

"Judge Freeman votes Aye."

"Ms. Elizabeth Freah?"

"No."

"Ms. Freah votes Nay."

"Mr. Frederick Hagood?"

"Yes."

"Mr. Hagood votes Aye."

"Mrs. Winifred Tremethick?"

"No, thank you."

"Mrs. Tremethick votes Nay."

William counted the votes. "The motion to have Mrs. Tremethick removed is defeated seven to five. I'll remind you that nine votes are required to pass a motion."

Winnie sat perfectly still, thinking about what had happened. She was irritated that Freddie Hagood had tried to throw her out while pretending it was for her own benefit. Winnie was increasingly curious about why she had been invited to America. Despite her inability to sleep at night, she felt as if she was in the middle of one of her beloved BBC detective stories and wanted to find out how it ended.

Freddie Hagood was disappointed his motion failed, but he was far from upset. He had gained useful intelligence about his fellow guests. He was surprised to discover he may be able to manipulate Camille Jolivet against the family and hoped Janice Elliot and Caroline Smith might be persuaded to join him. Freddie leaned back in his seat and calculated the angles as those around him prepared to continue.

Chapter Ten

Philip Thurwell was not used to being restricted in one place. He longed to be outside in the fresh air and felt as if he were suffocating in the conference room's turgid atmosphere. He looked around. No one wanted to take charge following the heated vote. Philip looked at William Bird who seemed content to sit and do nothing. The bastard was collecting his fat fee no matter the outcome for the rest of them.

Philip rapped the table with his knuckles to get everyone's attention. His nervousness made him rap too hard, and he not only startled the group, he also hurt his hand. He grimaced but realized everyone stared at him. He tried to morph his pained expression into a smile, but it looked as awkward as it felt, and Philip felt his face redden. "This is going nowhere. We'll sit here and propose motions, and none of them will pass, and before we know it all the money will be gone."

He spoke too fast, but his point was clear and he saw some agreement for it. He felt good until a voice challenged him. "So what do you propose, Phil?" Freddie's question startled Philip. He didn't have a plan, only a feeling that they weren't getting anywhere. Now Freddie had put him on the spot with the obvious question and seemed amused at Philip's unpreparedness.

Philip felt anger rise in his chest and looked away from Hagood's smug expression to the lawyer. "We need a person to take charge of this, a Chair." Bird nodded. "Good idea Philip, whom do you suggest?"

"Well, I don't know who..." Philip was flustered, he was afraid he'd given Freddie a chance to grab a powerful position. He scrambled. "Junior should do it. What do you say Junior? You're the oldest, you should be in charge." Junior smiled and prepared to accept his brother's nomination when he heard several objections. Caroline and Freddie noisily talked over each other, both objecting to a family member as Chair.

Junior began to argue, and the volume of their fight rose quickly until he found himself on his feet shouting at Caroline amid sudden silence. Freddie had stopped cold, and everyone looked at Junior with shocked expressions. Caroline Smith sat stunned. Her face was pale, and her eyes were wide with revulsion.

Junior's mind raced. What had he said? He had a hot temper and sometimes would fly off the handle. He cast a desperate look at Bethany, who stared into space, unable to look at him. He glanced at Philip, who looked defeated. Finally, he looked at Caroline Smith who glared back at him as hot color rushed back to her face.

Junior remained on his feet but felt suffocated by the weight of the silence around him. Then he understood. He recalled his words to Caroline and groaned as he sank into his chair. He had never liked Smith. He was suspicious of her rampant ambition. He'd once incurred his father's wrath for referring to the woman as *a monstrous cunt*. He had just used the same epithet, to her face, in front of everyone.

William broke the silence and tried to gloss over the incident. "Philip has a valid point, but the choice of Chair is yours. We have three volunteers for the job so far, Mr.

Hagood, Ms. Smith and Junior. Are any others interested?"

MacLean raised his hand after a glance at Bethany, who nodded quickly. Junior had blown his chance to gain the position and had tainted the rest of the family too. If anyone was going to watch over the interests of the philanthropist's family, it would be have to be Larry MacLean.

William acknowledged MacLean's raised hand. "Okay, we have four candidates. We'll settle this by voting, but we can make do with a show of hands as you are not deciding any monetary shares. If we need more than one round, the candidate with the lowest number of votes will be dropped until we have a candidate with a super-majority."

The group agreed, and more than a few of them wished William could lead the group with his efficient organization and no-nonsense manner. He called them to order. "Let's begin. All in favor of Mr. Thurwell raise your hands." Junior raised his hand and looked at the others. Not one other hand was raised in support. Even his siblings could not look at him. He felt anger rise, but bit his lip. It was his temper that caused his humiliation in the first place.

William noted the sole vote for Junior and called the next name. "Those in favor of Mr. Hagood, raise your hands." Freddie raised his, the Judge followed suit and Camille joined them. Three votes. William noted the count and moved on to Caroline Smith. Like Junior, she received only her own vote. She looked embarrassed but had the sense to say nothing.

William called Larry MacLean's name, and seven hands went up. Bethany, Philip, the Elliots, Betty Freah and Winnie Tremethick added their votes to MacLean's own. He recorded the votes. "Mr. Thurwell and Ms. Smith are eliminated. The choice is between Mr. Hagood and Mr.

MacLean. You'll need to vote again. Those in favor of Mr. Hagood, raise your hands."

Freddie saw the Judge and Camille vote for him again, joined this time by Caroline Smith. Four votes. William called for a show of hands for Larry who received the same seven votes as before, plus the unhappy addition of Junior. MacLean took eight votes. "The tally is eight votes to four in favor of Mr. MacLean, so you have no winner. I recommend you break to allow candidates to lobby for support. It's almost noon, we'll break for lunch and resume this afternoon."

The lawyer stood to leave, but was stopped in his tracks by Camille Jolivet's unmistakable accented voice. "There is no need for such a delay, Monsieur Bird. I am happy to change my vote in favor of Monsieur MacLean. If my dear sister is so confident in him, then so am I."

Freddie Hagood was frustrated but did not object. He realized his chance to lead the group was over, but that would not stop his bid for control of the voting. He looked at Bird and smiled his most agreeable smile. "I don't object to Ms. Jolivet changing her vote, but I think we should formalize it, don't you, William?"

Bird nodded. "I agree, please vote again. Those in favor of Mr. MacLean, please show your hands." Ten hands rose. No-one was surprised to see Camille vote for MacLean, but everyone was taken aback to see Freddie's hand rise. The lawyer announced the winner. "Ten votes. A super-majority means you have a Chairman. Congratulations Larry, I hand it over to you."

MacLean thanked the lawyer and immediately proposed a lunch break, suggesting the afternoon would progress more agreeably after a good meal.

* * *

As the group rose for lunch, Caroline marched to Freddie and challenged him. "Why did you switch your vote Freddie, not even supporting yourself?" He smiled slyly. A potential ally had come to him. "I decided it was a hill I didn't need to die on. Let's face it, the influence of the Chair goes only so far."

He took her elbow and steered her toward the dining room. "Why don't we have lunch and a chat and perhaps we'll find a way for those of us outside the family to help each other to a fair reward." She smiled and allowed him to escort her, already calculating how best to take advantage of this sly man.

Bethany hissed for Junior to join her. He looked even unhappier than he had during the voting. Bethany sent Philip to ask Camille to join them. Junior looked at his sister and muttered an apology. He realized his outburst had cost the family an important position of influence. Larry joined them, and Junior turned on the older man. "Well Larry, you greedy prick, you'll at least earn your extorted fee now."

Bethany shot her older brother a look. "Junior, for God's sake shut up. You did this to yourself. Your filthy mouth and rotten temper just cost us dearly, so don't yell at Larry. He's our best shot at getting what's ours, you idiot." MacLean raised his hands and petitioned for peace. "Its okay, Beth. I don't blame Junior for being upset. I didn't want the Chair, but I didn't want Freddie to take it either. I'm happy to represent the family interest, but we do have an agreement, and I expect it to be honored.

"Junior, I only volunteered after your blow-up. Before that, I was with you all the way. You lost everyone's support with your outburst and I felt as if I had to step in to make sure you had someone to look out for your interests. What I get out of this does not change my love for this family, it's that you can count on, not how much money I get out of it."

Junior glared at MacLean. "Fine, I get it. I fucked up, and you saved the day. Great, thank you. But let's not pretend this is about anything other than money, Larry. You're as greedy as the rest of them. You better make damned sure the family gets the lion's share, or I'll..."

He trailed off, his voice quivering with anger. Larry raised an eyebrow but said nothing, Philip approached with Camille at his side and Maclean decided it was a bad time to start another confrontation with the mercurial Junior.

Bethany suppressed a shudder as her half-sister approached. She couldn't decide it was jealousy she felt, or something else. She had lost her lifelong status as her father's only daughter and discovered her revered father had been ordinary enough to sire an illegitimate child. Bethany knew she would need to get over her emotions and concentrate on the big picture. To hold on to her inheritance.

Camille had helped them by switching her support to Larry. If it were an attempt to build a bridge to the family, Bethany would accept the gesture. She knew future motions were a numbers game. Whoever controlled the most votes also controlled who got the money. She would reluctantly accept Camille for the benefit of gaining her valuable vote. Bethany figured she would never need to see the French girl once the negotiations were over, and she greeted her half-sister as warmly as she could manage.

Camille saw Bethany's smile but noticed how its warmth failed to touch her sister's eyes. She had been instantly rewarded for her gamble to throw her lot in with the family, when Philip begged her to join them. She had been looking to be included from the moment Junior insisted they should take the largest portion of the fortune.

The vote for Chair had been the perfect opportunity for her to demonstrate her value to them. She had voted for Freddie Hagood because she had accurately guessed no one would gain a super-majority in the first round. She had planned to change her vote in the second round to support the Thurwell's candidate. She could explain her first vote for Hagood as logical support for the most experienced candidate for the job.

Bethany fussed over Camille and took her by the arm as they walked to the dining room. The brothers crowded around their new sister, anxious to win her over. Larry followed alone as he thought about the French girl's changed vote. He made a mental note to pay close attention to what she did and said in the coming hours. He suspected her to be a mercenary who would attach herself to whomever offered the biggest payday. He would need to make sure Freddie did not find a way to turn her away from the family.

Larry recalled Dennis and Janice Elliot had supported his bid for Chair, so too had Winnie Tremethick. He suspected the old lady had voted against Hagood, rather than for him, but if he could add those three votes to the family bloc it might be possible to eject the Judge, Freddie and Caroline.

He smiled at the prospect of seeing Freddie and Caroline tossed aside with little or nothing of his friend's fortune, both were grasping hyper-achievers. He didn't know much about the Judge, and he didn't care. There was something suspicious about the man, and for that reason alone, MacLean would see him off as quickly as possible.

Larry found a quiet spot for the family, so they could talk away from the curious ears of the others. He saw Freddie with Caroline Smith and suspected he was working some angle to get her to join a rival bloc. The Judge sat alone but stared at Freddie's back wearing a dejected expression. He seemed to have the weight of the world on his broad shoulders.

Freeman had voted for Hagood in both rounds, and Larry was certain the Judge had already been recruited into Hagood's camp, but he had no idea what he might have been promised. Larry would need to answer that question if the Judge proved difficult to eliminate. MacLean did some quick calculations. He assumed Freddie would secure Smith, and if he already had the Judge, Freddie controlled three votes. For his part, Larry had the Thurwells plus Camille and Betty. With his vote, that gave his group six solid supporters.

The three people not affiliated with a faction were the Elliots and Winnie Tremethick. If Freddie recruited any one of the three, he would have the ability to block any motions and the situation would get messy, fast. Larry had to convince all three to join his group, or at least ensure they did not join Freddie. He saw Jeremy escort the old lady to an unoccupied table and saw an opportunity. He excused himself and moved to join Winnie Tremethick.

* * *

Winnie looked forward to a roast beef sandwich that Jeremy promised would be served with proper English mustard rather than the pale yellow liquid she had endured last night. She would have liked a pickled egg on the side, but not even the capable Jeremy could conjure up obscure English delicacies in the middle of a winter storm.

She saw MacLean's approach and tried to suppress her irritation at his timing. He asked if he could join her and since she could not refuse without being rude, she agreed. Jeremy delivered the old lady's sandwich and inquired about Larry's lunch. He nodded at Winnie's sandwich. "I'll have what she's having, thanks."

Winnie looked at her food and her stomach growled with anticipation. Her manners would make her wait until her companion's food was served, but she was pleasantly surprised when he asked her not to wait. She took a large bite and smiled with satisfaction. Jeremy had delivered on his promise.

"Hello Mrs. Tremethick, we haven't spoken directly and I'd like to introduce myself. You might remember that I am... I was... Mr. Thurwell's lifelong friend. We were close before we started University together, by the time we graduated, we were inseparable. I feel his loss keenly, but I am concerned that his money be divided fairly."

Winnie nodded. She might be old, but there was nothing wrong with her memory. She'd be happy if some people would give her consideration for not being a fool. "I remember very well what you said before, Mr. MacLean. I know your next question is how I knew your friend. I'll repeat my answer, I didn't know him."

Larry made no indication she'd guessed his next question correctly, but what else did he have to ask? They all wanted the one thing she couldn't provide, a satisfactory explanation. MacLean understood the exasperation behind the old woman's words. He paused while Jeremy delivered his sandwich. "I am interested; no... more than interested, I'm *intrigued* by how my friend knew you. I don't doubt he knew you, and you him. It's odd that you don't remember, but I think I'm in a position to help."

Winnie listened and forgot her irritation at his interruption. "I knew Johnston all his adult life. There were very few times we didn't stay in touch and most of the time we told each other everything. I'm certain you must have met Johnston during one of the times we weren't in touch. You say you have never been to America before?"

"Mr. MacLean, I never owned a passport before Mr. Bird fetched me up one. I went to Wales on holiday once, but it rained the whole week. Apart from that, I ain't been anywhere." Larry smiled. He found the old woman's directness charming. He took a bite of his sandwich and thought ahead, becoming excited at what he thought might be some progress. "Exactly, Mrs. Tremethick. If you and Johnston met, it would have been in England, and it would have been during one of the periods he and I were not in contact."

He stopped talking and realized his mouth felt as if it was on fire. He reached urgently for a glass of water and drank it fast. His face turned red, and beads of sweat glistened on his brow. Winnie looked at him with concern. "Are you quite well?" Larry nodded and poured a second glass of water from the pitcher, unable to answer her until he had drained it. He looked at his sandwich, then at her. "What's in that?"

She laughed. It was a good natured explosion of mirth that caused the rest of the people in the room to turn to see what was funny. There had been no laughter in the mansion since their arrival, and it was almost an alien sound. MacLean managed a smile despite his discomfort as Winnie drew a big breath and fanned her hand in front of her face to calm herself. Her eyes sparkled mischievously. "I expect that'd be the English mustard, Mr. MacLean. It's a mite stronger than the stuff you're used to."

He put his food down and pushed the plate away, he'd rather go hungry than experience that again. She snorted a little and took a big bite of her own sandwich as she regarded him carefully. She liked this fellow, he didn't mind being laughed at, and that was something in a man she liked. "If you would continue, I think you had a good idea about how I might have known your friend."

Larry drank one more glass of water, he was embarrassed that everyone had stared but recognized the old lady's humor had not been unkind. He gathered his thoughts and continued. "I can pretty well remember the times Johnston and I were out of touch for any length of time. Unless you and he met before he was fifteen, which is unlikely, I should be able to narrow down the times you could have met.

"I'll make notes of the periods Johnston and I spent apart for extended periods, and give them to you. If you recall anything unusual or eventful during one of those periods, we might figure out when you and he met. Or we'll know for certain that you didn't and that this is all a big mistake."

Larry was excited to have found a way to solve the mystery of the connection between the old lady and his dead friend. They agreed to talk again after Larry delivered the list of dates and finished lunch in companionable conversation.

* * *

The Thurwells and Camille Jolivet shared a guarded conversation over lunch. There had been a moment of hostility when Camille tried to light a cigarette and Junior objected, but otherwise the four of them strived to maintain a polite veneer throughout the awkward meeting. Philip asked Camille about life in Paris, and she told a vivid, but entirely fictional, story of her life in the French capital. Her tale was of a life she had desired but never known.

Camille knew her half-brothers were trying to determine if she had money of her own, or if she was a gold-digger. It didn't matter. Her DNA proved she was Johnston Thurwell's daughter and had every right to share in his wealth. Bethany finally asked Camille a direct question. "Camille, we need to know if you will support the family. There are some people that would like to see us stripped of a proper proportion of our father's fortune, and we must defend our inheritance."

The Frenchwoman sat quietly for a moment before responding. "Oui, I see. I think you are correct. Monsieur Hagood is one you fear, non?" Bethany and Philip nodded, but Junior just watched without expression. Camille continued. "I am happy to help you. After all, we are family now, non?"

She smiled as she saw Bethany's face flicker with annoyance. "I was not as lucky as you. I knew our Papa such a short time, but I too am his daughter. I will always support our family, as long as my family is willing to support me." With that, she staked her claim to an equal share in the fortune. Junior sat forward, and his voice contained an edge of irritability. "What exactly does that mean?"

Camille knew they needed her more than they despised her. "Dear brother, I mean of course that we all get the same. You want most of the money to go to the family, non? All I ask is for an equal share." Philip knew the conversation had to lead to this. They had all understood this would be their fate from the moment William Bird confirmed Camille's claim as their father's daughter. The Thurwells did not relish the idea of including a fourth claimant. It meant a considerable reduction in their own share. Yet, if they denied Camille's claim, they risked losing even more.

Bethany was first to agree to Camille's demand. For her, it was less about money than her father's decision to hide the French girl from them. If everything she had heard was true, then her father had discovered Camille's existence only recently. She didn't like it, but they were no longer children, and she could not understand why he had not told her or her brothers.

Philip threw his hands up. "Whatever. She's got every right to want an equal share, right? If it was one of us, we would demand the same thing." Junior looked at his brother and sighed, but there was no point arguing a lost cause. Camille was his half-sister at least as much as Philip and Bethany were also his half-brother and half-sister. The philanthropist had been married twice, and now they knew he'd fathered children by three women. That the

French girl had only just been revealed to them did not make her inconvenient existence any less real, and Junior knew it. It was more important to secure another vote than to deny her claim.

He was forced to accept it, but he didn't see why he had to be graceful about it. "Fine. You win Ms. Jolivet. I agree you'll get an equal share with the rest of us, as long as you vote with us. If you cross us or in any way undermine our ability to get our rightful inheritance, the deal's off, get it?" Camille smiled broadly, she had won. The wealth she had craved since she discovered her father's identity would soon be hers. She pulled a solemn face. "I agree. We are together, a family. I am glad to know you wonderful people at last. We will succeed together, I am sure of this."

She offered her hand across the table, and Junior gave it a brief shake. Philip was far more gentlemanly and kissed the back of her hand in the European way. Bethany offered a tight smile, and they exchanged an awkward sisterly hug. Camille felt Bethany shudder as she kissed her cheek and smiled at her discomfort.

* * *

Judge Freeman watched the family from his solitary position. He was angry, disappointed and afraid. He could see what was happening as he looked around him. Freddie was talking to Caroline Smith, recruiting another person to his cause. Larry MacLean and the old woman were talking. He was probably recruiting her into the family bloc.

Freeman was worried about Hagood's alliance. He suspected they were badly outnumbered. Betty Freah and the Elliots sat together, but there was no conversation, not even between the husband and wife. Could Hagood get those three? He was certain that if Hagood suspected any of them had anything to hide that he'd use it to blackmail them into joining him. The man was ruthless and Freeman hated him for sniffing out his secret.

The prostitute might be a target. She was the only one doing anything overtly illegal, but everyone knew of her relationship with Thurwell which undermined Freddie's ability to use it against her. The Elliots probably felt some degree of loyalty to the dead man's family and would be tough for Hagood to recruit. The more Freeman ran the numbers, the less happy he became. For the second time in his life, he had been coerced to act to benefit a wealthy man against his better judgment, and he hated it.

If Hagood did pull off his alliance, Freeman's reward would be tainted with the knowledge he would always be looking over his shoulder for Hagood. He shivered. His career was in jeopardy and his chance of leaving this place with money was slim. He might even face disgrace and perhaps jail if his interference in the Thurwell case was revealed. He saw few good options and grew increasingly nervous as the clock ticked toward the start of the next session.

Chapter Eleven

William Bird signaled Jeremy to return the guests to the conference room. As the family walked in together, Bethany hurried to catch Larry and update him. "We're set Larry. Camille is with us. We have five votes."

"Good. We should try a motion this session. Let's test our allies and see how others may be aligned."

Junior interrupted, and his voice was full of malice. "Let's lose the Judge. I don't know why he's here and I don't like him. I don't care what he did for Phil. It doesn't justify his taking our money." Larry saw no reason to object. "Okay, then we'll see if we can pull this off. I'm interested to know how the Elliots will vote. My guess is they'll do whatever you do as a family as it's their best chance for a payout."

Ron Freeman was on his way back to the meeting when he caught a look from Philip Thurwell. The look turned the Judge's heart to stone. Philip had a triumphal look in his eyes that Freeman knew held no good news for him. He looked around for Hagood. He must warn Freddie to defend him. He saw Caroline Smith looking into a large mirror, adjusting her hair. Freeman stepped quickly in her direction, and she saw him in the mirror. "Judge Freeman, how are you?"

He ignored the pleasantry. She cared about the price of tea as much as she cared how he was. "Where's Freddie? I need to talk to him." She raised an eyebrow and, admired herself one last time before turning to face the Judge. "I don't know where he is, but I do know that we will all be in the same room soon. You'll see him then." She offered a thin smile. She didn't know much about the Judge other than that Freddie had recruited him into his group, but the man seemed flustered about something.

"It'll be too late once we get in there. We have to delay the meeting." She snorted. "I don't think you'll enjoy much success getting Bird to delay again. Remember there is a penalty at midnight and people want a quick result. They won't take kindly to another delay. We'll talk after this session, and you can tell Freddie and I all about your concerns then." She waved him off as if she were royalty dismissing a subject.

He followed her into the large room where everyone already waited. Freddie seemed relaxed, and Freeman hoped that perhaps there was nothing to worry about. If Hagood was calm, perhaps it was because he had enough votes to protect his people.

The Judge's mind raced as he heard the session called to order and saw Larry MacLean rise. "Ladies and gentleman, I propose a motion for a vote." William and Freddie looked up in surprise. Freddie had expected the meeting to begin with a discussion about how to split the money, not a vote. William wondered if it were possible the family had already formed a large enough group to force motions. He heard Larry ask a question. "We can propose any motion we like, as long as it is seconded, right Bill?" The lawyer nodded.

"Good. And our decisions are binding, provided we achieve the super-majority, correct?" Bird nodded agreement again, and MacLean smiled. "The family and I believe there are too many people present that have little or no business being included in the Thurwell fortune and we propose to do something about it."

The Judge shot a concerned look at Freddie, who returned the look with surprise on his face. Freeman's panic rose as he saw Hagood had not anticipated this turn of events. Larry looked around the table, making eye contact with each person as he continued. "There are family members, lifelong friends and devoted servants here today. There are others whose presence we do not understand, but are willing to try and understand. But we have already decided about the Judge and my old friend's rival."

Freddie sat impassively and knew he was unable to avoid what was coming, even as MacLean delivered the proposal. "The family moves that we remove Judge Freeman from this group, with immediate effect and without compensation." There was silence as William Bird asked for a second to the motion and acknowledged Junior's raised hand. William looked at Freeman. "Do you have anything you wish to say before the vote, Judge?"

Freeman sat wide-eyed and mute, too shocked to formulate a defense. Freddie Hagood interrupted, he had one chance to save his ally and he appealed to the lawyer. "William, is it entirely within the spirit of this meeting to have a person removed without any share at all?" The Judge looked at William Bird as a desperate hope rose in his breast. *Surely the motion is not within the rules?*

But Bird dashed his hopes. "Whatever is carried by super-majority is within the rules, Freddie. The entire fortune can go to one person, or no one, if it is the will of the majority. To reject a person without a share is well within the authority of the group." Bird looked at Freeman once more. "Judge, speak now, or we'll vote without hearing from you, sir."

Ron Freeman tried to gather himself, he needed to be persuasive. "This is a hasty motion, and I oppose it. Mr. Thurwell invited each of us for a reason, reasons that are in some cases still unclear. I believe we should wait until we understand why our benefactor invited each of us here." He paused but saw no sign of support. He became desperate. "Or, perhaps it's not necessary to know the reasons. Perhaps we should just agree that the family can take most of the money, and the rest of us will share the remainder?"

He saw Freddie shake his head, and Caroline dropped her eyes as he made a desperate plea to be saved. He felt the burn of humiliation in his gut. He realized he was begging white people for the crumbs from their table. He closed his eyes, no longer able to look at those who would decide his fate. "That's all I have to say. Do what you will."

William repeated the motion as he opened his laptop. "We have a motion to remove Judge Ronald P. Freeman without a share of Mr. Thurwell's fortune. Please record your vote as I call your name."

"Mr. MacLean?"

"Yes."

"Mr. MacLean votes aye."

"Mr. Johnston C. Thurwell III?"

"Yes."

"Mr. Thurwell votes aye."

"Ms. Bethany Thurwell?"

"Yes."

"Ms. Thurwell votes aye."

"Mr. Philip Thurwell?"

"Hell yes."

"Mr. Thurwell votes aye."

"Ms. Camille Jolivet?"

"Oui."

"Ms. Jolivet votes aye."

"Mrs. Janice Elliot?"

Bird looked up when no vote came. The housekeeper looked at Bethany, decided something and cast her vote. "Yes."

"Mrs. Elliot votes aye."

"Mr. Dennis Elliot?"

"Yes."

"Mr. Elliot votes aye."

"Mrs. Caroline Smith?"

"No."

"Mrs. Smith votes nay."

"Judge Ronald Freeman?"

"No. Of course not."

"Judge Freeman votes nay."

"Ms. Elizabeth Freah?"

"Aye."

"Ms. Freah votes aye."

"Mr. Frederick Hagood?"

"Nay."

"Mr. Hagood votes nay."

"Mrs. Winifred Tremethick?"

There was a pause and everyone looked up at the old woman. Her vote would determine the Judge's fate. She saw them staring, and it made her extremely uncomfortable. She heard the lawyer ask again. "Mrs. Tremethick, you must vote."

She offered Freeman an apologetic look before she whispered. "Yes. I'm sorry."

"Mrs. Tremethick votes aye."

William made a show of reviewing the count, but he knew the result. Everyone knew. "The motion is passed, nine votes to three. Judge Freeman, sir, please return to your suite. I'll contact you later about the arrangements for the rest of your stay." Freeman was numb to his core. He walked unsteadily from the room, unable to look at anyone. He need not have worried about making eye contact, no one dared look at him. As the doors closed behind Freeman, Bird broke the silence and recommended another short recess.

* * *

The family gathered together but wasted little time celebrating their victory. They whispered about whom to target next. Junior was excited and whispered Hagood's name. Larry was voicing agreement when Bethany noticed Janice Elliot standing close by, trying to listen without seeming too interested.

She stepped away from the others and greeted the housekeeper warmly. "Janice, thank you for supporting us, it's so important to us that only those closest to my father should share his wealth." Janice smiled at Bethany, but her instinct was to remain wary. She had voted against the Judge with the goal of the family giving up a fair share for her and Dennis. She heard Bethany thanking her, but found her words ambiguous.

"Miss Thurwell. Dennis and I supported your father in everything we did, over many years of service. I hope that will be remembered, when the time comes." Janice saw no reason to be shy about what she expected. Dennis and she both knew further employment with the Thurwells was not in their future. They needed as much of the Old Man's money as they could get.

Bethany smiled but was annoyed at the housekeeper's shrewish response to her genuine thanks. She hid her irritation and patted the housekeeper's arm to reassure her. The women parted, and Janice returned to her husband. "We did well voting with the family, Dennis. Keep it up and we'll be looked after, I'm sure of it." Dennis nodded but seemed distracted. She poked him in the ribs. "What the hell is the matter with you, Dennis? You look like a boy who just lost a puppy, not a man on his way to a fortune." He looked at her, and she was shocked to see his eyes were moist. It stopped the rising tide of her invective, but there was no sympathy in her heart, she was ashamed of him. Janice shook her head in contempt and walked away to refresh her coffee.

Dennis watched her go, relieved. He was frightened at how easily the Thurwells had gotten rid of the Judge. Dennis had almost voted against the motion. He had been undecided how to vote when his name had been called. He figured his employer invited all of them to the mansion for a reason and Dennis thought that gave everyone a claim to the Old Man's money.

To throw a person out with nothing seemed to go against the philanthropist's wishes. In the end he simply copied Janice's vote, and now he realized how close he had come to making a costly error. He worried that he and Janice might face the same fate as the Judge and it terrified him. He needed money to pay his debts, perhaps enough to escape his life and wife. He saw the old lady looking at him and gave her a polite smile. She returned it, but neither spoke, each was lost in their own thoughts.

Winnie had watched the Elliots terse conversation and could tell there was tension between them. The husband's shoulders sloped, and he wore a permanent hangdog expression in stark contrast to his wife, who seemed energized by recent events. Winnie observed without judgment. She had seen plenty of couples fall apart. Both her children were in second marriages. She wondered if Janice knew her husband hated her, or if she had stopped paying attention to him so long ago that she had no idea her marriage was over. She folded her hands in her lap and waited for the session to resume. She did not understand why another break had been called. None of these people would last a day on a farm if they needed to take a break after every twenty-minute conversation.

* * *

William had telephoned the Judge in his suite, but the call had not been picked up. Jeremy confirmed he had seen Freeman enter his room, but said that he had refused to answer the door. William would have to wait until the close of the day's business to talk to the Judge. It was another problem he didn't need. He had plenty to do already. He set his fresh coffee down carefully on a coaster and nodded a greeting to Mrs. Tremethick as he shuffled papers to get the group's attention.

The last to return to their seats were Freddie and Caroline, both of whom looked nervous. Bird turned the meeting over to Larry MacLean, and the room instantly hushed. There was palpable tension in the room, but Larry needed a technical question answered and turned to the lawyer. "Bill, we have eleven people left, we want to know if the super majority requires eight or nine votes." The lawyer had anticipated the question a week ago. "You need nine votes, we round up any fraction. You need nine for the next vote and then eight when you have ten people left, and so on. Clear?"

MacLean nodded and shot a glance toward Junior, who was upset but managed to keep his mouth shut. They had argued about the math, but it was Larry who had correctly anticipated the answer. The ruling made their job more difficult, but they had removed the Judge and could do the same again. Their major disagreement had been over whom to target.

The family decided not to target Winnie Tremethick again. She had survived Hagood's motion and Larry asked the others to keep the old lady around to give him an opportunity to figure out her connection to their father. Bethany worried that trying to remove Caroline Smith might be an issue for the Elliots, who may see the removal of an employee as a precursor to their own rejection.

Larry knew Freddie was the logical next target, but was concerned about the risk if they lost. Hagood was a vicious opponent who could cause a lot of trouble if he survived a motion. When they agreed to go after him, Larry hoped the voting would be as straightforward as the motion against the Judge.

Freddie knew what was coming and that he was powerless to stop it. His effort to form a voting group to counter the family had been delivered a fatal blow with Freeman's elimination. He was not surprised when Larry rose to speak. "William, I have a new motion for consideration. I propose the immediate removal of Freddie Hagood, without compensation." He spoke in his clear, deep voice as he looked directly at Hagood. Freddie returned the stare but showed no emotion.

The lawyer entered the proposal into his computer and asked for a second. Philip seconded and William began the roll call. "Mr. Lawrence MacLean?"

"Yes."

"Mr. MacLean votes aye."

"Mr. Johnston C. Thurwell III?"

"Yes."

"Mr. Thurwell votes aye."

"Ms. Bethany Thurwell?"

"Yes."

"Ms. Thurwell votes aye."

"Mr. Philip Thurwell?"

"Yeah."

"Mr. Thurwell votes aye."

"Ms. Camille Jolivet?"

"Oui."

"Ms. Jolivet votes aye."

"Mrs. Janice Elliot?"

"Yes."

"Mrs. Elliot votes aye."

"Mr. Dennis Elliot?"

"Yes."

"Mr. Elliot votes aye."

"Mrs. Caroline Smith?"

"No."

"Mrs. Smith votes nay."

"Ms. Elizabeth Freah?"

"Yes."

"Ms. Freah votes aye."

"Mr. Frederick Hagood?"

"Of course not."

"Mr. Hagood votes nay."

"Mrs. Winifred Tremethick?"

"Yes."

"Mrs. Tremethick votes aye."

William tallied the results, nine votes to two. He looked at Freddie, who was already rising from his seat. "I know. You'll call me. I'll be in my room." He buttoned his suit coat, smiled at the group with a look that suggested he would happily gut any one of them like a fish and left with his head held high.

An excited buzz echoed through the room. Bethany, Philip and Junior smiled widely, and gave each other congratulatory looks. Relief was all over MacLean's face. Bethany thanked Dennis for his vote, and he accepted her gratitude with a smile, but no comment. She thought he showed more class than his wife had earlier.

Caroline Smith was unhappy. She had tried to leave Hagood's diminished group at the last recess, but he bribed her with the promise of an extra million dollars on top of whatever she took from Thurwell's fortune. He'd said he could secure another vote to make them safe, so she had accepted his offer. She had been dreaming of the riches she would enjoy, but either Hagood had lied or his other vote had betrayed him. Now she was the only person left at the table who had voted against the family twice.

She needed to save herself to survive the next inevitable vote. She looked at the recently vacated chairs of the Judge and Freddie and felt close to despair. If the next motion was to remove her, it would be nine to one against. She needed to change two minds, fast. She saw Janice Elliot smiling and knew what she needed to do. If Smith had any hope at all of making it through the day, it was with the Elliots. But how to persuade them to keep her in the game?

Chapter Twelve

William informed the group he needed some time to organize the aftermath of their votes. He had not expected Hagood to be so easily outmaneuvered, it was out of character for the ruthless businessman. Bird needed to get to his safe and open a yellow envelope.

The dying philanthropist had considered many scenarios that might arise from the group's deliberations, including the possibility that Freddie Hagood would be tossed aside without compensation. Thurwell had left a stack of sealed yellow envelopes with handwritten instructions for his lawyer. Each could be opened only if the circumstance described on the envelope occurred.

William had no idea of the envelopes contents, only the conditions that required him to open each one. One envelope concerned Freddie Hagood and Bird needed to read what the Old Man had to say immediately.

* * *

Caroline was relieved when the lawyer called another break. She needed time to speak to the Elliots. She looked for the housekeeper and was alarmed when she did not see her. She stood and turned to head to the lobby but was startled to find Janice standing behind her. "We need to talk."

Smith nodded, and they left to find a place to talk privately. As soon as they were seated, Caroline wasted no time. "You can see where this is going, they are going to get rid of everyone who's not family." Janice waited for Smith to reveal her intentions before saying anything.

"They tossed the Judge and Freddie aside . Who's to say I'm not next? Or you and Dennis? We can't let them get rid of anyone else without a share. Do you agree?" Janice thought for a moment. She had the same concern, but not to the same degree. She and Dennis had voted twice in support of the family, Smith had not. The housekeeper saw Smith was impatient for a reply. "I agree things cannot continue as they are, but I don't believe Dennis and I are immediately threatened, unlike you."

Smith opened her mouth for a retort, but Janice held up a finger and quieted her. "However, if you were voted out, the family would be tempted to do the same to the rest of us. So I agree, we have the same interests, at present."

Smith realized she needed to revisit her appraisal of the housekeeper. She had thought of Janice as a simple servant with no grasp of the situation, but she had been wrong. Janice had worked out the problem, through cunning or guile. Caroline needed to be careful. If Janice suspected she and Dennis were to be used, it could end badly for her. They were the two votes that could keep her in the money, perhaps the only ones she could get. Janice knew she needed to keep Smith in the group, but she did not have to give away her support freely. "I guess you want Dennis and I to vote against the family, if they try to remove you?"

Caroline nodded, but Janice had more to say. "My question to you is why would we? If we support you, we have to vote against the family. That may not be good for us. We need the money, Mrs. Smith. We don't have high-paid jobs. So why should we risk our future for you? You never said one word to Dennis or me when you called at Mr. Thurwell's home. We didn't matter, except if your coffee was cold. So, Caroline, why should we risk anything for you?"

Janice was pleased with herself. She had never cared for Smith. She had seen the way the career woman tried to get the Old Man to notice her. A button carelessly undone on her blouse, darker lipstick, her flirty laugh and light touches. Smith was like a lot of women in the Old Man's world, they wanted money and influence, and they'd earn it on their backs if they had to. Janice had tried to seduce Thurwell once, to no avail. But she was always aware of attempts by other women. Women like Caroline Smith.

Thurwell had insulated himself from temptation with his arrangement with Betty Freah. There wasn't a social climber or would-be wife that didn't hate the whore for it. Smith understood the unspoken question. "Okay Janice. What do you want?"

"I want a million dollars, in addition to whatever share we get. If you agree, you're safe. They need eight votes, and they can't get them without me and Dennis." Smith listened as the cunning housekeeper laid out her demands. Janice had anticipated that she and her husband might be approached for their votes and had prepared for this conversation. Caroline had no choice and the women shook hands on their deal.

* * *

William retrieved an envelope from his safe. The scrawl on the front was plain enough, '*For Freddie, if he gets nothing.*' He slit the dark yellow envelope and read the short note. He was stunned by what he read, but he was also obedient to his late employer. He reached for the telephone and dialed Hagood's extension.

Hagood answered immediately. "Bird? Is that you?" William opened his mouth to tell Hagood the news when the other man took the breath from him. "How much do I get Bill?" The lawyer read the number out. "How did you know you'd get anything Freddie?"

Hagood chuckled. "You don't need to concern yourself with the how or why Bill. Your job is to do what you're told. And you've been told to pay me, right?" Bird confirmed his instructions. He was shocked the Old Man wanted his rival to be rewarded with a large settlement. "It says I'm to process your payment when the others are done, and shares are decided. You are required to remain at the mansion until it's over, I'm afraid."

He heard Hagood grunt assent and continued. "It says there are some conditions to this money and that you know some of them. You have me at a disadvantage Freddie, it seems I don't know as much as you." Hagood laughed, and Bird wondered if he was being laughed at. "You have no idea how much I know Bill. You'd do well to remember that. I'll be a good sport and stay up here in my suite. The pay is worth a few days of my time. Have Jeremy send up a good bottle of champagne, I feel like celebrating."

Hagood hung up, and Bird stared at the phone with a bemused expression. He was still astonished as he called Jeremy with Hagood's order. The major-domo could tell something was wrong, and asked if the lawyer was okay. He said he was fine, but his mind was a jumble of unanswered questions. He had no idea why the Old Man would want to reward his rival. He had not understood why the man had even been invited. Now he realized Hagood always knew he would get some money, as if it was guaranteed. Bird had questions but unless Freddie felt like explaining he may never get answers.

He slipped the handwritten note back into the envelope and placed it back in the safe. He needed to reconvene the group. There was plenty of time for further discussion before dinner. He didn't think the group would need an evening session if they continued as they had started. Bird assumed they would attempt to wrap up the business today and avoid the midnight penalty. He hoped it would be over soon, for all their sakes.

* * *

Junior sat with Bethany and Philip in the dining room where they sipped tea and discussed their successes. Larry sat with Camille one table away and chatted about her transition from Parisian to New York life. Junior suspected Larry was flirting with the French girl, and it looked as if she was flirting right back.

Junior shook his head in disbelief as his brother finished a thought about Caroline Smith. "She's voted against us twice, it's obvious she made a deal with Freddie. Why should we care about her? Let's dump her like we did the Judge and Freddie. I bet we can get rid of the Elliots for cheap too."

Philip stopped talking as soon as he caught Bethany's sharp look. He heard the housekeeper's voice behind him and his face reddened as he realized Bethany's warning had come too late. "How cheap do you think we might be, Mr. Philip? I'm especially interested, since that's my future you're talking about." Bethany stepped in quickly. "I think Philip was only suggesting your share would be smaller than ours. He just worded it poorly, right Phil?"

Her brother nodded, he had no idea how to extricate himself from the moment. Janice looked unconvinced and stood with her arms folded. It made her appear stern, but she did it to stop her hands from trembling with fright. Bethany offered Janice a seat at her side, which she accepted after a sufficiently dramatic pause. Philip stuttered anything that came to mind, his voice as small as it was when he was a boy. "I'm sorry Janice, really sorry. I really didn't mean anything by it, you know." Junior told him to shut up and compounded the image of Philip as the little boy who messed up.

Janice ignored Philip and turned back to Bethany. "I came to talk to you. To all of you." There was anger in her voice, but she controlled it. Bethany took the role of spokesperson, just as she did for her father's business whenever the shit hit the fan. She used her kindest voice but was careful not to sound condescending. "What did you want to say Janice?"

The housekeeper paused again. She was enjoying the family's discomfort. Her timing could not have been better. She had arrived just in time to hear Philip's indiscretion and the family was put on the back foot before they even realized they were in a negotiation. "I have information for you. Information that will save some of your precious money." She shot a look at Philip, and he blanched under her direct glare.

Bethany nodded. "I'm sure we'd be grateful for any information you have." She was not prepared for Janice's frank reply.

"A person has offered money for our votes. For Dennis's vote and mine. This person wants a share of your father's fortune, and they want Dennis and I to help them get it." Junior swore a nasty epithet before remembering his sister's earlier admonition and he immediately apologized to Janice. She waved it off, she heard worse every day of her life.

Bethany knew where this was going. "This person would be Caroline Smith?"

Janice did not acknowledge the guess. "I want guaranteed money before I tell you anything more. Dennis and I were loyal to your father, but we've lost our jobs and our home, so this is as serious for us as it is for you. We want a fair settlement or we'll take our chances and our votes elsewhere."

Junior balked, suddenly furious. "That's goddamn blackmail. You can't demand to be paid to tell us something we might find out ourselves, you ignorant bitch."

Janice shrugged. "As you wish. Good luck keeping your inheritance." She stood and walked toward the lobby, but slower than her usual pace. She smiled when she heard Bethany hiss at her brother, followed by the scrape of a chair and the rapid click of heels behind her.

Bethany caught her by the arm. "Janice, wait. Junior's an idiot, but you already know that, right?"

The housekeeper allowed herself a small smile. "I do know, but I'm serious. Dennis and I have nothing left. Our apartment is gone with our jobs. We have to get enough money to be comfortable."

Bethany was relieved her brother had not entirely ruined another chance for the family to take control. "How much have you been offered?"

"Five million. A guaranteed payment for both votes instead of a share in God knows how much or little your father left." Bethany was shocked to hear how much Smith offered. She was clearly a threat they had to remove. "We'll double it. You'll get no percentage, but the ten million is guaranteed. Now, tell us about Smith."

Janice took Bethany's offered arm and walked with her back to the family. She knew they needed her. Not as a servant any more, now they needed her. She felt giddy, and wondered if the feeling was power. If it was, she suddenly understood how people who possessed it always wanted more. Janice had their rapt attention as she told a tale of Caroline offering cash for the Elliot's votes. She lied about the amount and she exaggerated Smith's intentions, but she and Dennis would be rich, so she didn't care.

She saw the family was worried about Smith and her plan. They realized if Janice and her husband sided with the Foundation's CEO, they could have a lot of expensive trouble ahead. The housekeeper decided to take full advantage of their fears. "Ten million dollars is a fair price for our votes. But I want a bonus. If we join forces with Smith against you, we can stall progress for as long as it takes you to agree to share the fortune equally.

It's in your interests to reach a quick settlement, so I want another two million dollars for each penalty we save you. In five days, all the money will be gone unless we agree how to share it. If it ends tonight, no penalty is incurred, and you pay me another ten million. If it ends tomorrow, I'll get another eight million." Bethany drew a deep breath. Janice demanded a lot, but she knew if they refused it could easily cost them more than twenty million dollars. She looked at her brothers. They looked shocked but offered no objections. Bethany forced a smile and agreed to Janice's terms. Junior didn't like it at all. He thought it was too much money for a couple of votes, but could say nothing.

For the second time that day, he had surrendered the right to speak because of his temper. Janice was ecstatic. If they could pull off an agreement tonight, she and Dennis would have a fortune, twenty million dollars. Her head swam and she puffed up with pride as the family swallowed theirs and made her feel important.

Philip brought them back to reality. "So we dump Smith at the next vote. Then can we decide percentages and get on with our lives?" Janice nodded, but she had to get to Dennis to make sure he did as he was told. She couldn't afford to have his ignorance mess up her brilliant deal. She excused herself and hurried off to find her husband.

* * *

William was walking back to the conference room when he saw Janice exit the dining room in a rush. She beat him to the conference room and headed directly to her husband, Dennis. He wondered what her hurry was and saw Caroline also noted Janice's hasty entrance.

Caroline looked pleased when she saw the Elliots whispering together. The lawyer guessed the three of them had made a deal to protect each other against the aggressive family. Bird was still shocked by the sizeable payout to Freddie Hagood. The fortune the others were fighting over was to be reduced by Freddie's settlement, but they would never know it.

He wondered if Bethany realized Smith was working against the family, but he could not interfere, his role prohibited it.

* * *

William brought them to order and handed control back to Larry. The group was spread out around the vast table after Jeremy's staff had removed two chairs. They remained in the same order as before, but both the table and the room seemed larger.

MacLean immediately got down to business. "We're making good progress, but I'm mindful we only have until midnight to get everything squared away. With that in mind I have a new motion." He looked at directly at Caroline, but she was unflustered as he played the hand she expected and was prepared against. "I propose we remove Ms. Caroline Smith with immediate effect and without compensation."

Smith maintained her serene composure and looked forward to the moment the family realized they could not screw her out of her share of the fortune. She wanted to watch Junior's face when he realized he couldn't beat her.

William asked if she had anything to say, but she smiled and shook her head. He accepted Junior as seconder of the motion and reminded them that they required eight or more votes to pass. He opened his spreadsheet and began the roll call. "Mr. MacLean?"

"Yes."

"Mr. MacLean votes aye."

"Mr. Johnston C. Thurwell III?"

"Yes."

"Mr. Thurwell votes aye."

"Ms. Bethany Thurwell?"

"Yes."

"Ms. Thurwell votes aye."

"Mr. Philip Thurwell?"

"Yeah."

"Mr. Thurwell votes aye."

"Ms. Camille Jolivet?"

"Oui, yes"

"Ms. Jolivet votes aye."

"Mrs. Janice Elliot?"

"Yes."

"Mrs. Elliot votes aye."

Caroline stared at Janice. Her face darkened, and she began to tremble, had she been played for a fool? Her mind reeled when she heard the next vote. "Mr. Dennis Elliot?"

"Yes."

"Mr. Elliot votes aye."

Caroline was betrayed. The scheming bitch housemaid had played her for a sucker. She had probably been sent by the family to mess with her. She heard Bird's voice, but it seemed a thousand miles away. "Caroline, I must know how you vote." It was clear he had been asking for a while, but she hadn't heard him. She gathered herself, trying to retain some dignity. "No."

"Mrs. Smith votes nay."

"Ms. Elizabeth Freah?"

"Yes."

"Ms. Freah votes aye."

"Mrs. Winifred Tremethick?"

"Yes."

"Mrs. Tremethick votes aye."

William looked at the tally. "The motion is passed, nine votes to one. Caroline, you need to leave the room. I'll call you later to... Caroline?"

Smith was rigid, she heard nothing. Her eyes were on Janice, glaring at the woman that only a few moments before she thought was her ally.

She saw Junior smirking. He had done this. It must have been his plan to send Janice to trap her. Rage boiled within her. "You smug pricks, I hate you."

Bird stood. "That's enough Caroline. You have to go. Now."

She shot a look at him. "Fuck you, lawyer. I bet you were in on this, you goddamn bloodsucking shyster." Smith lost control, her hands balled into tight fists as she turned to Janice. "You bitch. I'll ruin you, you back-stabbing, trailer-trash whore."

William summoned help and with relief saw Jeremy enter the room with one of his female staff. They took Janice by each arm, but she didn't fight. She was still shouting insults at Janice as she was escorted out, her voice full of malice even as it grew fainter in the lobby. Caroline's voice became more distant until quiet returned, but a thick tension hung over everyone at the table.

Janice held her hands under the table to stop them from shaking. She repeated *twenty million, twenty million, twenty million* to remind herself that enduring Smith's vicious outburst was worth it.

She saw Dennis look at her with a mix of shock and fear. She had not told him the entire plan, she had not had time before William called the group to order, but he agreed to

116

follow her lead. She would need to fill him in on the details later, but it didn't matter. The deed was done, and their future was now secure.

* * *

William was surprised how efficiently the family had removed three people without sharing a single dollar. They had no idea the pot had been reduced by Freddie's settlement, and they never would. The group would decide shares by percentages and would only learn the dollar value of a person's share if they worked it back from their own settlement after everyone was paid.

Bird looked at MacLean and raised an eyebrow, wondering if they were done removing people yet. Larry saw the look and addressed the whole group. "Ladies and gentleman, on behalf of the family, thank you for your support. I can reassure you there will be no more votes to remove anyone without a share of the money. However, the family maintains its claim to the majority of the fortune. The balance is to be shared equally among you. To be clear, we are discussing shares for Betty and Mrs. Tremethick. Mr. and Mrs. Elliot have agreed to a fixed settlement in return for their support."

Dennis was surprised and shot his wife a sharp look. He had no idea he was involved in a plot, and he hoped Janice had sold their support for enough. He desperately wanted to talk to his wife, but he couldn't interrupt Larry, so he held his tongue and worried. MacLean was talking to Betty. "Ms. Freah, we understand your relationship with Johnston, and while some in the family disapproved of it, we will respect his wish for you to share his wealth."

He looked quickly at Bethany as he spoke, but she offered a quick smile to the woman she had hated for demeaning her father's reputation. Betty was far more generous with the return of her smile because she could sense an offer was coming.

Larry turned to the old Englishwoman. "Mrs. Tremethick, we really have no idea why you are here and you claim the same lack of knowledge. I'd very much like to chat with you about your role in Johnston's past. I don't doubt there was one and that it meant enough to him to bring you here."

The old lady nodded, she was tired from listening to people argue. Jetlag had caught up to her again, and she wanted to close her eyes for a few minutes rest, but no one seemed ready to stop talking. "Sir, I'll be happy to have that conversation, but can we just get this business over with? I'm tired."

MacLean nodded, he could see the end in sight. "Betty, we propose you get five per cent of the fortune and Mrs. Tremethick the same. The family and I will share the rest and pay Janice and Dennis out of our settlement. Seven people will share ninety percent. You two share the balance, ten percent."

Betty answered with a smile, but there was an edge to her voice. "I think five points is a bit low, Larry. I agree with getting the same as Mrs. Tremethick. However, we helped you get rid of three people. I think you can do better than ten percent." Winnie looked in wonder at Betty, she hadn't dreamed of asking for more and she marveled at the younger woman's courage in asking.

Larry contemplated Betty with a small smile on his lips, he had figured it was worth a shot to go for a lowball offer. "How much is enough, Betty?" She shot back immediately. "Ten percent. Each."

MacLean shook his head. "No, that's too much. Remember, this is a huge fortune. Five percent of a lot is still a lot. Seven and a half percent, each." Betty sat back and thought about it. She could hold out and push them toward midnight until they cracked, but what if they didn't. The old lady was no help. She just sat and let Betty do all the work. The problem was that Betty did not know how much she was negotiating for. It was frustrating to deal in percentages and only guess at the dollars.

JT had been a billionaire, so it had to be a lot of money and she had already got her share up to seven and a half, but she hated to give MacLean the last word. "Eight points then, I'll agree to eight." MacLean took a quick look around the family and saw some frustration but no one voiced an objection.

He looked at Winnie Tremethick. "Mrs. Tremethick, will you settle for an eight percent share?" She looked at him and nodded. "If it gets us finished so I can go home, yes."

Larry looked at William who furiously scribbled notes. "Bill, I think we're done. The family takes eighty-four percent and will see to the payment of the Elliots and myself out of their share. Betty and Mrs. Tremethick will take eight percent each."

William smiled. "Of course, but you must vote on it. The motion is the family receives 84% of the money. Betty Freah and Mrs. Tremethick each take 8%. Mr. and Mrs. Elliot and you, Larry, will be rewarded from the family's share. Do I have the details correct?"

"Yes, I'll propose the motion."

Junior seconded and William reached for his laptop for the last time.

"Mr. MacLean?"

"Yes."

"Mr. MacLean votes aye."

"Mr. Johnston C. Thurwell III?"

"Aye."

"Mr. Thurwell votes aye."

"Ms. Bethany Thurwell?"

"Yes."

"Ms. Thurwell votes aye."

"Mr. Philip Thurwell?"

"Oh yeah."

"Mr. Thurwell votes aye."

"Ms. Camille Jolivet?"

"Oui."

"Ms. Jolivet votes aye."

"Mrs. Janice Elliot?"

"Yes."

"Mrs. Elliot votes aye."

"Mr. Dennis Elliot?"

"Yes."

"Mr. Elliot votes aye."

"Ms. Elizabeth Freah?"

"Yes."

"Ms. Freah votes aye."

"Mrs. Winifred Tremethick?"

"Yes."

"Mrs. Tremethick votes aye."

Bird looked up and smiled. "Congratulations. Well done indeed. I will prepare the settlements this evening. We will meet tomorrow morning, when I set up your accounts and distribute the money. You will find out then what your share is worth. Larry, I'll need the distributions for the family, please make sure you have those ready when we reconvene."

MacLean nodded, it wouldn't take long to figure out. William saw happy faces all around and was quietly relieved at the swift conclusion of the *Danse*.

"Since you reached an agreement on the first day, the clock is stopped. There will be no penalty at midnight. You will receive shares of the entire fortune in the morning and then we'll have a formal dinner tomorrow night. Once that is over, you are free to leave."

They broke into spontaneous applause to signal the successful end to a stressful day. Even Winnie Tremethick smiled though her tiredness. Bird shook MacLean's hand and then everyone else's in turn. A quick peck on the cheek from Bethany surprised him, and it was soon followed by another from Camille Jolivet. As he left them,

Bird looked over his shoulder and saw nine smiling faces. Even the old lady had been caught up in the moment as her arm was pumped energetically by Betty, who squealed. "We're rich!"

Chapter Thirteen

William Bird closed his office door behind him, ensuring that the lock engaged so he wouldn't be interrupted. The room was cool and quiet, a welcome change from the charged atmosphere of the conference room. He opened his master spreadsheet on his laptop and began to calculate each person's share.

He entered zeroes next to Ron Freeman and Caroline Smith's names and punched in the amount of Freddie Hagood's settlement. He entered an eight percent share for Winnie Tremethick and Betty Freah. The rest would have to wait until Larry gave him the numbers for the family and their payoffs in the morning.

His next task was to check the current value of the philanthropist's fortune with the bank. He had no idea how much interest would have accumulated since he moved the philanthropist's assets to one offshore account, but it would be significant. William pulled up a secure web interface for a discreet bank in Zurich, Switzerland and plugged a USB fingerprint reader into the laptop. After he entered a sixteen-digit password, he placed his thumb on the pad and slowly counted to five.

Within moments, his private telephone rang. Bird answered and spoke his password at an auto-prompt. The bank's security system verified his password, voiceprint and thumbprint, and he was granted online access to the master account.

William saw the twelve accounts he had set up before his guests arrived at the mansion. Each numbered account held only $25 and had no name associated with it. In the morning, ten of the twelve accounts would receive large transfers, the remaining two he would close.

He smiled in satisfaction. Everything was in order at the bank. He entered a request for an up-to-date balance to be provided at 8am the next morning and logged off.

It was time for William to visit the people who had been eliminated. Freddie would be easy, for he was taking a secret share of the money with him. The Judge and Caroline Smith would be more difficult. Both were to leave with nothing, and the lawyer did not relish the thought of meeting either one of them.

* * *

Judge Ron Freeman had made his way to his suite in a daze after his humiliating eviction. He was ruined, his political future was ashes, and he may still have to live with the threat of Freddie Hagood's curiosity. He barely made it to the washroom where he threw up in the tub. He sank to his knees and wept angry tears with his shoes and pants splattered with vomit.

He did not recall how long he stayed in that position. He was aware of someone knocking at the door, but he ignored it and after a while the person stopped. Freeman figured it was Hagood, but Freddie could go to hell. When the telephone rang, he ignored it. *Fuck you, Freddie*, he thought, *you didn't lift a finger to help me.*

Eventually, pain in his knees from the cold marble floor made him move. He lifted his head off the cool surface of the tub and rose to his feet. The tub was a mess and he'd gotten puke on the floor, and his clothes were smeared in filth. Freeman grimaced when he caught sight of himself in the mirror. He turned the shower on and waited for the hot water wash away the mess before he stepped in and scrubbed himself clean. He let the water wash over him for a long time.

His telephone rang every 30 minutes, but he didn't answer it. He was thinking about his bleak future when suddenly he knew what he must do to save himself. Sauce for the goose was also good for the gander, or so the saying went.

Freeman stepped from the shower a renewed man. He felt refreshed and wore a determined expression. He may have been forced into his desperate plan, but he felt ready for the mission ahead. He toweled himself dry and picked out a dark suit, a crisp white shirt and red silk tie. He looked at his puke-stained shoes and decided to wear another pair. They were not as new, but he was in no mood to clean up his best pair.

He looked at himself in the mirror and was pleased to see a Judge again, calm, confident and ready for the world. He took a seat and waited for the telephone to ring. When it did, he let it ring six times, braced himself for Freddie Hagood's voice and picked up the receiver.

He was surprised to hear William Bird's concerned voice. Freeman had been convinced Hagood was the one calling. He told the lawyer he would join him directly and hung up. It was good the lawyer called. He was the very man the Judge wanted to talk to. Perhaps it was a sign that his luck had changed.

Freeman found Jeremy waiting outside his suite, ready to escort him to Bird's office. The major-domo led the Judge through the Library to the almost-hidden door and let Freeman in. He made inquiries about refreshments before leaving the two men to their business.

William looked at the Judge and was surprised by the man's composure after his earlier anger at his elimination. "Judge Freeman, thank you for joining me, I was concerned you would never answer the telephone."

Freeman offered no reply, but inclined his head slightly to encourage the lawyer to continue.

"Well, no matter. I need to discuss arrangements following the decision to deny you any share in Mr. Thurwell's fortune."

The Judge's face twitched, but he remained silent. The lawyer read from prepared notes, ensuring he followed his instructions to the letter. "The meeting has been concluded. There will be a formal dinner tomorrow night, to which you are invited, and the following morning you and the others will return home. I will, of course, arrange transportation."

The Judge was surprised to hear the meeting was over. What had happened after he'd been kicked out? He gave William an odd smile. "Mr. Bird, thank you for the update, but I have no intention of leaving empty-handed."

William's eyes narrowed as the Judge continued. "I do not accept the motion to dismiss me, and I expect the group to reconsider their decision. I expect you, Mr. Bird, to see that this happens." The Judge spoke in the clear, precise voice he used for sentencing. His face was set in stone as he executed his desperate gambit.

Bird slid his note pad to one side, buying time to gather his thoughts before he responded. "I see. Perhaps you could explain to me, Judge Freeman, why I would intervene on your behalf and why, even if I were to do so, the others would reconsider their decision?"

Freeman knew the moment of truth had arrived and did not hesitate. "Mr. Bird, do you recall the first time we met, in my chambers in Macon?" William nodded and realized what was about to happen. He closed his eyes as the Judge continued. "You will recall that we came to an arrangement that was to the significant advantage of Philip Thurwell. I expect you to intervene on my behalf, because if you do not and I am denied a fair share, I will ensure the world hears about what happened in Macon. I am sure neither yourself nor your client's family would want Philip's crime to become public?"

The Judge delivered his demand without emotion, his deep voice even and calm. Bird thought for a moment before he responded. "Judge, if you bring our agreement into the public eye, I am sure you understand what will happen to your own career. You could even face jail for your role."

The Judge's eyes blazed in a moment of fury before he gained control of himself. "Mr. Bird, I have nothing to lose. Freddie Hagood suspects me of something, and once he is free from this place, I have no doubt he will work until he has discovered the truth. I have no future, Mr. Bird. I have nothing to lose. But I do have something to gain."

William suddenly understood that the threat of exposure by Freddie Hagood had driven Freeman to act recklessly to save his skin. "Very well, Freeman. The group has adjourned for the day. The morning session will begin at nine tomorrow morning, I recommend you be there."

Freeman smiled. It had been far easier than he dared imagine. No wonder he presided over so many extortion cases. When it paid off, it was worth it. He thanked Bird, who dismissed him but refused to shake his hand. He left the lawyer's office and returned to his suite, smiling broadly at a startled cluster of the family who were on their way to the dining room. Their smiles faded as he passed them and none could meet his eye.

* * *

William waited for the Judge to leave his office, sighed deeply and rested his head on the soft leather back of his chair. His job had just become more difficult, and things would no doubt take a turn for the worse when the others heard about Freeman's demands.

He walked to a small reproduction Monet painting on the wall and pulled it open on a hidden hinge to access his safe. He punched a code into the keypad and heard the click of the locks as they released. The safe was neatly organized, with stacks of cash in various currencies on one side and a pile of identical yellow envelopes on the other. For the second time that day he reached for the envelopes and flipped through them until he found the one he needed.

Bird already knew most of what was inside. It was one of the few envelopes the Old Man had discussed in detail with him. He ran his finger over the envelope as he read the words, *In Case of Blackmail.* He took his ornate brass letter opener, slit the envelope open and removed the handwritten pages.

Johnston Thurwell and William had spent many hours trying to anticipate the reactions of twelve people given the opportunity to share a fortune at the expense of others. They knew blackmail was a possibility, among many other things that people driven by greed might do to one another, so they had prepared for the worst even as they hoped the envelopes would not be needed.

Thurwell had spent his last best days stooped over a small desk writing detailed instructions for his lawyer in the event of numerous outcomes. He had forbidden William to open them unless the specific condition on the label was met. Bird knew only the contents of the envelope in his hand now, and one other.

A death would cause any one of three envelopes to be opened. There was one set of instructions for murder, one for suicide and one for natural causes. Other envelopes existed for the nonattendance of one of more of the guests and for refusal to abide by the contract agreed prior to the meeting. Several were dedicated to more bizarre scenarios, and William hoped he'd never have to open those.

William remembered the night he had collected the sealed yellow envelopes. The Old Man would live only thirty more hours and his ability to remain lucid through the painkillers diminished with each hour. Bird had shuddered when he accepted the envelopes. The firelight reflected in the Philanthropist's eyes made him appear already ethereal. "These instructions will guide you William. If any bastard disrupts the *Danse*, this'll fix them."

William felt a sharp stab of sadness at the loss of his friend and client as he read the neat handwriting that detailed his next move.

Bill,

If you're reading this then one of the leeches has threatened blackmail, or you are a prick who cannot be trusted to obey simple rules. I'll assume the former, it seems more likely one or other of them will have tried to gain an unfair advantage. Well, this is what you'll do about it.

Each person, my damned children included, has something they would prefer not be public, something that, if discovered, could be used to blackmail them. On the enclosed pages, I've listed the details of their secrets. The secret shames they don't dare think about.

Your task is simple Bill, though I don't envy you. Each of them must admit their secret to the whole group. A secret shared loses its power, so we can neutralize the blackmailer.

If the threat was made publicly, then get to it as soon as you've finished reading this. If the threat was made privately, make them wait until the next scheduled session before you tell them. If that means they lose some of my money to the penalty, tough luck. The Foundation will be the richer for it.

If anyone cannot or will not share their secret from my list, throw them out with nothing, no matter who they are. I mean it, Bill. I don't even care if they're family. No secret, no money.

These are my instructions, now go do your job, God knows I'm paying you enough.

JCT2

He continued on and read the collection of secrets, petty larcenies and major crimes of his guests. When he was finished, he slipped the pages back into the envelope and returned it to the safe. He would not forget his simple instructions, nor would he forget the details of his guest's transgressions.

Some were shocking and new to him, others he was familiar with. One secret was a great surprise, though he did not see a threat to its holder if it became public. Perhaps there was more to it. Tomorrow, he and everyone else would find out. William shuddered and knew the next morning would not be easy.

* * *

The lawyer heard a knock at the door. Jeremy brought Caroline Smith to his office. William had forgotten about her appointment, he had been so absorbed in his new instructions. He beckoned Smith in. She said nothing and her mouth was a tight white line, she was still furious. William knew the emotion would not last. "Caroline, thank you for seeing me." He survived a glare that might have destroyed a lesser man and continued. "I have some news for you."

She was suddenly interested, her eyes alert. "What news? Am I back in?" She was a shark, and she was focused, he admired her for that. "Circumstances have changed, that's all I can say for now. You may rejoin the group for the morning session, we start at nine." Her eyes narrowed, she was excited but suspicious and unable to conceal it. "How do I know I won't be humiliated again?"

"Simply put, you don't. But if you want a share in Mr. Thurwell's fortune, be in the conference room at nine tomorrow." She stared at the lawyer, uncertain if she could trust him, but agreed to attend. Her heart raced at the implications of what Bird told her. She needed to return to her suite to think. She practically ran from the room and left the door open behind her as she left.

William stood to close the door and saw Larry MacLean in the library with, an antique book in his hand. But his eyes were on the lawyer. He'd seen Smith leave and was curious to know why she had shot a triumphal look his way as she ran from Bird's office. William said nothing and closed the door, he had to call Freddie.

Freddie answered the phone on the eighth ring. He sounded tipsy, and William could hear music in the background, Freddie was celebrating. "I need to see you Freddie. Can you come to my office?"

Hagood told him to wait, and William heard the receiver drop to the floor and feet padding on carpet. The music was silenced, and the sound of feet returned to the phone. "What do you want Bill? What do you need from me now that can't wait to morning?"

"Freddie, it's important, I need to see you, now." Hagood was in no mood to give up his celebrations. "Why?" William was becoming exasperated. "I'll tell you when you get here, but it is important."

"You can't come up here?"

William thought about that. It might be better to see Hagood in his room, rather than have him wandering through the mansion drunk. "Sure, I'll be right up." Bird hung up, not waiting for an answer. He left his office and was careful to lock it after him. Larry had left but the book he'd been looking at was left open on a chair. The careless treatment of an old book irritated William, and he picked it up. It was a first edition Charles Dickens' Bleak House. There was a gap on the shelf where it belonged, and William lovingly returned it to its place. He adored old books and envied the Old Man's collection. When the

Danse was over, he thought he might make the family an offer for some of the works in this room.

After a few moments of peace among its literary treasures, he left the library and heard a buzz of happy voices from the dining room. He guessed the nine survivors of the day were enjoying a celebratory dinner. He grimaced, they would not be happy when morning came, and they heard about the cancellation of their deal.

* * *

William knocked hard on Hagood's door, afraid Freddie might have cranked the radio again. He need not have worried, Freddie was waiting. He answered the door in his suit pants, but his crisp shirt had been replaced with a t-shirt, and he was barefoot. He held a large glass of wine in his hand, but his eyes were sharp. Freddie's sixth sense had tingled as soon as the lawyer had called. He knew something had happened, and now he was all business. "Come in, Bill."

William refused a glass of wine but accepted an easy chair as Freddie got right to the point. "What happened? Is my deal off?"

William saw no reason to delay the news, so he was direct. "Yes, your deal is off. I'm afraid certain circumstances mean a new set of rules is in effect."

He winced when Freddie shot out of his chair and spilled expensive red wine on the white carpet. "Goddamn it. It's that fucking Judge isn't it? I knew he was trash." Freddie looked at William and saw confirmation in his face. "That man is a useless bastard. Did he know about my deal, is that what caused this?"

Bird shook his head. "No one knows about your settlement Freddie, just you and me. The Judge acted only after he was removed without a share. He didn't know the others had come to an agreement, which is now voided, by the way. You start over in the morning, with new rules and twenty percent less money."

Freddie looked at the lawyer with surprise. "The penalty will be applied? Why can't you call us back now and let us try again before midnight?"

"Sorry Freddie, the Old Man was specific in his instructions." Hagood whistled softly. "The Judge will not be a popular man in the morning. When do you tell the others?"

William grimaced. "Not until the session starts. They'll find out when they see you, the Judge and Caroline back in the group." Hagood snorted. "They kicked her out too did they? I bet she took that well."

The lawyer shuddered at the memory of Caroline's departure. "Not really. But she knows she's back now, and she'll be looking for revenge." Freddie nodded absently. "I bet. That woman cannot take rejection. I know that all too well." William decided he didn't want to know what the other man was talking about. "I have to go, just be in the conference room at nine tomorrow morning."

Hagood was remarkably calm for a man that had just lost millions of dollars. William could see why Freddie was such a formidable businessman, he had already moved beyond his disappointment to the next problem. He was already planning for tomorrow.

William left Freddie standing with his left foot in a puddle of expensive red wine. If he saw or heard the lawyer leave, he made no sign. Bird returned to his office, noting there was still celebratory noises coming from the dining room. Happy sounds that made the lawyer blanch. The morning would not bring fortune to those happy people, but instead a whole new set of problems. William did not look forward to telling them the news.

Chapter Fourteen

Larry MacLean sat with Bethany and Junior to discuss the outcome of their efforts. The family had secured an impressive eighty-four percent of their father's fortune. Tonight they could only guess what that meant in dollars, they would learn that in the morning.

The conversation had turned to Larry's percentage. "You agreed to give me twelve percent, Beth." MacLean was desperate, Bethany was angry. "But Larry, I can't give you twelve percent of the entire fortune. You take your cut from our share, not the whole amount."

"I disagree. You made no such conditions when you needed my help. I got you everything you wanted, the majority of your father's money and an early settlement. We even avoided the penalty, and now you that got everything, you're trying to nickel and dime me."

Junior looked at MacLean, unable to remain quiet any longer. "Shut up Larry, we're not talking about nickels and dimes, we're talking about millions of dollars here, be reasonable."

MacLean glared at Junior and Bethany and felt his anger rise. "Look, I told you what my help would cost, and you agreed to pay me twelve percent. Of it all, not just your share. You took eighty-four percent of your father's money, so my cut is a fraction over fourteen percent of your settlement. Shit, I'll round down, give me fourteen, and we'll call it even."

"But we still have to pay the Elliots, Betty and the old lady." Bethany's original disappointment at MacLean's unexpected demand for money flooded back. She resented his new demand to take even more of their inheritance.

"I don't see how your promise to pay the others is my problem. You made a deal, either keep it or break it. If you renege, I'll tell William that we have no deal, and you can get used to the idea of giving up twenty percent to the penalty. It's cheaper to pay me what you agreed."

"You wouldn't? You'd undo it all, just to spite us?" Bethany was incredulous but knew she had lost. He was right. They stood to lose more if the deal fell apart. It was better to pay MacLean his increased demand. She whispered to Junior, who was red faced and looked ready to explode. "We have to give it to him, we have no choice."

Junior nodded, he didn't trust his temper and dared not speak. Bethany's voice turned to pure ice. "Fine, you get what you want, Larry, fourteen percent of our share. But when we're done here, I never want to see you again." MacLean winced, he loved Bethany as the daughter he never had. Her words stung because he knew she meant it. At that moment, Larry hated his brother more than ever for emptying the family trust and leaving him no option but to take from Thurwell's family.

* * *

Philip approached his siblings to find out what had happened. He saw that an argument had broken out. He had been talking with Camille and both could see a fight going on. Bethany told him about the fight, and Philip gave her a hug, he could see she was saddened by the situation with their once kindly 'uncle' Larry. Philip was also interested to know how their agreement affected him. "So what do we get? Each, I mean?"

Bethany laid it out. "We take our share and give MacLean his fourteen percent. Betty and the old lady take eight points each. The Elliots get twenty million, and we divide what's left four ways. We won't know the dollar value until William tells us in the morning." Philip shrugged. He knew it would still be an enormous sum and he could continue his life as he always lived it, never worried about money, or where it came from.

He noticed Bethany's sadness. "Hey, sis, it's okay. You did well today. We saved the Old Man's money and we're set for life."

A single tear rolled down her cheek. "But he's still gone Phil, and he didn't want me, or any of us, with him at the end. Why?" Her brother wiped her tear away and smoothed his sister's hair. He leaned closer until their foreheads touched. He had no answer to her question, and there was no comfort in words.

Junior watched them, and a spark of something ugly grew in him. His brother and sister had always been close, and their relationship made him feel like an outsider. After Junior's mother's divorce, Thurwell remarried, and his new wife bore him Bethany and Philip. But their mother never allowed him inside the cocoon of her family. He saw his French half-sister, and joined her with his back to the others, so he wouldn't have to look at them.

* * *

Dennis Elliot sat on the bed as his wife called for a meal and wine to be brought up. She acted as if she was a big celebrity. He was stunned at how Janice had persuaded the family to pay them for their votes and was alarmed at how close he had been to voting the wrong way and wrecking her deal. He was also upset because she wouldn't tell him how much she'd sold their votes for.

He heard her slam the phone down. "My God, Dennis, you wouldn't believe how stupid the staff here is. They never would have made it in New York." She was so full of herself that he was unable to bear her self-satisfaction.

"What did you get for our cooperation today, Jan?" He asked for the sixth time. "At least tell me that you got us a good deal?"

Janice could barely look at her husband with his hangdog eyes as he implored her to tell him how much they had earned. She didn't want to say yet because she was trying to figure out a way to keep the bonus for herself. She would split the ten million with him, but she wanted the other ten million dollars for herself.

"I got us a lot of money Dennis, you'll see. Stop worrying and just be happy. The Old Man is gone, but we won't have to work again, and we'll be able to afford a place of our own in the City." Janice intended to leave Dennis for good at her earliest opportunity but had no idea he longed for the same. Even if she had, she wouldn't have cared. She spoke of a future together neither of them wanted, but she didn't know it.

Dennis watched Janice prowl the room as they waited for supper. She was plotting how she might persuade William Bird to give her the full amount of the bonus. The lawyer wasn't a bad looking man, and she was attractive enough, perhaps he could be persuaded in the oldest way of all.

Janice went to her closet and looked at the clothes she had brought. Her best dress was a dark blue satin dress with a deep neckline. It was on a hanger covered in dry cleaner plastic. *That might do the trick*, she thought.

She heard a knock on the door and the bed creak as Dennis rose to answer it. If she let Dennis drink most of the wine, he'd be asleep in an hour, and she could slip out to see William Bird. It was a good plan, and she smiled at her own reflection in the mirror as she heard Dennis call her to come and eat. "I'll be right there, dear."

* * *

Betty Freah sat with Winnie Tremethick in the dining room. She was happy, but her mood was dampened by the knowledge that her good fortune came at the loss of the man she had liked and even loved a little bit.

Their conversation was sparse, Winnie never said much as far as Betty could tell. The old lady had refused wine with her dinner. She was so much like an elderly nun Betty thought it a miracle she had ever been married with children. She took a breath and tried once more to start a conversation. "I guess you'll be heading home soon, Mrs. Tremethick?"

The old woman looked at her and cracked a small smile. "That would be lovely, I miss the farm." She offered no elaboration and stared into space as she ate her food, apparently uninterested in further conversation. Betty gave up and ate the rest of her meal in silence with her memories of JT for companionship.

Winnie was relieved when the prostitute finally stopped talking. She had been trying to think but had no time to herself to do so. According to what she heard, she would be rich tomorrow. Winnie had no idea what she might do with a lot of money. She wouldn't abandon the farm. She supposed her kids might like some money, but they still wouldn't visit. They might call more often, but she doubted that too. She heard from her son three times a year, on her birthday, Christmas and Mother's Day.

Her daughter called every month, but never for long, and Winnie was never able to talk to her grandchildren. Her daughter thought her mother too provincial for the artsy life she led in Scotland as a sculptor and Winnie knew she was seen as an embarrassment. She sighed, there was no one else to give the money to unless she donated it to the church, but she did not care for the new vicar. Winnie had disapproved of the 'new' vicar since he arrived in her parish twenty years ago. It was unlikely he'd see a donation.

Winnie thought about these things but what concerned her most was why she had been invited to America at all. The question was at the forefront of her mind. Who was the man that had insisted she be here and why was she receiving his money? She worried there had been a terrible mistake and that a different Winifred Tremethick should be in her place.

Perhaps she would just go home and forget all about it, just put the money in her savings. She had no idea how she'd explain her riches to Mr. Chambers, the post office manager who kept her savings book updated. The idea made her smile. A commotion broke out behind her, and she turned to see what the fuss was.

* * *

The noise that had broken into Mrs. Tremethick's thoughts was Larry MacLean's hurried return to the dining room. He ignored Philip and Bethany's protests and pulled up a chair to join them, breathless from his sprint from the library. Junior and Camille saw his hasty arrival and joined the others where MacLean was fending off objections to his re-appearance.

Junior decided to take charge. "What are you doing back here, Larry? Haven't you done enough for one night?"

"Shut it, Junior," the older man barked. "We might have a problem. I just saw Caroline Smith leave Bird's office and she looked much too happy for a woman leaving here empty-handed." Philip scoffed. "What are you talking about you old fool? Bill said he'd talk to the losers after we were done, it was no big secret."

"Maybe, kid, but I was in the library when Smith left his office and she looked straight at me, as if she had won something. Maybe something important."

Bethany interrupted. "Perhaps she just wanted you to think that? She's proud. We all know Caroline would never admit defeat."

"I thought the same at first, but I decided to watch to see if anything else happened. I moved to a corner where I couldn't be seen and soon Bird came out of his office. He damn near looked right at me when he put a book back on the shelf, but he didn't see me. I was lucky."

He paused, still hardly able to believe Bird missed seeing him in the shadows. "Anyway, William left the library, and I followed him. I thought he was coming here, but instead he went to Freddie's room." Larry had their complete attention now, and they all leaned in to listen. "I had to follow carefully so he wouldn't see me, but I was able to run up and listen at the door, and I heard Freddie shouting, he sounded pretty mad."

Junior was torn between interest in what MacLean had to say and his distaste for the man. "Why would Freddie be mad at Bird? We were the ones that got rid of him."

"I know, Junior. I agree, but Freddie was plenty mad about something and I don't like not knowing what it could be."

Bethany pulled a face, still angry with him. "You're paranoid Larry, or you have a guilty conscience. Caroline would never let you see she was upset, especially not after her meltdown today. She'd pretend it never happened and was probably showing you a brave face. As for Freddie, who cares if he was mad? We threw him out and denied him a share of our father's cash, of course he's mad. William told Caroline and Freddie he'd speak to them later. Now we know he did. So what?"

MacLean recalled the expression on Caroline Smith's face. He knew in his gut that something was going on. He also knew he had failed to convince the family anything was wrong, he needed more evidence. "Maybe. Perhaps Beth's right and I read too much into nothing." Philip grunted. "Sure, Larry, that's it. You over-reacted. Now fuck off, you're upsetting my sister."

MacLean left to the sound of Philip and Junior laughing at him. He returned to the library and found a chair in the darkest corner of the room where he could watch Bird's office unobserved. Larry trusted his instincts enough to invest some time in surveillance.

Janice leaned in to the bathroom mirror as she applied her eyeliner. She heard soft, regular snores from the bedroom where Dennis slept. She looked at her reflection. She looked good in full make-up. Once she stepped away from the mirror's bright light, ten years melted from her face.

She was in good shape, she carried no extra weight to spoil her figure, and her breasts had filled out with age. She admired them in a dark bra, full and round. Janice reached for the hanger on the back of the door and stepped into her best dress. She liked the deep-vee front that showed enough cleavage to make most men look twice. She figured William Bird was like most men. She was counting on it.

Janice smoothed her dress and gave a flirty half twirl, watching herself in the mirror. She felt good, she looked good and would feel even better when the lawyer agreed to give her the bonus. She peeked into the bedroom. Dennis was flat on his back, still wearing socks even though his pants were neatly folded on the bed. His breathing was deep and regular. He would remain in that position until the early hours when his bladder would rob him of a full night's sleep.

Janice had more than enough time to execute her plan. She picked up her shoes, tiptoed past Dennis and slipped them on in the hallway. The high heels made her legs seem long and slender, and she smiled. Most men liked legs, too.

* * *

Larry was almost asleep in the library. He had removed the light bulbs from the nearest lamp to create an entirely dark section of the room where he could observe Bird's office without being discovered. He had not given up the idea something was wrong, the look he'd seen in Caroline Smith's eye had unnerved him.

He heard the click of a woman's shoes in the lobby and wondered if whoever it was would head to the dining room or the library. He pressed himself back into the chair, unconsciously trying to make himself invisible as he saw a woman enter the library. Whoever it was had a very appealing silhouette.

The woman walked to the lawyer's office, and as she entered the wash of light over the door, he saw it was Janice Elliot, his old friend's housekeeper. His eyes widened, he had known she was attractive, but Janice looked stunning. He watched as she looked around the room. Her eyes moved over his position, but she didn't see him in the darkness. She stepped up to the lawyer's door and knocked lightly.

There was a short delay before Bird opened the door. Larry could not see his face or hear what they said, but, after a few words, Janice stepped inside and the door closed behind her. Larry leaned forward in his seat, and a dim light caught his intrigued expression, just what was going on?

* * *

William was surprised by Janice's late visit. He knew her well from the Thurwell's New York home, but had never seen her as she looked now, in a cocktail dress that showed more flesh than he was comfortable with. She stood in front of his desk and smiled in a way that made him more uncomfortable. Her dress rode up too high on her thigh when she took her seat, but she made no attempt to fix it. He pretended not to notice, but he had, and his heart raced.

He was curious about the reason for her visit but felt a surge of excitement too. "Mrs. Elliot, you said this was urgent?"

She smiled, and her eyes sparkled as she bit her lower lip. "Yes, it is a matter of great importance to me. You see, I made an agreement with Mr. Thurwell's family to vote in their favor, in return for payment."

William nodded. "Yes, I understand. It was within the rules. But the family will pay you from their share, so how may I assist you?"

Janice was annoyed by his condescension but didn't let it harden her voice. "The deal was for a fixed amount plus a bonus for an early end to the negotiations. We did conclude early, so the bonus is rather large." William sat with his fingers tented as he listened. He didn't know the exact details of the deal, but what he heard sounded reasonable. He was distracted by the way his desk lamp's light fell on Janice's cleavage, and had to concentrate to make sure he looked at Janice's face.

She noticed his furtive glances and allowed herself a sly smile. "You see Mr. Bird, I want to you instruct the family to give me all the bonus money."

He didn't understand. "You think the family will renege on your deal?"

She shook her head. "No, the family will honor the deal. What I want is to not share the bonus with Dennis." She looked at him directly, making sure he had a good view of her chest as she delivered her demand.

He looked surprised and repeated. "You want to keep the bonus from Dennis?"

Janice smiled through her frustration. She was unsure if the lawyer was being slow or playing hard to get. "Yes, exactly. The Thurwells agreed to pay us ten million dollars, which I'll share with Dennis. They also promised a bonus, which is worth another ten million dollars. I want all of it. I'm leaving Dennis when we leave this place, and I want all of that money, William. I want you to see to it, for me."

She leaned forward to give him a good view of her curves and ran a finger through her hair flirtily. "I'll be so grateful, if you help me." She saw his eyes run over her figure, and her heart pounded in her ears, now was when he would decide to do it, or not.

William was under no misapprehension about why Janice was in his office and dressed so provocatively. She wanted Bird to help her cheat her husband and was willing to reward him in return. She looked almost eager to reward him. He was aroused by the thought even as he knew he could not accept her offer. He leaned back in his chair and closed his eyes.

Janice knew enough to say nothing. She'd done what she could. Either she would secure the money and have some fun with the lawyer into the bargain, or she would leave disappointed. If she was rejected, there was always Junior or his brother. She thought Junior would take the bargain, Philip probably not. She was too old for him.

William was briefly tempted by her offer, but knew he would never go through with it. What Janice did not know was that her plea was for nothing. Judge Freeman had undone the deal she thought was in place, but she would only discover that in the morning. His immediate concern was to get her out of his office without an awkward scene.

Janice watched his face and saw the exact moment of her failure. She was disappointed but said nothing. She pulled the hem of her dress down, there was no point showing William her legs for no reason. He offered a weak smile and told her what she already knew. "I can't do it Janice, it would be unethical. I'm sorry. You should leave. I hope you understand."

He stood and opened the door for her. Janice smoothed her dress as she stood to let him take a good, long look in case he had a last-minute change of heart. She stopped in the doorway and caressed his cheek with her fingertips. "I would have been so very, very grateful. You don't know what you missed, William." She brushed her lips lightly over his and left. Bird closed his door and leaned against it, breathing hard.

* * *

Larry saw the lawyer's door open again, and Janice reappeared. She stroked the lawyer's cheek and kissed him before she left. Larry admired the way her hips swayed under her dress as she walked out of the library. He wondered, did Janice Elliot just sleep with Bill Bird? It looked as if she might have, though they had barely enough time. She had been with him almost fifteen minutes. Had Larry stumbled onto a long-term affair or did she just do the lawyer for a favor? He sat in the dark and wondered what he had witnessed.

Larry had never suspected Bird of having an affair with anyone, let alone Janice Elliot. The Old Man was keenly tuned to undercurrents amongst his staff and had never mentioned that his lawyer might be banging the housekeeper. So what had Larry witnessed, and did it mean anything? He realized he should have followed Janice, but now was afraid to move from his place in case William came out of his office and caught him. He had missed his chance and was stuck where he was, for now.

* * *

William was shaken by Janice's visit. While he did not regret passing up her offer, he thought about it nonetheless. He had been surprised but relieved that she had given up so easily, she could have made a scene and claimed just about anything. No matter what he said, a provocatively dressed married woman in his office late at night would not have looked good.

He replayed her visit in his head, every word. She had been serious about taking the bonus from Dennis, and he had no doubt she would have had sex with him in return. So why give up after his first refusal? He realized Janice must have another target, someone else who could give her what she wanted. It would have to be someone with influence on the family, most likely Junior or Larry MacLean.

William knew MacLean would not hesitate to take Janice's offer, but he was less certain Larry had the authority to give her what she wanted in return. The better option was Junior. He had the most influence, and it made sense for Janice to try her ploy on him. William had to warn Junior, but needed to be careful not to reveal the deal was off. He thought about the pros and cons for a minute and picked up the telephone.

* * *

Junior heard the phone ring but ignored it.

He turned to his visitor and looked her up and down. He had never paid attention to his father's staff, why should he? Now Janice Elliot was in his room, dressed in a cheap party dress and offering him God knows what in return for cheating her husband out of some money. "What do you want me to do? Give you Dennis's share of the bonus? Why?"

She looked at Junior. She was frustrated and less sure of herself. The plan to offer herself to the lawyer was one thing because William Bird was polite and passably attractive. Junior might help achieve her goal, but he made her nervous. She wasn't even sure he liked women. She flicked her hair and stood as tall in her heels as she could. She was pleased the heels made her a little taller than Junior.

"I want you to give me the bonus money. Cut Dennis out of it. He doesn't know about it, and it needs to stay that way. I'm leaving him, and I need that money."

Junior rubbed his chin, his eyes cold and calculating. "You could leave him anyway, why take more than you deserve?"

She closed her eyes, he was toying with her. "Mr. Thurwell, I have put up with Dennis's incompetence and gambling. I want the money because if he gets it, it'll go to bookies. It will be wasted on him."

She looked into his eyes and suppressed a shudder as she tried to close the deal. "I'm willing to be grateful. If you give me what I want, I can give you something in return." She traced a finger along the soft curves of her cleavage and felt his eyes follow it. She felt exposed as he watched and rocked back and forth on his heels. His eyes on her skin felt like a burn and she suddenly wanted to run, but the thought of the money made her stay.

Junior didn't care about Dennis any more than he did Janice. It would be easy enough to do what she wanted. Beth wouldn't understand, but since the cost remained the same, he didn't think she'd make a fuss.

As for Janice, she was offering herself to him. He leered as his heart raced. It had been a long time since he'd been with a woman. Most society girls wouldn't go near him once their little gossip circle heard about his tastes. He grunted agreement and Janice's heart skipped with excitement as she realized she'd get her fortune. But when she looked into Junior's eyes, her happiness died. Janice reached for the drink he offered and was surprised when instead of handing it to her, he grabbed her wrist. She looked up, frightened by his tight grip. He was hurting her.

Junior saw fear spark in her eyes and laughed as she began to struggle.

* * *

William tried again, but Junior didn't pick up the call. He thought about going to Junior's room, but reconsidered. If he was wrong about Janice, he'd have to make some excuse about his visit and he preferred to avoid seeing the family until morning. If he was right about her, it was already too late. He had wasted too much time deciding what to do.

He sighed. Tomorrow morning would be a mess, and he needed some rest. He clicked off his desk lamp, checked everything was secure and left his office. He didn't look into the library as he walked to his room and even if he had, he would not have seen Larry MacLean watching from the shadows.

* * *

MacLean watched Bird lock his office door. He looked tired and was probably heading for bed. Larry waited a full five minutes before he dared to move. His legs were stiff after sitting for too long. He screwed the light bulbs back into the lamp and walked out of the library, deep in thought about what he had witnessed.

He was startled by a voice and turned to see Jeremy, the major-domo. Larry wondered how the man always simply appeared, did he never rest? "I'm sorry, what did you say?"

Jeremy smiled as he repeated the question. "I wondered if you might care for a drink or a snack, it's been some time since supper."

Larry looked at Jeremy again. Did he know what he had been doing? He politely refused the offer and headed toward the stairs. He turned to say something to Jeremy, but the man had disappeared. *He moves like a cat*, Larry thought, *you never hear him coming or going*.

* * *

Janice slipped into her room a few minutes before three in the morning. Dennis was in the same position she had left him in, unaware that she had been gone for hours. She felt rage at his somnolent figure. He didn't care about her and hadn't cared for years. She walked unsteadily to the bathroom and closed the door.

She turned on the shower and sank to the floor. Quiet sobs escaped from her lips. Her body was sore and abused. She sat on the floor as steam from the hot shower filled the room. She tore the cocktail dress off. She'd never wear it again. Janice saw a ghost of herself in the fogged mirror and was glad of the obscured reflection. She was sure she could not look herself in the eye right now.

Janice stepped under the scalding shower and prayed it could make her feel clean again, but she knew no amount of hot water would wash away the memory of the past hours. The extra money had not been worth the price Junior exacted from her. She hugged herself under the hot water and cried until she had no tears left, then scrubbed at her body until the skin was raw.

Eventually Janice stepped out, dried herself and crawled into bed next to her snoring husband. The clock showed it was almost five-thirty, but sleep would not rescue her from the horrors of the night, and she watched the minutes tick away until the alarm sounded at seven.

Dennis woke and rolled off the bed and went to the bathroom to urinate. Janice closed her eyes as she heard Dennis pee and fart loudly. He'd never learned to close the bathroom door before he went in. She hated it, it was another constant irritation, but this morning it didn't seem like such a big deal, so she rolled over and pulled a pillow over her ears. She lay in a world of muffled sound and darkness and wished she were dead.

* * *

Larry sat at the desk in his suite with a pencil poised over a blank sheet of paper. He was thinking about 1952, when he had been seventeen years old. He had promised to help Winnie discover how his friend had known her, so he ignored his distraction over what he'd seen in the library and creased his brow in concentration.

147

He would run through the chronology of his life with Johnston Thurwell to find the time his friend could have encountered Winnie. He listed every year from 1952 to present and filled in the details of where he and Thurwell had been. He worked without a break for two hours before he was finished.

His heart was heavy with melancholy, and he regretted his decision to extend his winter sailing trip and skip Christmas with Johnston. His shipmate had wanted to stay on the boat and had been persuasive, so he had called and cancelled. She was a waitress MacLean met in a Bahamas yacht club who had achieved the high but fleeting status of essential crew on his boat.

Larry fell in love with every woman he slept with and was always sincere in his devotion. His problem was that his attention span was limited to a few months. Inevitably, his roving blue eyes would settle upon a new beauty that would instantly steal his heart, and he'd replace the old girlfriend without a second thought. Larry's attention span had spared him from any marriage and the divorce that would surely have followed.

He and Johnston had laughed about that the last time they spoke. Larry realized now that his friend had been dying, but had said nothing about his condition. Larry had spent Christmas on a waitress instead of with his dying friend, and that guilt would haunt him forever.

Returning to the present, he leaned back in his chair and reviewed his work. There were only a few gaps on his list that would have allowed enough time for Thurwell to go to England. There was a three-month gap in 1957 after graduation when MacLean had gone to Mexico and lost himself on a tequila bender. The next was three years later, a ten month gap in 1960 when Larry went to Australia to follow a yacht race and enjoy the hospitality of the local ladies.

The only other viable gap was 1965. Larry paused as he remembered the lowest time of his life. He had just turned 30 when the police hauled him from the family home and charged him with dealing drugs. He'd been partying hard the previous weekend and had shared his generous stash of pot and pills with a couple of girls. One girl turned out to be a local councilman's daughter, and when her father found his daughter shirtless and passed out on his front lawn one Sunday morning, he had demanded to know who gave her the drugs.

The charges against Larry had been reduced to possession, but he still spent three weeks in the county jail. He'd been ashamed to tell his old friend and only admitted what happened years later. He hated the memories of 1965.

There were no times when Johnston could have met Winnie after the mid-sixties. Johnston entered the business world and his time was no longer his own. Johnston worked for a while as an analyst in an investment bank before he decided he could do better on his own and formed Thurwell Industries.

It was an arrogant name for a one-man start-up, but Johnston C. Thurwell II had vision. He started with $3,000 of his own money and persuaded a few others, including Larry, to invest a few thousand dollars each.

Thurwell Industries opened in 1966 with sixteen clients and $50,000. Forty years later Thurwell Industries was a global enterprise managing $300 billion in assets with an unparalleled record of success. In the early seventies, Johnston had diversified into the information business, going head to head with another entrepreneur, Freddie Hagood. They had been bitter rivals for decades, which made Freddie's presence at the mansion all the more confusing.

Larry looked at the dates on his page again, he was certain if his friend had ever met Winnie Tremethick, it had been in 1957, 1960 or 1965. He folded the paper and put it next to his watch on the desk. He'd give it to Winnie in the morning.

Chapter Fifteen

The residents of the mansion awoke to a clear day. The storm had broken in the night, and the dark clouds of yesterday were replaced by bright sunshine. The vast house looked like a cheerful Christmas card, but there was little goodwill within its walls.

Ron Freeman lay in bed and thought the sunshine was a good omen. His second chance at sharing in Thurwell's fortune began with the sun warming his face through the window. This day he would make sure he was not humiliated. He'd get his share of the Thurwell fortune and the family would pay for the trouble they had visited into his life. They would pay dearly. He padded to the shower with a spring in his step, a determined smile and a cold heart.

* * *

Bethany watched the sun rise, happy the storm was over. She loved the way the world looked after a snowfall. She watched the sky turn from a deep red glow in the East until golden light spilled over the snow-covered forest that surrounded the mansion.

Her heart soared when a deer appeared at the tree line. It sniffed the air, ears moving in quick twitches as it listened for danger. But the woods were silent, all sound muffled by the fresh snow. Bethany watched the deer step into the clearing and gingerly push its nose into the deep snow to find some grass. She watched the graceful animal feed and felt it was a good way to start a new day and a new chapter in her life. A life without her father.

The ugly business would be over today. William only had to divide the money and she would be free to grieve her father, and try to understand why he had shunned her. The deer looked up and met Bethany's eyes before it launched itself into the trees and was gone. Bethany smiled and took it as a hint to get moving herself.

* * *

Dennis Elliot was shaving and called his wife for the third time to get out of bed. The silly bitch would miss breakfast if she didn't move. He had a headache. He'd finished a whole bottle of wine last night and had passed out on the bed. He'd woken in the clothes he'd been wearing at supper and was stiff from sleeping at an awkward angle.

Janice had been awake when he got up, he was sure of it. Her breathing was different when she slept. He knew the difference, but went along with the pretence to eke out a few more moments of peace before she started on him again. He scraped at his face, dipped the razor in the hot water and called for her to get her ass out of bed. He sighed when she didn't move, today was the day they would become rich and yet she wanted to sleep in. He toweled his face dry, pulled the drain plug and watched the water swirl away, leaving dark bristles on the white porcelain sink. He didn't bother to wash them away. He was done with menial chores.

Dennis went to the bedroom and poked the covers over his wife's huddled shape. She grunted and pulled a pillow around her ears. He had enough and grabbed her arm to pull her out of bed, just like he'd done a thousand times before. She hated mornings and often needed a physical tug to get her moving.

He was shocked by her scream as she threw the pillow aside and fought his hand away. Her eyes were almost feral as she screamed for him to get away from her. He stepped back, alarmed by her reaction as he held out his hands to show he meant no harm. She stopped screaming but glared at him, breathing hard. "Don't touch me. Don't you come near me."

He backed off. There was something in her eyes he did not like. What the hell just happened? He opened his mouth to say something, but she shot out of the bed, slapped his face hard and ran into the bathroom, locking the door behind her. Dennis looked after his wife and rubbed his cheek where she had struck him. He knocked on the door, but she screamed again and he decided it was better to leave her alone until she calmed down.

He dressed quickly and left the room. If his crazy wife didn't want breakfast, so be it. He'd get his share of the money soon, and then he'd be rid of Janice for good. Her behavior this morning would make the break-up easier.

* * *

William Bird finished his eggs and toast before the first guests drifted into the dining room. He nodded to Camille and Bethany as they arrived together. They made to join him, but he stood and indicated he was leaving, he preferred to avoid any conversation. He made his apologies and left, taking a fresh coffee with him to his office.

The two daughters chatted amicably. After the meeting yesterday Bethany and Camille had enjoyed their first real conversation and Bethany discovered she might enjoy having a sister. Camille was still guarded, but had also been surprised by how well she and Bethany got along. They had nothing but their father in common, but were close in age and found that fashion, men and gossip crossed oceans both geographic and cultural.

* * *

Winnie Tremethick entered the dining room with Larry MacLean. They had met in the hallway on the way to breakfast, and he had gallantly offered his arm to escort her. He looked around for either William or Janice, still wondering what the scene he witnessed last night meant.

Winnie was as animated as he'd ever seen her and chatted excitedly about returning home. He noticed she never mentioned the fortune she'd take with her. He wanted to know her story before it was too late. He was intrigued to know how his old friend had ever come to meet such an unlikely woman.

* * *

Junior strode into the room with lightness in his step and a satisfied smirk. He was hungry and snapped his fingers at one of the staff to bring him some coffee. He looked around the room, his sisters were sitting together, and Larry was chatting to the old English woman. He was disappointed not to see Janice, he wanted to look her in the eye to complete his dominance over her.

He remembered he had to talk with Bethany about the new arrangement for the Elliot's payment, but he'd have time, it was not urgent. He grinned when he saw Dennis enter the room, but it faded when he realized Janice was not with him. *Perhaps she's lost her appetite* he thought, and stifled a giggle with a discreet cough.

* * *

The genial hum of excited conversation ended suddenly, as if someone pressed a mute button. Everyone stared at the door where an immaculately dressed Ron Freeman stood. He shot a hostile look at the assembled people before he took a seat and made a big show of shaking out his napkin as he ordered a large breakfast.

Bethany and Camille looked at one another, surprised that the Judge possessed enough nerve to appear. Why would he subject himself to embarrassment when he could have taken breakfast in his room? Unless it was an act of pure bravado, there was no need for him to appear in public.

The Judge's presence killed the atmosphere and people finished their breakfasts and left quickly. There was a half-hour wait before the meeting would begin, and the spoils would be divided. Most of the guests went back to their suites to freshen up. Dennis decided not to return to his room to receive more abuse from his wife and instead wandered around the lobby. He shot anxious glances up the stairs and hoped Janice would not be late.

* * *

Freddie Hagood sipped hot coffee in his room. He would wait until the last minute to arrive at the meeting. He wanted to make an entrance and see the family react to his return. They did not know he had been set to receive a generous payment and had lost it when Freeman tried to blackmail William. Freddie's new goal was to secure more than he had lost. He plotted how he might manipulate the group to his advantage, he knew more about each of them now, and he would not make the same mistakes he'd made yesterday. Freddie Hagood was used to winning, and he was damned well going to win now he had been handed a second chance.

* * *

Caroline Smith was excited. Her anger at being humiliated had passed. She looked at herself in the mirror with pride. She was no weakling that could be kicked around. The selfish Thurwells would cough up a fair share of the Old Man's money today. She'd make sure of it.

Her mouth twisted as she thought about how to handle the backstabbing Janice Elliot. She needed to exact a revenge for the housekeeper's betrayal. No one lied to

Caroline Smith and got away with it. She'd find something. She would make it her life's work to destroy Janice if she had to. Caroline checked her wristwatch, a few more moments, and she would head out. She wanted to be in a position to watch the other's reactions when they saw her at the negotiating table again.

* * *

Janice still trembled from Dennis's effort to get her out of bed. She knew she had over-reacted, but his touch had brought the memory of long hours in Junior's suite back and she had lost control. She forced herself to dress and sat in front of the mirror and tried to summon the courage to look at her reflection. When she finally met her own eyes, she felt the shame burn and looked away quickly. She had to pull herself together and endure being in the room with the others, with him, until the money was hers.

Once she was rich, she could run far from this place and forget. Or try to forget. *Focus on the money*, she told herself, *forget last night and focus on the money*. She repeated the mantra in her head as she stood and left the room, her stomach as jumpy as a shy girl on the first day of high school.

Janice made it to the top of the stairs on shaky legs and saw Dennis in the lobby, hopping impatiently from one foot to the other. She saw his relief at her appearance and allowed herself a smile. He was like a big dumb puppy, and that made her feel safe. Dennis was no threat. She would use him to stay strong. Her knees wobbled as she walked down the stairs, but she made it. To her husband's surprise, she folded her arm through his as they entered the conference room together.

They were the first to arrive and took their assigned seats at opposite ends of the table. Dennis noticed all thirteen chairs were set, just as they had been when they first arrived. He wondered why that might be. Surely the people who had been rejected would not be forced to watch as the others were given their money? Dennis couldn't imagine what cruel twist this might foreshadow. The Old Man had already unleashed so many surprises, who knew what yet was to come?

Dennis thought his suspicions were confirmed when he saw Caroline Smith enter the room. She wore a tailored Vera Wang suit and looked every inch a CEO. He saw her shoot a hostile look toward Janice, but his wife was not looking and missed it.

Smith was irritated she was not first to arrive, but she had been pleased by a suitably shocked expression on Dennis's face. The bitch housekeeper never looked up, she didn't have the nerve to face her. Caroline could be patient. She took her seat and smiled. She faced the door and would have the satisfaction of seeing each person's reaction as they saw her.

* * *

Betty Freah and Philip chatted animatedly as they entered the conference room, but stopped abruptly when they saw Smith. Philip looked at her with a puzzled expression. He recalled the Judge's surprise appearance at breakfast. Was this part of the philanthropist's plan?

He guessed Billy Bird would sort it out, so he nodded in Smith's direction and took his seat. He felt awkward and looked to his right where Betty was seated, then smiled as she gave him a shrug and a grin. Not much bothered Betty and today she was so happy that not even Caroline's surprise appearance could spoil her mood.

* * *

Bethany and Camille came in to the room, with Junior behind. The two girls glared at Caroline, but Junior didn't even see her, he was busy looking for Janice. He saw his target and leered, but it was wasted because she never looked up. She would look at him soon enough. His conquests always had to look him in the eye eventually. That she made him wait just extended the thrill.

He noticed Bethany had stopped and was staring. He looked and for the first time saw Caroline Smith in her seat and for a moment, he was as confused as his sister. "What are you doing here Caroline? This meeting is for people who will share my father's money. I believe the losers get to go home. That would include you."

She did not reply but shot him a venomous look. Junior snorted, if the rules said she had to watch him get rich, so be it.

Bethany and Camille watched Smith warily and were taking their seats when Judge Freeman strode into the room. He had expected to see the room full and was disappointed that only half the people had witnessed his entrance.

He was even more surprised to see Caroline Smith at the table. He had overheard a conversation at breakfast and was certain that both Smith and Hagood had also been thrown out. He must have heard wrong otherwise there was no reason for her to be here. His deal was not for the benefit of any other rejects. If William Bird had misunderstood, Freeman would soon correct him.

* * *

Larry MacLean and Winnie Tremethick strolled in together. She was on his arm and clearly enjoying his company. She expressed no curiosity that the Judge and Caroline Smith were back, but Larry did. He shot a look at Bethany and Junior, who both shrugged, confusion apparent on their faces.

MacLean had a sense of growing dread and was afraid the events he'd witnessed last night were connected to the reappearance of both Caroline Smith and the Judge. William Bird appeared at last, carrying a yellow envelope and his laptop. He showed no surprise at the presence of the two rejected guests but took his seat and began to tap away at his computer. Larry's heart beat faster, something was badly wrong. He could feel it.

The tension around the table ratcheted up another notch when Freddie Hagood strode in. MacLean's heart sank, Hagood's arrival was confirmation that something was seriously awry. He'd heard Freddie's anger when he listened through his door last night, yet now the magnate appeared calm and collected. He was in business mode and for Larry that meant storm clouds on the horizon.

* * *

William knew the exact moment Freddie arrived, without needing to turn. He heard Bethany's sharp intake of breath and other's exclamations of surprise and felt nine pairs of eyes land on him at the same time, all with the same question behind them.

He closed his laptop. He didn't need it. It had been something to keep his hands busy until this moment. He saw he already had every person's undivided attention and cleared his throat. "Good morning, I'm sure some of you are surprised to see you are reunited as a group."

"Jesus H. Christ, Bird. Are you deliberately understating it, or do you think we're morons? Of course, we want to know why the losers are back. What the fuck is going on?"

William held up his hand and waited for Junior to shut up. "I'm afraid there has been a change of plan. The deal you reached yesterday is no longer valid. It was rendered void by the actions of one person last night. Today we start a new process that requires all twelve of you."

The room exploded in noise and fury. Only the Judge, Freddie, and Janice said nothing. The Judge's face was set in stone, but he wondered what the hell Bird was talking about, this was what not he had demanded.

Freddie watched the family as they yelled abuse at the lawyer with faces twisted into ugly visages of greed and anger as they realized their inheritance was once more up for grabs. Janice sat with her hands folded in her lap, as her nails cut into her palms and hot tears ran down her cheeks.

William did not respond to the tide of outrage. He raised his hand, but it made no difference, so he sat and stared straight ahead until people realized they'd get no answers until they let him speak. As the last voice fell silent, inevitably Junior's, he continued. "Your agreement was voided before midnight yesterday, therefore, the fortune has been reduced by the twenty per cent penalty."

Larry MacLean was furious and led renewed howls of anger. "What the fuck do you mean, Bill? We could have reconvened if you'd told us last night. What is going on here?" He pointed a finger at Caroline Smith. "This is your doing Caroline, I saw you march out of Bill's office last night, what have you done?"

She shot to her feet and yelled back at MacLean. "I've done nothing, you idiot. Bird wanted to see me. I didn't make this happen, but I'm damned glad it did!" She snarled, but Larry saw the truth in her eyes. She was mean and triumphal, but she was telling the truth.

William raised both hands and pleaded for quiet. It took a full five minutes before he got them under control. He took a breath. "I work under a set of strict instructions left by Mr. Thurwell. I have little control over what happens, and I ask you all to remember that."

He looked around, they were angry, but they were listening. "Your deal was voided last night when I received a blackmail threat. My instructions for dealing with such a threat are simple. Before any discussion of dividing the fortune can proceed, each of you must satisfy conditions demanded by Mr. Thurwell."

He raised the yellow envelope, so they could all see it. "In this envelope is a collection of secrets. Each of you has something you would prefer remain secret from the world, and the people in this room. That is no longer an option if you wish to share in the fortune."

He saw the color drain from his guest's faces. Even Freddie Hagood looked worried. "Mr. Thurwell's idea is simple. Blackmail has been threatened, and he calculated the safest way to neutralize the threat, is for you to share your secrets. By doing so, each of you loses the power to use blackmail to manipulate the negotiations.

"The midnight penalty remains in effect, so I recommend you decide quickly if you wish to participate. If you refuse to share your secret, it will remain safe, but you will no longer be eligible to continue."

William heard more protests, but their fury had been extinguished. Now the sound of complaints was tinged with fear. Every person was scared about losing a share of the money but at the same time they were terrified about what they might be forced to reveal. Some had many secrets and did not know which one mattered. A few could think of nothing in particular. All of them were concerned about losing the chance to share in the Thurwell fortune.

* * *

A thin voice rose above the din and asked a question that stopped the noise. Everyone looked at Janice Elliot, who stood, pale and shaking. "Who? Who was it, William? Who did this to us?"

Judge Freeman was afraid. He was shocked at how his desperate play had turned out and wished he could turn the clock back. These people would hate him if Bird revealed his identity. He closed his eyes and prayed the lawyer would not reveal the blackmailer's identity, but his hope was in vain when he saw Bird point at him.

"The Judge came to see me in my office last night and threatened to reveal a secret that would have severely damaged Mr. Thurwell's reputation. Judge Freeman's demands voided your agreement."

People screamed at the Judge, and he stood to escape the angry mob, but found his way blocked by Janice. She trembled with anger as she looked up into his face. Freeman tried to slide past her when he felt something hot on his cheek.

Janice had spit in the Judge's face. He stood still, shocked, as her thick spittle dripped onto his immaculate suit. Janice turned to walk away, but her legs buckled under her. Dennis was close enough to scoop her up before she hit the floor. No one spoke as they watched him carry his wife away.

A high-pitched giggle startled everyone, and they turned to see Junior laughing uncontrollably, his face twisted into something so cruel, his laughter seemed horrific. Bethany shuddered as she watched her brother. Her skin crawled and she eventually looked away. But no-one could block out the sound of Junior's laughter.

Ron Freeman reached into his pocket and removed a silk handkerchief. His wife insisted he always carry one. She thought a clean white handkerchief was something a man from the South should always be armed with along with his manners. He wiped his face clean as the others watched and took a step forward. The angry group parted to allow him a narrow passage to the door.

He had to get to his room and remove the wet shame of Janice's spittle. Freeman also needed time to think, his plan had gone seriously awry. He had no idea a settlement had been negotiated last night. The people who had expected to be rich this morning would not forgive him for robbing them of their settlement. The lawyer had also said the penalty reduced the fortune by twenty percent. They would not forgive him for that, either.

Chapter Sixteen

Dennis carried his wife to their suite and set her down gently on the bed. Jeremy had appeared in time to open the door for Dennis and was now talking softly on the telephone in the other room. Dennis ran cold water over a face cloth and dabbed at his wife's forehead. "Wake up, Jan, please. Wake up."

He felt a hand on his shoulder. Jeremy was back with a woman at his side. He introduced her as Sarah, a nurse. Sarah firmly moved Dennis out of the way to take a look at the semi-conscious patient. "Leave us, I've got this. I'll take good care of her."

Dennis thought about protesting, but Jeremy steered him from the room before words came. Before he knew what was happening, Dennis was perched on a wooden stool downstairs in the main kitchen, sipping a hot coffee as Jeremy moved among the kitchen staff, issuing orders in his calm, efficient manner.

Sarah assessed Janice's condition. The woman was pale and her skin was clammy, but her breathing was regular, and her pulse was normal. Sarah figured she had simply fainted, Jeremy had told her there had been some sort of shock. She reached into her first aid kit and found a bottle of smelling salts. She cracked the top and wafted the bottle under Janice's nostrils.

Janice coughed and tried to sit up but failed and began to cry in deep racking sobs that seemed to come from her very soul. Sarah soothed her, talking gently all the time. Eventually Janice quieted and looked up. "I don't know you."

There was fear in her voice, but Sarah introduced herself and Janice laid her head back down. "Do you know why you passed out?" Sarah asked because she should, not because she was interested. "I didn't get much sleep. I got no rest last night. Then, this morning, it was all for nothing. I got nothing."

There was a lot Janice was not saying, but if she wanted to keep her business to herself, it was none of Sarah's concern. "Well, you'll be fine. Get some rest and I'll have soup brought up. Do you want a valium?"

"I just need to sleep, thanks." Sarah packed up her small bag of medical items, pulled the drapes closed and quietly left Janice to rest.

* * *

The conference room was filled by excited, often angry voices. Larry, Bethany, Philip, Camille and Junior huddled together in a tight family group near the window, where Bethany tried to make sense of events. "What just happened? Our deal is void, we lost twenty percent of Father's fortune, and now we have to share secrets. I don't have secrets. Do you?"

She looked at each of them, but none could meet her eyes. Bethany did have a secret, they all did. She could not believe hers might be written on a piece of paper in Bird's office. Surely no one knew? She was frightened and in that emotion, was in good company.

There was a moment of quiet until Larry spoke. "Whatever's happened, it's in our interests that these damned secrets are shared quickly. According to William, we lost twenty percent of the fortune last night, and the penalty clock is ticking again. I don't see why we can't put together the same deal as before, but first we have to get through this nonsense. Do you agree?" Philip pulled a face. "Do you think we can get the same deal Larry? Won't Freddie and Caroline work against us? They did before."

"No, Phil. They failed yesterday. All we have to do is keep our supporters loyal, and nothing has to change. We'll still have the Elliots, Betty and even old Mrs.

Tremethick on our side. Even if we have to increase their share a little, we'll still win."

Philip was reassured by Larry's assessment, but Junior felt sick. He couldn't tell the others, but he was certain that at least one of the Elliots would not vote with the family again. Bethany rallied them. "Okay, everyone stay focused. When you talk to anyone that supported us yesterday, make sure you shore up their support, we'll need them all again. Let's get this sordid blackmail thing out of the way and move on."

Camille nodded but was concerned, her soft voice serious. "But, sister. What if the secrets we hear change the way we feel about each other? That could be a problem, non?"

Bethany shuddered. The same idea had occurred to her, and she was afraid Camille had raised a very real problem. "We'll have to agree to not let whatever we hear affect our resolve." Bethany worried that if the secret she feared most was in William's envelope, the family might never understand.

She offered a nervous smile and saw the same reaction echoed on the other's faces. Only Junior didn't react, he seemed lost in his own thoughts. Bethany had been shocked by her brother's outburst after Janice spat on the Judge. He had delighted in Janice's reaction. Bethany was worried. Her brother had always been odd, but his laughter had sounded almost insane. She would keep an eye on him, the death of his father and the stress of losing their settlement may have gotten to him.

Larry interrupted her thoughts with a plan. "I suggest we break up and make sure we get everyone we can to pledge their support again, before we hear these secrets. Phil, you take Betty. Beth, you take the Elliots, and I'll talk to Mrs. Tremethick. I think her secret will be whatever link she had with your father, and I can help her. I'm also going to talk with Bill to see if we can get last night's penalty reversed, we might be able to resolve this quickly and still keep the entire fortune. Any questions?"

Bethany raised her hand. "Larry, what if Camille is right and our secrets change the way people feel about their allegiance?"

"Look, we can't know how it all will play out, but if we can get a declaration of support now, it might make it harder for people to change their minds later. It's a long shot, but we have nothing to lose by trying, right?" MacLean was pleased to see the group nod in agreement. "Okay, go circulate and be charming. Let's get what we need and we'll meet back here before William calls us back into session."

* * *

Larry left the family to talk to the lawyer. He saw Freddie and Caroline chatting together and smiled. It seemed he was correct about the group dividing along the same lines again. That was good news for the family.

William watched as his guests organized into groups and huddled in whispered discussions, each looking to find a way to screw the others out of a share. They all had to meet the new challenge and Bird suspected the old alliances would not survive the telling of the secrets. He felt a brush against his elbow and turned to see Larry MacLean. "Can we have a private word?" The lawyer nodded and led Larry to his office. The two men looked at each other across Bird's desk.

"What can I do for you, Mr. MacLean?"

Larry leaned forward in his leather chair. His voice was conversational, but his words betrayed his deep anger. "If you'd told me last night the deal was off, we might have been able to sort this mess out. It's not right the penalty was executed and that you gave us no opportunity to stop it."

"Larry, I told you already, I operate under strict instructions. Mr. Thurwell left a lot of notes detailing how I should act in circumstances that might or might not occur. Blackmail was one such situation, and my instructions were clear. Freeman threatened to blackmail the family in private, after you had adjourned. Mr. Thurwell's instructions were to wait until the next scheduled session to inform you. That's it, no arguments. Is there anything else?"

Larry shook his head in answer to the question but then changed his mind. "Yes, about this demand that we tell our secrets. What if someone has more than one secret, Bill? How are we supposed to know which one Johnston wants us to share?"

"They don't. If they have a lot of skeletons in their closet, they better make the right guess. Otherwise, you will all hear more than you need to, and the process will take longer. I can't offer any clues. You need to decide for yourself what secret you hold that will satisfy the Old Man's requirement."

"Why did he do it, Bill? Why make us fight over the spoils? Did he tell you why?"

"No comment, Larry. Maybe you'll find out, maybe you won't. It's not my decision if you get to know the reasons or not. Now, if you're finished, I need to get organized before we start again." MacLean accepted the kiss off and left the lawyer's office, he wanted to find Mrs. Tremethick to see how she was coping with the new turn of events.

* * *

Bethany came across Dennis Elliot in the lobby. "How's Janice, Dennis?"

The manservant shrugged. "I wish I knew, Miss Bethany. A nurse took a look at her and kicked me out. Jeremy gave me a coffee in the kitchen, but I can't sit still not knowing what's going on. It's not like Jan to get upset

166

like that. She's usually the calm one. Something's wrong." She nodded and made noises of condolence, but was she useless trying to help a domestic situation she couldn't relate to.

She saw Jeremy and called him over. The major-domo complied at once and told them both that Janice was resting comfortably. "Can I see her?" Dennis sounded so wretched that Bethany's heart almost broke, but Jeremy was professional.

"I don't think it's a good idea, sir. Let her rest. You can look in on her later, when Sarah's satisfied with her condition."

Dennis nodded, chewed his knuckle and wandered off. Bethany watched him go, and only too late she realized she had forgotten to ask the couple to support the family again.

* * *

Freddie watched as Caroline calculated the angles of joining him again. They had failed before, so perhaps she should find a way to get in with the family. Yet if she tried and they rejected her, Freddie might recruit others and she would be left out in the cold with no one looking out for her. The family had blindsided her before when they turned Janice against her.

It was clear they gave her no credit for her years of service at the Foundation. Hagood saw the moment Smith decided to partner with him again and smiled. He needed at least one more person to avoid a repeat of yesterday, but whom? Freddie was nervous about revealing his secret, but didn't see how it would affect anyone else who might ally with him. Only the family would care about his secret.

* * *

Larry found Winnie still in her seat. She looked confused and upset. "May I join you?" She looked up and smiled for the first time since the morning session began. "Mr. MacLean, there you are. I suppose I'm not going home now?"

"I'm afraid not Mrs. Tremethick. Not under current circumstances, but I do have something for you. You remember I promised to think of the times I wasn't in touch with Johnston?" The old lady nodded, her eyes fixed on the folded paper in Larry's hand. "Well, I was up late last night and wrote out what I remembered. Here, take this but don't look at it now, I don't want others to see. Read it when you can do so in private and let me know if anything sparks any memories."

Winnie took the paper, and it disappeared into the large handbag that was her constant companion. "Bless you, Mr. MacLean. I hope it helps both of us."

He smiled and found the old girl charming. They chatted about the surprises of the morning. She told him that while she didn't agree with what the Judge had done, the family had to take some responsibility for trying to send him away with no share. MacLean wouldn't have agreed with her assessment yesterday, but today she seemed like a pillar of wisdom. It would have been easier and cheaper for everyone to share the whole fortune. He could not undo what had been done, but he could do his best to rescue a bad situation. He patted the old woman's arm and excused himself. He had to find out how Philip and Bethany had made out on their missions.

* * *

Larry found it remarkable that the family had unexpectedly increased in size from three to four and how quickly the events of the past twenty-four hours had bonded them into a tight group. Junior, Philip, and Bethany would have ostracized the French girl in any other circumstance, yet here she was at the heart of the family unit. Philip grinned and gave two thumbs up to show Betty's support was solid. They looked at Bethany, who shrugged. "I don't know. I saw Dennis in the lobby, but he was too distracted and Janice hasn't come out of their room since her meltdown. I'll ask them later."

When Junior spoke, there was something about his voice that made them stare. "I could go and see her, if you think it would help." He had a faraway look in his eyes, and Larry wondered if he had been drinking.

Beth shook her head. "No, I said I'd take care of it and I will."

Her brother looked irritated but said nothing else. Larry watched the exchange and wondered why Junior would offer to see Janice. He had acted strangely all morning. His hysterical laugh had sent chills down MacLean's spine. It had sounded inhuman. Larry suspected the stress of having their settlement pulled out from under them had rattled Junior. He wasn't good under pressure which was why he had never been given a permanent portfolio in the family business. Instead, Junior was shuffled in and out of meaningless meetings as the token Thurwell. Larry decided to keep an eye on Junior in case whatever it was that disturbed him was something other than stress.

* * *

William entered the conference room and saw his guests waiting. There was palpable tension in the room, and when people looked at him, few of them could look him in the eye. They knew he had read their darkest secrets, and it bothered them.

He knew each of them dreaded the revelations that would come in the next hours. Some secrets would seem harmless in the light of public scrutiny while others may change lives or fracture relationships forever. Only time would tell, but it was up to William to get them started down that road. He called the meeting to order, and it took no time for them to take their seats.

William noticed two empty chairs. "Where are Judge Freeman and Janice Elliot?"

Dennis raised his hand, as if he needed permission to speak. "Jan's in our suite, sir. She took a bit of a turn after the last session."

William frowned. Janice had spit in the Judge's face, but he had no idea why she was so upset by his blackmail. Everyone who had been part of the first day's agreement had cause to be angry at Freeman, but she was the only person to react so viscerally. William waited, but no one spoke for the Judge. He was irritated and did not bother to cover it.

"We can't continue until everyone is here. The idea is to share your secrets. Each of you has to reveal your secret to the entire group. All of you, at the same time."

"But the nurse said Jan should rest-"

Junior interrupted Dennis. "For God's sake man, go and get her. We don't have all day, there's a clock ticking in case you forgot. Go get your wife, or I'll do it for you." He finished his sentence with a leer and again Larry wondered about Junior's state of mind. What was it with him and the housekeeper this morning?

Dennis flushed deep red and went to fetch his wife. As he left, Freddie Hagood also rose and headed for the door. "Where are you going, Freddie?"

Hagood stopped and looked down his nose at William. "I'm going to get the Judge. You did say we'd need everyone."

The lawyer nodded, but Larry was on his feet. "Wait a minute. We should let Jeremy get the Judge, someone neutral. Who knows what Freddie might say while we're not in earshot?"

"For God's sake MacLean, I can say whatever I want to him, whenever and wherever the hell I like. If you want, come with me. See if I care."

Hagood turned on his heel and left the room. Larry moved to follow him, but then changed his mind. He would stay. He needed to keep an eye on the family more than he was interested the Judge. A long as Larry held his group together, he could control the agenda.

* * *

Dennis slipped into his suite and waited until his eyes adjusted to the darkness. Three narrow shafts of sunlight poked through chinks in the heavy curtains, and dust motes moved lazily through the light. He found Janice still in bed and assumed she was sleeping. He padded across the carpet and her voice startled him. "Dennis, is that you?"

"Yeah, it's me. How are you feeling?" He sat on the edge of the bed and looked at her. He struggled to understand his feelings as he saw her afraid and vulnerable. He had long fallen out of love with his nit-picking wife, but this fragile version of her reminded him of the affectionate person he'd thought he'd married.

Dennis felt his resentment and anger fade and was surprised to see his own hand reach out and touch her cheek. Janice recoiled, and her voice regained its familiar edge. "What are you doing, Dennis? For Christ's sake, I don't need your sweaty hands all over me."

He sighed as the tender moment faded to dust, and he opened the drapes. The room flooded with bright sunshine and Janice groaned and pulled a blanket over her head, cursing him. Dennis' temper flared, he'd had enough. He was angry for his moment of weakness, how could he forget what she was and how she treated him? He tugged the blankets off her roughly. When he saw her, he gasped and sat down on the bed, hard. "What the hell? Janice, what happened to you?"

Her back was criss-crossed with angry red scratches and peppered with bruises. She tugged at the sheet to hide her body and buried her head in the pillow. She cried something he didn't hear. He rolled her over gently. "What happened, Jan? Where did these marks come from?" He could see she was frightened, there were more bruises on her wrists and he let go of her arm, afraid of hurting her. Janice's eyes squeezed shut, and she hugged herself as tears began to flow. "Talk to me Jan, who did this to you?"

Janice lay on the bed and looked up at her husband and wondered why he could not have been this strong all the time. If he'd been a real man she never would have wanted to leave him, never would have gone to Junior's room. Last night would never have happened.

Now Dennis was upset, and she could see anger in his eyes, but not at her. Dennis wanted to know who did this to her, and for a brief moment she wanted to tell him and see Junior suffer. She sniffed and wiped her eyes, she could see a better way to use Dennis's anger and get back at Junior. "If I tell you what happened, you must promise to do what I say, nothing more. I mean it Denny. If you want to help me get the man who did this, you have to do what I say."

Dennis's face reflected the rush of emotions that ran through him. Part of him quailed at the return of his carping wife, but a larger part was filled with rage that someone had hurt her. Something bad had happened to her last night, and Dennis suspected the Judge had something to do with it. It would explain why she spit at him.

He balled his fists as anger filled him at the thought of the Judge violating his wife. Dennis would kill him. He'd choke the life out of the prick. "Did that goddamned Judge do this? Is that what happened?"

Janice shook her head and knew she had to get her husband under control. "Promise you'll do what I say, Den. We'll get revenge and our money. More money than we were promised yesterday. A lot more." He stared, bewildered at her sudden coolness. She had been beaten yet was talking calmly about money and revenge. All he wanted to do was to kill someone for touching his wife. "I don't know Jan. Tell me why I shouldn't just kill whoever hurt you?"

"Don't be a moron Dennis. Listen to me. I'll tell you what happened, but you have to understand that taking his money is our best revenge. Better than you going to jail for a few moments of satisfaction. Better than jail for him for what he did to me. Now, are you ready to help me, or do I shut my mouth and let you imagine what happened?"

Dennis sighed, she was implacable, and he couldn't resist her overwhelming personality. If he had ever possessed the ability to stand up to her, he had surrendered it with a thousand small concessions during their marriage. "Fine. I'll do what you want. But tell me the truth."

Janice allowed herself a smile, her first that day. She would get her revenge on Junior. She patted the bed for Dennis to sit with her and started talking. "I took a call last night, after you fell asleep. It was Junior. He wanted to talk about money. He said he had a proposition for me." She saw her husband's eyes narrow at the mention of Junior, but he said nothing and she continued. "I went to his room. I don't know why I did, so don't ask. I knew better, but I was so happy about us becoming rich, I wasn't thinking."

Dennis opened his mouth to speak, but she silenced him with a finger on his lips. "No, just listen, Dennis, please. When I arrived, he said he could arrange to give me more money. I didn't understand at first, I thought he meant for both of us, that we could get more money than we had

173

been promised. But he didn't mean that Denny. Not at all."
She took a deep breath to calm herself.

Dennis was completely engaged in her story, he had no
suspicion she was making it up as she told it. "He told me
he'd give me a larger cut than you, if I would leave you and
go with him. Junior promised to give me your share of the
money Denny, if I ran away with him. He said he'd wanted
me for a long time. I said no, of course, I'd never betray my
husband. I tried to leave, but he grabbed me. I fought him.
I fought as hard as I could Denny...but... he was too strong
and I was so scared and I got so tired. I'm so sorry."

She cried, and her body shook with deep sobs that
wrenched at Dennis's heart as he tried to make sense of
what she said. He was shocked, but it was easy to believe
Junior was capable of both the offer of money and the
assault. Dennis knew he was going to kill Junior. Janice
felt his hand tighten around hers and saw her husband's
jaw stiffen. She had to calm him down, this was going far
better than she could have expected.

"Dennis. Dennis, look at me. Remember your promise.
We get revenge by taking his money, Den. Not by hurting
him, not physically. Beating him will achieve nothing, he'll
recover, and you might go to jail. If we take his money, it
will burn him forever. Help me take his money Denny. I
know how to do it." Dennis saw the resolve in his wife that
had crushed his spirit. At least this time it was directed at
a different target. She made sense, but even so he had no
idea how he could not beat Junior to a pulp when he saw
him.

He closed his eyes and breathed slowly. Okay, he'd play
it her way. If they got more money, he would be able to
escape more easily. Dennis felt like a traitor for thinking
about deserting her while she was covered in bruises, but
one look in her eyes told him that while her body may be
beaten, her spirit was as strong as ever. He had to find a
way to escape her, but first he and Janice would take every

dollar they could from Junior. Dennis had loved the Old Man. He'd been a loyal and true servant and had been deeply saddened to learn of his employer's death.

But the great man's family was a different matter. They could rot in hell as far as Dennis Elliot was concerned. He stood and looked down at his wife. "Get dressed Jan, if we don't get started soon I'm likely to run down there and choke that prick out of existence." He reached out a hand and helped her out of bed. He took a seat in the living room while she showered and dressed and did everything she could to make herself as attractive as possible.

Her first strike against Junior would be to show him that he had not broken her. He nearly had, but that was before she figured out a way to get back at him. That she had diverted her husband's anger with a fabricated story was no problem. Dennis would do as he was told, he always did. She'd leave him and start over to forget this whole sordid business. Janice thought about the beaches of Southern California, that's where she'd go. Where it was warm and no-one knew her. She smiled at her reflection in the mirror, a happy smile that was accompanied by eyes as hard as flint. If Junior had seen her at that moment, his heart would have quailed.

* * *

Freddie knocked on the Judge's door and was surprised when it opened immediately. The Judge was dressed in a new tailored suit that Freddie admired at once, it was not easy for big men to wear formal clothes, but the Judge had it nailed. "It's time to rejoin the rat race, Judge. I thought I'd come and collect you and take a moment to talk."

Freeman leaned on the doorway. His head almost touched the top of the doorframe and Freddie took a half step back, his neck hurt to look up at the big man at close quarters. "Judge, you delivered us another chance at some money. I can't say I'm impressed by your methods, but I can't say I blame you either." Freeman said nothing, he just listened. "We need to do the secrets thing, but then the scramble for the fortune is back on. I think we need each other again Judge, don't you?"

Freeman grunted. "I don't see why I should align myself with anyone. It did me no good last time around."

"That was unlucky. I should have seen it coming. Freeman, before they threw you out yesterday you voted against the family. They won't forget that, or forgive it. And that was before your clumsy blackmail threat voided their agreement. Unless you see a way to protect yourself, I'm afraid you're options are limited. Very limited."

Freeman knew he was correct, even though he hated to throw his lot in with Freddie again. "Very well, Mr. Hagood, I agree, we will be allies once more. I expect you to do better for our cause this time, do not let me down." Freddie bristled at the dig at his effectiveness, but let it pass. The Judge was pointing out the truth as he saw it. He could not know how much his blackmail cost Freddie. Only William knew the Judge's blackmail had derailed a small fortune.

Freddie had an idea that he might be able to do even better than the large settlement he had been gifted and since lost. He needed one more person to secure them against a repeat of the first day. Freddie hoped as people revealed their secrets he would gain candidates for his alliance. He offered his hand, and they shook on their new deal. As they headed to the conference room, the Judge smiled for the first time since his earlier humiliation. The others may hate him, but he was back in with a chance at gaining a fortune. His plan had taken an unexpected twist, but he was back at the table and that was all that mattered.

* * *

There was silence in the conference room as the group waited for the others to return. Philip and Betty engaged in soft conversation that was inaudible except for an occasional tinkling laugh that Betty was unable to suppress. She seemed unburdened by the weight of the task to come and Bethany hated her for being so relaxed while she was sick from fear.

Bethany did not want to share her secret. She was shocked that her father might have discovered it. She had known his views and his Foundation actively reflected his personal beliefs. If her secret was ever revealed it would have caused her father a lot of problems, but that wasn't the worst of it. Bethany knew in her heart that her secret was the reason her father never called for her as he lay dying.

* * *

Janice stepped from the bathroom, fully dressed and with perfect make-up. She stood tall and proud, and Dennis felt an old feeling stir in his chest as he looked at her. She was still a fine looking woman. "You look great, Jan. Really good." She accepted the compliment with a smile even as her heart fluttered with nerves at what was to come.

She joined her husband, who offered his arm in a chivalrous gesture. "Thank you Dennis. Now let's go and nail that bastard to the wall." Dennis smiled, he couldn't help it. His wife had suffered God knows what at the hands of Junior Thurwell, yet her focus was on Junior's fortune and how much she could hurt him back.

Chapter Seventeen

William turned in his seat to see Freddie return to the conference room with Judge Freeman. Freeman did not look left or right, but quietly took his seat and folded his hands in front of him and stared into space.

Freddie was nonchalant and took his place between Camille and Bethany, effectively ending their conversation. He smiled at those that looked at him and noticed Dennis and his wife had yet to make it back. He was annoyed at having to wait, he was used to being the person everyone else waited for.

Philip returned to his conversation with Betty and ignored a disapproving look from his sister. Philip didn't care that Bethany disliked Betty. She was unable to accept her father had been sexually active and blamed Betty, which Philip thought a ridiculous argument. Philip took his father's virility as a good sign that he had good genes for a long sexual career.

He was asking what Betty might do when all this was over. He didn't dwell on what they had to endure before sharing the fortune was discussed again. He would worry about that when it was his turn to tell his secret.

He was about to whisper something funny about his new French sister when the Elliots returned. He fell silent, interested to see what drama might unfold at the housekeeper's return.

Janice appeared to be an entirely different woman to the one Dennis had carried out of the room. She was dressed in a fashionable suit, and her hair and make-up were immaculate. She possessed the air of a confident businesswoman, not the simple housekeeper he used to see in his father's home.

Junior had waited eagerly for Janice's return. His thoughts had been on nothing else since she'd spit on the Judge. He wanted, no, he *needed* her to look at him and acknowledge his power over her. When she appeared on Dennis's arm and looked directly at him, anyone studying Junior's face would have seen it transform from triumph to disappointment and, finally, deep anger.

His complexion turned the dark red hue that signaled danger to those that knew him well. Janice had met his

178

eyes, just as he needed, but instead of submission and shame, he saw contempt. The slut even dared to look down her nose at him.

He wanted to slap her but then he noticed Dennis glaring at him. He felt a deep chill run down his spine. Dennis knew. There was hate in his eyes, and Junior had no doubt Dennis now knew all about last night. Junior's anger bled away and left him with a sick feeling deep in his stomach. He was suddenly terribly afraid.

No woman had dared to tell a soul what happened after they had been alone with Junior. Sometimes their silence cost money, but most times shame and his veiled threats were enough. Now Dennis knew about him. Dennis was a slow thinker, but he was a big man. Junior could not allow Dennis to corner him. He'd need to stay around other people for safety. Junior was sweating and could not hold Janice's gaze. He dropped his eyes in defeat as fear and rage battled for dominance in his heart.

Winnie Tremethick saw a flicker of fear in Janice's eyes as she sat next to her. She was afraid of something or someone, but was putting on a decent show of being confident. Winnie reached out and patted Janice's arm and offered a little smile made warmer by her kind eyes. Janice returned the smile, it was natural, but Winnie saw the effort required to make it. The old lady wondered what had so upset her, but now was not a suitable time for questions. She heard the lawyer call them to attention and turned to listen.

* * *

William was relieved that everyone was present, if not entirely happy or comfortable. "Since you are all here, it's time to continue. Larry, I'll run things until the sharing of secrets is complete, at which point you may Chair the group again. Let me be clear, there is no debate about what you must tell each other. I have a list from Mr.

Thurwell that describes information each of you would prefer to remain secret, but that you must share.

"If you provide an accurate description of your secret, you may remain to negotiate your share in the fortune. If you obfuscate or try to misdirect the group, I will give you one final chance to correct the record. Failure to share the truth or refusal to participate is your choice but will cost you the opportunity to win Mr. Thurwell's money."

The lawyer looked in turn at each person until they acknowledged him. The heavy silence was punctuated only by an occasional pop from the fire that still burned robustly across the room. William was satisfied they all understood. "Is there anyone who prefers not to participate? If so, now is the time to leave. Once we begin, there will be no backing out."

No one volunteered to leave. "Very well, then we can begin." He looked up as he sensed a hand was raised, it belonged to Camille Jolivet. "Monsieur Bird. How do we decide who goes first?"

"The order will be random. I'll write your names on pieces of paper and pick them out one at a time. If your name is called, you talk." Camille gave a grimace, a one in twelve chance of going first wasn't too bad. She hoped that she would not be the first to talk.

Larry MacLean interrupted. "Bill, how do we know it'll be random? You could have a pre-arranged order and manipulate it, why don't you let one of us draw the names?"

"Would that make you feel better, Larry? Is that what you are really worried about right now?" Bird snapped.

MacLean looked away, feeling foolish. He had felt he should say something to retain his authority with the group, but his question had been meaningless and Bird had made him look petty. He wished he'd kept his mouth shut. He mumbled an apology and tried to look like he hadn't just acted like an ass.

Bird stared at Larry for a few long seconds to make a point about who was in charge, then opened his notebook and tore out twelve strips of paper. He took his time, knowing all his guests watched his every move. He wrote a name in neat print on each piece of paper, taking the time to look directly at the person whose name he wrote, then folded the paper twice and dropped it into an empty water pitcher. He dropped the last name into the glass and saw each person trying to guess who might be unlucky enough to go first. William shook the glass pitcher to mix up the names and placed it in front of him. Twelve people simultaneously stopped breathing as Bird reached into the glass and picked one out. "Freddie Hagood. Freddie, you go first."

Hagood shrugged. His face was expressionless, and his voice even. "So be it, I get to go first." He sipped his water, refilled the glass and set it down again, giving it a quarter turn. He liked to be the center of attention and knew these moments would be his last as Johnston Thurwell's legendary business rival. Freddie scanned the others' faces. Some of them had worse things to share than him. One he knew about already. It was time to end many years of secrecy.

"You all know me. I own the largest network of business information sources in the world. If you have a business making more than a few million dollars a year, I know about it, and I will sell what I know to the highest bidder. It's good business. It was so good that Johnston Thurwell and I competed hard to control it. We banged heads for a lot of years. I won some contracts, and he won others. But over time he won more as I lost more. By 1987, our firms had a lock on the market. Over 75% of all commercial business information came from one or other of us."

Freddie took another sip of water. He had everyone's complete attention. "At the end of the eighties, Johnston and I met in secret. We met in these woods, in fact. He'd bought this land, but the mansion hadn't been built yet, there was just an old lodge that was barely standing. We came here, and we made a deal. He gave me a staggering sum of money and I gave him my business.

"We knew we'd never get regulatory approval, we controlled too much of the market. So we pretended to operate separately. We fixed prices and bullied customers into each other's arms. At the end of each year, I took ten percent of HBN's profit and stuffed it into an offshore account for Johnston. I put five percent into my own account, and we carried on, until now. I'm far wealthier than you know, and Johnston took twice what I did every year, for twenty years. And he had the rest of his empire making him money too."

Freddie saw shock on the faces looking at him as they quickly re-evaluated their estimates of Thurwell's fortune. Others were aghast at the deception of the two magnates. William, when he had read the secrets in the yellow envelope, had at last understood why he had never been invited to the Old Man's private meetings with Freddie.

Junior turned deathly pale, he had trouble comprehending what he'd just heard. He realized with horror that the secret he would need to reveal was far worse than the one he'd thought he would be telling. It would be a mess when the family heard it.

Larry MacLean was the first person to recover his wits. "Do you mean to tell us that, for twenty years, you and Johnston colluded to manipulate the market? How? I mean, how did you pull it off?" Freddie grinned. He felt no pressure now his secret was out. He'd spend the rest of his days in jail if the news left this room, but that would mean someone else risking a secret being revealed. It was mutually assured destruction. "Larry, you've know Johnston most of your life. How come you never suspected your oldest friend was in cahoots with me?"

"You hate each other, everybody knows that." MacLean's reply was out of his mouth before he thought about it. Their bitter rivalry was no secret. Then, understanding came. "Oh my God. You two kept up the pretence of rivalry, of despising each other. None of it was real?" Freddie grinned as he enjoyed the disbelief on their faces. It underlined the success of the grand deception he and his dead friend maintained for decades.

Bethany was rocked to her core. She was the face of public relations for her father's empire. She had issued vicious press releases about Hagood, even started rumor campaigns to cost him market share. She recalled leaving her father's office with him raging in the background about the charlatan Freddie Hagood. But none of it had been real. The war between the two business giants had no losers except their unsuspecting customers. She was shocked. Her father had never once hinted at such a deal and had used her like a pawn. She had a hard time believing her father could be so cold toward her.

Then she remembered her own secret. She didn't know how he had found out, but she had no doubt about the cause of the chill in their relationship in the last year and a half. Her head dropped, and she concentrated on breathing, she had to stay calm.

Hagood smiled. "So, William, did I forget anything?"

"No, Freddie, you laid it all out. You've met the requirement and may continue." Freddie leaned back in his chair. He felt light-headed with the thrill of telling the secret he and his friend shared. That the world thought of them as bitter enemies had been a great source of amusement to them. They had joked together as they made up stories about each other to escalate their rivalry in the press.

When they met in public, they enjoyed a thrill at the crowds that gathered while they pretended to be barely polite to each other. That they became fabulously wealthy while they had so much fun was a bonus. Freddie never minded collecting only half of what Johnston did. The fortune Thurwell privately paid him for HBN was more than he could spend in a hundred luxurious lifetimes.

* * *

William mixed the eleven papers in the pitcher as his eleven guests held their breath. The lawyer carefully unfolded a slip of paper as people prayed it would not be their turn.

"Ms. Freah. It's your turn. Betty, please share your secret."

Betty Freah sighed. This was a chore, but nothing to be feared. She took a quick look at the faces focused on her, skipping quickly past Bethany's. "I already shared my secret, sort of, in our introductions. But I understand why I have to do it again. The simple fact is Johnston paid me to have sex with him. He was my only client for over ten years. I also run a small operation with some girls of my own. I like the term escort, but if you prefer whore or prostitute, I can live with it. I stopped worrying about other people's labels a long time ago.

"That's all there is. It's no real secret. I had sex with a rich man who paid me well in return. I refuse to share intimate details, and I hope you won't try to make me." She looked pleadingly at the lawyer who shook his head. "That won't be necessary, Betty. You can proceed to the next session, thank you."

Betty sat with her hands folded in her lap as she endured everyone's scrutiny. No one spoke to her, some of the men looked at Betty with interest, but she was used to that. The women looked down their noses at her, with the exception of Winnie, but Betty was used to that. There were no questions so William dipped his hand into the glass and stirred the papers before he picked out the third name.

"Larry. Larry MacLean, it's your turn."

MacLean was relaxed. The people he might have wanted to keep his secret from already knew it and the others did not matter. He drew a deep breath. "I'm broke. My family is flat broke. Johnston has been supporting me for several years. My brother, who we trusted to manage the family trust, went rogue and stole or lost all our wealth. I turned to my oldest friend for help. I'm not sure how that might be used against him, or me, but there it is. Larry MacLean is heir to no fortune and needed his best friend's charity to sustain his lifestyle."

He leaned back in his seat and watched the reactions. The family showed no surprise, they already knew about his family trouble. Freddie chuckled quietly which made Larry angry, but no one else cared. Most of the people were too consumed with dread for when their own time in the spotlight came to worry about Larry's minor revelation.

He looked at the lawyer. "Did I miss anything, Bill?"

William looked at MacLean and shook his head. "Actually Larry, while that was an interesting story, it is not the secret Mr. Thurwell required you to share."

The color drained from MacLean's face. "What do you mean, not the right secret? There are no other secrets." Larry's mind reeled. He did have another secret, but he never suspected his friend knew about it. Surely, he could not have found out? Larry's heart raced and fear gripped his stomach as he tried to think of another secret, any secret, that was not the awful truth.

"One more chance, Larry, or I'll take you out of the group immediately." Bird's voice was flat, there was no room for negotiation, his required task was quite clear. Larry tried to stall. "I... I... Might I take a moment? I need to think."

Junior snapped. "Get on with it Larry, time's ticking away, just get on with it. How bad can it be?" Larry looked at his friend's eldest son and swallowed hard, it was quite a lot worse than Junior suspected.

Bird warned him again, but Larry hardly heard him through his rising panic. "Larry, start talking or you're out." MacLean tried to calm himself and took a deep breath. "Fine. I'll do it."

"Damned right you'll do it MacLean. If I did it, you damned well can too." Larry shot a venomous look at Hagood's gloating face and clasped his hands in front of him. "I committed an indiscretion in my past. It was not a small indiscretion by any means, and I wronged my oldest friend in committing it."

William frowned and interrupted. "Larry, speak up so everyone can hear you, or get kicked out, I'm serious."

MacLean nodded and looked at Bird with an unspoken appeal in his eyes but was met with an uncompromising stare. Larry started over, raising his voice so everyone could hear. "In 1968 I began an affair with Julie, Johnston's first wife and Junior's mother. I persuaded her to leave him and she did but after their divorce, I lost interest in her and moved on. I didn't know Johnston ever found out."

He drew a breath to continue, but Junior was on his feet, his face deep red and his mouth flecked with spittle. "You prick MacLean. You... you cheap fuck." Junior was so angry words failed him. Larry looked into his eyes and saw pure rage beneath the surface. "I'm sorry, Junior. Truly sorry."

"You broke up their marriage, you monster. You ruined my life, and all this time you let me blame him. I should kill you-"

"Enough. Junior, that's enough. Let him finish."

Junior glared at Bird, but sat down and bored his eyes into MacLean as if he wished he could kill with a look. He had blamed his father for the divorce. No one had ever suggested his mother was the reason for their break up. She must have told her ex-husband of the affair, either to get her divorce, or sometime before she died ten years later. He had found out about his friend's betrayal and had never said a word to Junior.

He saw MacLean's weary face, the so-called great family friend who turned out to be nothing more than a cheat and a liar. He'd had the nerve to remain friends with the man he'd cuckolded and later even beg for money. Junior's chest burned with deep rage, but he waited for MacLean to complete his confession.

"I thought I loved her, I really did. Julie was a special woman, and I thought Johnston never treated her well enough. In the end, though, it was I that did her the most harm. I caused the breakup of my best friend's marriage. That is my secret. That is my shame. I'm sorry." Larry's head drooped as he finished. He felt old and tired and wanted to be anywhere but in the room with Junior and the rest of the family.

William Bird shook his head at Larry, but acknowledged his secret was shared. "Thank you Larry. You get to move on to the next session."

Bethany looked at the person she thought she knew so well just twenty-four hours earlier and realized the man she called 'Uncle Larry' was almost a total stranger. She shook her head and looked at Junior. He had always been screwed up about his parent's divorce. Thurwell's second wife, Bethany and Philip's mother had never made room for Junior in their family.

Larry MacLean had caused the break-up and the knowledge tore Junior up inside. As a boy, he had transferred the love he withheld from his father to his kindly Uncle Larry. The double betrayal was astounding, and Junior found breathing difficult as he tried to comprehend it.

William asked if the group wanted a break. Larry looked relieved and stood to leave when Junior's voice stopped him in his tracks. "Don't move, MacLean. We're not jeopardizing any more of my father's money so you can slink off and feel sorry for yourself. Sit down, all of you. We're ending this circus today, sit down and let's finish."

Larry meekly returned to his seat and tried to ignore the judging eyes on him.

* * *

Bird watched the drama play out, he knew a break would be necessary at some point, but he had no desire to contradict Junior when he was volatile. He brought the focus back by reaching into the glass and selecting the next name.

"Judge Ronald Freeman. Please share your secret with us, sir."

Freeman took a breath and started talking. He saw no reason to delay after watching MacLean's self-destruction. "You may remember I said I had previously met William Bird. It happened that Mr. Bird came to Macon to negotiate Philip Thurwell's release from jail. He had been arrested following a traffic accident. What I did not mention was that I refused Mr. Bird's request. I had no reason to intervene in the case, which the police department was still investigating. The accident was far more serious than Philip described, a young man died at the scene and manslaughter charges were possible."

There was a hiss from Junior, who shot a look at his younger brother. "You told us that you totaled your Porsche, Phil. You killed someone?"

Philip shrugged, but Bethany knew her younger brother best and noticed a tightness in his face, Philip was hiding something. She turned back to the Judge who glowered at Junior for interrupting him.

"I refused to go along with Mr. Bird's request. In fact, I was more determined than ever to see justice served. Unfortunately, shortly after my refusal I found myself in an impossible situation and regretfully agreed to Mr. Bird's demand that Philip not be charged. In exchange, I would receive financial support for my political career."

Freddie Hagood listened intently, he had guessed most of this, but it was interesting to hear it firsthand. He interrupted Freeman. "Bill blackmailed you, Judge? Is that what happened?"

Freeman nodded and sent an accusing glare at William Bird. "I was coerced into dropping the case, but I accepted the offer of political support."

Freddie looked at the lawyer. "Is that true, William?"

The lawyer held Hagood's gaze without flinching. "I did what I had to do to get Philip out of there. The Judge had a family member that provided some leverage."

"You took advantage of a young girl's poor judgment." Freeman snapped.

Freddie was still interested in the details. "So your secret is that Bill Bird blackmailed you into letting Phil walk from a car wreck that killed someone? How did you do it, exactly?"

"I called in a favor. I didn't want to, but the Chief of Detectives owed me and I called it. The police had already determined there was no DUI, and the victim was a known felon. It seemed like there was little actual harm if we let it slide."

Freeman saw looks of disapproval as the others listened to his story and he felt the need to defend himself. "Look, it's not a perfect system. In fact, it's swamped. Chances are that Philip would have gotten a fine, if that. So I did little more than expedite the process. Yes, I was blackmailed into getting the case dropped and yes I accepted political help in return, but I've seen worse abuses."

Freddie turned away, embarrassed for the Judge as he tried to justify his behavior. Others looked at Bird with disapproval. William didn't care to make excuses, he had done what his boss wanted and he had gotten it done fast and easy. That was all that mattered, not the judgment of people who all carried dirt of their own. Freeman sounded defeated as he asked the lawyer to pass him to the next session. "Am I done? There's nothing more to tell."

"Yes, Judge, you will continue. It's time to select the next person."

* * *

"Johnston Thurwell III. Junior, you're next. Please tell your secret."

The philanthropist's eldest son felt his heart quail. He had dreaded this moment from the moment he heard Freddie Hagood's secret. He swallowed and darted a quick look at Bethany. "I want to say, in my defense that I didn't know then what I know today. If I had known, if I could have seen the truth, things would be very different."

Philip groaned. "Just get on with it, brother. It's not like you're the only scumbag at the table, is it?"

Junior looked at his brother and sighed, he was right. There was nothing to do but tell the story. "I sold Thurwell Industries' information to our competitors. Freddie himself paid me a lot of money. Today I just found out he and my father were in secret partnership. Which means father knew of my betrayal." Junior's head dropped as he talked, felt small and weak, like he used to as a boy.

"How could you, Junior? How could you sell us all out? Why, for money?" Bethany was unable to keep the contempt from her voice. She had worked hard to make the business successful and was shocked to discover her brother had sold them out, undoing the work of thousands of good people. "Why Junior? Tell me why you did it."

Junior lifted his head and looked at Larry MacLean with pure venom. "I hate you Larry. I spent years trying to take revenge against my father and all the time it was you that I should have punished. You ask me why, sister? I hated father. I blamed him for dumping my mother and making me feel like a second-class kid when you and Phil came along.

"You were so close to him, and I was never included. I plotted my revenge, and when I got to where I could hurt the Old Man, I acted." Bethany and Philip shook their heads, Junior's rant hit a nerve, yet Junior still sounded petulant as he spoke of his boyhood. Junior looked at Freddie with desperation in his eyes. "Did you tell him? When I came to you with my offer, did you tell my father?"

Hagood smiled, but there was no compassion in his eyes. "Yes, of course. As soon as you called me, I told your father. The funny thing was that if I had not been working with your father, I would have told you to get lost. I've no interest in being used as a pawn in family squabbles.

"Johnston told me to both pay and encourage you. He used you, Junior. When I sent you to meetings, you were being played. Your father made sure you only saw information he wanted leaked. You sold falsehoods and misinformation to his competition, and we made a rich profit from your efforts to ruin him. "We used to laugh about how much money we made from your treachery. He always knew you were a weak kid, which is why you never got a proper job."

Hagood laughed as he mocked Junior, who flushed crimson. Junior wanted to say something to get back at Freddie, but withered under the other man's cruel laughter. A fat tear rolled down Junior's cheek and landed with a splash on the table in front of him. He wiped at it with his sleeve, his mind numb as he tried to process how badly he had been misled about his mother's divorce and how his revenge had been turned against him. "I need a break. William, a break now, please?"

Freddie Hagood pre-empted Bird's answer. "Suck it up Junior. Larry didn't get a break, why should a family traitor get to hold up our progress?"

There were mutters of agreement and William made it official. "No break. Not until we get to lunch. Sorry Junior, but you refused Larry's request for a break and I'm going to be consistent."

He felt some small sympathy for Junior. The man had carried his childhood anger into adulthood and in the last hour had seen that both the source of his anger and his attempts at revenge had been misdirected. Bird recognized Junior's qualification to move to the next session and picked the next name from the glass.

* * *

"Janice Elliot. Janice, if you please, move us forward and share your secret."

She seemed surprised to hear her name. She looked at William, then at Dennis. Her husband gave a slight nod. "Mr. Bird, my secret is a shared one. Dennis and I have the same thing in common, I think we should only have to say it once, for us both. Would that be okay?"

Bethany was surprised, she had an interest in what her father's servants had to say and was increasingly nervous about more potential bombshells. William looked from Janice to Dennis and conceded the point. It would save time to have it told only once. "Go ahead, I don't care which one of you tells it, or if you share, but make it as brief as you can, please."

Dennis nodded and took over, a small kindness to Janice. It was the second time in a few hours she had been pleasantly reminded of the man she had once fallen in love with. "Jan and I were asked to do something for Mr. Thurwell. He told us that we'd do it for loyalty, not payment, but he promised eventually we'd share in his estate. Which is why we're here, I guess. "Mr. Thurwell discovered a betrayal that wounded him enormously. We helped him get retribution."

Bethany's face was a picture of barely controlled fear as she interrupted. "Who? Dennis, who was he angry with?" Dennis looked at her strangely. It was as if she suspected he was talking about her, but as far as he knew she was guilty of no betrayal.

He pointed at the philanthropist's oldest friend. "Mr. MacLean was the target. The first Mrs. Thurwell died ten years after their divorce. A package arrived for Mr. Thurwell. There were letters written by Mr. MacLean to her and pictures of them together. What caused the most hurt to Mr. Thurwell was a letter she had written to him while they were still married, but she never sent. In it, she told him of her love for Larry MacLean and she, well, let's just say she was not shy about sharing intimate details." MacLean turned white as a ghost as he listened to Dennis. He had discovered the method by which his dead friend had learned of his illicit love affair.

What worried Larry was Dennis had mentioned retribution, but Larry could recall no harm caused to him. He listened fearfully as Dennis continued. "Jan and I agreed to help Mr. Thurwell. He had paid for our wedding and was always good to us. We hated to see him upset. It took some time and a few payoffs before we found what we needed, a weak link in Mr. MacLean's life. Once we found that one loose thread, Jan and I went about unraveling it."

MacLean was angry. He knew no action had been taken against him, which meant Dennis was a liar. "Bullshit Dennis. You never touched me. Julie died over twenty years ago, and Johnston was my friend until he died. This is just crap you're peddling to avoid telling something embarrassing about yourself."

Dennis shrugged, and Janice took over the narrative. "Mr. MacLean, you make the mistake of assuming the package Dennis spoke of arrived directly after Mrs. Thurwell's death. In fact, he only received it a few years ago. When her old apartment building was renovated, a package was found hidden in the walls and was forwarded to the building's owner. Mr. Thurwell still owned the building. It was a coincidence he ever got it. It lay there a long time, unremembered and unwanted. When he received it, it was unwelcome even then. His hurt was awful, and his rage was terrible to witness. So, you see Mr. MacLean, it's only in the past few years your betrayal was uncovered, and Mr. Thurwell began actions against you."

MacLean shook his head, not believing them. The only thing that had happened recently was his idiot brother blowing the family trust. He still thought the couple was lying. "Go on. What did you do? You and Dennis, in this absurd fantasy of yours, what did you do to me?"

"I'll let Dennis talk about it. It was his idea, after all."

She nodded at her husband, who smiled and turned to MacLean. "Mr. Thurwell wanted to take your life apart, Mr. MacLean. He knew he couldn't do it without first making you dependent upon him. So we stole your family's money. Or, to be more accurate, we had Robert, your brother, give it to us."

Larry's mind reeled. "You're lying. Johnston was helping me. I asked for help, and he never hesitated."

Dennis shook his head. "No, sir, I'm telling the truth. Your brother owed money to bookies all over the country. Let's just say I have a bookie or two in common with Robert. Mr. Thurwell set me up with a lot of cash. I was to become Robert's friend and that's what I did. We gambled together, but I kept pushing up the stakes and encouraging him, until eventually Robert was in debt to some very bad folks. "Then we acquired some pictures of Robert with a hooker. Jan did a good job taking pictures and Betty provided the girl."

Larry looked at Betty Freah, who sat with a stone expression. "Betty? You were in on this? But I introduced you to Johnston for Christ's sake. You owed me."

She scoffed. "You killed any loyalty I owed you when I found out what you did to your best friend's marriage. You prick Larry, how could you sleep with your best friend's wife? What you got, you had coming, I was happy to help JT out."

MacLean shook his head, unable to believe the plot they had worked against him. "Okay. Robert's an idiot. I know that about my brother, but if what you say is true and you took my family's money, why would Johnston help me? It makes no sense. There are too many holes in your story Dennis, I'm not buying it."

Dennis chuckled. "Robert MacLean owed a lot of money to a loan shark he thought was involved in the local mob family. He believed it because that's what I told him. He was scared and desperate. We showed Robert pictures of him snorting coke from a hooker's thigh, and some that were a bit more sordid, too. Then we told him to pay his debts in full, or the last thing his kids would see was pictures of their father up to his naked balls in coke and girls. "It was like turning on a spigot, the money flowed from your trust so fast that, in less than six months, we had it all. Robert was given enough to disappear, and all Mr. Thurwell had to do was wait for you to come looking for a handout."

Larry shook his head, it couldn't be true. Yet he had not been able to reach his brother since his lawyers called to tell him there was a problem with the trust. He looked at Dennis again, grasping for anything to make the man a liar. "Then why would he help me? It makes no sense."

Dennis nodded and passed off the story to Janice. "You were lucky Larry, that's what happened. You've lived beyond your means, even after Mr. Thurwell started helping you. He was waiting for your debts to grow, for you to finish digging a deep enough hole, then he was going to cut you loose and watch you fall. Your time was coming too. You know how much you need his money. You're about done already. But Mr. Thurwell died before his plan was completed. I don't know why you've been given a chance to save yourself by being included here, but I'm sure Mr. Thurwell had his reasons. Like I said, you got lucky."

Freddie Hagood whistled. "Goddamn, Larry. I thought the man was tough as a rival before he took me out, but you reaped the whirlwind Larry. Damn."

Larry's heart pounded in his chest. He accepted what the Elliots said was true. He had been living too high. Even cutting allowances to the rest of his family had not been enough to stem the tide of his accumulating debt. When Bethany asked for his help, he had seen his chance and demanded a large share. He looked now at Bethany, who looked away. Larry knew he would be lucky if he saw a penny of the Thurwell fortune and panic filled him. He was ruined. He heard Bird passing the Elliots into the next round, their secret successfully shared at his great cost.

* * *

Judge Freeman watched the undoing of Larry MacLean with the same morbid interest of a person watching a bad car wreck. His attention had been caught by something said at the end of the last exchange, when Janice suggested her employer had not had time to remove MacLean from this group before his death. Freeman had an excellent ability to follow complex arguments and to pay attention to details, an invaluable tool for a Judge. There was something so jarring in Janice's statement, he knew instantly she was wrong.

Whatever else the dead Mr. Thurwell had been, he was not careless. If Thurwell had plotted as carefully as he had to bring about the ruin of his treacherous friend and to plan the blackmail clause the Judge himself had triggered, it was unlikely he had forgotten to disinherit MacLean. Something else was going on, something Thurwell had not shared with his loyal servants.

* * *

William picked the next name from the pitcher. "Caroline Smith. Ms. Smith, it's your turn. You know what to do."

Caroline was frightened. What she had to say would end her career. A cold bead of sweat ran from her armpit down her torso and made her shiver. She feared the judgment of the family, so rushed to get it over with. "As you know, I am Chief Executive Officer of the Thurwell Foundation."

She put her usual emphasis on her title and then realized how hollow it would sound in a few seconds. "I am afraid I was not as honest in my position as I should have been, and as much as Mr. Thurwell could have expected of me."

She heard Philip snort. "Get on with it Smith. If you're a crook, just say so."

Smith flushed at his description, but he was right. "I allowed some decisions about Foundation grants to be influenced by lobbyists. I accepted gifts to ensure the Board looked favorably on certain applicants." She stopped and waited for condemnation, but there was quiet. The silence was more unnerving than the outcry she had expected.

Bethany was the person whose reaction she feared most, but she was lost in her own thoughts. Junior was distracted and worried at his fingernails. What might have been a bombshell revelation a few hours ago was nothing after the dramas they had already witnessed. Her indiscretion was severe, but it paled by comparison to the family betrayals and back-stabbing. She breathed a sigh of relief and looked at the lawyer to see if he would pass her confession. "Well, William? Is that it?"

Bird nodded and pronounced her eligible to progress.

He was as surprised as she that there was no comment from the family. They all knew how important the Foundation had been to the philanthropist. Johnston Thurwell had been a deeply flawed man, but his public persona was greatly improved by the work of his great charitable enterprise. Sick children, struggling artists and dedicated educators, among others, had benefited directly from a man who would have terrified them had they known him in different circumstances.

Thurwell relied on the Foundation to give him an appearance of humanity, and when he discovered Smith sullied the Foundation's purpose, he had been livid. She had been fortunate the information had only come to her employer's attention a few weeks before his death, or he would have exacted a high price for her greed. Instead, for some reason he included her in this gathering. She would have to fight for anything and maybe get nothing. The lawyer had enough information to know what the broad outline of the *Danse* was, but he still had no idea of the end game. He'd find out in time, they all would. He reached for the next name.

* * *

"Camille Jolivet. Ms. Jolivet, if you please."

He offered a half-smile and indicated for her to start. Camille was coy, she was not certain her deepest secret had been discovered and did not intend to blurt it out if there was a lesser misdemeanor she could admit. "Monsieur Bird, may I have a hint as to the general nature of what I am to say?" She gave the lawyer a coquettish tilt of the head and hoped her charm might make the lawyer agreeable. He looked at her in such a way she had no doubt that her attempt failed miserably. "Share your secret, or lose everything. That's all the help I can offer."

She pouted and gave a shrug. She saw some people were listening while others, including Bethany, seemed not to be aware of her at all. She took the time to light a cigarette, drew deeply from it and started to tell her story into a cloud of blue smoke. "I shared the story of how I came to America to find my father. It is true, he was my father. But, some parts of my history are not so true. I said my mother told me my father's identity at the end of her life, and that is so, but she was not as strong and proud as I said. Mama had been an alcoholic for many years. She had no money and lived on the charity of the Church and her sister."

She waved her hands around as she spoke, the dark smoke of her cigarette curled upwards in an acrid spiral. So far, most people paying attention found her smoke more offensive than anything she had said. "So, I found one day, a diary. It was Mama's journal, and she had written the name of my father in it, with a few notes about his success in America. I looked him up, and that's how I came to be here today." She stopped and drew long on her cigarette.

Freddie was incredulous. "That's it? You had a drunk for a Mom? Bill, I'm not seeing much there, is she for real?"

The lawyer shot a look at Camille. "Wait for her to finish, Freddie."

Camille was suddenly frightened, he did know her deepest secret, and now she knew must finish the story. Camille had no idea how they had uncovered the truth, but she guessed rich people could learn anything if they really wanted to. She shook her head, lit another cigarette with trembling fingers and began talking, chewing her knuckles nervously between sentences.

"I see. Then, Monsieur Bird, you know everything. So be it. My mother, she was a drunk. She lost her mind long ago and only existed to shit and piss over my life. I found her diary one day. I discovered a rich American was my father and wanted to escape Paris with all my heart." She paused and smoked for a moment.

What she had to tell the group was a memory she had suppressed since being accepted by the Old Man as his daughter. "My mother, she was sick from the booze, you see? She was not able to travel. She had no passport, no money. She had no dignity. Her health was failing, I could see her each day getting worse and the messes I had to clean, so disgusting. I wanted a new life, but Mama kept me chained to hers." She took another drag of her cigarette, she was pale and there was silence as they waited for her to finish.

Some thought they knew what was coming next, but even they were shocked by the truth. "Mama often spent nights on the street. She would escape the apartment while I slept and would beg on the streets until she had enough money for a drink. She would drink until she passed out, sometimes in the gutter. We did not live in the best arrondissement, and there were plenty of bad people there. One night I woke, and she was gone. I took a flashlight and looked for her. When I found her passed out in a doorway, she had shit herself again. It was disgusting, and I was so angry I hit her, but she did not move, so I hit her again."

Tears welled up as she described the last moments of her mother's life. "I used the flashlight, and I beat her and beat her. I was so angry at her for keeping me in poverty while I had a new life waiting for me. She was a wicked, selfish old drunk, and I hit her again and again. When I stopped. I saw what I had done. It was horrible. I ran home and waited for the gendarmes to come."

Camille's tears flowed freely, and her voice cracked with emotion. "When they came in the morning, they told me mama had been killed in a robbery. They had no way to know she had nothing to take, not even her dignity. They did not suspect me. She was a street person, and they did not care so much about her, only that they could not explain why she was attacked. I told them that she wore a silver chain that was precious, and they said it was gone. It gave them a motive for the attack, and they never asked another question. I buried her and left Paris forever." There was horrified silence after she admitted her matricide.

William was about to announce Camille's task complete when a soft voice broke the quiet. "You're going right to hell, my girl. You wicked, greedy creature." Winnie's voice was low, but it carried so everyone heard her. No one could recall a time when she had spoken without first being asked a question. She was clearly upset and pointed at Camille, her face set in stony disapproval. "Hell is waiting for you. To kill your own mother, can there be a worse crime-"

Bethany stood and screamed. "Don't. Don't you dare say that. Do not judge her, you have no right. Stop. Stop it now."

Winnie did stop because she was surprised by Bethany's outburst. Bethany dropped back into her seat, spent. She made no attempt to look at Camille but just trembled in her seat. Philip moved to his sister's side and knelt next to her. "I think it's time we took that break, don't you Billy?"

The lawyer looked up, but Junior seemed shocked into agreement with his brother. Freddie shrugged, and Bird took it to be tacit agreement. He acknowledged Camille was eligible for the next session and called an adjournment for lunch. It took a moment for anyone to move, but Camille stood and quickly exited the conference room, headed for her room.

Larry MacLean went to Winnie and helped her out of her chair. "Take the time to look at that list now Mrs. Tremethick, it might be the only chance you have before you are asked for your secret."

"I will, Mr. MacLean, I will. Thank you."

Chapter Eighteen

William hurried to his office to take a few minutes away from the others. It had been a rough couple of hours, but so far, everyone had successfully confessed their secrets. How could they not when the lure of Thurwell's fortune was so strong? Already he'd heard admissions of corruption, blackmail and even matricide, and there was more to come. The group would not be the same after this phase of the *Danse*.

Three people still needed to share their secrets, Bethany, Philip and Mrs. Tremethick. William opened the yellow envelope and reread the details of each secret. There was every chance the mood would become uglier than it already was, and that might cause more problems when it came time to divide the fortune.

The alliances of the first day would not survive to the next round of negotiations. The things they learned about each other would make old relationships untenable. Bird saw no way for Junior and Larry to remain allied after MacLean's admission of his affair with Junior's mother. The family alliance was in trouble. The first day had gone well for them because they had controlled the outcome of every vote, but that advantage evaporated with the revelation of Larry's secret shame.

William worried about the next session and read Winnie Tremethick's secret again. He was apprehensive the old lady might be unable to share it, he believed her when she claimed no memory of Johnston Thurwell. There was a yellow envelope in the safe to open in the event the group rejected her with no share, but he was ignorant of its contents beyond the hand-written note on the envelope.

* * *

Bethany sat alone in her suite, exhausted after her emotional outburst. She was revolted by Camille's admission of matricide and still reeled after learning of Larry and Junior's separate betrayals of her father. She felt drained and her growing anxiety made her snap at the old woman. Bethany feared she too would be judged harshly for her behavior. Her stomach tightened into a painful knot at the coming trial.

Her two brothers would understand that her betrayal of their father was greater even than Junior's. She had no doubt her father had found out the truth, it explained why he had not wanted her near him when his end came. She also realized the cruel process he had designed for their inheritance was their punishment.

After listening to the secrets from those close to her father, she was shocked that his employees had treated him with more love and respect than his closest friends and family. The Elliots helped put Larry MacLean into a position where he could be destroyed at will, even Betty had aided the effort. Freddie Hagood had turned out to be a close friend and partner, not the ruthless rival they had believed. She shook her head and thought of her father. She was as guilty as the others.

She closed her eyes and prayed for strength, but the only words she heard were Winnie Tremethick's condemning Camille to hell. She shuddered and hugged herself closer.

* * *

Philip sauntered into the library. He knew he was going to have to tell his secret, but he couldn't change that fact and so he didn't worry about it. He was worried about his

203

sister, she was not herself and he wondered what possible indiscretion she may have committed that had her so rattled. She had loved her father and had been much loved as his favorite. Philip could barely imagine anything she could do to cause his father to reject her.

His thoughts turned to his own pending admission, and the Judge popped into Philip's thoughts. He smiled, the self-righteous prick was going to be mighty pissed after he heard what Philip had to say, perhaps even more pissed than the Old Man had been.

Philip didn't care. He had moved on, the events in Georgia seemed a lifetime away. He would tell his story, tolerate the obvious reactions and wait for his share of the money. Then he could get back to the mountains and find some fresh, deep powder. He smiled at the thought just as Jeremy appeared to announce a buffet lunch was ready.

* * *

Winnie Tremethick sat at the small desk in her room. The sun shone across the teak surface and brought out the wood's rich glow. She reached into her enormous handbag and found the note Larry MacLean had passed to her. She pursed her lips and prayed it might reveal a connection between herself and the mysterious American.

She unfolded the single sheet of paper and looked over the neatly written list. Her attention was immediately drawn to three dates MacLean had circled in red. He'd told her earlier he thought he'd narrowed it down. She adjusted her glasses and looked at the first date.

1957, October - November

Winnie thought back to the late fifties. She'd been married with two young children and a husband who returned home from the pub later each night. Her son's birthday was Halloween. He would have turned ten in 1957. There was nothing unusual about that year. No memory of an American. It was just herself, the kids, the farm and Arnold and his drink. She thought about how her life had been when she was 28. She wondered if she might have been happier if she had been stronger and insisted that Arnold not get drunk every night. *If wishes were fishes*, she thought. She moved her finger down the page to the next red-circled date.

1960, January - October

Winnie moved her life story ahead three years and thought about 1960. Her son Ken became a teenager in 1960, a strong young man at the beginning of the decade that would almost ruin him. Joy, her daughter, would have been 12. Shy for her age but already a beauty. Arnold had stopped his nightly visits to the pub, but spent the evenings with a bottle of cheap scotch until he passed out in front of the fire.

Her life had been unimproved from 1957. Her only pleasure was the children. She thought hard, but there had been no American. She shook her head in frustration and moved to the last dates MacLean had highlighted.

1965, February – December

Winnie's life had changed in the autumn of 1964 when Arnold stumbled and fell into a threshing machine he was repairing. She was a widow at 36. Ken had been gone for two years, drawn to 1960's London like a moth to a flame. Winnie feared he'd be as consumed, she never heard from him. Joy was seventeen and had taken a job in Glasgow as a hotel receptionist.

Both children wanted to be as far from the farm as they could get. They blamed her for the premature death of their father. It was unwarranted, but a cruel fact nonetheless. Winnie's heart was heavy as she ran through the memory of her lonely year.

Then her heart skipped a beat as she recalled events that occurred in the springtime of that year. Yes, it had been April or May of 1965. Her memories flooded back, and her eyes opened wide as she remembered a long-forgotten but remarkable time.

She recalled being woken one rainy night by a noise, but being unable to see anything outside in the darkness, had gone back to bed and forgotten about it. The next morning she'd thrown a waterproof over her head to go out and feed the chickens. The percussion of rain on the coat was loud, and at first, she missed the faint sound from the lane as her hens flocked greedily around her feet.

When she heard the noise again above the sound of raindrops and chickens, she went to the gate and looked up the lane. She couldn't see anything, but she heard something. Whatever it was, it was out of place in her familiar surroundings. Winnie turned to get out of the thick weather and back to the house, convinced she was hearing things, when she heard a voice calling for help.

Winnie left the yard and walked up the lane, cursing the foul weather. She stopped when she saw torn up grass at the side of the road and a much-disturbed hedgerow. She peered into the undergrowth and saw a motorcycle on its side. There was a young man pinned under it, and he was calling weakly for help. Winnie dropped the coat and plunged into the hedge immediately, calling out to the boy. He was so relieved to see a helper he began to cry, which Winnie thought a bit soft until she saw his mangled leg.

It took an hour of hard physical effort to free his leg and Winnie was soaked by the time she dragged the man free of the wreck. She sat him against a tree and gave him a thermos of hot tea and hurried to fetch her sturdy horse. Winnie was a strong woman but she knew that, after the effort of freeing the man, she had no strength to carry him back to the house. Eventually, with the young man grunting with pain at each bump and jolt, she got him slung over the horse and into the dry barn.

She piled straw deep on the floor and helped the stranger onto its softness. She looked at his leg, tutted, and went to get her kitchen scissors and first-aid box. When she returned the man had passed out. It was a mercy for the poor fellow, and she quickly tended his wounds. Nothing felt broken, but he groaned through his unconsciousness when she touched his left shin where the skin was torn and ragged. Winnie cleaned the wound with warm water and stitched the worst of the cuts. When she was finished, she threw thick blankets over him and made her trustworthy dog lay next to the stranger. If the young man tried anything foolish with her, the dog would give him a whole new set of wounds to worry about.

Winnie called her horse to duty once more and together she and the animal retrieved the broken motorcycle. It looked like a complete wreck as it lay on her cobblestone yard, but she covered it with a tarpaulin and returned to the barn to check on her patient.

Winnie trembled at the memory. She had not thought about these events for many years, but the images flooded back with clarity now. She closed her eyes and remembered the rest.

Her patient slept in the barn for the rest of the day, the dog never left his side. She sat in Arnold's broken old rocking chair that she had intended to chop for firewood and watched the two of them. When the young man's eyes opened, he looked around and saw the dog, then the barn and the horse before he finally saw Winnie.

"How are you feeling dear? You took a tumble off that bike of yours, been out of it all day." He sat up and winced at the pain in his body. His leg felt as if it was on fire. He lifted the blanket and saw his pants cut off above the knee and a mess of black and blue bruises, with neatly stitched cuts.

He looked at the woman in the broken chair. "You did this?"

She nodded.

"You're a nurse?"

"No dear, I'm a farmer. Around here, we make do. The hospital's a long ways away, and I got no phone for an ambulance." She pointed at his leg. "Nothing's broke, you're just banged up a bit. You're a lucky young chap, no mistake."

He looked at his leg again. It hurt, but it looked clean and the stitches were tight and neat. He hurt all over, his arms were covered in scratches, and he felt his face and guessed he was scratched there too.

She watched him closely. "You're no picture, deary. You must have gone through that hedge headfirst, I reckon. Might've got killed if'n your leg hadn't caught in the bike and kept you from flying too far. There's a big old oak a few feet from where I found you. I'd guess it's a mite stronger than your head."

The young stranger looked at his savior. He couldn't place an age on her. Her face was naturally tanned and lined from exposure to the weather, but her eyes looked young and kind. He would never forget the kindness in the eyes of the woman that saved him. He stuck out his hand, ignoring the pain.

"I'm Charlie. Charlie Wells. Thank you for your kindness, Miss-"

"Tremethick. Mrs. Tremethick. But you can call me Winnie, everyone does." She paused and regarded him with a quizzical look. "Where are you from then, Charlie Wells? It ain't from around here."

He smiled, but that hurt too. "My accent gives me away I guess. Well, Winnie, I'm Charlie Wells from Toronto, Canada."

Her head tilted to one side as she thought about that. "A colonial? Funny, I never met me a Canadian before.

My Arnold used to talk about you fellows after the war. Said you was all brave lads." She looked at the scratched face and tried to judge his age. "But you'd be too young to have been mixed up in that."

He nodded. "My father served. His unit went to France from Plymouth which is why I was there. I wanted to see it. Then I had a notion to visit Land's End, borrowed this bike and, well, here I am."

Winnie trembled as her memories came to her in a flood as the dam that had kept them contained for decades opened. A Canadian man called Charlie Wells had fallen into her life in late spring of 1965. Could Charlie Wells of Toronto have been Johnston Thurwell of New York? If he were, she had no idea why he would need to make up a name, but Charlie Wells was her one and only connection to this side of the Atlantic.

She reached for the telephone and immediately heard Jeremy's voice. She told him that she needed to speak with Mr. MacLean. Jeremy made no comment, but she heard a click, followed by the unfamiliar American single ring-tone and Larry MacLean's voice. He sounded angry about something, so she talked fast. "Mr. MacLean, it's me, Winnie. I think I've remembered your friend."

She heard a sharp intake of breath. "Mrs. Tremethick? You have? Tell me, what have you remembered?"

Winnie recounted her memory of the young Canadian Charlie Wells and heard a curse word followed by a laugh. "Yeah. I think you've got it, Mrs. Tremethick. Johnston's middle name was Charles, and it's not too much of a stretch that he may have used Wells instead of Thurwell. He did pretend to be Canadian from time to time, especially with girls if he thought he could get, um... well, never mind. He sometimes thought it sounded more interesting to be foreign rather than just another guy from the City."

He agreed to join her and have lunch brought up, so they could talk about what she remembered. Larry slipped on his shoes and hastened down the hallway to see the Englishwoman, his heart beating fast. Winnie's memory sounded right. It sounded like Johnston.

The old lady was excited when he saw her. Her blue eyes sparkled and she looked more alive than he'd ever seen her. Larry squeezed her hand, and they sat together on the large couch. Winnie held on to his hand, he could feel the excitement in her grip.

"Do you think your friend Mr. Thurwell might have been my Charlie Wells? It was so long ago. I had almost forgotten Charlie. Almost."

She said it with a quietness that made Larry look twice. She had a naturally kind expression, but there was something else there now. He could investigate later. First, he had to find out if the Canadian man she remembered was Johnston Thurwell. "Do you remember what he looked like? Was he tall or short? What color were his eyes? Tell me what you remember, tell me all of it."

Winnie nodded, took a sip of a tall glass of water, closed her eyes and started to talk. "He was a good-looking young fellow, quite tall as I recall. I think he might have been a bit shorter than you, but not by a lot. I'm short myself, so anyone taller than 5'6" looks big to me.

Larry squeezed her hand to encourage her. "He had lovely eyes. Light blue, like cornflowers. He was pretty scratched and bruised, but had a good, strong face. He looked healthy, you know. At least I thought he looked healthy enough for a young man that fell off his motorcycle."

Larry nodded, so far nothing she had said had ruled out Charlie Wells from being Johnston Thurwell. He felt his own excitement grow. "Was he a large man, or slight?"

"Oh, he wasn't a big man like my Albert was. Not at all. But then I imagine he hadn't worked the land all his life.

He looked fit. He had meat on his bones, as we say in the country."

Larry was happy with everything he heard. His old friend would have been twenty-nine and facing thirty in 1965. He recalled Johnston had been upset at the approach of his hallmark birthday, so much so that he left his young wife and took off to Europe.

Johnston had told no one about his trip. Larry had only discovered he was gone when he arrived at his friend's house for a surprise visit and found Julie alone. That was the visit he first allowed himself to get too close to his friend's wife. That spark would later lead to their affair and her divorce. Johnston never spoke about where he had gone or what he had been doing in his time away. It was a topic those close to him soon learned to avoid if they wished to be spared his temper.

"Did Charlie Wells talk about his wife, or any details of his life back in America?"

"You mean Canada, Mr. MacLean. Remember he told me that he was from Toronto. Not that it mattered, Toronto meant as much to me as Timbuktu. I never traveled. Until I came here, I never even rode in an airplane before."

He prodded her to answer his question. "I don't think Charlie was married. He never mentioned a wife and didn't strike me as the kind of man to have ties. He was a bit wild I think."

Larry saw the odd look on her face again and did some quick mental arithmetic. Winnie Tremethick had to be in her late seventies, so when she met Charlie Wells she would have been in her early to mid-thirties. It wasn't impossible something could have happened between them.

"Did your children meet Charlie?"

She shook her head. "My kids left home before '65 and my husband died the previous autumn. There wasn't

211

anyone left but me. Charlie kept to himself. He wouldn't come to Church on Sundays, never wanted to see anyone. He was quiet. He never even went to the pub of an evening."

Larry realized she must have had her children when she herself was only a girl. She was living alone on a farm when a mysterious Canadian fell, literally by accident, into her life.

"How long was he with you, Mrs. Tremethick?"

She looked at Larry and her eyes narrowed. "You think your friend and me got friendly do you, Mr. MacLean?" He flushed, it was hard to imagine the elderly woman next to him as a sexual creature forty years ago and he felt embarrassed to have asked. But she was still talking, unaware of Larry. "And what if we did? Would it matter? He was hurt, and I was alone. It's not so wrong for two people to find some comfort with each other, is it?"

MacLean shook his head, she was right. But if Charlie Wells was Johnston Thurwell, he had been married while he was with the Englishwoman. At the same time, Larry had begun his slow seduction of his friend's wife. "Tell me what happened, Mrs. Tremethick. When did he leave? I know when Johnston came home but when did he leave you?"

She looked at him with deep sadness. "I drove him away. I felt guilty about falling for another man so soon after Arnold died. I didn't know what I'd tell the kids if they came home and found another man in their father's house. He stayed with me until the end of the summer and then we fell apart. It was lovely, but it wasn't meant to last. He was too young in his heart and country life was too slow. He never said so, but I saw the look in his eyes when we walked the cliffs in the evenings.

"We look out over the Atlantic, Mr. MacLean, but I could see Charlie wasn't looking at the sea, like I was. He was looking over it, at where he belonged. He was gentlemanly enough to ask if I'd return to Toronto with him, but it wasn't for me. I had my chickens and the farm. I was born in the village, and I'll probably die there. It's all I ever needed.

"I was the wrong girl for him to go adventuring with. One night, right around the start of September, we had some words and then Charlie was gone. There was a tramp steamer in port that week, from France, I think it was. It was gone the next morning, and so was Charlie. I think he just climbed aboard and sailed away."

She dabbed her eyes with an old handkerchief as Larry watched her and felt the depth of her emotions as she remembered. She looked at him, her eyes red and with a shy smile on her face. "Look at me, a silly old woman crying over something like that. It was a lifetime ago, and it never would have worked. If my Charlie is your friend Mr. Thurwell, I wouldn't have fit in his world."

Larry nodded, but wondered if Johnston's life would have taken the same direction if Winnie had returned to North America with him. Perhaps the man that made a fortune would have made a different life with this simple, honest woman. "Johnston returned home in late November that year. He never said anything about where he spent his time. His wife stopped asking when she realized she didn't want to know the answer."

He caught the sharp look from the old woman. "Yes he was married. I'm sorry." She shook her head. "It was a long time ago. There's no harm in it now." He took her hand and gave it a comforting squeeze. "Johnston was different after that trip. He was focused, driven. He quit his job before he took off in 1965 and when he returned he started his business and never looked back."

Larry wondered if that last part was true, his friend had been decidedly different after he came back to his life and his wife. It was time to find out for certain if Charlie Wells was Johnston Thurwell. Larry reached into his breast pocket and pulled out an old black and white photograph he'd found in the library. Pictured were two young men laughing on the dock at the MacLean's lake house. They had just climbed out of the water, and the camera had captured a pure, happy moment.

It was taken in 1962, it would be close enough for Winnie to recognize if the fellow next to Larry was the man she had met, or not. He saw she was looking at him with nervous anticipation. "Is that a picture of him? May I see it?"

She pulled her reading glasses from her handbag and slipped them on as Larry passed her the photograph. She looked at it for a long time. She said nothing but stared into the picture. Larry was bursting for her to confirm it, but he already knew from her expression that she was looking at Charlie Wells.

Eventually, Winnie looked at Larry as she gripped the image tightly in her aged fingers and whispered. "That's my Charlie. That's him, no doubt about it. May I keep this, please?" She traced her finger over the smiling face in the photograph. "I forgot how handsome he was. You both are, two young men in their prime. Oh Charlie."

She hugged the picture to her breast and tears flowed down her cheeks. Larry was suddenly uncomfortable, unsure if he should try to hug her or hold her hand. He was saved from making a decision by a sharp knock at the door.

Jeremy stood in the hallway with a waiter. Larry had quite forgotten he asked for lunch to be brought up. He stood aside to let the two men in, putting a finger over his lips to indicate they should be quiet. Jeremy understood immediately, as always, and took the tray from the other man and sent him out. He quietly placed the tray on the table and poured a cup of tea for the old lady. He handed it to her without a word, and she took it with a grateful "Bless you, love" and then he was gone.

Larry marveled at the major-domo's ability to do everything exactly right, every time. He had done the one thing Winnie needed most. He delivered the ancient salve to all English hurts, a hot cup of sweet tea. He watched as she sipped her drink and held the picture of Johnston next to her heart. She was lost in her thoughts, and Larry, having helped her discover her secret, left her in peace.

Chapter Nineteen

William finished a sandwich and looked at the antique clock on his desk. It was time to get the group back together. He hoped the final three would not take long to tell their stories, but he feared it was a vain hope. He knew what Bethany and Philip would say and that it would be unpleasant, but he had no idea what the group's reaction to what Mrs. Tremethick had to tell would be.

He telephoned Jeremy to gather everyone back in the conference room in five minutes. He picked up his laptop and papers and headed there to prepare for what was to come. He saw no one else on his walk to the conference room. There was a dull drone of conversation from the dining room, but it was nothing like the celebratory sounds he had heard at breakfast.

His guests drifted back into the room. Freddie arrived with Janice and Dennis Elliot, the three of them talking quietly. Junior arrived solo, as did the Judge and Larry MacLean. The others arrived with serious faces. They all wanted the ordeal over with. There was a pause while the guest's took their seats. William saw Winnie Tremethick's seat was still vacant.

He was about to ask if anyone knew of her whereabouts when she appeared on Jeremy's arm. The major-domo helped her into her seat, whispered something in her ear that made her smile, and left. Silence settled as William swirled the remaining three pieces of paper around and picked one out.

"Bethany Thurwell. Beth, it's your turn." When he looked at her, she seemed as if she was in physical pain, and he worried about her health. She sat still, not moving, not talking. Everyone waited for her to start and she felt the unbearable weight of every pair of judging eyes on her.

"I can't do this. It's not right, I can't do it." She blurted the words, her mind frozen with fear. Philip tried to help. "You have to tell us, sis. You have to, or you lose your share. Come on." She looked at her younger brother. He loved her, she knew. Would he still love her after she shared her secret? Did it matter? She had not loved herself for a long time. What difference did it make that others might not?

William cleared his throat. "Bethany, please. You have to share your secret, or I will remove you." She looked at the lawyer and knew he meant it. She took a deep breath and told herself the humiliation would pass. She needed her inheritance. It was hers, no matter what her father had thought of her at the end.

Bethany summoned her courage. "It's not a long story, although the path to how it happened is a long one. I was in a relationship, and it became serious." Bethany looked at her brothers. They had met and liked Anton.

"Anton asked me to marry him, but I refused. More than once. My father did not care for him and made his opinion very clear. I don't know why I just didn't defy him and marry the man I loved, but my courage failed me. Anton asked a third time, and I refused for the last time. I think I broke his heart, he was gone within a few days. He did not return my calls or emails. I sent a gift that was returned unopened."

Bethany stopped to wipe a hot tear from the corner of her eye. Her hurt was real again and with it came an old anger. "I became angry. Not at Anton, but at father. I should have been angry with myself, but it was easier to be angry at him.

"It wasn't long after Anton left that I realized I was pregnant. I didn't know what to do, Anton would not respond to any of my attempts to contact him. The doorman at his building turned me away. I heard he left New York to be with his family in Moscow. I was so angry with father I couldn't even talk to him about it. So I got rid of the baby."

Junior and Philip gasped, unable to believe what they heard. Her brothers knew Johnston Thurwell had yearned for a grandchild. He was also a staunch supporter of pro-life groups through his philanthropy. Neither Junior nor Philip shared their father's views, but understood he would have seen Bethany's abortion as a cold betrayal. She had aborted his grandchild, the one thing in the world he had desired but could not buy.

Larry looked at Bethany in a new light. He shared his dead friend's views and felt the same shock that must have torn Johnston Thurwell apart when he learned of it. He saw Beth looking at him, but he didn't know what to say. She had something she wanted to say, however. "It was his own fault Larry, he never thought Anton was good enough for me, and I lost the man I loved. Why would Anton's child be good enough, if the father was not?

"It was quid pro quo, Larry. I lost my love, father lost his grandchild. But I ran out of courage and couldn't tell him. When I next saw him, my anger had passed, and I felt empty and drained. I decided it would be my secret alone. Until this morning, I believed I had kept it safe. I was wrong. When William told us that we each had a secret to share, I knew father had found me out. It's the only reason I can think of that would make him reject me at the end of his days."

Even those who listened with sympathy looked at Bethany with discomfort. She had aborted her baby to punish her father. Winnie Tremethick lowered her head and whispered a prayer for Bethany. She believed the girl had mortally sinned and prayed for her soul. Judge Freeman did the same and sat with his eyes closed, deep in contemplation.

Junior was shaken by his sister's admission. He realized his thoughts on the matter were filtered through his father's own strong feelings. Now he was faced with the harsh truth of his sister's actions, he found he couldn't condemn her out of hand. "You're right, Beth. The Old Man cut you out of his life for what you did. You know it, and I know it. So now we know why he didn't want you at his bedside. Me too, I guess. We both betrayed him."

Bethany looked at him, her eyes filled with tears, but he held up a finger to stop her saying anything. "Wait, Beth. I'm figuring this out. I'm not judging you, I'm not saying anything about what you did, or why. I never will."

He shrugged as he finished, but Bethany knew it was as close to a selfless act as Junior was capable of and she smiled through her tears, grateful for his words. She looked at Philip, who shrugged. "We're cool, sis. Just remember that, okay? Forgiveness is important." She smiled, but didn't understand what he meant. That would come soon enough.

William decided it was time to move on. He was not interested in hosting a debate on morality or religion. He had business to manage and brought everyone back to the job at hand. "Thank you, Bethany, you will continue. We only have two people left, Mrs. Tremethick and Philip. Once we've heard their secrets you may return to the business of dividing the fortune."

He looked up and was satisfied their lust for a share of the money overrode any moral outrage they might feel, with the sole exception of Winnie. She looked like she had plenty left to say, but William acted to cut her off before things turned ugly. He reached into the pitcher and pulled a name out with a dramatic flourish.

He read Philip Thurwell's name, but decided he needed to divert the old lady in case she was planning on making a scene.

"Winnie Tremethick. Mrs. Tremethick, it's your turn." Winnie looked dazed, as if she had not understood. "Mrs. Tremethick? Do you have any idea yet about your connection to Mr. Thurwell?"

She looked at the lawyer, he had always been friendly, but now seemed stern and businesslike. "Yes, I think so. Mr. MacLean helped me, and we're sure that we've discovered my connection to Mr. Thurwell." A flutter of excitement went around the table as they leaned forward to better hear the old lady. William was pleased that he had moved the group beyond Beth's explosive secret. They were all eager to hear the story of the old lady and the dead philanthropist.

"I met Mr. Thurwell in the spring of 1965, by accident. He was traveling through the south of England under a different name, which is why I never heard of your Mr. Thurwell. Mr. MacLean helped me figure it out, he gave me some dates when he and his friend were out of touch and for most of 1965 they never saw each other. Right Mr. MacLean?"

"That's right. Johnston took off without a word. He told Julie he was going to Europe and left. He just quit his job and went. He returned home at the end of the year, but never talked about where he had been or what he had done. It quite upset your mother, Junior, as you might imagine."

Junior was silent. He hadn't even been conceived in 1965, and it was odd to hear about his parents in a time when he wasn't even a thought. He shot a look of contempt at Larry. He did not want him to mention his

219

mother's name with such familiarity. Instead, he looked at Winnie. "You said my father was traveling under a different name? Why?"

"I can't say why. I knew your father as Charlie Wells. I only learned that he was really Johnston Thurwell in the past hour. I can't explain something I wasn't aware of, not forty years after it happened."

William paid close attention to the conversation. In his safe was a yellow envelope with a name written on it, *Charlie Wells*. He would need to look at the contents of that envelope as soon as the next break came. He made a quick note to himself and then leaned in to hear the rest of the old lady's story.

"I said I met Charlie by accident and that is exactly true. He crashed his motorcycle near my farm, and I found him in a very sorry state the next morning. I rescued him, patched him up pretty good, and he stayed with me until he was healed."

"So he stayed with you and your family? Is that what you're saying?"

Winnie looked at Junior, she knew the reason he wanted to know, and she knew she would disappoint him with her answer. She studied him, looking for any family resemblance, but she didn't see it. Charlie had possessed a strong face with kind eyes and a manly frame. His son looked mean and weak, not at all like his father. "Charlie. Your father, I mean. He stayed at the farm. I was alone, my husband had died, and my children had already left home. I had them young. We didn't used to hang around, like women do today."

She shot a sharp look toward Bethany, but Junior interrupted and spoiled her chance to say something. "So you were alone with him? For how long?"

Winnie sighed, she guessed Junior would not care for the truth, but since he was insistent, she'd give it to him. "He stayed through the summer. As he healed and grew stronger, he started to help me out on the farm. I didn't mind a strong back around the place, and he was good company. If you're asking if there was more to it, the answer is yes, there was."

She looked at Junior with unwavering eyes, and he dropped his gaze. His father had cheated on his mother even before he was conceived. It hurt, even though it was ancient history. Larry asked Winnie a question, one she had not fully answered in their time together. "How close were you and Charlie, Mrs. Tremethick?"

She looked at MacLean. She had been shocked at his flirtation and later affair with Thurwell's wife, only to learn she'd committed the same sin, albeit unwittingly. Still, she liked Larry. He had been a gentleman to her. "Charlie asked me to go to Canada with him. I said I couldn't and we parted soon after."

She paused and remembered a late-summer evening on a cliff top. "Actually, that's not quite accurate. Charlie asked me to marry him and go to Canada. But I had been widowed less than a year, and I had two children out in the world. I couldn't just pick up and leave. He couldn't understand why I had to stay, and he was angry when he left. We both said some things we didn't really mean and they were the last words we said to each other, to my regret. I never saw or heard of him again, until this week."

Larry whistled and Junior sat back, shocked. The others tried to imagine the old Englishwoman forty years earlier, having an affair with a man that would become one of the richest in the world. It seemed an incongruous match. Junior needed clarification. "You say my father asked you to marry him? But he was already married, to my mother."

Winnie looked pained. "Yes. I'm sorry, dear. I had no idea he was already married. I didn't even know he was American, he told me he was from Canada. I'm sorry. I never suspected there was a different truth to what Charlie told me."

Junior was upset, but it was hard to be angry with the old lady. His father had been the problem. His father had always been the problem. He had abandoned his wife for almost a full year, carried on an affair with a farmer's widow in England and returned without explanation to start a family. What kind of man had his father been? Junior realized he didn't know his father, his friends or his siblings as he thought he had. *We've all been hiding*, he thought, *none of us are who we seem to be.*

"Is there anything else, Mrs. Tremethick?"

The lawyer asked the question as his own mind tried to absorb the new facts about his dead client. "No, dear. Unless you want me to tell you the details about his accident, I told it all to Mr. MacLean earlier though."

William decided the details could wait, even though he was intrigued by the details of her story. "Not now, you've done what you needed to. We should move on."

* * *

William looked at the sole piece of paper in the pitcher. He knew the name on it was Winnie Tremethick's, but only Philip remained, so he left the paper where it was and invited Philip to speak.

Philip took a long look at Ron Freeman. Philip had already heard everyone else's secret, but only one had anything in common with his own. He glanced at Camille, his new half-sister. He hoped her confession would be judged worse than his when all was said and done. It was time to find out. "Judge Freeman already told some of my story. He got caught up in it and is sitting at this table now, looking to profit from his involvement. Billy Bird was involved too, weren't you Billy." He sneered at the lawyer, who looked back with a blank expression.

"See, the thing is, I did kill a guy. I hit him with my Porsche, and he died. I used my phone call to call Dad, and he called Billy. Billy flew down to see the Judge, and I was sprung and life went on. That's right, isn't it, Bill?" Bird made no acknowledgement. He was puzzled and wondered where Philip was going with his story.

"There was only one detail you clever legal minds missed. I know Dad sent you to get me out of a jam Billy, and that was nice of you to get the Judge to see it your way. I don't know what you said or did, but I appreciate it. The problem is, you keep calling it an accident. It wasn't. I killed the motherfucker on purpose."

Judge Freeman felt like he was going to have a heart attack. His mind was numb as he tried to comprehend what he had heard. Even William stared in horror at the youngest son. He had intervened in what he had thought was a tragic accident, not a murder.

Philip laughed as he watched the two men react. "Yeah. I killed him with my Carrera. The crooked fuck sold me some dope that had been cut so many times I would have needed to snort a pound of it to get a buzz. When I bitched about it, the prick pulled a gun on me and told me to leave town. So I did, but as I was heading out, I saw him crossing the road, strutting like he owned it. It was too easy. I floored it, and it was game over for him.

"You have to admire German engineering, he must have gone twenty feet in the air, but there wasn't even a dent in the Porsche. They build cars even tougher than street dealers. They should use that in their fucking commercials." Philip slouched down in his seat, he was done talking and now waited for the shit storm to hit, hoping it wouldn't last too long before they got back to talking about money.

Freeman jumped to his feet and pointed at Philip. "I risked my career, my life to get you a pass on that incident." He turned to Bird, who watched with some difficulty, his own face betrayed deep dismay. "Did you know about this Bird? Did you know that this... this thug killed that man deliberately?"

William shook his head, he had no words. He'd been as duped as the Judge had been. Even the Old Man had not suspected Philip of his crime. It was not the secret Philip was required to reveal. "No, I had no idea. I'm sorry, Judge. Philip has surprised me as much as you, this shocking news isn't the secret he is required to share."

Philip sat up quickly. "What? What did you say, Bill?" He looked frightened. He had no idea what other secret he could have. He'd done nothing worse than what happened in Macon.

"While your story is compelling and difficult for me to hear, it's not what you're required to share. I'll ask you one more time, Philip. Share your secret with the group." Bird's voice was pure ice and his eyes filled with cold fury. He saw confusion on Philip's face and felt a cruel pleasure as he realized Philip did not know what to say. "Philip, last chance. Start talking or you're done."

Bethany wanted to tell Philip to say something, to say what he had to say to make William stop threatening him, but she couldn't find the words. Her brother had killed a man and did not care. She knew she should turn to her brother's aid, but remained silent, she may have committed her own sin, but what she had done was at least legal.

Philip's mind raced, he had been so sure the Old Man had found out the truth about Georgia. He had listened to the people around him tell their dark secrets, and it occurred to him his father had discovered all the worst things there was to know about those around him.

Only one other person in the world knew Philip had run down the drug dealer on purpose, but he had forgotten about her. He had convinced himself the girl must have emerged and sold the information to his father. Now he knew he had been wrong. There had been no need to tell the story of the murder, but he had no clue what he had to say to meet the condition. "I don't know, what could be worse than killing a man? Jesus. Billy, give me a hint. Please?"

His plea was met with an impassive stare. Philip's heart sank. He'd just taunted the lawyer and would get no sympathy there. He cast a wild look around the room, but no one could meet his eyes. "You can't do this, Bill. I'm family, you need to help me. I don't know what I'm supposed to say."

William was angry, but kept his voice as even as he could. "Philip Thurwell, you have not met the requirements for continuing. You will leave this room and will have no further involvement in negotiations. You will not share in your father's fortune."

Philip paled as his panic rose. "Junior, you got to help me, man. Can't you see what's happening here?" Junior looked away, unable to meet his brother's eyes. "Beth? Come on Beth. It's me, your little bro. Stop him from kicking me out."

Bethany shook her head. "I don't even recognize you, Phil. You killed a man and look at the consequences."

Philip's panic stripped away the last vestige of his civilized veneer. "Yeah, Sis, I did. But you killed your baby, so tell me that we're so different. Now help me out, you self-righteous bitch."

Bethany recoiled as if he had slapped her. William's voice cut through the silence. "Philip, will you remove yourself from the room, or do I need to have you removed?"

"Sure and who are you going to get to move me, Bill? I'd like to see you try and make me leave."

William keyed a small button secreted under his desk. The door opened immediately, and Jeremy walked into the room. William nodded toward Philip, who stood defiantly in place. "Jeremy, Philip needs to be escorted to his suite, if you'd be so kind."

The major-domo smiled perfunctorily and approached the youngest Thurwell. "Please, come with me, sir. There's no need for trouble."

Philip snorted and looked down his nose at the servant who stood calmly with his hands at his sides as if he were at attention. "I don't think so. You'll need to do better than this creep, Billy." As he sneered, Philip aimed a powerful punch at the major-domo's jaw. Without apparent movement, Jeremy avoided the blow and suddenly had Philip's face buried in the tabletop with his arm raised painfully behind his back.

"Never mind sir. We'll soon have you up in your room and comfortable." He marched Philip from the room. The young man whined in pain as his nose dripped blood onto his shirt. He was forced to walk briskly or risk getting his arm broken. Another staff member closed the door behind them and left the group in a stunned silence.

"Was that really necessary, William?" Bethany broke the silence, her voice a whisper.

Bird saw everyone looking at him. He tried to smile but found his mouth was dry. "I'm sorry for the violence, but we would not be able to continue until Philip was removed. He was rather belligerent."

He checked his watch, it was mid-afternoon, and he needed to call a recess to get to the yellow envelope labeled *Charlie Wells*. He wrapped up the meeting. "Each of you has met the requirements to continue, Philip has not and will receive nothing from Mr. Thurwell's estate. I recommend we take a short break, it has been a rather intense session."

Chapter Twenty

The group broke up slowly, but William left them and hurried to his office. He needed to see what was in the envelope with Charlie Wells' name on it. The Old Man had made it clear that when an envelope was 'triggered' there was to be as little delay as possible before opening it.

Bethany made a move to follow the lawyer, but found her way blocked by her older brother. "Where are you going, Beth?"

"Junior, we can't allow Phil to be disinherited. I know he was a monster, but he's our flesh and blood." She moved to rush by him, but he grabbed her arm. "No, Beth, he's out. William said so, and I agree. Besides, he's only my half-brother, remember?"

Bethany looked into Junior's eyes and saw no forgiveness in them. He squeezed her arm again, hard. She winced in pain as his fingers twisted her skin. "You do agree with me, right sister?" His face was so close to hers that she could smell old coffee on his breath.

"Please, Junior, you're hurting my arm. Just let me talk to William?" Junior sneered and opened his mouth to speak but instead made an odd gurgling sound. He went pale, and his strong grip released her as he sagged at the knees. She saw Dennis Elliot close behind her brother. The manservant caught Junior under the arms before he hit the floor and helped him to a chair.

She looked at Dennis, confused by what happened. Had he attacked Junior? Then, just as suddenly, Janice was at her side. "Come with me, Miss Beth. Let the men talk." Bethany allowed herself to be led away, still uncertain as to what had happened. Junior sat in the chair, trying to catch his breath. His ribs felt as if they were on fire. Dennis stood next to him and offered a glass of water. "Drink this. You'll feel better in a few moments."

Junior sipped the water and realized Dennis had jabbed him so hard it had taken his breath away. "Dennis? What the fuck? Did you hit me?" He sounded incredulous, and his temper flared until he looked up and saw the hate on Dennis' face. His rising color faded to paper white again as Junior realized that Janice undoubtedly had told her husband what happened the previous night. The Elliots must have seen him grab Bethany's arm and Dennis had jumped in to save her.

Junior was afraid. He had not expected to have to deal with Janice's husband. Dennis took the glass away from Junior and leaned down. His face was so close to Junior's he could feel his hot breath on his cheek. "Your days of bullying women are over, Mr. Thurwell. You understand me, don't you? Or do I need to explain things more fully, in private?"

Junior nodded quickly, saying nothing. He had to get away. He needed a place to be safe, so he could think. Dennis offered his hand to the winded man. Junior took it and was helped to his feet. Dennis squeezed the hand in a vise-like grip. It hurt like hell, but Junior tried not to show it. "Run along now, Mr. Thurwell."

Junior scurried from the room, no longer concerned with finding his sister but headed to the safety of his own suite. Caroline Smith had been looking for Junior and saw him rush from the room. She wanted to speak to him before the next session and hurried after him.

Dennis took a casual glance around the room and was pleased that no one had witnessed the quiet drama. He had remained in control of his temper, but he had wanted to beat Junior to a pulp. He stood for a moment and calmed himself, but when he turned, he saw the Judge's deep brown eyes regarding him from a few feet away. "That was nicely done, Mr. Elliot."

Dennis smiled as if he had no idea what the other man was talking about, but knew it was pointless. He had missed seeing the Judge because he had been seated, but the big man had enjoyed a ringside seat. The Judge pushed the chair next to him back, an invitation for Dennis to join him. The manservant hesitated for a few seconds and then took the seat.

"I assume there is a history between you and Mr. Thurwell?" The Judge spoke as if he were recounting a known fact instead of asking a question.

"I don't like to see women pushed around by a bully. I've heard that Junior is a particularly nasty bully."

Freeman looked at the manservant with curiosity. He was trying to figure out why Dennis had moved so quickly to intervene in what appeared to be nothing more than a squabble between siblings. The Judge had watched the entire scene play out, but until Dennis jabbed Junior in the ribs, hadn't noticed how cruelly Junior had twisted Bethany's arm.

How did Dennis see that from across the room, with Junior's body blocking his view? *He couldn't have seen it*, the Judge thought. *Even Janice would have only been able to see Bethany's face, not her brother's grip on her.* Suddenly Freeman understood. Janice has seen something in Bethany's eyes and alerted her husband. Dennis had not hesitated, and the pair rescued Bethany with seamless efficiency.

They've seen this behavior before, the Judge realized. Or Junior has subjected one of them to similar treatment. That would mean it was Janice. Junior was too small and cowardly to strong arm a man like Dennis, but his wife, perhaps. "You've seen his cruelty before."

Dennis noted the Judge made statements, he did not ask questions. He nodded but said nothing. Dennis did not trust himself to keep his anger in check if he started telling what Junior had subjected his wife to. Janice would not thank him for sharing her shame, it was best not to say anything. "It would seem the Thurwells have an affinity to violence. Was that also the case with their father?"

Dennis looked up sharply, and Freeman saw a flash of his hot temper. "Mr. Thurwell was a gentleman, always kind and gentle natured. His children though..." Dennis shuddered.

Freeman was moved by the fierce defense. Dennis was a loyal servant of the old school. The Judge did not share Dennis's faith in his dead employer's goodness. The philanthropist had sent his lawyer to get his youngest son out of trouble and had not been particular about the tactics his lawyer used.

The Judge leaned forward and patted Dennis on the back. "What you did for Bethany was good, Dennis. Would you and your wife consider working with me to ensure fair shares for everyone are ensured as we go forward?"

He needed allies. Freeman could not rely on Freddie and already knew Caroline could be bought. She admitted it in her confession. Dennis thought about it but didn't see any angles. He needed Janice, she was the schemer. "I'll ask Jan and let you know." Dennis stood and walked out of the room without looking back. The Judge caught a questioning look from Hagood but ignored it and went to find something to eat.

* * *

Janice steered Bethany to the dining room where she spotted Camille and headed to her. When Camille saw Bethany's frightened face, she immediately rushed to meet them, helping Janice seat her half-sister. Janice told her to sit and keep an eye on Bethany before leaving them, she needed to find Dennis.

Camille poured a tall glass of water for Bethany and made her sip it slowly. As her sister calmed, Camille teased the details of the story from Bethany, as she was able to recall them. "I don't understand any of it, Camille. Junior has been selling out the firm to our competitors and Phil's admitted to a horrible murder, God help him. Then Junior hurt me when I said I was going to talk to William about getting Phil back in. Dennis did something to Junior, I know he did, but I can't say I'm sorry. I was frightened by my own brother. I'm so confused."

Camille had been surprised when Bethany defended her against the old woman's attack, but understood her sister's reason after hearing her own confession. Camille did not care for either of her new half-brothers. She suspected Philip would have tried to sleep with her if they hadn't been related, and Junior acted like he hated her.

They both scared her, though Camille was not easily frightened. She had not been afraid of anything since that dreadful night in Paris and the next morning, when the gendarmes came. She hugged Bethany to comfort her, and Bethany enjoyed the closeness. Despite the acrid smell of strong cigarettes that clung to her sister's clothes, she was warm and soft and made Bethany feel safe. She returned the embrace and a bond was forged. From that moment, the Thurwell brothers would no longer be the dominant force in the family.

* * *

Freddie looked around the conference room and felt out of place. Since he had revealed his secret, his cover of being the great rival was stripped away, and he felt naked and exposed. He saw Betty Freah and smiled across the room.

She accepted his unspoken invitation and joined him. "Quite the day, Freddie, don't you think? Whoever would've suspected you of being one of the good guys?"

"I guess, but don't let the SEC know. I don't think they'd share your high opinion of me." She nudged him in the ribs. "My silence will cost you, Freddie." He laughed. "Sure. You declared your income to the penny, I suppose?"

They laughed at the standoff, then Freddie sighed and shook his head. "Johnston knew what he was doing, right to the end. By getting us to tell our stories, our secrets, he's made us all equally vulnerable."

Betty nodded, her thoughts too had been on JT. "I hadn't seen him for a few months, but he still paid me. I thought maybe he'd switched to a younger girl and paid me out of kindness, but he was too busy dying to get laid. I miss him."

Freddie nodded, he missed his friend too. They had spent much of the past twenty or so years pretending to hate each other, but in their private meetings, their mutual respect and warmth was real. Now Freddie had no peer left, no person he could be himself with. "Do you want to grab a quick bite to eat, before we get going again?" She agreed, and he was surprised as she folded her arm into his, but he liked it.

* * *

Larry MacLean sat alone. His friend's family was lost to him as allies. Even Johnston had turned out to be his enemy. Larry knew he deserved punishment for his betrayal, but Johnston had stolen his family's entire wealth. God only knew what Thurwell had planned for Larry had he lived long enough to complete his scheme.

Philip had been thrown out, and Junior would never forgive Larry for wrecking his mother's marriage. Bethany was lost to him since yesterday. The family alliance was dead, and Larry had no idea what to do next. He spotted Winnie, still at the table. She might be his last friend in the world, so he joined her. She gave him a look. "I want to say I do not approve of your behavior with regard to your friend's wife."

His heart began to sink, and he made to leave but she put a hand on his arm to stop him. "However, since I committed adultery against the same marriage, knowingly or not, I can't very well hold it against you." She offered a sly smile, and he felt relief flow through his body. "Thank you, Mrs. Tremethick. I need a friend. All my others have abandoned me."

"Just call me Winnie, dear. I feel old when you call me by my married name. My days with Charlie seem so real again, I almost feel like a girl. But when you call me Mrs. Tremethick it brings all the years back in a rush."

"Okay Winnie, that's a deal, as long as you call me Larry."

They sat in silence and watched the others drift in and out of the room. Winnie sighed as she watched. "What a den of thieves and villains. I've never known such a bunch of people to make my skin crawl. Do you realize, Larry, that we are locked away in a remote location with people who have committed murder, fraud, blackmail, robbery and prostitution? My goodness."

"It sounds bad when you put it like that." He deadpanned.

She looked at him, confused for a moment before she laughed. Too loud. It was a release of tension, but it brought sharp looks from the others. The two of them fell into an easy chat and remembered a time when Johnston Thurwell, or Charlie Wells, had been their friend and lover. There was more unpleasantness ahead, but for now, they lived in the past to forget the present.

* * *

William held the yellow envelope in his hand and ran his fingers thoughtfully over its seal as he contemplated what surprises might be inside. The safe was open behind him, and his office door was locked against interruptions.

The lawyer had received two surprises in the last session, the first was the details of how Winnie Tremethick met his employer and the second was Philip's confession to murder. He was still trying to cope with Philip's revelation. He would never have approached Judge Freeman if he had known the truth. In fact, he was certain the Old Man would never have sent him under those circumstances.

Thurwell would have lived with the shame of having a murderer for a son rather than allow Philip to use his wealth and power to escape the consequences.

Bird was still stunned Philip had not told his secret. All he had needed to admit was his complicity in Junior's betrayal of their father by acting as courier and providing his brother with alibis for taking time away from the office. But Philip had kept a worse secret than his betrayal, and it had finally caught up with him. William would keep Philip restricted to his suite so he could not cause trouble.

William turned his attention back to the Charlie Wells envelope. His orders were unambiguous. If Winnie remembered Charlie Wells, Bird was to open the envelope and carry out the instructions within. It had never occurred to him that Johnston Thurwell and Charlie Wells were one and the same, but he had no reason to suspect it might be the case.

William slit the envelope with his letter opener and tipped its contents onto his blotter. A small silver key fell out, followed by a single sheet of paper and a second envelope, delicate and white.

Bird picked up the envelope, it was addressed *To Winnie*. He looked at the key. It looked old but was untarnished, as if it had been handled often. Finally, he turned to the handwritten sheet and read his instructions.

Bill,

If you're reading this, then you should know I'm happy. You will have had the pleasure of meeting Winnie Tremethick, and she will have remembered Charlie Wells.

I'm sure she told you about the summer we spent together in England. She might even have told you how she saved my life. What I am certain she never told you, was how much she meant to me. She could never share that, because she never knew.

I should have told her, I should never have left her. There is a letter to Winnie in this envelope. I want you to give it to her only if she seems strong enough to read it. I haven't seen her in forty years and have no idea of her health or state of mind. I hope and pray as I write this, that you think her well enough to give her my letter.

There's a key with this letter, but that is for you, Bill. In the boathouse is the old chest we used to sit on to change our shoes. You can't miss it. Under that chest is a loose floorboard and under that, you'll find a box. The key unlocks that box. You're to take the contents of the box and give it to Winnie. Do not delegate this task Bill, do it personally.

Then transfer forty million dollars to Winnie and make sure she gets home safe. I have no wish to keep her from the farm. She wouldn't leave it forty years ago, and I'm certain she misses it now.

Destroy these instructions when you've completed them. Do the work as soon as possible and keep her safe. Once the Danse is over, I want her out of the vipers nest as soon as you can make it happen.

JCT2

William turned the paper over, but the reverse was blank. The instructions were straightforward enough, and he already knew he would give the letter to Winnie. There was no doubt in his mind that she was strong enough to read whatever was inside.

He checked his watch, he had told the group their break would be thirty minutes and the time was nearly up. Should he start the session and go to the boathouse later, or did the Old Man mean right now? He had said as soon as possible, so he had some latitude. He decided to collect the box later. He would face a revolt if he delayed progress much longer.

William replaced the key, letter and his instructions in the yellow envelope and locked them back in the safe. He checked over the room, and when he was satisfied everything was secure, headed back to the conference room.

Chapter Twenty-One

The mood among the group was guarded. Their secrets had changed the way the participants looked at each other. Old alliances were irrevocably broken, but no one had yet had time to forge new ones. Tension and suspicion were dominant as people filed back into the room. Bird saw Philip's seat had been removed. Jeremy had seen to it that an empty chair would not distract them.

He saw Larry finishing a conversation with Winnie Tremethick, the old lady looked happy, and William felt a sharp pang of regret. He should have taken care of her first, to hell with the others. It was too late now, he was committed to the session. He'd take care of her at the dinner break.

"Ladies and Gentlemen, you may continue to determine the division of the Thurwell fortune. At midnight, whether you are in session or not, the money will be reduced a further twenty percent. There are eleven of you remaining and motions must be carried by seventy-five percent. You need nine votes to pass a vote."

A murmur rumbled around the table. They were all aware the family bloc had fractured. Nine was a large number to reach, and they were nervous about the way forward. "I recommend you elect a Chair, unless you wish to continue with Mr. MacLean as your leader."

Junior snorted and waved dismissively. "As if that snake will decide what I get to vote on or not, fuck that."

Caroline made a show of clearing her throat to get attention. "I'm sorry Larry, but I think we need a new

236

Chairman. One who hasn't made as many enemies as you."
MacLean didn't argue, though Smith openly sneered. He knew his time as the group's leader had ended. He simply nodded and accepted his new pariah status.

"We need someone neutral, someone we can still trust." Everyone looked at Dennis. It was out of the ordinary for him to say anything unless he was spoken to first. Junior glowered, he wanted to tell the manservant to mind his place, but was afraid of him. He rubbed his ribs where Dennis had jabbed him, it still hurt like a son of a bitch.

"Like who, Dennis?" Bethany was willing to listen to the man who saved her from her own brother.

Dennis looked bewildered, he hadn't expected a follow-up question, but Janice came to his rescue. "What about the Judge? Judge Freeman is about as neutral as we could find and he's used to being in charge, right, sir?"

Freeman was surprised by Janice's endorsement, they had only had a brief conversation about his offer to Dennis and she said she needed time to consider it. Apparently she had decided. He was pleased. "I am used to controlling a courtroom, that is true. It would be an honor to be your Chair."

Freddie interrupted. "Just wait a minute, before we get ahead of ourselves. Judge you were blackmailed into setting a murderer free. Then you blackmailed William to save your own skin and put us all through hell. That raises questions about your integrity." Betty voiced her support of Freddie, but no one joined them.

Freeman counted three full breaths before responding. It was a trick he learned as a young lawyer to ensure he remained in control of his emotions in front of a jury. Juries liked to know that lawyers were in charge, just as people in general liked to know that those given positions of authority were trustworthy with the power they wielded. "I was forced to make a decision I would have preferred not to have made, that is true.

However, you must recall it was only in the past hour we learned Philip Thurwell committed murder deliberately."

Freddie conceded the point, but was not yet ready to give his approval. "Okay, fair enough. How do you feel about the Thurwells, Judge? This family may be responsible for the destruction of your career. Can you be fair to them?"

Junior interrupted before the legal man could respond. "Just wait a second, Freddie. We're not going to make the Judge our Chair on your say so, or based on whatever bullshit he says. There might be someone else who can take the job on."

Freddie was annoyed by the interruption. "Who, Junior? You? You don't have the temperament to lead a parade, let alone these negotiations."

Junior flushed scarlet as Freddie landed a solid blow to his delicate ego. "No, not me. I was thinking of Caroline. She runs the Foundation and is as qualified as the Judge." Smith sat up and looked pleased to have been picked, if not surprised. It was obvious she and Junior had arranged the attempt to chair the group.

Freddie snorted. "Caroline Smith, the woman who rubber stamps Foundation grants based on how much you can line her pockets? That's an outstanding recommendation, Junior."

Smith felt the need to defend herself. "I believe the Judge and I may be seen as equals, if you compare our past indiscretions. I don't think you should be so quick to dismiss me as a candidate, Freddie."

Hagood shrugged, he didn't like Smith and never had. "How about a show of hands, let's see how others feel about the choice. William?"

Bird agreed and as there were no objections he started the process without pause. "Your nominated candidates are Caroline Smith and Judge Freeman. I'll call the name.

Raise your hand if you support that person for Chair. Those in favor of Caroline Smith?"

Junior and Smith raised their hands, but they were alone.

"That's two votes for Caroline Smith. Those in favor of Judge Freeman, raise your hands." Dennis and Janice Elliot raised their hands simultaneously, joined by Larry, Winnie and Betty Freah. Ron Freeman raised his own hand as William counted. "That's six votes for the Judge. Those in favor of another candidate, raise your hands."

Freddie raised his hand and looked at the two sisters, who had not voted. Bethany raised her hand and looked at Camille, who raised hers after a quick smile at her sister. William recorded the vote. "Three for another candidate. You have no majority. I recommend you find an alternative candidate for your three votes. When we have a full roster, you can vote again. The person with the lowest count will be eliminated in each round until you reach a super-majority."

William took charge to steer them toward the next step. "So who will you nominate? Freddie, Bethany and Camille, you voted for an alternate choice. Who?"

Beth looked at Camille, and a look of understanding passed between them. Bethany addressed the others. "I think Freddie should get the job. He turned out to be a true friend to my father, I trust him." Camille added her agreement.

William turned to Hagood. "Freddie, do you agree? Do you wish to be considered for the Chair?"

Hagood accepted the sister's nomination with a gallant nod of his head. "Do you need to vote again, or will you accept the results of the last vote, with the three votes for an unnamed candidate being given to Freddie? If you don't repeat the vote, Caroline will be eliminated and there will be a choice between Freddie and the Judge."

Junior began to object but caught a look from Smith and fell quiet. She knew they were beaten and did not want Junior's mouth costing them more goodwill. "I accept the results of the first round, I concede. Proceed with the second vote."

William was grateful for any unpleasantness Smith had averted. "Thank you Caroline. You now have a choice between Freddie Hagood and Judge Freeman. Nine votes are required for a decision. Those in favor of Freddie, raise your hands now."

Camille, Bethany and Freddie raised their hands again, but no-one joined them. William counted and announced the result.

"Three votes for Freddie. Those in favor of Judge Freeman, raise your hands."

Eight hands were raised, the original six plus Junior and Caroline. William sighed. The situation was predictable but tedious. Junior would never support Freddie after his humiliation and Caroline would vote with Junior every time. They had come to an impasse.

"Eight to three, there is no super-majority. Do you need a break to figure this out?"

Freddie coughed looked at the sisters. "Ladies, I appreciate your trust, but I think it is in our best interests to move on. Let's start this off right with a unanimous vote for the Judge. I think he may be a decent man who was caught in terrible circumstances. He has everyone else's support. If I change my vote to support the Judge, will you join me?"

Bethany knew they had lost. Eight to three was too large a gap to overcome. What Freddie recommended was an elegant way to proceed. It built a bridge between the two factions instead of increasing tensions. She agreed and was joined by Camille.

William was impressed by Freddie's offer and acted before any dissent could break out. "Let's make it formal, those in favor of Judge Freeman for Chair, raise your hands."

Eleven hands rose in unison and a half-hearted cheer went up from Freddie, which drew a laugh and broke the tension as William announced the result. "It's a unanimous decision. Judge Freeman, congratulations sir, you have the Chair." The Judge was surprised by a spontaneous round of applause. He realized every person wanted a quick resolution to the day. They had spent too much time in this room, under too much pressure.

"Thank you. Especially to Mr. Hagood, Miss Bethany and Miss Camille. Thank you all for your trust. I will attempt to wrap up our business as quickly as possible. I suggest we first agree there will be no attempts to remove a person without a share?" He looked at each face with trepidation, but saw no one willing to start a fight on the matter and was pleased. "Good, then I think we stand an excellent chance of finishing before the midnight penalty. I'm sure we all approve of that goal."

Junior was furious, but dared say nothing in case he further damaged his cause with the group. He needed to get to Bethany and persuade her to work with him to secure a suitable share of their father's money. He knew Caroline would support him. If he added his sister and she brought along the French girl, he would control a powerful alliance.

Junior could achieve none of this without some private time and for that he needed a break, but not yet. He risked raising the ire of the others if he called for a break just as the Judge was getting settled as Chair. The Judge was talking. Junior listened and adopted an air of relaxed indifference. "There are eleven of us, and we need nine to approve a final decision. I recommend we consider equal shares, it was an idea defeated yesterday, but I submit that what happened yesterday is no longer relevant."

Junior watched the reaction to the Judge's speech. Too many people were in agreement that equal shares were a good idea. He had to say something, he would not allow servants share equally in his inheritance. It was inconceivable. "No. No one agreed anything of the sort. I insist the family gets most of the wealth. It seems only proper that our father would want us to be well taken care of."

He heard a snort from Larry MacLean. "Junior, you still don't get it, do you? If Johnston had wanted you to get more, he would have bequeathed it to you in a Will, but he didn't. You and Beth are trying to salvage what you can, like the rest of us. Considering what we all heard earlier, I can't say I'm surprised. It seems to me his family was the cause of more heartache for Johnston than the rest of us combined."

"Well, you'd know something about causing father heartache Larry. I don't think you're in any position to point fingers." Junior's retort was out of his mouth before he had time to think and only Bethany's interruption saved him from saying more.

"Stop it. Both of you, just stop." Bethany's voice trembled. She was angry and could not bear to listen to them bicker for a moment longer. "Most of us could be accused of abusing my father in one way or another. Only a few of the people around this table told secrets that did not reflect badly on them, and of those, even fewer could claim to have been noble."

She glanced at Dennis, the one man who had acted selflessly to help his employer. He'd broken the law to do it and had even involved his wife. She imagined he had not even considered refusing her father's request for help. Bethany looked at Freeman. "Judge, can I ask for a show of hands for who might support the family's claim to the largest share? I don't mean an official vote, just an indication?"

The Judge glanced at William, who shrugged. "Nothing says you can't do an informal poll, it's your call."

The Judge called the question and Bethany's heart sank as she saw eight people keep their hands in place, the only raised hands were hers, Camille's and Junior's. Freeman sounded conciliatory as he read the show of hands. "I think you have your answer. There is no support for your claim."

She was prepared to make another suggestion, but her brother interrupted. She recognized the anger in his voice and closed her eyes, dreading what he would say. "You ingrates. You leeches. You took and took from my father, all of you were into him for something, and now you stab us, his family, to get your grubbing, greedy fingers on a few more dollars of his money." Junior's face was crimson and his mouth twisted into a vicious expression of hate.

Bethany feared he would go too far and risk getting voted out with nothing if he upset them all too much. She tried to calm him, but he turned on her. "Don't try and shut me up, sister. I'm speaking for you here, not just me. Sure, we're not perfect, we have flaws. But damn it, we're his flesh and blood. We carry his name, and sure as shit we should get most of his money." He pointed at the others, moving an accusing finger at every person, his rage barely contained. "Not one of you can tell me you're worth more than me, the son who bears his name. I am worth more than all of you put together, just remember that." He sat down, and his chest heaved as he struggled for breath through his rage.

"Or what, Junior?" Janice was flushed with fury. She had suffered at Junior's hands and was not prepared to let him have the last word about his perceived worth. "What are you going to do if you don't get your way? Cry?"

There was a twitter of laughter from Betty, who was not silenced by the look of pure venom Junior shot her. Janice pressed on. "Come on, big man, what are you going to do if we don't give you what you want? Tell us, we want to know." Janice taunted him, and Junior's face turned to its darkest shade of red. It signaled danger, but she kept baiting him.

"We're waiting for an answer-"

Junior rose and balled his fists as a red mist filled his vision, but Judge Freeman cut him off before words came to his strangled throat. "That's enough. Quiet down. Everyone just be quiet, this is not going to get us anywhere. I should not need to remind you that we have a deadline. I'm calling a break. I strongly suggest you calm down and start thinking about how we are going to resolve this impasse. It's almost four, we'll return to our business at five. I want everyone back here, ready to make decisions in an hour. Do what you have to do to calm down, talk to whom you must about how to proceed, but be here and ready to deal at five. Now, go."

Junior was already exiting the room as the Judge finished his sentence. He needed to be alone, his head hurt with the fury he felt at the Elliot slut. How dare she talk back to him? He thought he'd shown her who was the boss last night, but it seemed she had already forgotten her lesson.

After only a few moments, the Judge and William were alone. William felt encouragement was called for. "You did well Judge, they might have gotten out of control had you not stepped in. You know a bunch of them want to make alliances again, and you gave them time to go do it. Well done."

Freeman grunted. "I meant what I said about trying to have everyone take something away, you know. I don't want to see another person tossed aside like I was and as Philip Thurwell has been. I have all the reason in the world to detest that boy, but to throw him out was an error. It raised tensions that might get in the way of an agreement."

William had sympathy for the Judge's opinion but could do nothing about it.

"I had no choice, my orders are non-negotiable. He didn't tell the required truth, and there was only one possible outcome. If it makes an agreement hard, so be it. Philip is out, and he's not getting back in. Sorry if it messes up your day, but there it is."

William left the Judge, he needed to get his papers under lock and key and go foraging for a box in the boathouse.

Chapter Twenty-Two

William looked out of his office window and noted the fading light. Dusk came early this time of year and the late afternoon gloom's dull pallor made even the fresh snow look gray. He collected his cashmere overcoat and a pair of rubber overshoes from his closet. He hoped he would not need any tools or he'd have to find Jeremy, and he preferred to keep this mission to himself. He scrabbled around in the bottom drawer of his desk until he found one thing he knew he'd need, a small plastic flashlight.

The boathouse was not far from the main building. In the summer, it was a pleasant walk under shade trees to the waterside. It was not so easy in January, and William found it difficult to put one foot in front of the other through the deep snow. The grounds keepers had not cleared the pathway to the boathouse, the lake was frozen over, and they'd been told no one would be skating this week.

Bird cursed, the snow was over knee height, and he had to throw his legs in the air in an exaggerated stride to get a decent step forward. He was only halfway to the boathouse when he lost his left overshoe and regretted its loss immediately. He had snow in his socks, but it made no real difference to his progress, which was glacial in its pace.

The trip would wreck his thousand dollar shoes and he wished he'd called on Jeremy for a pair of boots. The dark shadow of the boathouse rose in front of him as he breathed hard and pushed though the snow drifts. Branches rested on its roof, weighed down with snow to form a dark canopy over the wooden door.

William fumbled with the flashlight but dropped it as he tried to switch it on. He cursed and went after the light. It was easy to find, it had lodged a foot down in the deep snow, but his fingers felt biting cold snow as he retrieved it. Snow had found its way into his sleeve and now William wished he had gloves in addition to boots.

He shone the flashlight into the gloom and trudged to the door, hoping it wasn't locked. He need not have been concerned, there was a bolt, but no padlock secured it. He pushed the door open and stumbled into the boathouse, glad to be out of the snow and on a firm wooden floor.

William had been to the boathouse many times, but never when the light was so poor. He had to pause to remember the layout of the place as he cast around with the flashlight beam. He soon found the old wooden chest and picked his way carefully through the dark to it. He sat down, he could at least take the time to empty his shoes of snow before he retrieved what he'd come for.

He tipped piles of snow onto the dry wood floor and was surprised by how much powder had jammed into his footwear. He slipped his shoes back on and stood to look at the chest. It looked heavy and had not been moved in a long time.

William would have to slide it away from the wall. He was just able to slot his fingers into the gap between the wall and the chest when he bent to move it. He braced himself and gave the chest a strong pull. It moved an inch and stopped. William expelled a loud breath and cursed, the chest was stuck.

He needed to find something to lever the chest aside. He shone the flashlight around until he found the oar rack, still loaded with stout wooden oars. He collected one of the strongest-looking oars and slid the blade into the gap between the wall and the chest, standing on it to get the blade as far down as possible.

He dusted his hands off and braced his feet for good balance and gave a hard pull on the oar. He staggered back as the chest slid easily away from the wall, the oar worked better than he expected. He bumped into the doorway as he fell backward, but the frame stopped him from tumbling back out into the snow.

He propped the oar against the doorframe and returned to the chest. He knelt on the smooth lid and used the flashlight to inspect the exposed floor. He saw one board with a knothole just large enough for a fingertip. It had to be the board that hid the box. He leaned down lower, jammed his finger in the knothole and lifted the board out of its place. It came up easily, and he felt triumphant, he had been right not to bother Jeremy for tools.

He peered into the void, it was deeper than he expected, and he was forced to stretch until his fingers found a shape. He grabbed what felt like string and pulled it up. When he could see what he had recovered, he saw a ribbon neatly tied around a small metal box. He'd found what he came for. Bird placed the box on the chest and gave it a shove to put it back in its place. The chest moved easily now it had been disturbed, and he was pleased to see it return as if it had never been moved.

He bent to pick up the box but was startled by a voice behind him. "Billy Bird the turd, what are you doing in here, I wonder?"

William knew the voice even before he turned to see Philip Thurwell standing in the doorway. The lawyer dropped the box into his overcoat pocket and hoped the other man hadn't seen it in the gloom. "Philip, what are you doing here?"

Bird was confused, what reason did the young man have for being at the boathouse? "I believe I asked first, Bill. Why don't you tell me what you found scrabbling back there?" William cursed silently, Philip had seen more than he would have liked.

"It's none of your concern what my business is here, Phil. Let's go back to the house, shall we?"

He approached the door, but stopped when Philip reached and took the oar William had left by the doorway. Something in the manner Philip hefted the oar made Bird afraid. It was heavy, and if Philip decided to use it as a weapon, he could maim or even kill him. The young man stepped into the boathouse, swinging the oar as he moved it from one hand to the other.

"Better start talking, Bill. I saw you get something back there. Maybe it's valuable. You know, it occurs to me if what you have in your pocket is worth anything, I might as well take it. After all, I won't be getting any of my father's money. Will I, Bill?"

William's mouth was dry, he was scared. Philip's voice was quiet, but he could hear simmering fury in it. William had disinherited him, and now he had the lawyer cornered alone in the remote boathouse. Philip had admitted murder only hours earlier, and a deep chill went down William's spine.

"Now, Phil, wait a minute. Those were the instructions your father left, I just followed them. It was nothing personal." William hated the fear in his voice but could not hide it. He knew Philip could knock him unconscious or worse and just take the box from him. Philip snorted, and the lawyer knew his appeal had been heard and denied. He reached into his pocket and felt the small box next to the flashlight when a desperate idea occurred to him.

"Okay, Phil. There's no need for trouble. Here, let me show you." Philip stepped closer as he drew his hand out of his pocket, but instead of the box, William drew out the flashlight. He flipped it on and shone it directly into Philips's eyes, momentarily blinding him.

Philip roared in anger and swung the oar in a scything motion at the space where Bird's head had been a second earlier, but the lawyer dropped to a crouch and dodged the blow. He scurried past Philip and saw his path to the exit was clear. Bird dropped the flashlight and ran. He heard a loud crack as the oar crashed into the doorframe, a vicious blow that could have killed him, had it connected.

The panicked lawyer waded through the snow, but it was like trying to run through quicksand. His legs were heavy, and his progress too slow. He felt like he was in a nightmare when he heard a wicked laugh as Philip came after him.

Bird looked around desperately. He was out of view of the main house, and the snow deadened sound so much that crying for help would be futile. He shouted anyway in the hope some brave soul might be outside. He turned and saw Philip close behind him, walking with ease through the deep snow.

"Say goodnight, Bill." Philip brought the oar over his head and prepared a devastating swing at the lawyer, who crumpled to his knees with a whimper. William covered his head with his hands and realized with horror that he was about to die.

But the blow never landed. Bird heard a grunt and a soft thud. He didn't dare move or look to see what had happened. He knelt, frozen by fear in the snow, and waited for the lights to go out.

A hand was on his elbow, gently encouraging him to stand. It took a while for him to react. "Come on, sir, it's all right. Stand up now, we'll have you back inside the house in no time."

William looked up and was amazed to see Jeremy's concerned face. The major-domo was dressed in outdoor gear. Behind him, William saw Philip face down in the snow. He was very still, the oar at his side.

"Is... is he dead?"

Jeremy shook his head. "Oh no, sir. Out for the count, yes. Dead, no."

"How? How did he find me? How did you find me?" Bird was talking too fast as adrenaline pumped through his body.

"Well sir, I don't know how he knew you were out here, but I'd hazard a guess he saw you leave the house. His room overlooks this pathway. He probably spotted you and decided to follow."

William nodded, he'd been careless. Jeremy continued explaining as he patiently waited for William's legs to stop shaking enough so they could head back to the mansion. "As for me, I saw Mr. Philip hurry out of the house dressed for the outdoors and curiosity got the better of me, I'm happy to say."

He owed his life to the major-domo, there was no doubt about it. "But, where were you, I didn't see you when I ran out of there."

Jeremy helped the lawyer walk slowly back to the house. "I heard voices in the boathouse and hid in the trees in case I was needed. When I saw Mr. Philip decide to put that oar into your skull, I took it away. I'm afraid I hit him harder than I should have, but it seemed like a good idea at the time."

Bird looked at the unruffled man and shook his head, bemused at how matter of fact Jeremy could be after so much violence. "Thank you, Jeremy. I owe you my life."

Jeremy waved the thanks aside as they reached the house. "Now you go on up to your room, sir and have a shower to warm up. I'll send up something hot for you. I had better fetch young Mr. Thurwell before he catches pneumonia."

Bird could take no more. He nodded dumbly and headed for his room as Jeremy returned to the gathering darkness to fetch Philip's unconscious body.

Chapter Twenty-Three

At the moment William Bird was wondering whether or not to ask Jeremy for boots before venturing outside, Larry MacLean and Winnie Tremethick took a table together in the dining room. Their mood was solemn. Winnie was tired, and Larry felt like an outcast. She looked at Larry's sour face and shook her head. "You look as if the whole world is on your shoulders."

He sighed. "I'm alone. For the first time in my life, I have no family or friends. My brother has disappeared and even though I now understand why he left, I still don't know where he went. My oldest friend is dead. I'll always think of him as my friend, despite what I did to him. And what he tried to do to me. "

Larry needed to get away from the mansion and back to his boat. He needed to find a new distraction with long legs and a deep tan. That would have to wait, however. If he was to have any kind of future, Larry had to take as much money as he could from the destructive vortex he and the others were caught in. His thoughts drifted to happier times when he and Johnston would sit together in easy friendship and chat long nights away with quality wine and cigars.

Winnie's voice cut through his melancholy. "If you don't start doing something, you'll leave empty handed, mark my words."

He started. "Pardon me? What did you say?" She looked at him askance, and he felt like a boy caught with his hand in the cookie jar. "Okay, I heard you. What do you mean?"

She raised an eyebrow and waved her finger in his face. "I mean, you need to find yourself some new friends, and soon. Look around you. Everyone's talking to anyone they think can help them get Charlie's money. Why are you sitting with me feeling sorry for yourself? If you want to go home empty-handed, stay with me. If you want to save yourself, you had better get on with it."

Larry looked at her with renewed respect. She was never quite the person he thought she was. He looked around the dining room, and saw the old woman was correct, many people were in the room and all of them were vying for friends or begging and selling favors. Winnie was right. He had to get back in the game.

He saw Freddie and Betty together. He could do worse than start there. Larry's indiscretion had not directly hurt either of them, and the worst Betty had done to him was to provide a girl in the plot that brought down his brother. He didn't like that she had participated, but he rationalized that if Betty had not provided the girl, someone else would have.

"What about you, Winnie? How will you manage? Do you want to come with me?" She smiled and shook her head. "I'll be fine, Larry. You go on and do what you have to."

He took her advice and walked with more purpose than he felt toward Freddie and Betty.

* * *

Winnie watched him go and was glad of the opportunity to leave the room. She was tired and needed to rest. The day had been too intense, and her head was filled with memories of Charlie Wells. She quietly slipped out of the dining room and walked to her suite. She closed the door behind her and breathed a long sigh of relief. She loved the quietness of her own space. Winnie was not used to being among so many people. At home, the only time she saw more than a couple of people in one place was at Church on Sundays. Most Sundays there were less people suffering the hard wooden pews than there were in the mansion.

She walked to the couch, slid her shoes off and flexed her old toes, happy to be out of her uncomfortable footwear. Winnie wore Wellington boots six days out of seven and had been in considerable discomfort wearing dress shoes. She closed her eyes, and when sleep came, Charlie Well's face appeared to her, as handsome and happy as he had been many decades ago.

* * *

Freddie saw Larry's approach and whispered a warning to Betty. She had been gossiping about MacLean, and how she had known him before her introduction to the Old Man. Her recollections were not flattering. Betty heeded the warning and turned to flash one of her best smiles at Larry as Freddie greeted him. "You look like hell, Larry. Sit down, won't you?"

Larry grimaced at Hagood's rough greeting but accepted the invitation. Freddie wasted no time. "So what can we do for you, Larry?"

Betty was happy for Freddie to take the initiative. They had agreed that adding allies to their group was a smart strategy. Betty had suggested Larry. Freddie had balked at the idea initially, but she had been winning him over slowly, so he was prepared to see how it played out now they were talking.

Freddie looked at MacLean and saw a beaten man, which pleased him. Beaten men were easy to manage and often cheap. "Larry? I assume you're not just here for our company, as sparkling as that may be." He smiled at Betty, who gave him a playful slap on the wrist.

"I need a couple of friends in the room with me. I think the family might try to short-change me in the negotiations, and I can't afford that. I suggest the three of us collaborate in a mutual protection of interests, as it were." He rushed through his unrehearsed plea and looked at the others with a worried expression. Betty was unreadable. She projected a friendly demeanor, but he had no idea what she was thinking.

Freddie showed interest in what Larry had said, but it was a cool, passing interest. "I see. Your idea has merit, Larry, but you are somewhat toxic as far as the family is concerned, wouldn't you agree? I don't know that Betty and I would be well served throwing our lot in with yours."

Betty appeared to be in complete agreement with Hagood, but Larry missed the sharp look she fired at her partner and the return glance that told her to be patient. MacLean sighed, he couldn't give up. Freddie and Betty represented his best chance of an alliance that could protect him. "I know, but while the two of you can protect each other now, you might need another vote, to be safe. I can be that vote."

Freddie pretended to consider the plea. He had already decided to accept MacLean, but he reasoned there was no need to associate his and Betty's interests with Larry for nothing. "We could get another vote with less baggage attached, Larry. I'm sorry, but I don't see why we should take you on and risk diminishing our own chances of success."

Hagood watched MacLean's shoulders sag under the weight of the rejection and knew he had him at his most vulnerable. "That is unless you can make it worth our while to support you."

Freddie was forced to suppress a triumphal sneer when he saw Larry making desperate calculations in his mind.

"How much? How much will it cost me to get your support?" Larry was trapped, and he knew it, if he walked away, he would risk being isolated and vulnerable. If Freddie and Betty could help secure him a fair share, he'd still be better off. He looked at Hagood and felt a flash of anger amid his desperation. Freddie was taking advantage of his weakness, and there was nothing he could do about it.

Freddie's eyes became slits as he laid out his demand. "I think half will do, don't you Betty?"

Betty's eyes widened, she had not thought Larry could be made to pay for their support. She looked at Freddie with admiration of his skill at exploiting MacLean's vulnerability. Larry knew he was defeated and agreed to Freddie's outrageous terms. She laughed inwardly, she might be the whore at the table, but Larry was the one who had been screwed.

MacLean knew he had no choice but to agree to Freddie's demands. Half of something was better than nothing. He would accept their terms and try to figure out a way to make it work. The three of them shook hands, and Larry left them. He needed to be alone, he was nauseated by the deal he had been forced to accept.

* * *

Ron Freeman was pleased with himself. Twenty-four hours ago, he had been thrown out of the meeting with no money and faced a ruined career. Now he was the leader of the group and Philip Thurwell, the cause of all his troubles, had been disinherited. He smiled as he reflected on his change in fortune when a soft tap on his shoulder disturbed him.

He turned to find Dennis Elliot hovering behind him. "Sorry to disturb you, Judge, but Jan and I were hoping we might have a chat, in private." Freeman saw no sign of the manservant's wife and wondered what was on their minds.

"I guess that would be fine, where is your wife?"

Dennis leaned down and spoke in a near whisper. "She's in the library, sir. We want to speak with you, but where there are fewer ears, if you know what I mean." Freeman saw interested looks aimed at the manservant and himself and understood perfectly. "Okay, let's go."

The others watched them walk out together, which made Dennis's attempt to hide their conversation redundant. It was obvious they intended to talk. Dennis led the Judge to a quiet reading nook where his wife waited in an overstuffed wing chair. She smiled when she saw her husband return with Freeman, she had been pleased with Dennis's solid resolve since she had told her story about Junior.

Dennis seated the Judge, but Janice was in charge of the meeting. "Judge Freeman, thank you for meeting with us." He offered a smile, despite his reservations about her.

"Dennis and I think it would be to our mutual advantage if we came to an agreement about how to vote in future sessions. I believe Dennis and I will be okay as long as we stick together, but it would be better to have three votes, than two."

She watched the Judge's face for any reaction, but detected nothing beyond polite interest. She made to speak again, but Freeman raised a finger to stop her. His easy air of authority made her obey. "Yesterday you both voted to have me thrown out. You do remember that, don't you, Mrs. Elliot?"

Dennis muttered something, and though Freeman did not catch what he said, he understood the apologetic tone enough to know what had been meant. He continued. "Perhaps you can tell me why I should trust you now, only a day later? Perhaps you could also tell me why I should have anything to do with you after you humiliated me this morning? Need I remind you that you spat in my face? I realize my blackmail was clumsy, but no one else acted so disgracefully."

Dennis gave Janice a concerned look. He had been worried about this morning's incident and had warned his wife they might be wasting their time.

She told him not to worry and to stay quiet. Those words would have angered him yesterday, but things were very different between them today. Dennis felt needed again, and he liked the feeling. In turn Janice had softened her attitude toward him, and there was less snapping orders and more actual conversation.

He held his breath as his wife leaned forward and patted the Judge on the knee. "Now Judge, you need to move past this morning. I apologize for what I did to you, unreservedly. I was upset, but that doesn't excuse my actions. I thought your blackmail cost Dennis and I our futures, I panicked, and overreacted. I am so, so very sorry."

Dennis held his breath. He had never seen Jan so contrite, and wondered if she meant it or if she was giving the Judge what he needed so he would join them. It worried him that he couldn't tell. He listened as she continued soothing the Judge.

"As for the votes yesterday, nine people voted against you. Only Freddie Hagood and that Smith woman voted to keep you. You might try again to get their support, but I think you need better friends. Dennis warned me that you might hold our vote against us, but something is different about you today than yesterday and that is why we should work together."

Freeman was interested, Janice was frank and honest. More than that, he was intrigued to know what she thought was different about him today. But first he needed to heal the rift and acknowledge her apology. "Alright, I accept your apology Mrs. Elliot. I accept some responsibility for how you must have felt this morning. Perhaps I even had it coming. And you are correct about the votes yesterday. You were far from alone in working against me. I will move on and put the unpleasantness behind me. If you can do the same, then I believe we can work together."

She smiled, and he knew they were agreed. "Now, perhaps you can explain what you think is different about me today?"

Janice breathed a deep sigh of relief that the Judge accepted her apology and was more than happy to move on. "We know a lot more about you, Judge, and you know more about us. Dennis and I helped Mr. Thurwell get to Larry MacLean's brother. Dennis had been a tremendously loyal servant to Mr. Thurwell and never hesitated when he was asked to help. I had some worries about the nature of the task, but we did it. Our reward for that loyalty is to be included in this meeting. That, Judge, is what the three of us have in common. You helped Mr. Thurwell when you got Philip out of a jam. Your reward is to be here too.

"That you had to be forced to help wouldn't have mattered to Mr. Thurwell, he would remember what you did. In short, the three of us helped Mr. Thurwell, and that puts us in a distinct minority when you look at the crooks in the midst of his family. You see my point, Ron?"

Janice patted Freeman's knee again as Dennis looked at her in awe. She had put it simply, and even Dennis saw the truth in her words. The Old Man received more support from his employees and a coerced Judge than any of his children. Dennis was proud of Janice for her bright mind and way with words. He watched the Judge, who sat with his hands pressed together in a steeple, his fingertips on his lips as he thought about what Jan had said.

Freeman was impressed. The housekeeper had put together a persuasive argument, better perhaps than some lawyers he had heard from in his courtroom. She had revealed a truth that had not occurred to him before. Freeman had previously only felt anger at the philanthropist for threatening him. Now that he thought about it, he wondered if he too might cross a line to protect a child in trouble.

Thurwell had tried to honor his promise to aid the Judge's career from beyond the grave by including him in the group that would share his fortune. It was twisted, but true. He and the Elliots had done more to help the dead man than his own flesh and blood. Johnston Thurwell had been surrounded with betrayal. His family betrayed him on many levels, his best friend had ruined his first marriage, and his Foundation's chief executive was a crook. Freeman saw Janice smile. She had seen a change in his face that told her they agreed.

The Judge considered his response carefully. Dennis held his breath, but Jan seemed calm. Eventually Freeman's deep baritone filled the silence. "You make a compelling case, Mrs. Elliot. I think, however, we might make more of your idea than you expect."

He paused and waited for her curiosity to build, Freeman had not lost his trial lawyer's instinct for a dramatic moment. But he was surprised when Janice interrupted. "You think we should invite the other two into our group, don't you?"

He looked at her, stunned. The woman possessed cunning that ran much deeper than he had given her credit for. He nodded, thrown off by her interruption but interested in where this was going. "Whom was I going to name, Mrs. Elliot? It's clear you have considered the angles, please share your thoughts."

Dennis was lost. His head swiveled between his wife and the Judge as if he were in the front row at a fast-paced tennis match. Their excitement was palpable, even if he had to wait to understand what was happening. Janice wore a wide smile as she responded to Freeman. "I believe we are thinking of the same people, Judge. The only other people that did anything for Mr. Thurwell when he needed it were Betty Freah and Freddie Hagood."

The Judge joined Janice in her wide smile and clapped his hands together in admiration of her performance. "Bravo. Well said Mrs. Elliot. I agree completely. We would have a powerful alliance with five people. There is perhaps one other that belongs in the group, don't you think? I refer to the old English lady, Mrs. Tremethick?"

Janice pulled a face. "Perhaps. She seems to be close to Larry MacLean, and that could be a problem. I think we're strong enough with the three of us plus Betty and Freddie."

Freeman nodded. "Can we agree not to entirely reject Mrs. Tremethick as a possibility? She may have a role to play yet."

Janice nodded assent and the three of them shook hands on their accord. She turned to her husband. "We should have time to persuade others to join us before the next session. Dennis, would you, please?" He stood without a word and finally understood what they had been talking about and was anxious to help. With a smile for Janice and a respectful nod to the Judge, he excused himself to go in search of Freddie Hagood and Betty Freah.

* * *

Camille Jolivet watched her sister through a cloud of blue smoke with one leg kicked up on the opposite chair. She took another long drag and carelessly flicked ash onto a plate where it turned into a black pool as it merged with left over juice from a fruit snack. Bethany was distracted, Camille would have to pull her together if they were to reach a successful agreement before midnight.

Bethany had been shaken to her core by her brothers' betrayals, more shocked than she had been at Camille's confession. Bethany was repelled by Camille's secret, but it seemed surreal, too horrible to be processed. She was thrown into turmoil by how little she had understood her brothers, the siblings she had known all her life.

Philip had been ejected and would get no penny of his inheritance. William had been harsh, but she found it hard to make a case to bring Phil back after he admitted murdering a man. She had not spoken to Junior. He had left quickly, and she had not been able to catch him. She needed to speak with him and patch the family unit back together before everything was taken from them.

Bethany hoped the revelation of her own secret would not be a problem for Junior. Camille seemed not to care at all, but Junior knew of their father's yearning for a grandchild. She coughed, and it broke the spell of her inner thoughts. She looked at her half-sister as she smoked one of her awful cigarettes. "Can't you go outside? Those things stink the place up."

Bethany sounded more cross than she had meant, but Camille paid no attention. "It's cold outside and warm in here. If you don't like the smoke, perhaps you should go outside, non?"

Bethany sighed. "Forget I said anything. I'm sorry. I'm tired. Tired and worried about Phil and Junior. We need them. You know that, right?"

"Philip is gone, Beth. Monsieur Bird has made his decision. It is unfortunate, but there is no way to bring him back. Junior, he is a mess. We need him, for sure, but we have to get others too. You should think about talking to your servants again, we could use them. They are two for the trouble of finding one, non?"

Bethany nodded. She was not prepared to give up on Philip, but Camille was right. They needed more allies to ensure they took the lion's share of their father's money.

She thought about getting the Elliots again, it would be a good move. They had helped her father against Larry MacLean. Perhaps they would transfer their loyalty to Bethany and the family.

Dennis and Junior had crossed swords earlier. Bethany did not understand the reasons for their animosity, but she felt sure the manservant would see reason if the family offered them enough money. It had worked yesterday, and nothing was different from then, as far as she was concerned.

She agreed Camille's idea was a good one. She would leave talking to Junior until later. He was flesh and blood, so she was not worried he would do anything other than support the family's claim. His betrayal of their father had been born of anger over his mother's divorce. She hoped he bore no ill will towards the rest of the family.

Camille watched her sister closely and saw Beth's shoulders regain their perfect posture. "Very well, I'll find Dennis and renew our offer from yesterday, agreed?" Camille drew another drag on her cigarette and nodded as she exhaled. "I'll keep the table warm." She flicked more dark ash onto the plate. Bethany shuddered in disgust at the mess on the expensive china and left in search of Dennis Elliot.

Chapter Twenty-Four

Caroline Smith needed to find Junior. She had searched the dining room, library and lobby, but he was nowhere to be found. She concluded he must have taken refuge in his suite, but was reluctant to look for him there. She had heard rumors of his encounters with women and preferred not to discover for herself if they were true.

She picked up the guest telephone in the lobby and asked to be connected to Junior's suite. After seven rings, she was about to hang up but heard the receiver pick up.

No voice answered. "Hello? Junior are you there? It's Caroline. We need to talk."

There was a soft click, and the line went dead. Smith was furious. She was not used to asking twice to get a meeting. She called again, but this time there was no answer. She put down the phone and looked at the grand staircase that led to the guest suites. She must make a choice, go and see if Junior would answer his door, or forget her plan and find another collaborator.

She was deciding what to do when she saw Dennis Elliot hurry across the lobby. It looked as if he was on an important mission, but had been derailed when he ran into Bethany Thurwell. Caroline could see the manservant was uncomfortable, even across the vast lobby.

She felt an uncomfortable crawling sensation at the back of her neck. She looked up and saw Junior standing above her with his hands on the solid banister rail, watching. Caroline felt a shudder trickle down her spine in slow motion. There was something reptilian in the way Junior looked at her. There was no life in his eyes, he looked at her like a wolf would observe its prey. She offered a tight smile and beckoned for him to join her, hoping he would not insist she go to him.

She breathed a sigh of relief when she saw he intended to come down. She could achieve her goal in the safety of a public area. He walked directly to her and took a half pace too far to invade her personal space. She knew from experience if she stepped back he would advance, there was no escaping Junior's mind games.

"What do you want, Smith?"

She stood her ground. "You need me, Junior. Your family needs a vote to replace your brother. I'm it." His face showed no emotion at her mention of Philip.

"There are still three of us Caroline. We're in no danger of being tossed aside like my unfortunate brother."

"Three is a good number, Junior. Four is better." He considered her offer and was tempted to take it. She had made a direct hit with her appeal to replace Philip's vote. Junior knew his brother's absence left his group weakened, but he didn't have to take Smith's offer. She needed him more than he needed her. She was alone unless she found some friends and he knew Caroline Smith had no friends in the mansion.

"If we take you in, you won't get an equal share of course. Family first, you know." He put a sneer on the last words and watched to see if she would fold or fight. He liked them to fight, it was better that way. She did not disappoint.

"No deal. Sorry, Junior, I might need friends but, I'm not stupid. I get an equal share or you can go to hell." It was a gamble, but Caroline was damned if she'd give up her vote for anything short of a fair deal. He flushed red, and she thought he was angry. She would have been repelled at the truth, that he had been aroused by her sharp retort. His mouth twisted into a cruel version of a smile.

"I'll talk to my sister. We'll see what we agree on. Decide how much you will settle for, Smith, but don't expect parity, you're not going to get it. Family comes first."

He turned on his heel and left her. She was excited and angry at the same time. Junior could be a total prick, but she had gotten him to talk to Bethany. Smith knew Bethany had no fondness for her and would hold her behavior at the Foundation against her, but she hoped the harsh reality of needing a fresh vote to replace Philip would overcome her objections. She had no choice but to wait for the family's answer, so Caroline headed to her room. She would feel better after she splashed some water on her face to clear her head.

* * *

Bethany was surprised when she walked into Dennis in the lobby, the very man she was looking for. Dennis, for his part, was near panic. He could not let Bethany discover the Judge with Janice in the library. He needed to find Freddie and Betty, but he would have to deal with Bethany first.

He followed her into the dining room and saw the two people he actually wished to speak with. He cursed his rotten luck, he had been so close to getting what Jan wanted but failed. He took a seat opposite the pretty French girl and almost sat on her foot, which rested on the cushioned chair. She moved her foot reluctantly and made him feel as if he had considerably inconvenienced her. He offered a shy apology and turned to listen to Bethany.

"We want to offer you and your wife the same deal as yesterday, but with a reduced bonus, if that's okay with you. We'll reduce it by twenty percent, in line with the penalty we suffered. Would that be acceptable to you, Dennis?"

Dennis wondered what Bethany was talking about. He knew Janice had made a deal to support the family with their votes in return for a reward for their loyalty, but he had not been told about a bonus. What was the bonus for, and how much was it?

Perhaps Jan had forgotten to tell him. With the upset over what Junior had done to her, he could understand how it might have slipped her mind. He had an uneasy feeling that there was another reason he had not heard about the bonus, but he pushed it to the back of his mind. He would tell Janice about the new offer, she would know what to do.

Bethany and Camille were looking at him, waiting for him to say something. "Well, thank you. Thank you both. I'm sure that will be just fine. I'll talk to Jan, but she's indisposed right now. Might I provide our answer to you later?"

Camille rolled her eyes in dramatic exasperation, but Dennis looked to Bethany as their spokeswoman. She nodded. It was the answer she had expected. She kicked herself for not discussing the offer with Janice instead of her husband. "Of course, please find your wife and discuss our offer, but we need to know your answer as quickly as possible. You understand that time is of the essence, Dennis?"

He nodded, he didn't appreciate her condescension but had become used to it over time. She had never seen him as anything other than a servant. He knew that was what he was, but the Old Man always managed to treat him in a way that made Dennis feel valued. His offspring, however, never learned the subtle art of dealing with people.

Dennis hurried back to Janice. He did not dare look at Freddie and Betty, it was impossible to invite them to meet Janice with the Thurwell sisters watching. He needed Janice to figure things out and walked as fast as he could toward the library.

* * *

Junior saw Dennis scurry through the lobby, but gave it no thought. It was no business of his why a servant was in a hurry. He sauntered into the dining room, saw his sister and the French girl and joined them.

"Where have you been Junior? Now is not a good time to get moody, we need to spend our time figuring out this mess."

He didn't bother to look at his sister. "Shut up, Beth, you give me a fucking headache." She threw her hands up in frustration. She started to bark at him, but he waved her off and talked over her. "If you'd just shut up, you might find out what I've been doing."

Bethany glared, but gestured for him to continue.

"Caroline Smith wants to join us to replace Phil's vote. I told her I'd talk to you and that she will have to accept less than equal shares. We're going to accept her, Beth. On my terms. Having four votes is a good idea. You agree, of course?"

Camille looked at her sister, who tried to maintain her cool and evaluate what Junior said. Bethany was irritated that her brother had been doing something useful, she preferred it when she was right and could admonish him. His play with Caroline was a good one, she saw no downside, but had a chance to go one up on him.

"Fine, whatever. It's great that you got Smith. One more vote will be useful when we add it to the two I've secured for us." Camille looked sharply at Bethany. Her sister was counting on the Elliots being on board before she knew it for a fact. Camille hoped Bethany was correct, if she and Junior were both successful then the family group would be powerful with six votes.

Junior feigned a yawn. "Who did you get, the Elliots? That's yesterday's news, sister. They have nowhere else to go. Of course they will support us. Is that all you've done?"

Bethany glared but swallowed her anger. It was pointless to start a fight, though he was spoiling for one. "Well, they might be old news to you, but we are a lot stronger with them." Junior shrugged as if he didn't care, and Bethany let it slide. She prayed that Dennis would be back soon with a positive response.

* * *

Janice saw Dennis return to the library and was alarmed to see he was both alone and upset. Something had gone wrong. Freeman saw her expression and turned in his seat to see Dennis arrive, breathing hard as he sat next to his wife. "What's wrong, Den? What happened, did you see Freddie?"

He struggled to catch his breath and nodded his head followed immediately by a shake, which confused her. "What? Did you see him or not? Denny, just tell me what happened."

The Judge shared Janice's concern, but tried to calm the flustered manservant. "Come Dennis, take a deep breath and tell us what happened, please."

Dennis looked at both of them, did as he was told and started his story. "I nearly made it to the dining room. That's where I thought I might find Freddie. And he was there, with Betty, but I couldn't speak to them because Bethany grabbed me."

Janice scowled at the bad luck. "What did she want? Did Freddie see you talking to her? What happened, Denny?"

He paused. "She was with the French woman. They want us to team up with them, like yesterday. She said the money would be the same."

Janice felt a stab of fear, had Bethany mentioned the bonus? She had said nothing of the bonus to Dennis. Her plan had been to steal it out from under her husband. But that was before she'd gone to see Junior. She shuddered at the memory and studied her husband's face, looking for any sign his distress was aimed at her. She relaxed when he looked into her eyes. There was no anger, just concern.

The Judge interrupted. "Would one of you tell me about the deal you had yesterday. Janice?" Freeman was curious, but not surprised, to hear the Elliot's had been aligned with the family. He had missed most of the previous day's negotiations and had not witnessed the voting.

Janice decided to be straight with her new ally. "The Thurwells offered Dennis and I a guaranteed settlement if we supported their votes. It all went to plan, and we would have been paid out this morning. Except your late night conversation with Mr. Bird blew that plan to pieces."

She looked at him, and a small smile crossed her lips, she knew he would try and steer her back on course by reminding her that she would gain more today. "Ten million dollars. Yesterday I considered that a pretty good pay day for servants."

"Small potatoes, I suspect, compared to what we stand to win today."

She smiled at the Judge's hopeful assessment and turned to her husband. Dennis was worried that Janice had not mentioned the bonus again. A nagging feeling began in the back of his mind, and he took a second look at his wife. Why had she failed to mention the bonus to either him or Freeman?

He would find out later, they'd talk when they were alone. For now, he had to listen. "I think we have an opportunity here, Denny, we can use Bethany's offer to advance our own cause. What if we pretend to accept the family's offer, but still ally with Freddie and Betty? Our group will be strong, we have five people. But the family will believe the situation to be more like six votes to three."

Freeman considered Janice's idea. The plan would leave the family vulnerable, and that would benefit the others, but he was worried about how far he could trust her. "It's an interesting idea, Janice, but what if you and Dennis change your minds and support the family against me? How do I know I can trust you?"

She smiled. "Why would we settle for less than we could get from an alliance with you and the others? The family offered Dennis and I a flat fee for our support, I expect that is all they will offer today." Janice hoped the Judge believed her. She had been surprised when he challenged her on the new plan. If it had been yesterday he would have been right about her motives, but he could not know how badly Janice wished to take revenge against Junior. She could no more support the family than she could gouge out her own eyes.

She waited for Freeman to think about her answer and flicked her attention to Dennis. She was alarmed to see the look on his face. Dennis wore the veiled look she loathed. It was a sure sign he disapproved of something she had said or done. She quickly ran through the reasons Dennis might feel that way. It was either the idea to play a double game against the family, or Bethany had mentioned the bonus.

Janice figured she could repair the damage in either case, but it was a sharp reminder of the fragility of her marriage. Yesterday she had plotted to run away and start anew without her husband. Today she had fallen a little bit in love with him again since her ugly encounter with Junior. A cold finger of doubt worried at her. Was she in love with Dennis again, or was what she felt a temporary emotion triggered by the extreme circumstances of the past twenty-four hours? She shook her head to clear it. She needed to pay attention to the Judge who was her best hope of achieving her goals.

Freeman had his own doubts. He figured Janice to be the kind of woman who would sell her own mother for a profit, so it was entirely possible she could turn on him. Yet, against his better judgment and instincts, he believed her. He knew enough to know he had not heard her real motives and perhaps he never would. But he trusted her.

He had an idea of his own. "Okay Janice, I agree in principle that it will be to our advantage to let the family believe they are in a stronger position than they actually are. However, before we give Bethany an answer we must shore up our own defenses. We must have Freddie and Betty's support, and they too must agree to your scheme. If that can be achieved, then I concur that Dennis accepts Bethany's offer, and we play for the win. Any objections?"

Janice smiled at the Judge. He was adept at this. She shook the Judge's hand, and even Dennis seemed keen on the plan. It was decided that Freeman would approach Freddie and Betty. If the Thurwells saw Janice or Dennis in conversation with the others, their plan might fail. The

Judge hurried from the library in search of Freddie and Betty, aware that time was slipping away before the next session would begin.

Chapter Twenty-Five

Jeremy dragged Philip Thurwell's unconscious body into the basement and across the stone floor of the mansion's vast wine cellar. The young man had not stirred when he had been lifted out of the snow and carried to the house by the major-domo, assisted by two male staff. Jeremy fetched a sack of sugar from the dry goods store and placed it under Philip's head. He threw a wool blanket over the prone figure because the cellar was cool, but there would be no other comforts.

Jeremy pulled the heavy oak door shut, turned the lock and dropped the key into his pocket. It would be William Bird's decision what to do with Philip, but in the interim Jeremy did not intend to allow him further opportunities to cause trouble.

* * *

In the dining room, Betty Freah saw Judge Freeman's imposing figure enter and look around. He was searching for someone and she was surprised when his eyes stopped on her. He headed over to join her and Freddie. Freddie had little interest in the Judge after the first day, but when Freeman was closer, Freddie saw he had a different look about him. Today he could believe the man was a Judge, he was not the broken man of yesterday. "Well, Judge, what brings you to my table?"

Freddie didn't hide his disdain, but was surprised it had no effect. "I have an offer you need to hear, Freddie. The same offer is extended to you, Ms. Freah." Betty was intrigued and was keen to hear what the offer might be, but she waited for Freddie to take the lead. Hagood wondered what the Judge was up to, but he would listen. He had made fortunes by listening when others were too busy talking.

"Okay, fine let's hear it, Freeman."

The Judge shook his head. "No, not here, Freddie. I have others that want to meet with you. We have a more private space in the library."

Hagood snorted. "No, they can come here, why should I move?" He flinched at a sharp pain in his shin. Betty glared at him and delivered another kick under the table. Hagood was amused, but he got the point. "Okay, we'll come with you and see what this is all about." The Judge smiled and waited for Freddie to help Betty out of her seat. Betty gave Freddie a sharp look and exaggerated smile as she folded her arm through his and Hagood uttered a gruff laugh as they followed the Judge.

* * *

Larry washed his face in cold water and looked at his reflection in the mirror. His eyes looked haunted, and his skin seemed paler than usual. He had to get out of the mansion, back to the outdoors and his boat. Sitting in his dead friend's country retreat in the middle of January did not suit him. MacLean desperately needed the torture to end, he felt trapped.

He would come to terms with his new financial situation soon enough. It would hurt to give Freddie half his share, but it was better than nothing. Larry pulled on a fresh shirt and glanced at his watch, he had another fifteen minutes to collect himself and then it was time to return to the stifling conference room.

He wondered if Mrs. Tremethick, his only remaining friend, could use some company. He caught a look at himself, who was he kidding? It was he that needed company, not the old lady. He left his room and headed down the hallway.

* * *

Freeman led Freddie and Betty to the nook where Janice waited. Dennis was busy repositioning seats he had collected from other areas of the library. Freddie said nothing, but was surprised to see who Freeman's new partners were. "Judge Freeman told us there was something we had to hear. What is it?"

Hagood directed the question at Janice. There was no doubt in his mind who was in charge of the small group. Freddie liked Dennis, but the manservant was not a schemer.

Janice did not hesitate. "We want you and Betty to join the Judge, Dennis and I. Allied, we will have five votes, which should safeguard us against any effort by the family to rob us. It will also give us plenty of influence when it comes to deciding who gets what."

Freddie knew safety in numbers was a sound plan. He glanced at Betty who looked tense but was listening. Freddie started to speak, but Janice held up her hand.

"There's more, Freddie. Yesterday Dennis and I sold our votes to the family for a fee. Bethany renewed the family's offer a few moments ago. We propose to accept it, but only to trick them into a false sense of security. Our real alliance will remain with this group. When the moment comes, Dennis and I will vote with you, Betty and the Judge. The family can go to hell."

Freddie heard a thin whistle escape Betty's lips as she looked at Janice. She never suspected the housekeeper capable of such devious plotting. He thought about Janice's proposal and about his deal with Larry MacLean. Perhaps he could keep it, make an extra half-share and still benefit from Janice's alliance.

"Okay, let me see if I understand this. You, your husband, and the Judge want Betty and I to join your group. At the same time, you and Dennis pretend to join

273

Bethany and the family, but will vote against them? Is that right?"

Janice knew it was time to let Freddie do the talking. He'd agree or he wouldn't. He looked at Betty who shrugged as if to tell him it was his decision. He turned back to the housekeeper. "I see a flaw in your plan, Janice. Splitting the fortune is unlikely to be achieved in one vote. I think it's possible there will be three votes, maybe more, before this thing is through."

She nodded, but Freddie saw she missed his point. He needed to spell it out. "You and Dennis can only surprise the family by switching your vote once. The first time you do it, the cat will be out of the bag and further votes will be tainted with suspicion, which would be counter-productive for all of us."

Freddie had everyone's attention now, even the Judge's. No one had thought the idea through as far as Freddie. Freeman interrupted. "Freddie makes a good point, Janice. I had not thought of there being more than one vote, but he's right. If you and Dennis switch the way you vote, it might hurt the family to the benefit of this alliance, but it will compromise any chance of success in the next round. It's no good if everyone is worried about double-dealing and betrayal."

Freddie nodded, the Judge had understood. He turned to Janice, who was upset. She wanted the satisfaction of seeing Junior's reaction the moment he realized she had fooled him. She wanted to hurt him and was not happy to hear Freddie tell her the idea was a bad one. "I see your point Freddie, but wouldn't we be better letting the family think they had two more votes? If Dennis and I refuse their offer, they'll know we have another plan."

Hagood nodded. "Yes, they will know, but it's better for everyone that we reach a successful outcome tonight, before we suffer another penalty. We have a better chance of reaching a deal if we don't play games. Think about the numbers, Janice. A motion needs nine votes to pass, the best we have is five. There are three family members left, and that's enough to block any motion they don't like, regardless of how you bait and switch.

"We could be deadlocked in the first round, and you and Dennis will have blown your play for no advantage. The family has the ability to protect themselves from being kicked out, what's the point of pretending you support them when you don't?"

Dennis whispered in Janice's ear. "He's right, Jan. It might be better to play this one straight."

She was irritated at being denied her chance to trick Junior, but there was more than one way to win. "Okay, you're right, Freddie. Dennis will refuse Bethany's offer, but can we agree that we don't let the family take one dollar more than the rest of us? No lion's share for them. At most, they get the same as the rest of us. If you accept that condition, we have a deal, Mr. Hagood."

Janice smiled as she spoke, a smile so full of malice that Betty felt a chill run through her. Freddie wondered what drove Janice's animosity toward the family, but he didn't care enough to worry about the details. She laid out a set of conditions he had no problem with and he agreed to Janice's terms.

There was an audible sigh of relief, and they all exchanged handshakes in a complicated cat's cradle of pumping arms. Freddie decided to come clean about his other deal. "By the way, we have six votes, not five. Betty and I have arranged a deal with Larry MacLean to make sure he is not thrown out empty handed. He will vote as I do, without question. I do not believe we need to include him in this agreement, let's consider his vote a bonus."

Judge Freeman looked at his watch and announced it was nearly time to reconvene. Dennis was dispatched to tell Bethany that he and Janice would not accept her offer, a duty he reluctantly accepted.

Winnie struggled to keep her eyes open as she listened politely to Larry MacLean reminisce about his old friend and her long-ago lover. Larry spoke of Johnston Thurwell, but she could only think of him as Charlie. Winnie was tired of Larry. He had woken her from a much-needed nap and now kept her awake with story after story about the past. She was too polite to say anything, but she was certain that a lot of what Larry was saying was pure fiction. She knew enough about men to understand that any opportunity to tell stories unchallenged led to embellishments.

Winnie looked at her wristwatch, they would head back downstairs soon, an idea she did not relish but which seemed less of a burden with each passing moment in MacLean's company. She was in no doubt that if Larry talked uninterrupted for much longer, she would hear about how he and Charlie had slain dragons in their youth.

* * *

William was finally warm again after a long shower. He had eaten the soup Jeremy sent and felt better for it, but he could not stop his hands from shaking. He looked at them, turning them palms up, then palms down. They shook from the wrists to his fingertips though the nauseous feeling in his stomach had quieted. He had puked in the shower when he realized how close to death he had come. If Jeremy had not seen Philip leaving the house, he would be outside, dead on the snow-covered pathway to the boathouse.

Bird sat in a thick terry-cloth robe and watched his hands shake. He had tried to dress, but shirt buttons were an insurmountable obstacle with his fingers in their current condition. So he sat and waited for them to stop shaking. A knock at the door made him jump like a frightened rabbit, and he stared fearfully at the door, afraid that Philip had come to finish him. He sighed audibly when he heard the calm voice of Jeremy.

Jeremy stepped into the suite, looked once at the lawyer and immediately took control. Bird was in shock and in no shape to return to the conference room. He walked to the telephone and quietly issued orders to his staff. A few moments later, there was a sharp rap on the door and Jeremy admitted one of his staff, a burly young man with a shock of red hair. Jeremy ordered the man to stand guard outside the door and allow no one into the room. He placed a gentle hand on William's shoulder and told him not to worry and then was gone.

* * *

Bethany's eyes were wide with shock as she looked at Dennis's apologetic face. The manservant had a hard time making eye contact with her. Camille had uttered some expletive in French and Bethany was glad her understanding of the language did not extend to gutter talk. Junior had left a few moments before, so she was spared the humiliation of his reaction. "Why, Dennis? Our offer was good enough yesterday, why not today? I don't understand."

Dennis mumbled an answer, but all she made out was his wife's name. Bethany wished for the second time that she had thought to speak directly with Janice. Her husband was a poor go-between. Her immediate thought was that Janice was negotiating, but Bethany needed Junior's agreement before she could increase her offer. He had left in search of Caroline Smith, there may not be time to figure out this unexpected reversal before they resumed.

She looked at Dennis, who seemed pitiful as he squirmed in his seat and rubbed his hands nervously. "How much will it cost today, Dennis? I assume that this is about money? Yesterday you would have received eighteen million dollars, but your bonus was conditional on finishing the business before the penalty was applied. Today's offer was ten million plus another six if we wrapped up before midnight. Apparently that is no longer enough, so tell me, how much will it take?"

He gave her a strange look, but she paid it no attention. He had been odd since he returned. Of course, he didn't have an answer. He would need to return to Janice, and the negotiations would drag on, perhaps too long. Bethany needed to negotiate directly with the housekeeper, but first she had to make Junior agree to increase their payout. She dismissed Dennis and left with Camille to find Junior. She saw the Judge and Freddie Hagood heading into the conference room and cursed, she was out of time.

* * *

Caroline saw Junior loitering in the lobby as she headed to the conference room, he was waiting for her. He fell into step next to her, and they walked together for a few paces before he whispered. "Okay, you're in, but you'll accept ten percent less than the family. It's still a lot of money, Smith, you owe me."

Caroline felt a surge of relief when she heard she was safe from any attempt to throw her out. For the first time that afternoon she allowed herself to relax and a bounce appeared in her stride as she entered the conference room.

Chapter Twenty-Six

The room filled quickly, and there was an excited buzz of conversation, punctuated by an occasional crackle from the fireplace. Judge Freeman waited to begin. He looked at William Bird's empty seat and wondered what kept the punctual lawyer from being on time.

He was about to make a quip about timekeeping when he saw a suited figure stride into the room, but it died on his lips. It was not William Bird he saw, but Jeremy, the major-domo. Jeremy closed the heavy doors behind him and turned to face the room. He saw the Judge look from him to William Bird's empty seat and back again, and he spoke before Freeman could frame a question.

"Ladies and gentlemen, I apologize for the interruption, but it cannot be avoided. Judge Freeman, I understand you are the Chair?" Freeman nodded. "Then I must ask you to call an immediate recess until further notice."

There was immediate uproar. Junior jumped to his feet and demanded to know what was going on. Others asked the same question, with varying degrees of volume and outrage. Jeremy held his hands up and waited for the noise to subside, he had no intention of trying to shout them down.

Eventually they got the message and quieted, and the Judge took charge.

"Jeremy, I'm not certain you understand that our business here is time sensitive. I assume you are here on Mr. Bird's instructions, we would like an explanation, please." There were murmurs of agreement, and everyone turned their attention to the major-domo.

"I am here on Mr. Bird's behalf, but not at his instruction. I regret to inform you that during the last recess, Mr. Bird was physically attacked and is badly shaken."

Jeremy waited as uproar drowned out his voice. He waited patiently for the room to fall quiet, making no appeal for calm but just waiting for them to settle. "Mr. Bird was outside when Philip Thurwell confronted him and attacked him with a weapon. Fortunately, I happened to be nearby and was able to intervene before Mr. Bird was injured. However, he is in shock and needs time to recover."

Bethany slumped into her chair, unable to believe what she had heard. She knew Philip was capable of violence, not long ago he had admitted murder, to her considerable distress. It did not require a stretch of the imagination to see he would blame the lawyer for his disinheritance. She looked up, her eyes brimming with tears. "Where is my brother now? Did you hurt him, Jeremy?"

Freeman was irritated at Bethany's interruption, but understood her concern and indicated for Jeremy to answer.

"I had to restrain him, Miss. I had little time to act. Your brother was close to killing Mr. Bird. I hit him, once. It was enough to stop the attack. He is locked in the wine cellar where I intend for him to stay until I receive instructions from Mr. Bird."

Bethany lowered her head and cried. She was fond of her younger brother, but recent hours had revealed a person she no longer recognized. A week ago, if she had been told the things she knew now about Phil, she would have laughed them off as wild fantasy. Today they were all too real, and she wept for the brother she thought she had known.

Junior stood and everyone took a collective deep breath, anticipating a fight. "You need to let my brother out of the cellar now. You have no authority to keep him down there."

Jeremy was calm, but uncompromising. "Sir, with all due respect your brother is a dangerous man. He would certainly have killed Mr. Bird had I not intervened. He stays in the cellar."

His resolve did not waver when he saw Junior puff up in indignation. "I said, let my brother out of the cellar. Now, do as you are fucking told."

Jeremy opened his mouth to answer but was preempted by the Judge. "No, Mr. Thurwell, Philip stays in the cellar. Jeremy's right, your brother is a menace. We need to know he is no position to attack anyone else. I imagine you have called the police, Jeremy?"

Junior was stunned into silence at the mention of the police. He instantly thought of the scandal if news of Philip's attack went public. "Now wait a minute, Freeman. No one said anything about needing the police here. We can take care of this."

Jeremy needed to get back to William, so he interrupted. "Please, everyone. I have not called the police. Judge, my instructions for this week are that no outside contact is permitted, short of a medical emergency. Mr. Bird will be fine, he is physically unharmed, but he is in shock. Once he feels better, he can decide how to handle the matter. Until then, I suggest you wait for him to recover and accept that Philip will remain in the cellar. Now, if you'll excuse me, I should see how Mr. Bird is doing."

He walked to the door but was stopped by Bethany's plaintive voice. "May I see him, Jeremy? Can I see Phil? Please?"

He turned and looked at his employer's beautiful daughter. He hated to upset her, but her request had to be denied. "I'm sorry Miss Thurwell, that's not a good idea. Perhaps Mr. Bird will allow you to see him, but it will be his decision, not mine."

He saw her head drop as he left in a hurry. Junior was preparing to launch another salvo and Jeremy left before he had to listen to it. The Judge could sort out the aftermath of the news, the major-domo needed to be with Bird.

* * *

Judge Freeman pleaded for calm. Junior was furious and paced back and forth in front of the fire with a thunderous expression on his face. He was angry with his idiot brother, but was far more upset at being defied by a servant in front of everyone. Jeremy would pay a price for that slight, Junior would make him sorry.

Bethany worried about her brother locked in the cellar and about what would happen to him if the police were called. No one else was thinking about Philip, other than reassuring themselves that if he was locked up, he couldn't hurt them.

Winnie whispered her concern for William Bird to Larry MacLean, a conversation that was picked up by Betty and Janice. Soon most of them were demanding that the Judge do something, anything. Freeman had no choice but to call another recess. They were unable to continue without William Bird. "Everyone, please listen. I'm calling another break, the length of which is uncertain, but which will be determined by how quickly William is able to rejoin us."

He raised his voice over their objections. "I know we have a deadline approaching. I don't know if circumstances allow for relief from the penalty, William can tell us that when he returns. But you all know we cannot continue without him. Anything we might decide in his absence would not be binding and would be a waste of our time. I will visit William and try to estimate when we might reconvene. Until then, please just wait patiently."

They knew what he said was true, but none of them liked it. Junior swore at the Judge, but made no attempt to argue the facts of the matter. Freddie wanted to get the situation under control as much as the Judge did. "Freeman is right. There is nothing we can do until Bill Bird returns. We might as well accept it and do what we can in the meantime. Thank you, Judge, you'll report back to us after you've seen him?"

Freeman agreed, grateful for Hagood's support. His intervention had quelled the uprising that had threatened to overtake the group. He thanked them and left to see William Bird for himself.

Camille comforted her sister as best she could, which was little. Bethany was more confused than upset. She had trouble accepting the ugly truth about her brother and her heart ached to see him. She was annoyed with those that only had thoughts about how the delay would affect their money. It was as if neither Philip nor William mattered at all, only the money. Bethany shook her head and whispered to her sister that she had to get out of there, away from the others. They left together.

The others left in search of places to wait. Junior took Caroline by the arm, and they left together. Larry offered to escort Winnie, but she declined and waited until he had gone, before heading to her room. She could not bear the thought of being cooped up with his stories for more long hours.

* * *

Jeremy watched the lawyer as he rested. He looked comfortable wrapped in the thick robe, but his face was haunted. The problem was in his head, not his body. Jeremy knew it could take a long time for a person to accept they had come close to death. He'd seen it before.

Accidents had a similar effect on the psyche, but almost being murdered by another man left a mark. It not only shook the soul to face imminent death, it stripped away any last vestige of preternatural pride. William had been defenseless and on his knees before his would-be killer. There was no more complete a defeat for a man to bear. When the facade of human civility was stripped away, and a man had fought for his life and lost, it left a scar on the soul. Bird was in shock from the attack and his defeat by a feral force against which he had no defense.

Jeremy heard a light tap at the door. The red-haired man opened the door wide enough for Jeremy to recognize the large frame of the Judge. He nodded and Freeman was admitted. "I was hoping you'd come up here, sir. I hope I didn't leave things too awkward for you downstairs?"

The Judge smiled, it was rueful but genuine. "It might have been worse. How is he?" Freeman walked to the bedside and looked at Bird. The lawyer was on his back, but his eyes were closed. If he knew the Judge was there, he made no sign.

"It's shock. He was close to being beaten to death. He needs rest. It's all I can suggest. We gave him a sedative to keep him out of it for a few hours." Freeman agreed with the major-domo's assessment of the situation even as his heart sank when he heard about the drugs.

"How long do you think he'll need?"

Jeremy shrugged. "He might be okay when he wakes up. It might take longer, perhaps days. He'll take a while to come to terms with the attack, but he should be able to function well enough for you to finish your business."

Freeman nodded. "I hope so, I have no idea how much patience I can expect from the others, but until our friend here is able to join us, there is nothing I can do."

The two men moved to leave, but Jeremy noticed the lawyer's clothes were scattered over the floor and asked the Judge to wait outside for him. He picked them up, throwing the soiled suit and other wet clothes into a laundry bag. He went through the pockets to empty them and found a small metal box in the overcoat pocket.

He placed the box on the nightstand where the lawyer would find it when he woke. The major-domo left the room and closed the door quietly behind him. He ordered the red-headed guard to admit no one without his permission and then he and the Judge headed downstairs. Freeman wanted to visit the would-be killer, and Jeremy wanted advice.

* * *

Philip Thurwell's head pounded. His jaw felt as if a truck had hit it. He opened his eyes and looked around the dimly lit room. He could see hundreds of bottles arranged in neat bins through the metal grille that separated him from his father's wine collection. He sat up and instantly regretted it as nausea washed over him. He barely avoided throwing up. He wondered what had happened, he had been about to end the scumbag lawyer and then, nothing. He remembered nothing.

Someone had hit him. The pain in his jaw had come from a punch, but he had no recollection of who had thrown it. Whoever it was, he was a tough son of a bitch. Philip had been punched before, but never so hard. Hell, he'd never been knocked out cold before.

He threw the blanket off. He still wore his outdoor clothes and was too warm. He heard the sound of a key scraping in the lock and scrambled to his feet. He shook his head to clear it, but winced as bright light flooded in. Philip saw two back lit silhouettes enter the room. The door closed, and the gloom was restored. No one said anything and Philip waited anxiously for his eyes to re-adjust to the low light. After a few seconds, he found himself face to face with the Judge and the servant, Jeremy.

"What the fuck happened?" Philip stammered. He was nervous, aware he had no friends in his makeshift cell.

Freeman stepped closer to look at the young man. "What did you hit him with?"

Philip looked incredulously at Jeremy. He would never have guessed the quiet man was the person that saved the sack of shit lawyer. Jeremy held up his right hand. "Just this. I had no weapon. I didn't think I would need one when I went after our friend here."

Freeman whistled a low tone as he turned to Philip. "Son, you're lucky he didn't take your head off." Philip recovered some of his bravado.

"Fuck you very much, Judge, for your concern. Now let me out of here, I've had enough of this place, I'm leaving." He made a move toward the door but ran into a rock hard finger in his chest. He looked up into the Judge's eyes and his heart quailed at the fury looking back at him.

Freeman growled. "You're not going anywhere, son. You might have gotten away with murder under my nose once, but this time I'll see you go to jail for trying to kill Bird."

Philip took a step back, frightened. He had not been thinking about anything other than getting back at the lawyer when he'd left his room. He hadn't meant to hurt him, but he'd lost his temper. "Hey, man. He's okay, right? I never touched him, so no harm, no foul."

Freeman shook his head. Philip couldn't tell if it was a rejection of his plea or an indication of disgust, but it was certainly a negative reaction.

The two men turned and left. He heard the key turn and their muffled voices disappearing into the distance. The quiet of the cellar pressed in on his aching head again. He had his back to the wall and slid down it to the floor where he held his head in his hands and wept, more from frustration than remorse. Philip was in a world of trouble and, for once, he knew it.

Chapter Twenty-Seven

Dinner was served at seven, but only Winnie Tremethick and the Thurwell sisters had chosen to eat in the dining room. The others ate in their rooms, if they could eat at all. Camille had suggested to Bethany they sit with the old woman when they saw her alone and her sister had reluctantly agreed.

Winnie had been surprised when they joined her. She had nothing to say to either girl, she thought of them both as heartless killers. She stared at them for a second and then picked up her plate and moved to another table, sitting with her back to them. The younger women had been too proud to leave the room, and now the three ate in awkward silence.

Camille stole a look at her watch. It was after seven-thirty, and there had been no word about William Bird's condition. She was anxious. The likelihood of the group reaching a consensus before midnight lessened with each passing minute. She shook her head. Another twenty per cent of the fortune could be lost because Philip had lost his head. It was not enough he had disinherited himself, now he had messed it up for all of them.

Throughout the mansion, similar thoughts about Philip were common. Meals that would have elicited enthusiastic praise in any upscale restaurant tasted like ashes in the guest's mouths. Those that waited in their suites cast hopeful glances at their telephones, and despairing ones at clocks, as precious minutes turned inexorably into lost hours.

* * *

William opened his eyes and blinked. He felt groggy and disoriented. His room was black except for faint flickers of orange from the fireplace in the other room. As his eyes adjusted to the light, he could see the drapes were open but that it was already dark outside. He had no idea how long he had slept, but he felt better. He checked his hands and was pleased to see they no longer shook.

He reached for the bedside lamp and turned it on. He immediately saw the metal box from the boathouse. The memory of Philip's attack flooded back, and he slumped onto his pillow. Bird shuddered and felt cold fingers of fear tickle his spine. He closed his eyes and counted down from ten, slowly, until the icy fingers withdrew.

He looked to see what time it was, but his watch was gone. It wasn't on the dresser, and he did not recall taking it off when he showered. He must have lost it in the snow during the struggle. He'd ask Jeremy to look for it tomorrow. You didn't leave a Patek Philippe wristwatch in the woods, no matter the circumstances of how it arrived there.

He looked again at the box on the bedside table. Collecting it had almost killed him. He needed to know what was inside. He inspected the box closely, it was small but heavy, and the lock looked robust. He cursed when he remembered the key was still in his office safe. There was no way to open the box until he retrieved it.

William climbed out of bed and stood gingerly, fearful he would feel nauseous again, but he felt surprisingly strong and dressed quickly. His curiosity about the contents of the box proved stronger than the aftershocks of Philip's attack. He suffered another flashback and saw Philip's face twisted with hate as clear as it had been in the woods, but mercifully it was gone almost as soon as it appeared. He shuddered, tied his shoes and looked at the door. He remembered his promise to Jeremy to call before he left his room. The major-domo had saved his life and, therefore, despite his curiosity and excitement, he lifted the phone.

Jeremy knocked on his door a few minutes later, and Bird was extremely happy to see him. They shook hands before Bird threw aside his usual reserve and gave the man an expansive hug.

"I see you're feeling better, sir. Do you intend to call the group together?"

William shook his head and picked up the small box from the bedside table. "No, I have to open this and do some work before I can get them together again. What time is it?"

"It's almost ten 'o'clock, sir. Are you sure you're feeling alright? I gave you a sedative, and you might feel a bit woolly for a while."

William was shocked when he learned the time, he had been out far longer than he suspected. The group would be frantic at the thought of the looming midnight deadline. "I can't afford to lose more time, I'm sure the others will be keen to meet as soon as possible. I have to get to my office, but it would be better if they didn't see me, I don't need a fuss right now."

Jeremy nodded and told the lawyer that everyone was waiting for the call to reconvene. He also mentioned he had fielded many angry calls as the hour grew later. William pulled on his suit coat, and Jeremy led him down to his office. As promised, they were unobserved, and William thanked and dismissed the major-domo at his office door.

Bird placed the box on his desk and retrieved his instructions and the small silver key from the safe. He read the hand-written note again and looked at the box. It was time to find out what he had nearly died for. Bird inserted the key and heard a gentle click as the lock released. He lifted the hinged lid to reveal a smaller wooden box and an envelope. Both were wrapped in sealed plastic to protect them from the elements in case the integrity of the outer metal box failed.

William used his letter opener to split the plastic and took out the two items. The envelope was secured with a wax seal that bore Johnston Thurwell's crest. William inspected it and found it to be intact. It was addressed *To Winnie*, and William knew she should be the one to break the seal. He turned his attention to the box. It was small and square, a wooden work of art with an inlaid pattern on the lid. The delicate hinge and front catch looked like they were gold. He did not open it. He knew that what was inside was not for his eyes.

Bird opened his laptop and waited for it to boot. He scanned the instructions from the yellow envelope once more to ensure he had interpreted them correctly. He reached under his desk and scrabbled with his fingertips to find the Ethernet cable hidden there. He plugged it into his laptop and waited for it to establish an Internet connection. The wireless network in the mansion was state of the art, but had been disabled to control his guests' contact with the outside world.

William logged into the Zurich bank account and with a few clicks instructed them to transfer forty million dollars to Winnie Tremethick's account. He paused and looked at the account assigned to Philip Thurwell. With a grim smile, he removed the twenty-five dollars he had used to open Philip's account and added it to the old lady's money.

He clicked the confirm button and waited. Exactly one minute later his private telephone rang. He picked it up and gave the bank his confirmation code. It was after 4 a.m. in Zurich, but there was always someone on duty to handle the requirements of the super rich. Bird closed the computer and returned the envelope and the metal box back to the safe. He picked up the letter and wooden box and called Jeremy. He needed an escort again.

* * *

Jeremy took Bird from his office to Winnie Tremethick's room. They saw no sign of another soul in the mansion, for which William was thankful. He knocked on the old lady's door and was surprised when Larry MacLean opened it. There was an awkward moment as the two men looked at each other, then MacLean broke into a wide smile and pumped William's hand. "God, Bill. It's good to see you up and about. We were all worried we wouldn't see you for days. Are you okay? We heard what happened."

William held up his hand to stop Larry's verbal torrent and assured him that he was fine and would reconvene the meeting soon. Larry seemed happy to hear the news and stood in the doorway, his attention now drawn to the items in Bird's hand. "What's this, Bill? Do you want me to give these to Winnie?"

He reached out to take the box and letter, but William took a step back. "Thanks, Larry, but this is something I have to do. May I?"

MacLean stepped aside to let the lawyer in, announcing him to Winnie, who craned her neck to see who was at the door. Larry tried to dismiss Jeremy at the door, but the major-domo asked him to join him in the hallway. "I believe a private conversation is required at this time, sir. Allow me to accompany you back to your suite."

Larry looked back into the room and saw William was waiting for him to leave. He was disappointed. He wanted to know what William had in his hand, but he accepted his dismissal and collected his jacket. After a soft word in Winnie's ear, Larry left her alone with the lawyer. William heard the door close and turned to Winnie with a smile. "Please don't be concerned Mrs. Tremethick, I'm here on instructions from Mr. Thurwell."

"Oh, I see. I was worried about you Mr. Bird. We all heard you was attacked outside. That nice Jeremy said you was unhurt, but it's nice to see you with my own eyes."

She invited William to sit next to her, but instead he drew up a chair and sat facing her. She looked at him with her honest eyes, curious to know what he had to say.

"Mrs. Tremethick, as we now know, the man the world knew as Johnston Thurwell was known to you as Charlie Wells."

She smiled. She had been with Larry MacLean for the past hour listening to stories of her Charlie. She had forgotten her earlier irritation with Larry and had invited him back to her room to tell her more stories of Charlie.

William cleared his throat to get her wandering attention back. "I have instructions, direct instructions from Mr. Thurwell about what I am to do now you have discovered that he and Charlie Wells were one and the same." Winnie leaned forward and hung on Bird's every word. "Mr. Thurwell wanted to be sure you would be comfortable financially, and I have just completed a transaction that has given you forty million dollars. That's about twenty-five million pounds."

She gasped and threw her hands to her face, unable to believe what she had heard. William continued, preferring to get everything in the open quickly. "Also, I have a letter and a box for you. Mr. Thurwell had hidden these away and asked me to make sure you received them as soon as you realized he was Charlie."

He offered the box to the old lady, and she took it from him gently, as if it were gossamer. Her shock at the money was replaced with a much stronger emotion as she recalled the summer of 1965 and her handsome Charlie. Heavy tears flowed down her pale cheeks. "I've seen this box before, Mr. Bird. It was a long time ago, but I could never forget it."

She caressed the ornate lid with her fingertips and wiped away a tear before she carefully flipped the latch and opened the box. A sob escaped her as she turned the box to show Bird its contents. He saw a diamond ring nestled on a blue velvet pillow. The ring was modest, which surprised William until he remembered that Johnston Thurwell had not yet made his fortune when he and Winnie met.

He looked from the ring to Winnie and saw pain and love on her face as she gazed at the engagement ring she had refused in the autumn of 1965. "I hadn't been a widow for a full year when he asked me to marry him. I couldn't accept it. I was too worried about what people would think. He proposed to me when we was out walking one evening. He even got down on his knee."

She shook her head as she looked at the ring, sniffing through tears. "I was surprised, pleased even, that he thought enough of me to ask. I couldn't marry Charlie though, not with my husband so fresh in the ground. Or I thought I shouldn't. Charlie was upset when I told him no.

I'd never seen him angry before, but he was very cross with me that night.

"He left me up there on the cliff. I wanted to explain but thought it better to wait 'til he calmed down. I should have run after him. I wish I had because Charlie never came home. I never saw him again."

Her tears flowed freely as she recalled her heartbreak and looked at the ring, but she did not remove it from the box. She could never wear the ring she should have accepted forty years before.

William sat quietly as he listened and felt her heartbreak. He handed her the letter, which she took with trembling fingers. She turned it over in her hand and saw the heavy wax seal. She looked at William with red eyes full of brimming tears. "If you don't mind, Mr. Bird, I'd prefer to read this in private."

"Of course, Mrs. Tremethick, but I do have one more piece of information before I go." She looked up, her face showed she was not ready for more surprises but he knew this last act would please her. "Your attendance at the meetings is no longer required. It is Mr. Thurwell's wish that you return to your farm as soon as possible. There is one event that you must stay for, but then Mr. Thurwell wants you to be back where you belong. I think he would be happy to know you have his ring at last. I suspect he has some kind words for you in that letter."

Winnie wept as she heard that she was soon to go home. Her homesickness flooded back, and she longed to see the green hills of Cornwall again. She whispered thanks to William, who excused himself and slipped from the room.

William met Jeremy in the hallway and told the major-domo to have the guests assembled in the conference room in ten minutes. It would be after eleven before they were together again. He was not hopeful an agreement would be reached before the penalty deadline, but he knew they would want to try. He walked quickly to his office while Jeremy roused the guests.

Chapter Twenty-Eight

The lobby filled with the sounds of hurrying people as they made their way to the conference room. There was excited chatter as they greeted each other, but many turned grim when they looked at the large grandfather clock at the foot of the stairs that reminded them of the late hour. William stood beside his chair as the group filed in, and acknowledged those that took the time to tell him they were glad to see he was not hurt.

Junior Thurwell was the last to enter. As usual he wanted to make an entrance. He stood in the doorway until people noticed him and only when he had their attention did he walk to his seat. He glared at the lawyer. William waited for him to either sit or speak, he knew Junior had something on his mind, and it was unlikely to be pleasant. "Please, take your seat, Junior. I'm sure you want to press on."

Junior sniffed. "Bird, I see you are uninjured. I hope you intend to remedy the injury you have caused us?"

"What injury would that be? I am not aware of anyone else having been attacked."

Junior waited a few beats to make sure everyone was watching. "I believe you owe us somewhere in the region of five hours lost time. We were prevented from making progress by your absence. It was an impediment to our prospects of reaching an agreement before midnight. I think we all agree?"

He waved his hand expansively over the room to indicate he was going to speak for everyone. Whether they agreed or not was of no concern to Junior. William heard mutters of agreement, most people quietly prayed Junior would prevail.

William shook his head. "I'm afraid that is a vain hope. The midnight deadline is not negotiable. I have no authority to change it. Now would you like to waste time debating something I can't change, or would you like me to call you all to order?" William tried to stay calm, but knew a note of anger had slipped into his voice.

Junior was having none of it. "Why should we suffer because of your inability to attend? We were all able to be here, the Judge was our Chair. I refuse to accept that we must lose another twenty percent of my father's money just because you were not here." He jabbed his finger at William as he spoke, punctuating his points as his voice rose in volume.

William had had enough. "Junior, shut up. I was incapacitated because your brother tried to take my head off. I'm lucky to be here and frankly, you're lucky too. Had your brother succeeded, you would have left here empty-handed. Your father left instructions for many circumstances and homicide is one of them. Had Philip killed me, the entire fortune would have gone to the Foundation. Every penny. If you prefer to grandstand and criticize me, I'll say goodnight and take a day or two to fully recover. It's your choice, Junior. Sit down and accept the way it is, or keep yapping and I'll see you in a few days, if I feel up to it." William's voice shook with anger.

He saw Bethany and others look at him in alarm and then at Junior who stood with his hands flat on the table as his face turned deep scarlet.

"Gentlemen, please. That's enough." Freddie Hagood broke into the argument. "William, I'm sure there is no need for this to escalate.

Junior asked a question, albeit not tactfully, but it was a question many of us had. If you say the deadline is unchangeable, so be it. It is unfortunate, but a fact nonetheless. I'd like to express my thanks to you for getting us together before the deadline, I'm sure you'd rather be resting."

Bird nodded, he was still angry, but Freddie had brought his temper down a notch. He sat down slowly and concentrated on his breathing.

Hagood turned to Junior. "I think we have our answer, Junior. William says it's out of his hands, so I suggest we waste no more time and continue our business?" Junior stood before them, trembling with rage at being threatened by the lawyer, but he heeded the warning. He knew a wrong word from him now would not only see Bird leave, it would turn others against the family. He and his sisters needed support. If he pressed the issue of lost time, it may come at a high price. He clamped his mouth shut and sat, gesturing at Bird to continue. He didn't trust himself to say a word.

William watched Junior's surrender and felt a thrill of victory. He had faced down one Thurwell brother after being defeated by the other. It felt better to win. It was time to move on. The clock was remorseless in its march to midnight.

William thanked Freddie for his sensible words and began to hand the proceedings to the Judge when Larry interrupted. "Wait a minute. Mrs. Tremethick is missing. We can't continue without her, where is she?" There was an outburst as people realized Larry was right. No one had noticed her absence in the drama of Junior's entrance.

William pleaded for quiet. "Mrs. Tremethick is no longer part of this group. She will remain in the mansion, sequestered from the rest of you until your negotiations are concluded." He was forced to wait again as people demanded to know the exact circumstances of her departure. William raised his voice to make his final point. "All I can tell you is that Mrs. Tremethick has fulfilled her duties. Tonight you must accept that your group is reduced to ten people and that the amount you will divide is reduced by a settlement Mrs. Tremethick has received by direct order of Mr. Thurwell."

A smile crept over Larry's face as he thought of Winnie in her room, probably thinking of home. He liked Winnie very much, she was a wise soul and the memories they shared had created something of a bond between them. He silently applauded her success and then turned his attention to the bedlam around him.

He saw Camille Jolivet on her feet, jabbing her finger at the lawyer, her face twisted in greed. Junior had lost his cool again and cursed Freddie who had risen to parlay for calm. Judge Freeman banged his hand on the table, adding to the mayhem and doing nothing to restore order.

MacLean laughed. It was a harsh, short burst of derision but soon turned into a full-throated laugh. He felt hot tears roll down his cheeks. He laughed at the thought of Winnie Tremethick's unlikely love affair and he laughed at the ridiculousness of people who would sacrifice millions of dollars because they were jealous of an old lady who might have been given something they had not.

Larry saw people staring, but he could not stop laughing. Junior swore at him, and he laughed harder. He sounded manic, but it was how he felt. He faced ruin. Whatever he took from the fortune, he would have to give half to Freddie. It was ridiculous how Johnston had made them fight over his money. All they had to do was agree equal shares, and it would be over. Yet their greed was robbing them of the very money they were fighting over. It was absurd.

"Just what is so funny, MacLean?" Freddie was furious. His tone had changed from the one that had been appealing for calm, only moments ago. Hagood had an idea Larry was laughing at him, and Freddie hated to be mocked. "Come on, Larry, let us all in on the joke."

MacLean looked at Freddie and wiped his eyes. The laugh died, and he fell serious. "Look at us. Just look.

We're fighting over money, yet even as we argue the fortune gets smaller. We're so busy trying to get more that we all get less. We're insane. Look at you all obsessing about an old lady who might have gotten something you didn't, when you're all just one vote away from having as much, if not more than her. You may never know what she was given, but if you're rich too, why do you care? The truth is we don't deserve Johnston's money. I think this is his way of showing us that."

Camille dropped into her seat and the others quieted. He had hit a nerve and injected a cold dose of reality into the boiler room atmosphere. Freddie calmed down when he knew he was not the object of MacLean's amusement. He shook his head. "Larry's right. This is senseless. It's 11.45, and we are fighting about something we have no ability to change. I'm right, aren't I, Bill? This Tremethick deal is done, and there's nothing we can say or do to undo it."

Bird confirmed the old lady's money was transferred, and there was no going back. Heads shook as people realized they had been foolish.

William took advantage of the sudden quiet to hand proceedings off to the Judge, who quickly took control. "Everyone, listen and listen well. We have just over ten minutes to avoid another penalty. I think we would all like to be able to join Mrs. Tremethick and go home. We have that chance now. All we need is eight votes for a deal."

Freddie interrupted. He had been shamed by Larry's words and wanted to end the nightmare. "I propose a motion. I propose each of us receive ten percent of the remaining money. An equal split. Regardless of whom you are or what your relationship to Johnston was. Equal shares for all, do I have a second?"

Betty Freah raised her hand. William acknowledged their motion. "You have a valid motion Judge, you should vote quickly."

There was a groan when Junior stood, his face red and angry. "I made it perfectly clear, the family must take a larger share. What part of that do you find so hard to comprehend? If it were your father's money, you'd feel the same, so why do you try to cheat us out of our own fucking inheritance."

"Junior, for God's sake man, if you defeat this motion we all lose, even you. Get a grip."

Freddie could not believe Junior would block a motion, but was shocked when Camille interrupted. "I think my brother is correct. It is the principle, no? Let the family take half and divide the rest between you. I will support that motion. But equal shares, no. I stand with my brother in this."

Freddie turned desperately to Bethany. "Beth, where do you stand? We need eight votes, if you support the rest of us, we can all go home. Are you with us, or with Junior?"

Bethany sighed. Her head was spinning, and her overwhelming sadness at her father's death flooded back. She looked at her brother and shook her head. "I'm sorry, really sorry Junior, but they're right. We can't keep doing this, I'll vote with the others."

Junior hissed, and Camille pleaded with her sister to change her mind, but the Judge called the vote. "We only have two minutes, people. I'll go round the table starting with me and working to my right, make your vote fast and make it clear, we don't have time for screw-ups." He looked at Bird and checked they were able to proceed.

Freeman started the roll call. "Judge Freeman votes Aye. How say you, Betty Freah?"

"Yes."

"Betty Freah votes Aye."

"Dennis Elliot?"

"Yes."

"Dennis Elliot votes Aye."

"Bethany Thurwell?"

"Yes. Sorry Junior, but this is the right call."

Bethany Thurwell votes Aye."

"Freddie Hagood?"

"Aye."

"Freddie Hagood votes Aye."

"Camille Jolivet?"

"Non."

"Miss Jolivet votes Nay."

"Janice Elliot?"

"Yes."

"Janice Elliot votes Aye."

"Johnston Thurwell III?"

"No! You goddamn swindlers, I won't give you what you want."

"Junior votes Nay."

"Larry MacLean?"

"Yes."

"Larry votes Aye."

"Caroline Smith?"

Smith did not answer but looked at Junior. William looked at his watch as the second hand ticked toward midnight. "Fifteen seconds. Caroline, you must vote. How say you?" She looked at William and the Judge, and a thin smile crept over her lips.

"No."

William called midnight and the fortune was reduced by another twenty percent.

Freddie stared at Junior, Camille and Caroline, stunned by what they'd done. Smith sat calmly as Junior nodded approvingly at his ally. He was pleased with Caroline but furious at Bethany's betrayal. William called an adjournment until morning. If anyone heard him, he could not tell. The room was silent as the fact of the loss sank in. He collected his papers and computer and left the throng of disappointed guests behind him.

Chapter Twenty-Nine

Camille glared at Bethany and Junior moved to stand with Caroline Smith as she endured a verbal beating from an angry group that included the Elliots, Freddie Hagood and Betty Freah. The French woman shook her head. "How could you vote against your own flesh and blood, sister? I am disappointed."

Bethany wanted to explain that she was tired and wanted it to be over, but she kept her thoughts private. She did not want a fight with Camille. It would be unpleasant enough with Junior. Bethany saw her brother sneer at the group that surrounded him and Smith. He had one hand around Caroline's waist. It was a gesture that should have been protective, but instead seemed menacing. Caroline looked as uncomfortable with his hand on her as she did with the insults from the angry group.

Judge Freeman left the table and took a seat on the wide window ledge and watched the scene before him. He was upset the vote had failed. He had not suspected that Caroline would support Junior so firmly. She must have been promised a terrific deal. Freeman was intrigued by Bethany's vote to settle and wondered if she might be the conduit through which a deal between the rival groups could be brokered.

A woman cried out in alarm. Freeman was on his feet and amid the group in a second. Dennis Elliot held Junior by the throat with one hand and was aiming to take a punch when the Judge stepped in and grabbed Dennis' arm and put a stop to it.

"Enough. All of you, that's enough. Dennis, take your wife and leave before this goes too far." The Judge glared at Dennis until he released Junior and led his wife away by the hand. Freeman turned to Junior, who was greatly disheveled and flustered. "Junior, you take Ms. Smith and get out of here too. Everybody needs to calm down, what's done is done. Tomorrow we'll have to start again."

The Judge pulled himself to his full height and looked at the crowd. "All of you go to your rooms or somewhere else, but break this up immediately. Nothing useful can be achieved tonight. The deadline has come and gone. We've lost the money we tried to save. It's over." His voice carried such authority that not even Freddie argued with him. Their disappointment was palpable, but they obeyed the Judge and broke the pack up.

Junior led Caroline away, indicating for Camille to follow them. Camille rose from her seat and beckoned to Bethany. "Come, sister. We must fix this." Bethany sighed deeply but accompanied her sister from the room, following a few paces behind Caroline and Junior. She saw her brother had his hand in the small of Smith's back, pushing her toward the stairway.

* * *

Freddie and Betty met the Elliots in the lobby and the four of them headed for the bar in the dining room. The only people left in the conference room were Larry MacLean and the Judge. They looked at each other but had nothing to say. Freeman turned on his heel and left, he needed to speak to William. Larry was alone, and Winnie was unavailable to him, which left him friendless until he could leave the mansion.

Larry thought Junior's insistence that the family take the largest share of the fortune was in part because he did not want Larry to be rewarded equally with the family he had betrayed. He looked around the deserted room, shoved his hands deep into his pockets and headed up to his suite. He passed Winnie's room with a wistful glance but went directly to his suite where the only company he could look forward to was a bottle of expensive brandy.

* * *

Philip was uncomfortable. He had tried many different positions on the floor, but the unyielding stone tiles made his body ache. He wrapped the blanket around him as defense against a draft, but still the room was cold and dark. The only light in his private dungeon came from the digital temperature gauges on the ranks of refrigerators beyond the iron grille.

He had no idea what the time was, he had not seen anyone since Jeremy had delivered a stark supper. He'd tried to sleep, but there was no hope of that. His head ached, and his jaw reminded him of its distress with each mouthful of his meal. The anger of his attack had left him, and now he was left with the aftermath. Philip sat in the dark and brooded about his future.

He saw a shadow move in the light under the door and heard the scrape of the key in the lock. The door opened and Jeremy stood in silhouette for a second before flipping a switch in the hallway and flooding the cellar with harsh light. Philip squinted against the sudden brightness as Jeremy came into the room. The major-domo was not alone. Another man was behind him, carrying something heavy.

Philip made no attempt to move. Jeremy intimidated him, and Philip had no wish to give him a reason to attack. The major-domo pointed to the man behind him. "We've brought a cot and a pillow. Your blanket will be enough to keep you warm. There's a bottle of water and some cookies, in case you're hungry. I'll bring breakfast in the morning. I don't expect to hear from you until then, understand?" As Jeremy spoke, the other man set up the cot and placed the rations where Philip could see them.

"Can you give me a flashlight at least?"

Philip hated how meek he sounded, but Jeremy shook his head. "You get nothing you might use as a weapon, son. What you have now is all you get. If you don't want that, we can take it away."

Philip wanted to be off the floor. "No, I want the bed, please." With a quick glance around the cellar, Jeremy seemed satisfied everything was safe and then he was gone. The light was extinguished and the door locked. Philip felt his way to the cot and fell asleep before he even had time to pull the blanket over himself.

* * *

Ron Freeman knocked firmly on William's office door and heard a call to enter. He pushed the door open and for the second night in a row entered the lawyer's inner sanctum. Bird was at his desk reading. A yellow envelope lay open on his desk. William waved for Freeman to take a seat while he finished reading, and the Judge complied. He took the opportunity to admire the study while he waited. Bird's office was dominated by dark woods, rich leather and lots of books. It was a comfortable room, designed for a man.

The Judge had taken no time to observe the décor when he had been in the office last night. He had been focused only on saving his prospects. He marveled at the difference in his situation twenty-four hours later. Freeman saw silver picture frames on Bird's desk, but they were turned to face the lawyer, so he was left to guess they were of the lawyer's family.

William looked up from his papers. "I was hoping you would come. We need to talk about the others. Emotions are running too high."

Freeman nodded. "Your experience this afternoon is evidence enough of that, William. You were lucky Philip didn't harm you, or worse."

The lawyer nodded, momentarily startled by a vivid flashback of Philip standing over him. He shook his head to clear it and returned his attention to the Judge. "The group is down to ten people, so the rules require eight votes to pass anything. But Junior and the family can block any motion, and they don't seem open to compromise. I was surprised to see Bethany break ranks in the last round, but I don't expect it to happen again. I imagine Junior and the others will straighten her out before tomorrow."

Freeman nodded, everything he heard confirmed his own thoughts, but Bird had more to say. "I can't tell you what to do. As Chair, you have limited ability to affect what motions are called, let alone how votes are cast. All I ask is that you try to keep their emotions under control. Tomorrow morning is likely to start with the fallout of the penalty. Both sides will blame the other, but if they can't get past recriminations, we are likely to repeat this discussion tomorrow night."

Freeman sighed, he felt guilty about his own role in raising the temperature. Now he was charged with bringing the situation under control. "William, the only path to a resolution is to solve the question of whether the family is entitled to a larger share than the rest of the group, or not. Either the family must accept equality, or the others must drop their demand for it. Until that question is settled, I see no opportunity for a motion to succeed." He scratched the back of his neck as he thought through the problems.

He decided to be open about what he knew. "William, there are six people, including me, who have agreed to work together. The only people not in our group are the three family members and Caroline Smith. To break the deadlock, two people from the family group need to change their minds, or four people from my group must defect.

"I don't believe anyone in my group is prepared to compromise. There are some very firm opinions among its members. I imagine the same is true of the family bloc. I cannot imagine Junior accepting equality. He seems more interested in a point of principle than his diminishing inheritance."

William nodded, he guessed the group had split into factions, but was surprised to learn only two existed. He had not suspected MacLean was included in a group. Larry seemed alone even in a crowded room. He looked at the Judge's troubled face. "I'm sorry I can't do more to help you, Ron. I'm pushing the envelope of my duties even with this conversation. If there is anything I can do within the rules, I'll try."

Freeman smiled. "Can you tell me how much we're talking about, Bill? It might help focus minds if we were dealing in dollars instead of percentages."

The lawyer shook his head even before Freeman finished the sentence. "Sorry, I can't. The sum won't be revealed at all. Of course, once the conversion from percentages to cash is made, you'll be able to extrapolate what the number was. My instructions are specific on this point, there is no negotiating it."

Ron Freeman offered a rueful smile. "I had to try, you understand?"

The two men understood one another, but with nothing else to say and afraid he may already have said too much, William stood. Freeman knew he was dismissed and left the lawyer's office. He hoped the other members of his group had not retired to their rooms yet, there was still serious talking to be done.

Chapter Thirty

Bethany sat in Camille's suite, opposite Junior and her sister. An uncomfortable silence had fallen as soon as the door had closed. Caroline fixed dirty martinis at the bar and the sound of her working was the only noise in the room. Bethany looked at her brother nervously. He was flushed, and she knew he was still furious with her. She saw some sympathy when she looked at Camille, but there was coolness in her sister's demeanor and their fledgling sisterhood was being severely tested.

No one said anything and Bethany did not feel like being the one to start. She knew whatever she said would provoke a verbal assault from Junior and was in no hurry to hear it. Caroline delivered drinks to Junior and Camille, then to Bethany before taking a seat across from her. The arrangement looked like a parole-board hearing, and Bethany was left in no doubt whom the petitioner was.

Camille was the first to speak, her heavily accented voice was soft, but her question was direct. "Why did you turn on your family, sister? Do you not agree we deserve more than the others? Please explain that we might understand."

Bethany swallowed and tried to delay suffering Junior's pent-up wrath. "I can answer that, but I think we should discuss this as a family, not in front of others." She looked directly at Smith who smiled over the rim of her cocktail glass without an ounce of warmth in her eyes.

Junior leaned forward and jabbed a finger at Bethany. "Really? You think we should ask Caroline to wait outside while we find out why she is more loyal to our family than you? You should be trying to explain why we should even listen to a single word that crosses your treacherous lips."

Junior's face was deep scarlet, and flecks of spittle hit her face as his temper broke through the frail dam of his self-control. Bethany tried to hold her head high, but as he rose to his feet and launched into a crescendo of furious epithets, her courage failed and she began to cry. Junior's mouth creased into a cruel sneer when he saw his sister break. This was what he craved, his unfaithful bitch sister cowering and begging for forgiveness. He felt the sweet rush of power fill his body and despite the subject of his fury being his sister, he was aroused as he watched her defenses crumble.

Caroline watched as Junior destroyed his sister with words. She was appalled by his withering attack, yet awed by his ability to use words to open wounds in Bethany's soul as surely as if he wielded a scalpel. She shuddered, but could not tear her eyes away from Junior's masterful performance in fury.

Camille was disgusted. Junior was out of control and had crossed the line. She had seen and heard enough but waited until she sensed Junior had crested the peak of his rage before she dared intervene. She had no doubt he would turn on her if she tried to stop him. When he paused to take a breath she reached and took his hand.

She quailed when he turned to look at her, but she squeezed his hand. "Enough, brother. She can see the error of her ways. It is clear to her now, non? We must repair the injury she has caused us. It is time to regroup and be of one mind again." She demurely flattered him with her lashes as she pled her case. He was breathing hard, and his hand felt clammy and cold in hers, it was an unpleasant sensation.

Junior did not answer. She did not see his hand move but felt a crushing blow to her head. She fell back with a cry and tried to cover her face with her hands but Junior held her wrist in a vice-like grip. She struggled to get away, but he stood over her and aimed a solid punch to her head. She went limp, the blow dazed her and Camille tasted blood and was terrified.

Bethany rose quickly, and grabbed her brother's arm to stop his attack, but he shook her off easily and she fell hard to the floor, her ankle twisted painfully under her. She looked pleadingly to Caroline, but Smith had turned away and covered her ears to muffle the sounds of Camille's beating.

Junior felt adrenaline pump into through system as he threw two, three more punches at Camille's face. Her panicked eyes filled with pain and fear. She was helpless, and his arousal grew with the power he wielded. If they'd been alone, he would have taken her. He tipped his head back and roared with primal joy, his face contorted into a dreadful mask of hate.

Bethany crawled to the couch and took the French girl's head in her hands. She used her sleeve to stem the flow of blood from a split brow that was swelling quickly. Junior looked down and sneered. "I'm alone in this fucking family. I have a halfwit brother, a traitor for a sister and a French slut who would dare order me around. You're not even a part of this family, you stupid bitch. We would have disowned you long ago if it wasn't for your fucking vote."

He paused when a needle of fear prodded him through his rage. He saw Bethany's tears mixed with Camille's blood on the white couch and felt the power drain from his body like air released from a balloon. He saw Caroline looking at him with frightened eyes. She looked like she wanted to run for the door but was rooted to her seat by fear.

Junior breathed hard. His temper had gotten out of control, and he realized he had gone too far. He stared at the scene before him. His sisters sobbed, and Bethany cradled Camille's bloodied head as she moaned in pain. He looked at his hand, still balled into a fist. The knuckles were red with blood, but it was not his. He left the room without looking back. He ran to his suite and locked the door behind him, wondering if anyone would come after him. Junior was suddenly acutely afraid that Dennis Elliot might knock on his door.

* * *

Caroline saw Junior leave and ran to the door and locked it, in case he decided to come back. She stood with her back to the door and trembled, she wanted to run and hide but the other women needed help. Caroline's partisan agenda was forgotten when she saw the two sisters in pain. She grabbed the ice bucket and some bar towels.

Bethany looked up when she felt a tender hand touch her. She was too stunned to be surprised who offered her aid, but gratefully took a towel and patted it on Camille's face to blot away the blood. Camille's cheek was already swollen, but Bethany was more worried about her right eye. The brow was badly cut, and blood seeped from the wound at an alarming rate. "Call for help, she needs medical attention."

Smith reached for the telephone and in no time Bethany felt strong hands lift her gently. She saw many people were in the room. A red-haired man carried Camille to her bedroom as others tidied the upset room.

Bethany was suddenly exhausted. She looked up at her savior and saw Jeremy's face, filled with concern. The major-domo carried her easily and laid her next to Camille. He pleaded for her to stay awake, but she was too tired to fight her exhaustion and embraced blackness as it descended.

* * *

William entered Camille's room and stopped in his tracks. Caroline was seated opposite a bloody sofa, hugging herself as she spoke with Jeremy. Her face was white with shock. The Judge stood in the bedroom doorway talking to a small gray-haired woman he recognized as one of the staff.

Bird walked quickly through the chaos to join Freeman, who looked relieved to see him. "Bill, you're here, good. This is Sarah. She's a nurse, and she's looked at both girls. Camille has sustained quite a beating but should be okay. I haven't been able to find out for sure what happened, but Junior is involved, that much is certain."

William asked the nurse if he could see the two women. She stood aside and permitted him entry to the dimly lit room. They lay side by side on the bed facing each other holding hands in the dark. Camille's back was to him, but Bethany saw him and offered a wan smile.

He saw a bandage around Bethany's ankle and wondered what injury had befallen her, but forgot about it when he saw Camille. He suppressed a gasp, the girl's face was swollen and a deep cut over her right eye was held together by five fresh stitches. Camille saw his shocked face and closed her eyes. Fresh tears flowed down her bruised and puffy cheek. He sat on the chair next to the bed, and Bethany turned to look at him. "What happened here, Beth? It was Junior, wasn't it?"

"I'm okay, Bill. Camille tried to stop Junior. He was angry with me. You know how he gets sometimes." Bird grimaced, he was well aware of Junior's temper, but he did not interrupt her. "She tried to stop him, and he beat her. He beat her, Bill, like she was a dog. He just kept hitting her. I tried to stop him, but he pushed me away and my ankle twisted. He hit her so hard. It was awful."

She cried as she described the attack and Bird took her hand in his. "It's alright Beth, he won't hurt you anymore. We'll make sure of that."

She was shaking and could not look up to meet his eyes. "What are you going to do, Bill? Have you called the police?"

He shook his head. "I can't Beth. Not for this, nor for Phil's attack on me. We have to stay isolated until a deal is reached, short of medical emergency. You and Camille are hurt, but Sarah says you don't need hospitalization."

She stared at him wordlessly before she turned her attention back to Camille and stroked her hair. William felt helpless and left them whispering comforting words to each other. Outside their room, he and the Judge stood together in silence and watched Jeremy wrap a blanket around Caroline Smith's shoulders before he joined them. "Gentlemen, I propose we chat outside, where we won't upset the ladies?"

The three men stepped into the hallway. Jeremy closed the door behind them and turned to the others. "Junior Thurwell did this. Ms. Smith says they came here to discuss something after your meeting broke up. Whatever was said led to the attack on Miss Jolivet and Miss Bethany. I called Sarah to attend to Miss Jolivet's injuries, and she tells me both women will be okay. They were offered sedatives but refused them. Miss Jolivet took a couple of painkillers, but that's all. What do you want to do?"

Freeman growled. "Now we find Junior."

William asked the others to accompany him. He was not fully recovered from Philip's attack and seeing the aftermath of Junior's assault had made him nauseous. He knocked on Junior's door with a firmer rap than he intended, but it went unanswered. He tried a second time and called for Junior to answer, but again there was no response. He looked at the Judge. "You don't suppose he's hurt himself, do you?"

Freeman grunted. "That man is too in love with himself to commit suicide. He likes to hurt others, not himself. He's a coward, and he's hiding."

Jeremy stepped forward and sorted through a large key ring. "Excuse me, sir, we can easily find out if Mr. Thurwell needs our assistance." He selected a key, slipped it into the lock and opened the door. The room was dark, and there was no sign of life.

Jeremy signaled the others to wait in the hallway and stepped into the room. Freeman noticed how the major-domo moved, slow and quiet, not a movement wasted or out of place. He disappeared from their view, and they waited anxiously.

Moments later, the lights came on, and Jeremy reappeared. "He's in the washroom. The door is locked, but I can hear him in there. He's hiding." He led William and the Judge into the room. There was no sign of occupation except a jacket tossed over the back of a couch. A sliver of light was visible under the bathroom door, and they saw a shadow cross once, then again in the opposite direction. Junior was pacing the length of the washroom.

William banged on the door. "Junior, come out of there. It's Bill. You have nothing to be afraid of. Come out, we need to talk."

The shadow stopped moving, and Junior called out. "I'm not coming out if he's there. Send him away and I'll think about it."

William was confused. He looked at the others and saw the same reaction. He shrugged and turned back to the door. "Send who away, Junior? I don't understand."

The shadow resumed pacing, and there was a delay as they watched it pass the door, three, four times before it stopped again. "Don't fuck with me, Bill. Is he there or not? Is Elliot with you?"

Junior wasn't making sense. "Elliot? You mean Dennis Elliot? He's not here Junior, why would he be? I'm here with Jeremy and Judge Freeman. We want to talk. Open the door."

The doorknob turned, and William stepped back. The door opened a crack, and a red-rimmed eye appeared. "No one else is with you?"

The three men nodded, and the Judge stepped to one side so Junior could see into the suite beyond him. Junior peered as deeply into the room as he could and only when he was fully satisfied did he step out into the room. William and the Judge followed him as he took a seat. His eyes were red, and he was pale, he had been crying.

Jeremy noticed scrapes on the knuckles of Junior's right hand. He had probably cut them on Camille's teeth when he was beating her. Freeman walked to the door and took a quick look in the hallway before closing it and turning the deadbolt, ensuring the four men had privacy.

William was in no mood to pander to a petty thug and got right to business. "Do you want to tell us what happened?"

Junior understood there could be no denying his assault. He saw from how they looked at him that they knew what he had done. Junior lowered his head and appeared to shrink as he sat on a couch identical to the one he had left covered with blood and tears in his sister's room. "I don't know. Bill, I don't know what happened. I was mad at Beth because she voted against the family. I was upset."

He looked up to see if there was an ounce of sympathy for him and dropped his eyes quickly when he saw the other's expressions. "Camille tried to stop me. I didn't hit Beth, I was only talking to her, but Camille was tugging on my hand and telling me to stop. I know what happened next, but it wasn't me. You have to believe me, Bill, I wouldn't hit a woman."

William felt his stomach turn into a cold knot as he watched his employer's eldest son grovel. He'd heard Junior had such a dreadful reputation among society women that few would allow themselves to be alone with him. Junior's protest fell on deaf ears.

Jeremy knew what he was looking at. Junior was a serial abuser who had gotten caught near enough in the act. He was a typical bully, full of cruelty and bluster when he was able to dominate his prey, but a coward when confronted. The major-domo felt his hands ball into fists. He had loved his employer as much as any loyal servant, to think the wretch before him was the Old Man's flesh and blood was too much to bear, and he took a step forward.

William saw the move and reached out, putting his hand on Jeremy's shoulder, stopping him. He saw the major-domo wrestle for control of himself, but soon the man's calm demeanor returned, and William relaxed. The Judge did the same. He had watched Jeremy warily as soon as he noticed his balled fists.

Junior looked afraid, which was fine with William. The bluster had left Junior, and he sounded like a small boy. "What are you going to do now, Bill? Can I talk to Camille? Let me tell her that it was a mistake."

William frowned. "No. You don't get to see Camille or Beth unless they want to see you, or until tomorrow's meeting. Assuming they are well enough to make it." He looked at the clock. It was after 1 a.m. "As for what I'm going to do? Nothing, though I wish I could. Any other time I'd already have called the police, but this is not a normal time and I am forbidden from breaking our isolation."

William felt his anger rise and let some of his frustration find voice. "What your sisters may do after we conclude the meeting is up to them. I will recommend that they charge you with assault. You're disgusting Junior. You have been a disgrace to your father for a long time, but for the first time you've given me an opportunity to tell you to your face."

Junior looked like he'd been slapped, but there was something else in his eyes. He heard there would be no police and realized he would have an opportunity to persuade his sisters not to press charges. He looked at Bird and in a sudden spark of cunning knew he was powerless to act, bound by rules that he would never break.

Junior stood and pulled his suit coat on, moving slowly as the others watched. He took a step toward William, and his eyes bored into the lawyer. "Don't talk to me like that, Bill. Not ever."

Bird took a step back, surprised by Junior's sudden change in mood. He realized Junior had spotted a weakness he could exploit. Junior took a step forward to stay in Bird's face when a hand as hard as steel landed on his chest and stopped him cold.

Jeremy had no intention of allowing Junior to gain an advantage and sat him down on the couch with a firm push. The major-domo saw a flicker of fear in Junior's eyes, his bravado had left him. Judge Freeman stepped away from the door and into Junior's view. "I have a question, Mr. Thurwell. Why did you think Dennis Elliot would be here? It's a curious thing, and I'd like an explanation."

Junior could not look the Judge in the eye. "I don't know, I just thought it might be him. He's never liked me."

Freeman frowned, the excuse made no sense. Dennis would have no cause to know about the events of the evening, unless one of the women had called him. Freeman wondered if the manservant offered protection to one or more of the sisters, or perhaps there was more to it. He shrugged as if he accepted Junior's explanation, but resolved at the same instant to find Dennis and ask what the real deal was.

William wanted to leave Junior and return to the sisters. "I'll have Jeremy leave a man at your door tonight. Don't leave this room. We'll have breakfast brought up, and I'll let you know if there is any change to tomorrow's arrangements. Until then, I'm confining you to this room."

Junior protested. "You can't do that. I have to talk to my sisters about how to deal with tomorrow's session. It's not fair to deny us preparation time."

William snorted. "Your sisters want nothing to do with you, Junior. You'll be lucky to survive a vote tomorrow, you may have attacked Camille, but I think you really beat yourself."

He savored the frightened expression that appeared on Junior's face. His barb struck home as Junior realized his loss of temper could have dire consequences when the group reconvened. William summoned the Judge and Jeremy, and the three of them left the room, locking the door behind them.

Jeremy called for a man to stand guard at Junior's door and told the lawyer and judge he'd follow them as soon as the guard arrived.

* * *

When Jeremy re-joined them, they were in conversation with Caroline. She had helped herself to a couple of glasses of wine and was calmer, but still badly shaken by what she'd witnessed. She retold what happened and left no detail out. To the horror of the men, she recalled exactly the verbal tirade against Bethany that preceded the attack on Camille.

Bird shook his head. He knew about Junior's temper, but Smith's recounting of the verbal assault was shocking. The lawyer thought Camille's physical wounds might heal faster than Bethany's mental wounds. If everything Caroline told them was true, Beth might have suffered severe emotional trauma. He asked Jeremy to escort Caroline to her room and noticed her relief when he told her Junior was confined to his suite.

The nurse told William that both women were asleep, and he could not disturb them. Something in her tone would have stopped him from insisting if he'd wanted to, but he was content to let them sleep. He and the Judge left the room and parted ways, the Judge to retire to his room and William to his office.

A deep tiredness came over him as he walked to his office, but he smiled when he saw Jeremy waiting at his door with a hot drink.

"Here you are sir, a little restorative for you, it'll help you relax."

William took it with a grateful nod and the major-domo disappeared in the dark library. Ten minutes later Bird emerged again, locked his office door and climbed the stairs to his suite.

Chapter Thirty-One

Philip was woken by the sound of the cellar door opening. A servant carrying a tray entered the cellar, followed by Jeremy. Philip rolled over in his cot and swung his legs out, only to be stopped by a sharp word from the major-domo.

"Stay there, son. You don't get up until we're out, understand?"

He stopped immediately and watched Jeremy clear a space for the other man to put down the tray.

Philip smelled eggs and bacon and his mouth watered at the thought of a hot breakfast. There was coffee too, and he thanked Jeremy. The major-domo ignored the thanks. "You've got a plastic spoon, no fork or knife. Find a way to manage. I'll come back in an hour, and I expect the food to be eaten and your spoon, plate and cup to be by the door. If they're not, this will be your last meal of the day. Any questions?"

Philip tried to sound confident. "Yeah, I have a question. What's going on? Are the cops coming? Because I'm pretty sure you can't lock me up in here like this."

Jeremy sniffed, he didn't like Philip's attitude. It reminded him of Junior's bluster. "Mr. Bird will decide what happens to you, when he's got time. Sit tight, don't make a fuss and maybe you'll be okay. Maybe."

The door closed, and Philip tumbled out of his cot and ate his breakfast sitting on the floor. As he ate, he worried about the fact that the man he'd tried to kill was responsible for deciding his fate.

* * *

Sarah let herself into Camille's suite quietly and saw no evidence the sisters were awake. She looked at her watch, it was after seven. Jeremy had asked her to find out if Camille would be able to make the meeting at nine. She had already assured him that Bethany's ankle would not prevent her from attending, but could not speak for her mental state.

She knocked lightly on the bedroom door and was surprised when Bethany opened it. "Oh, Miss Thurwell. Good morning. How are you? I hope you rested well?" Bethany just nodded and walked to the washroom. She favored her ankle, but her limp was not pronounced.

Camille lay awake, staring at the ceiling. Sarah breezed into the room with a cheery attitude and opened the curtains wide. Snow was falling again, and yesterday's sunshine was just a memory. The dark clouds looked heavy enough to bury the whole state in snow.

Camille winced and covered her eyes as light flooded the room. She still suffered from a bad headache. Sarah took a look at her patient. The stitched brow was neat and clean. She would have a small scar when the swelling went down, but careful application of make-up would cover it. Sarah was most concerned about Camille's cheek. It had swelled so much that her right eye was completely closed. The eye itself was blackened, but the bruise was already yellowing.

"How do you feel, any blurry vision or headaches this morning?" Camille groaned. "My head hurts." Her words were distorted by her swollen lips.

Sarah reached into her bag for painkillers. "Can you swallow these without water?" Camille shook her head, so Sarah called Jeremy for a glass of water.

Bethany joined them, and Sarah checked her ankle while they waited for the water. "You're fine, it's a mild sprain. We'll keep a bandage on it for a few days, but you should soon be back to normal."

Bethany asked about Camille, and Sarah assured her the injuries looked worse than they actually were, though she would need medication to dull the pain. Sarah saw the shock of the night's events still reflected in Bethany's eyes. "Do you think you and your sister will be up to attending the meetings today, Miss? Mr. Bird is concerned to know."

"I can do it, but Camille? I don't know. I'll talk to her, but no promises." Sarah nodded and answered a knock at the door. She received the glass of water and a tray of breakfast foods and juices. She gave Camille her painkillers and slipped out.

* * *

Dennis stepped out of the shower and toweled himself dry, he felt happy this morning. He was well rested and ready to start the day. Last night he and Janice had enjoyed a bottle of wine, talked about the settlement and remembered their employer with kindness. They had spoken about what their future might hold and had ended the night making love, the first time they had been intimate in many months. Dennis smiled broadly as he hummed a tuneless ditty.

Janice listened to her husband in the shower and was troubled. They had spent a beautiful evening together, the best for a long time. Was she in love with Dennis again? Her thoughts were jumbled, and she couldn't tell if her feelings were gratitude for his help after the nightmare in Junior's room, or something else.

Dennis had questioned her about the discrepancy between her and Bethany's account of the first deal, and Janice had convinced him that she had not mentioned the bonus because it was not guaranteed. She thought he believed her and was glad. If he found out what she had actually tried to do, their fresh start would be over just as Janice was beginning to believe she wanted them to make it.

Dennis came out of the washroom and saw his wife with her eyes open, deep in thought. He surprised her when he jumped onto the bed and tickled her through the sheets. She squirmed and giggled, telling him to quit being a fool. She sounded annoyed, but he kissed her and muffled her protests. "We don't have time for this, Den." But Dennis wasn't listening, and soon she wasn't protesting.

* * *

Junior was still dressed in yesterday's suit. He had not gone to bed, and his mind was a confusion of thoughts. He was afraid of what might happen when the group met this morning. He wasn't concerned about their reaction to what he had done, but he was worried how it would affect their votes.

He had rigidly promoted the idea that his family should get a larger share than the others, but now he was afraid of being voted out with nothing at all if they turned on him. His anger sparked. The people in the mansion had no business dealing with money that was not theirs. He felt diminished by having to plead to strangers for his own inheritance.

His thoughts were interrupted when Jeremy knocked and entered his suite, followed by a waiter.

"Your breakfast, sir. The meeting starts at nine, I will come back and escort you down." Jeremy waited for the other man to uncover the plates and pour a cup of coffee and then both left without another look toward Junior, who fumed at the major-domo's ignorance.

He looked at the tray of food and decided he was hungry. As he ate, he worked at finding a way to save himself from thieves who were trying to cheat him of his birthright.

* * *

Freddie had been up for a couple of hours and had already visited the gym. He picked up the phone and asked to be connected to Betty's room. When she answered, he invited her to breakfast and they agreed to meet in the dining room at seven-thirty. He smiled, she was an agreeable companion. He now understood why Johnston had kept her around so many years.

Betty had rebuffed his clumsy advances so skillfully last night that he hadn't minded the rejection at all. He looked out of the window and watched the snow fall. He hoped today would bring an end to the negotiations. Last night had turned ugly after the penalty had been triggered and he was worried about how much more they could take.

* * *

William sipped a strong coffee at his desk as he flipped through the stack of unopened yellow envelopes. He hoped to find one that would provide a clue about what to do with Philip and Junior. If he could find one with circumstances close enough to actual events, he'd let the Old Man guide him.

The phone rang, and he answered on the first ring. It was Bethany. He listened, thanked her and hung up. He was pleased to hear that Camille felt well enough to make the meeting on time. She asked for assurances Junior would not be able to hurt them. He promised Bethany there was no need for concern, he personally guaranteed their safety.

He returned to the envelopes. The Old Man had hoped events would not take a violent turn. Even as he had anticipated such events, he would never have believed his sons would be involved. However, Philip was locked in the wine cellar, and Junior was under guard in his room. But what could William do with them?

* * *

The dining room was sparsely populated when Freddie walked in. Betty gave him a friendly wave, and he joined her. He nodded a greeting to Larry MacLean, who sat alone. Judge Freeman sat at another table but had his back to the rest of the room. Freddie thought about offering a greeting, but decided Betty's smile was more inviting than the Judge's broad back.

* * *

Camille and Bethany said little as they ate together in their room. Camille tried to drink a protein drink through a straw, but detested the taste and switched to coffee, which she discovered tasted odd when drunk through a straw. Bethany poked at the food on her plate, she had no appetite. She blanched when Camille lit a cigarette, but said nothing. Her sister looked terrible in the morning light, her face was bruised and swollen, and her right eye was entirely closed. The pretty face with the mischievous Gallic charm had been devastated by Junior's handiwork, and even her good eye was haunted by fear and pain.

Bethany reached out and held her sister's hand as she smoked, letting her know she was there.

Camille squeezed her hand and mumbled a sound that might have been "Thank you." She had difficulty expressing anything clearly.

Bethany was worried. "Are you sure you can do this, Camille? I can call Bill again and postpone, if you want."

Her sister shrugged, which gave Bethany no significant clue as to what she meant. Camille saw Bethany's confusion and mumbled. "The money, we cannot lose more. If I attend, we finish."

Beth nodded, she understood. None of them wanted another penalty. They had lost too much already. Forty percent of the fortune had been wasted because of their inability to agree.

Bethany felt sure everyone must be as tired of the mansion as she was, and hoped the group would come to an agreement today. The problem that worried her most was her brothers. She did not know what William intended to do about Philip, and now there was also the aftermath of Junior's attack on Camille. She had been prevented from seeing Junior. The man at Junior's door was polite but firm and refused to admit her without William's permission.

She sighed. Twenty-four hours ago, the family had been united. First they lost Philip, then she had voted against Junior and the result had been disaster. Bethany looked at her watch. It was almost eight and time to get ready.

Chapter Thirty-Two

William emerged from his office at eight forty-five to check on Mrs. Tremethick. He understood that, of everyone in the mansion, Johnston Thurwell would have wanted William to pay her most attention. He would see to her needs personally if he had to.

He passed the Elliots on his way up the grand staircase. They gave him a cheery greeting, and he saw Janice's arm enfolded in her husband's. William wondered what had changed between them since Janice had appeared in his office to seduce him into cheating Dennis.

He knocked on the old lady's door and was pleased to see she looked rested when she opened it. She invited him in, but he explained he had only a few moments and was just checking in. "Did they finish voting last night Mr. Bird? Will I be heading home soon?"

He shook his head. "The business is not settled, Mrs. Tremethick, so I'm afraid not. If it's any consolation, the bad weather has closed the local airport anyway, so no matter how the others did, you'd still be our guest." She smiled, but felt a tug of regret that she would not be returning home yet. She had spent a large portion of the night admiring Charlie's ring and reading and re-reading his letter.

Winnie wanted to visit the cliff walk where he had dropped to his knee and asked her to marry him. She wanted to look at his ring and apologize to his memory for her cowardice. "Perhaps they will reach an agreement today, and we can all go home tomorrow then?"

"Let's hope so, Mrs. Tremethick, there is nothing I would rather do than see you successfully returned home." He gave her his best smile, the one he had often used as a defense attorney when he needed charm, in addition to a clever argument, to get his scumbag of the week acquitted.

She sighed. "I suppose you want me to stay in my room?"

"Yes, you can't see the others until they are finished. Jeremy can provide anything you need." William promised to look in on her when he could and excused himself. It was time to begin another tough day.

* * *

Bethany and Camille entered the conference room together, each holding onto one of Jeremy's arms. A stunned silence fell when the others saw them. Jeremy sat them next to each other. He had unilaterally decided to change the seating arrangements to ensure the sisters could offer each other mutual support.

The Judge entered the room and walked quickly over to the sisters as Jeremy seated them. Freeman spoke with them quietly to assure himself that they were well enough to continue. When he saw they were determined to proceed, he gently patted each on the back of their hand and told them not to worry. He would ensure Junior posed no threat.

He moved to take his seat but was stopped by Dennis, who wore a dangerous expression. "Junior did that to her, didn't he."

Freeman noted the manservant was not asking a question, but stating a fact. "I can't say, Dennis. Mr. Bird will explain when he gets here." Dennis made a move to press the matter but saw the lawyer enter and backed off. William looked around the room. Everyone was present except Junior, who would be escorted down when he called for him.

"Please, everyone, be seated. I have a statement that should address your immediate questions." He took his place at the table but remained standing while he waited for others to settle. They looked from Camille Jolivet's ruined face to the lawyer and to Junior's empty chair. William cleared his throat and read from his prepared note. "Last night, after your meeting broke up, an unfortunate series of events led to an attack on Miss Jolivet in which Bethany was also injured, though less seriously.

The attacker was Junior Thurwell, who will join us shortly." As he expected, there was immediate uproar and William raised his hands in an appeal for calm, but was forced to wait until it was granted. "I understand how you feel, believe me, I do. No matter what happened last night, or how we feel about it, Mr. Thurwell is still a legitimate member of this group and votes will not be valid without his attendance."

A voice growled. "Then we have an easy bit of business for our first motion." Everyone looked at Dennis, who sat, white-faced with fury. "Bring him down here, Mr. Bird. Bring him down here so we can throw his sorry ass out of here and not have to look at his face again." There were murmurs of approval and a smattering of applause.

William had expected their anger, and there was nothing he could do to influence their votes. But he needed to ensure Junior's physical well being. "I will call for Junior as soon as I am satisfied that no one here presents a threat to his safety. I will not tolerate physical attacks. If I could have prevented last night, I would have. The consequence of any physical violence will be an immediate twenty-four hour suspension of proceedings, do I make myself clear?"

"Bill, how can you stand to defend him? He deserves a beating, just look at her." Freddie pointed at Camille, who turned away, ashamed.

William shrugged. "Freddie, I've defended worse people in my time. I mean what I say. Any assault will cost you another twenty percent penalty." William looked at Dennis, who quietly glowered. "Dennis, we're clear on the consequences if you make a move, right?"

The manservant nodded, but William was nervous. He didn't like the mood in the room. It was worse than he'd expected. But he needed to bring Junior in, and there was little point waiting any longer. He indicated to Jeremy to fetch Junior and the major-domo was gone instantly. "I recommend you try to remain calm and focused on the goal, not on what you feel about Junior or his actions. Please, do not add to the trouble already caused by this."

He spoke to fill the silence and had no idea if anyone paid attention. Everyone waited and looked alternately from Camille to the door. Tension heightened when footsteps approached and then Junior was in the doorway, flanked by Jeremy and the guard who had spent the night outside his room. Both men were taller than Junior, and he felt small as he walked into the room. His stomach fluttered when he saw Dennis Elliot glaring at him, but his butterflies settled once he saw the defeated look in his French half-sister's eye.

She looked awful. He'd done a real job on her. He was not displeased. He took his seat and waved away his guards, who did not move until the lawyer dismissed them. Junior tried to appear relaxed even as he worried Dennis might launch himself across the table and choke the life from him. No one moved. It seemed that no one was even breathing as they stared at Junior.

William broke the silence. "I declare the meeting in session. Judge Freeman, you have the Chair." The Judge nodded and looked around the room. "Ladies and Gentlemen, it's time to see if we can bring an end to these proceedings and make our-"

Dennis interrupted. He stood and talked over Freeman. "I propose a motion that we remove Junior Thurwell immediately, without a penny of his father's money. Let's get rid of this beast, right now."

Janice immediately seconded the motion. Freeman looked at William, who shrugged. He had expected this and had no inclination or ability to stop it.

Junior turned pale as his worst fears were realized. He had to stop their revolt. "Now wait. Just wait a minute. You can't throw me out, I'm family. You have no idea what happened last night because you weren't there. I was provoked. None of you have the right to judge me." His defense had sounded more dignified when he practiced it, now he saw only disapproval as he pleaded his case.

Freddie Hagood pointed a bony finger at him, his voice thick with rage. "You don't beat a woman, Junior. I don't care how much you were provoked. You don't lay your hands on a woman. Right, Larry?"

MacLean looked at Junior. He was repelled by him, but also saw a glimmer of opportunity. He looked at Freddie and agreed, but his mind raced. Freeman called the room to order. "We have a motion, properly seconded. The question is whether or not we remove Mr. Johnston Thurwell III from this group. We require eight votes to carry the motion. I will vote first, and we'll go around the room. I vote Aye. How say you, Betty Freah?"

"Yes."

"Betty Freah votes Aye. Dennis Elliot?"

"Oh yes."

"Dennis Elliot votes Aye. Freddie Hagood?"

"Yes."

"Freddie Hagood votes Aye. Bethany Thurwell?"

Bethany looked at her feet. She couldn't betray her brother again, no matter what he had done. She thought much of what happened last night was her fault. If she had been loyal, her brother would not have been so angry. "No. What happened was as much my fault as his. Please, don't do this."

Camille looked at her sister in mute horror. She tried to speak, but it hurt too much and she turned away, unable to face her as the Judge registered Bethany's vote.

"Bethany Thurwell votes Nay. Camille Jolivet?"

The French girl raised her head and turned so Junior would have to look her in her good eye. "Oui."

"Miss Jolivet votes Aye. Janice Elliot?"

"Yes."

"Janice Elliot votes Aye. Johnston Thurwell III?"

Junior bristled with rage. "No, this is a travesty. It's vindictive. You've never liked me, any of you. You're a bunch of losers and crooks."

"Mr. Thurwell votes Nay. Larry MacLean?"

Larry didn't answer, but looked at Junior.

The Judge called again. "Larry? I need your vote, please."

Larry waved his hand to silence Freeman. "I can save your miserable ass, Junior. You're one vote away from oblivion. You understand that, right?" Junior nodded, he was furious but knew he was doomed.

Dennis stood. "What the hell are you doing, MacLean? Vote the prick out. Kick his sorry ass out, right now."

Freddie growled. "Larry, if you vote for him, our deal is off."

MacLean shot Hagood a bitter look. "Well, Freddie, you offered a particularly crappy deal as I recall. I think I might get a better offer from Junior about now." Larry turned to Junior. "Junior, here's my offer. You agree to equal shares for everyone, and I'll keep you in. If you hold out for more, you're gone. What's it going to be?" He ignored the howls of protest from the others.

The Judge called for his vote again. "Larry MacLean, how do you vote?"

MacLean pushed Junior. "Let's tell the man, shall we? How do I vote, Junior? Do you agree to my terms?"

Junior was furious, but knew he was defeated. If MacLean voted against him, he would lose all of his inheritance. If he agreed, he would get ten percent. When faced with nothing, suddenly it sounded like a great deal. He looked at MacLean and nodded. Larry shook his head. "Say it, Junior. I want to hear you say it. We all do. Then we can vote and go home."

"Okay, I agree. Equal shares for everyone." He said it through gritted teeth, aware there was a changing mood in the room.

Freddie interrupted. "Larry, forget it. Betty and I will forgo our agreement. You can keep your full share. We won't take a penny, just don't save this sadistic prick. Kick him out and you'll get a fair share. It'll be worth more too, with him gone. Don't do this."

A panicked look crossed Junior's face as Larry considered the new offer. "So it's different now Freddie? Now I have some power, you want to be fair? Well fuck you. You should have treated me with a bit more respect. I vote Nay."

A hiss went around the room as the Judge called the vote. "Larry MacLean votes Nay. Caroline Smith?"

Smith was upset, she had been allied with Junior yesterday but after witnessing his cruelty last night she wanted nothing more to do with him. She avoided looking in his direction. "Yes."

"Caroline Smith votes Aye."

William read the result over a background of angry mumbling. "The tally is seven votes for and three against. The motion fails."

Freddie fumed. "Goddamn you, Larry. We would all have benefited from him being gone, in more ways than one." Larry heard the discontent around the table, but he didn't care. He had saved himself.

Larry looked at the sisters and saw a rift had opened following Bethany's support of her brother. Camille had turned in her seat to ignore Bethany. It was as perfect an illustration of a cold shoulder as Larry had ever seen.

Freeman called them back to order, and Larry saw his chance. He gave a significant look to Junior and interrupted. "I'd like to propose a motion."

Freeman was surprised. "Larry, I was going to suggest a short break, so we could all calm down. Why don't you wait a half hour?"

MacLean shook his head. "I don't think so. Why would I give Freddie a chance to arrange it so I get screwed again? No. You all heard Junior agree to equal shares. We can end this now. I propose the money be divided equally among the ten of us."

MacLean looked William. "Bill, I proposed a motion and that's within the rules, right?"

Bird nodded. "It's valid, if you have a seconder."

Larry looked at Junior and raised an eyebrow, but it was Bethany who spoke. "I'll second the motion. I just want this to be over. Please, everyone, let's end this torture and get back to our lives."

William looked at the Judge. "They've proposed and seconded a valid motion. You have to call the vote, Ron."

Freeman pulled his chair in and sat upright. He could sense the tension in the room. "Before I call the roll, let me say I respect Miss Thurwell's request. We should all think about our vote and whether it is likely we will have another opportunity to come to an agreement as we do now. I, Ron Freeman, vote Aye. How say you, Betty Freah?"

"Yes, let's end this now."

"Betty Freah votes Aye. Dennis Elliot?"

"I'll agree, but only out of respect for Miss Bethany's wishes. I vote yes."

"Dennis Elliot votes Aye. Bethany Thurwell?"

"Thank you, Dennis. I vote yes."

"Bethany Thurwell votes Aye. Camille Jolivet?"

The French girl looked at her sister, her swollen face streaked with tears. "Oui. Yes, I vote yes. Let this be over. I cannot fight any longer, not with you." Bethany took Camille's hand and smiled, her own eyes brimmed with tears.

"Miss Jolivet votes Aye. "Freddie Hagood?"

Freddie was upset. He did not like to be outfoxed, but he knew the time for maneuvering had run out. "Aye."

"Freddie Hagood votes Aye. Janice Elliot?"

"Yes."

"Janice Elliot votes Aye. Johnston Thurwell?"

Junior paused. "I don't agree with this. You are all no-good parasites taking the family's deserved wealth."

Larry was on his feet, and his face took on a dangerous look. "Junior, don't fuck this up. You made a promise."

Junior waved a hand dismissively. "Oh relax Larry, I'll support it, I just want to make it clear I detest these leeches for stealing my inheritance. I vote yes. Happy?"

"Mr. Thurwell votes Aye. "Larry MacLean?"

"Yes. Thank God, yes."

"Larry MacLean votes Aye. Caroline Smith?"

"Aye, yes."

"Ms. Smith votes Aye."

The Judge looked at the tally sheet though he did not need to.

William confirmed what they all knew. "The motion is passed unanimously, ten votes to zero. You have agreed the fortune will be equally divided among the ten of you." Genuine smiles broke out on faces that had been grim for days.

The Judge and the lawyer shook hands, and William stood to address them. "I offer my sincere congratulations to all of you. I need time to process the payments. I'll soon provide you the details of how to access your money and advise you of the amount you will each receive. Until then, relax. I'll ask Jeremy to send in champagne."

His announcement was met with applause as he picked up his laptop and papers to leave. He stopped when he got to Junior. "Come with me Junior, you can't stay here."

"Fine, why would I want to celebrate the destruction of one of the world's great family fortunes?" He turned to the others. "I hate you all. Burn in hell you greedy bastards."

Junior followed William to the door where Jeremy and two staffers met them. Junior was escorted back to his room, and Jeremy sent for champagne as the lawyer disappeared to his office.

Chapter Thirty-Three

Dennis walked to the conference room window and looked out into what little light filtered through the falling snow. He was upset, even though he would be a rich man before the day was out. He was upset he had not seen Junior punished. He looked over his shoulder at the people shaking hands and congratulating each other. He saw Janice in conversation with Betty Freah, both glowing with the promise of enormous wealth.

Dennis was excited too, but the Old Man was in his thoughts. Johnston Thurwell was gone, and the last vote had divided his vast fortune. Everyone would move on with their lives, except for his old boss. Dennis faced an entirely new life. He had no home or job but would not need to work again. He could settle his debts and... And what? The question bothered him. He did not know what came next. He turned to look at Janice, was his future with her? He had doubts about the story she'd told about her deal with the family. Dennis shook his head to clear his mind. He needed to return to the others. Freddie watched him with a puzzled expression, and Janice was trying to get his attention. Dennis folded his face into its familiar manservant smile and walked back to the happy group.

* * *

Larry sat and marveled at his good fortune in saving his situation from certain ruin. He felt a strong hand on his shoulder and looked up to see Freddie. Larry stood and faced the other man, their faces impassive as each weighed the other. "You played that well, Larry. I don't know how you could stand to support Junior after seeing what he did to Camille. I guess it's always about what you need, right?"

Freddie's eyes were hard as flint, but MacLean returned the look unflinchingly. "Are you upset because Junior wasn't thrown out, or because you're not stealing half of my share? Perhaps if you hadn't been such a prick when I needed help I wouldn't have been forced to do what I did. So fuck you, if you don't mind."

Freddie smiled. "Perhaps, Larry, but I'll be able to live with myself. I doubt the same can be said for you. Enjoy your victory." He turned on his heel and walked away.

Larry thought about leaving the others to visit with Winnie when a light touch at his elbow made him turn. Bethany leaned on the back of a chair to rest her ankle, and her eyes were moist. "I don't forgive you, Larry. We're no longer friends and never will be again, but thank you. You saved my brother from losing everything when he

334

deserved to lose it all. It would have broken my heart to see him cast out, even after what he did. You stopped that from happening. Perhaps it was for your own selfish reasons, but you stopped it. Thank you." She brushed his cheek with her lips and was gone, moving across the room to join Camille who was struggling to her feet with the help of Judge Freeman.

Larry watched her go with a heavy heart. Bethany was a gentle creature, and he had lost her forever and regretted it bitterly.

* * *

Camille wanted to return to her quiet suite. Her head pounded, and she felt weak. Ron Freeman had seen her distress and had excused himself from Betty to get to her side. She looked at him helplessly, and his anger rose as he thought about what her brother had done to her. "Let's get you out of here." Camille tried to stand, but her legs buckled with the effort.

The Judge picked her up in his arms without effort. Others turned to see what was happening, and Freeman felt a stab of self-consciousness, which to his relief ended with Bethany's arrival. "She needs rest. Will you carry her up to our room?" Camille protested that she could walk, but Bethany interrupted her weak attempts at argument. "You need to rest, Camille, and we need to talk. Alone. Let the Judge carry you, I think he can manage." She winked at the Judge who flushed and followed her.

Betty watched the small drama from across the room. The Judge had rescued Camille with a gallantry she found quite romantic. Janice watched with a hard expression in her eyes. Betty turned to the housekeeper. "That poor girl will have a scar over her eye forever, Junior really beat her badly."

Janice waited until the Judge carried Camille out of earshot. The cold fury on her face shocked Betty. "Her brother is a sick pig, she's lucky he didn't rape her too. She got off easy."

Betty looked closer at Janice. She had known lots of abused women in her life, most of whom polite society never listened to. Ordinary people often considered rape an occupational hazard for working girls, but that didn't make the hurt and shame less real. The look on Janice's face was a look Betty had seen before, and suddenly she realized there was a history between Janice and Junior.

Betty took Janice's hand in hers and led her away from the others until she was certain they could not be casually overheard. "Does Dennis know?"

Betty saw Janice's shock at her blunt question. She felt an urge to deny everything, but when she looked in Betty's eyes she saw understanding. "He knows some of it. He knows enough."

Betty looked at Dennis and realized why Janice had been late to yesterday's meeting. "My God, it was here, this week? Did Junior attack you here?" A tear rolled down Janice's cheek. It was the only answer Betty needed. "We have to tell William. Junior cannot be allowed to get away with this too."

Janice shook her head. "He already has. I can't tell William Bird. You don't understand. I just can't. Junior will get his money, and no one will care what he did to me, or his sister. I have to live with what happened. Dennis wants to hurt him, but the rich always get away with everything. You heard how Philip killed a boy and walked away from it. Do you think anyone will care about what happened to a servant? There were no witnesses. It'd be his word against mine." Tears flowed down her cheeks. "People will say I was asking for it."

Betty sighed, she had heard the same argument from every abused woman she'd met, and it infuriated her. "Oh come on, it's not like you went looking for it, is it. He wanted it and took it. That's the way it always goes."

Janice saw Dennis looking at her across the room and shame flooded her. "But I did go looking for it. He took what I offered, and more besides. That's what happened." She shuddered as she remembered that night. "He's an animal."

Betty had no idea why Janice would want something from Junior, didn't she know his reputation? Was it possible she had never heard the dark whispers about him? "Did he rape you, Jan?"

Janice shrugged. "I don't know. I don't know what you'd call it. I can't tell you. I won't tell you. Dennis can't know that I went to Junior's room voluntarily, neither can William. What happened, happened. It's over. I just saw Camille, and it all flooded back. I'll be okay." She offered a small smile as a thank you for Betty's concern and excused herself.

Betty watched her go and saw Dennis scurry after her, his face a portrait of concern. She didn't hear Freddie's approach until he nudged her playfully.

"What was that all about? Did you girls have a fight?" Freddie was surprised when Betty rounded on him. "Shut up, Freddie. Sometimes you'd do better to mind your own business." She stalked off and left him speechless. He was disappointed. He had taken time to get close to Betty. He liked her a lot and was sorry he had caused her to get angry with him. He figured chasing her was not a wise move, so he let her go. Making up was easier if you didn't throw gas on the fire.

He saw Caroline and decided to join her. Smith saw Hagood's approach, but her mind was not in the room. It was on last night, and the horror she had witnessed. She had voted twice with barely a thought to what she was saying or thinking. When Camille had entered the room, she realized she had not dreamed the attack. Her memory played it over and over again, and she shivered as she recalled the fear that had transfixed her and made her unable to help. Freddie noticed the odd look on Caroline's face and wondered what was up with the women this morning.

He understood Camille would be shaken, Bethany too. But what made Janice leave in a hurry and then Betty blow up? Even Caroline Smith, the usually unflappable executive looked as if she'd seen a ghost. He sat next to her but if she noticed she gave no sign and he hesitated to say anything after the reaction he'd gotten from Betty. After a moment, she looked at Freddie. She showed no sign of being pleased to find him sitting with her, but no displeasure either. She simply didn't care he was there. "What do you want, Freddie?"

He shrugged. "Nothing, really. Are you alright?"

Smith looked at him, and there was a long pause while she thought about the answer. "Yes, I'm fine, thanks." He was surprised, she looked far from fine. She stood and left him without another word. He found he was alone in the room, even MacLean had left.

A waiter appeared and asked if he required anything. Freddie shrugged. "Not unless you have any idea what's going on this morning."

* * *

William locked his office door. He needed to be free of interruptions. He fumbled the key code to his safe in his haste and cursed as he waited the programmed three-minute delay before he could try again. He entered the code with more care on his second attempt and pulled the yellow envelopes out of the safe. At the bottom of the stack was the thickest one of all, labeled *The End of the Danse*. He would look through them all to be certain he had not missed anything.

He settled into his chair when he heard a soft knock at the door. He waited and hoped whoever was there would go away, but then he heard Betty's soft voice through the door. "Mr. Bird, please open the door, I need to speak with you, please."

William swore under his breath and stashed the envelopes in a desk drawer before he unlocked the door. He invited Betty in with as much grace as he could muster, but was unable to restrain himself from checking the clock as she took a seat. "What can I do for you Betty? I have a lot to do if you and the others want to get your money today."

She nodded and bit her lower lip. "I think Junior has hurt someone else, in fact, I'm sure of it."

Bird grunted, surprised. "That's not possible, Betty, he's been under guard since last night. He's had no chance to get near anyone."

She shook her head. "No, you don't understand. It must have happened before last night. He hurt another woman before he beat up Camille."

Bird was concerned. "Did he hurt you, Betty? Did Junior do something to you?"

She shook her head. "Not me, someone else. I don't know if I should tell her name, she doesn't know I'm here, but she's been hurt, and I'm sure it was Junior."

William was frustrated. "Betty, you cannot make accusations against Junior without some foundation. I can't do anything unless whomever you think was attacked comes to me herself." His hard tone took her by surprise.

"If I tell you who it is, will you follow up? Will you find out what happened?"

"No, I won't. Unless this person complains to me, I'm not going to dig up more trouble. Listen, Betty, the group just agreed a deal. You all want to collect your money and get out of here. If I start looking into an attack that might or might not have happened, no one gets paid today, and no one goes home tomorrow." He realized he sounded harsh and mellowed his tone. "You speak to this woman. If

339

she wants to tell me, I promise to listen. If that happens, I'll look into it, but not before. You'll excuse me, please?"

He stood and opened his door, indicating their meeting was over. Betty knew the lawyer was right, unless Janice wanted to make something of it, there was nothing to be done. She thanked him for his time and left, frustrated and embarrassed. She had acted in haste, upset William and achieved nothing to help Janice.

* * *

William returned to his desk and flipped through the envelopes. He had passed a half-dozen before he realized he hadn't read any of them. His mind was on Betty's visit. She claimed Junior had attacked someone else, a woman. If it had happened like Betty said, then the victim had to be Caroline or Janice. Camille and Bethany had both been attacked, and he was sure Winnie Tremethick was untouched. Caroline had witnessed Junior's attack on Camille and he felt sure she would have said something if she had been the victim of another attack.

He frowned as he ticked off the events as they could have happened. If Betty was correct, the only other woman Junior could have hurt was Janice. But why? He remembered the night the housekeeper had appeared at his door and offered herself to manipulate her reward. He had refused, of course. But did Janice make the same offer to Junior?

It was hard to believe she would be so desperate, but it was possible. She had wanted to steal the bonus from her husband badly enough to offer herself to him. Perhaps she had seen Junior as the next best option. Junior might have agreed to help Janice, but if Betty was right, he had exacted a high price in return.

William returned to the envelopes. He knew none addressed sexual assault. There was also no envelope with instructions about what to do about Philip's attack. He

340

snorted as he came to the envelope labeled *In Case of Murder*. He and the Old Man had laughed about that one. William had called his boss paranoid.

It seemed ironic that had Philip been successful in his attempt to murder him there would have been instructions about how to deal with it, but because he had failed, there were none. William had an idea of how to deal with Philip. He would determine Junior's fate once he heard Camille's decision about whether or not she wished to press charges. He thought if Junior had assaulted Janice, it might make Camille's decision easier.

He thought about calling Janice, but had no idea if Dennis knew anything, or if there was anything to know. He decided to heed his own advice. If Janice wanted to complain, he'd act, but not before. He put it from his mind and opened the last envelope to find out what to do now the guests had reached an agreement.

Chapter Thirty-Four

Winnie Tremethick read the letter from Charlie Wells and cried. His words reminded her of the days she'd enjoyed at a time in her life when she had thought the best had already come and gone. Her memories of being a widow in love were fresher now than they had been in forty years. She was no longer afraid to remember, there was no pain left in the memories, only the joy and love from a long ago place. She couldn't recall a day spent with Charlie when the sun hadn't shone and the meadows weren't laced with flowers. She knew it was a ridiculous trick of the mind, but she didn't fight it.

She read Charlie's words again. They seemed so vibrant she could almost hear his voice speaking the words as her eyes moved across the page. Winnie held the letter close to her chest, closed her eyes and fell asleep in her chair.

Janice and Dennis Elliot sat in uncomfortable silence. He had followed her to their suite from the conference room, but she didn't want his attention. She was upset by her conversation with Betty and needed time to think. Dennis had refused to leave until she explained what had upset her and the angry silence had begun.

Dennis was confused. This morning he had felt so close to her, it was like the start of their marriage again. Now a familiar coldness had returned, and Dennis pondered the things that bothered him in the last few days. He was still troubled by Janice's explanation about their bonus. When he thought about why she might have tried to keep it secret, none of the possible answers made him feel better.

He thought about Junior's attack on his wife and wondered again how she had come to be in his room. She claimed Junior called her and offered her money if she went with him after the deal was done. But what if that were not true? Dennis realized the arrangement might have been initiated by his wife, not Junior. His mood darkened as he thought through the timeline. It was possible she had made an offer to Junior in return for more money and that Junior had only taken what was offered. She had said nothing to Dennis about the attack until after he discovered the marks on her body.

He had let the details slip by him in his anger at Junior, but now he looked at his wife and worried she had played him for the fool. He felt nauseous and knew that as soon as his wife felt better, they would have a frank conversation.

* * *

Bethany sat on the edge of the bed with her sister lying behind her. They were physically close, but there was animosity between them. Bethany sighed and tried to start the conversation over. "Camille, please let me explain why I had to stop Junior getting thrown out. Please. Just listen, I beg of you?"

Camille rolled on to her back, and Bethany flinched as she saw her pretty sister's beaten face. She had trouble talking through her swollen mouth. "Look at me Bethany. He beat me like a dog and you let him off the hook. I understand. I do. I am not really your family, even now. I'm your second-class half-sister. Deny it, if you can."

Camille's words stung, but she was mistaken and Bethany had to make her see. "No Camille, you're wrong. I hate Junior for what he did to you. I've heard rumors that he treats women badly, but I've never seen it, you must believe me. I will have nothing more to do with either of my brothers when this is over. I don't know who they are anymore. Philip killed a man in Georgia and tried to kill William, and I will never forgive Junior for what he did to you."

She wiped a tear from her cheek as she spoke and she saw through blurry eyes that Camille was listening. Bethany hoped her appeal would be enough. "I had to stop Junior from being disinherited, or I would never be free of him. Do you understand? He would always be after me for support. I needed Junior to receive his share of my father's fortune. He can look after Philip from his share. I want nothing more to do with either of them."

Camille listened and in her heart knew the explanation was true. Bethany had secured a better future for herself by allowing Junior to keep a share of his inheritance. Her injured face softened, and she reached out and touched her sister's arm gently. "You are cutting yourself off from your family? That is your plan?"

Bethany turned, her eyes brimmed with tears. "Not all of it, Camille. I wish we had met under better circumstances. Truly, I do. But I find having a sister to be

343

a comfort and I want us to be friends. Can we still be friends, even after all this?"

They looked at each other for long seconds before Camille opened her arms and welcomed Bethany into a warm embrace. They each dissolved into tears and hugged and whispered comforts to each other. Bethany's heart broke at the idea of abandoning her brothers, but it was soothed by the hope of a better future with her sister.

* * *

Caroline Smith sat alone in her suite. Her shoes were kicked carelessly across the floor, and her head was a jumble of thoughts. She should be celebrating, her goal of being rich had been realized, but instead she was numb. She missed her family, something she had not done all week and was suddenly ashamed to think of.

Their lives would be better now that they had real money. Her husband could retire from the teaching job he hated. Caroline smiled as she thought of him, but the smile faded as her mind replaced his face with Junior's on the night he attacked his sister. Caroline held her head in her hands. The images and sounds of that night haunted her.

She looked at the telephone and prayed for it to ring with news that William Bird had completed his task, and she could get out of this place. The mansion made her feel sick, despite its luxury. It was a cold, evil place, and she would not be sorry to leave it.

* * *

Ron Freeman came across Larry MacLean in the hallway. He had escorted the sisters safely to Camille's room and was headed to his own suite. The Judge stopped and waited for Larry to reach him. They regarded each other coolly, and then Freeman offered his hand. Larry looked surprised but took the offered hand.

"Congratulations Mr. MacLean, on our settlement. I see no reason for unfriendliness now the worst is over. I'm pleased you got a full share, I must say I had no idea Freddie had tried to take advantage of you so cruelly."

MacLean relaxed. "Thank you, Ron. I guess we both overcame the odds when they were stacked against us, right?" Freeman invited MacLean to his room for an early shot of something strong and Larry happily agreed. He would visit Winnie later.

The men each nursed a large glass of good whisky in Freeman's room. "What do you think will happen to the Thurwell boys, Ron? Do you have any idea what Bill intends to do with them?"

Freeman looked at his glass as he considered the question, and then drained its contents in one large gulp. "I can't say what is on William's mind, and it may not matter. He says he has instructions of what to do in certain circumstances. If orders exist for either situation, his hands will be tied. Mine, however, are unencumbered by any allegiance to a dead man."

His deep voice rumbled with anger and Larry noticed it immediately. "What do you mean, Ron? Are you going to do something?"

The Judge's dark eyes glowered as he leaned forward. "Yes. I was complicit in allowing Philip Thurwell get away with a murder. I will not allow him to escape justice for his attack on William. I swore an oath to uphold the law, and I let myself down when I broke that promise. I won't do it again. This time I intend to see Philip tried for his crimes."

Larry nodded, he understood the Judge's anger at being duped over the Macon incident, but he saw a problem. "Phil knows too much, Ron. He could bring you down with what he knows. Hell, with what he's heard this week he could cause problems for a lot of people if he wanted to. Freddie might go to jail, Camille may be deported to face

345

charges of her own, and I'm sure most of the others would not like the world to know their misdeeds."

The Judge nodded but seemed set in his decision. "That's true, Philip could cause problems, but I don't think he will. Either way, I cannot let him off the hook, he must face a trial." He reached for the open bottle and refilled his glass, offering it to MacLean, who declined.

Larry was worried, the Judge was not thinking straight, Philip was exactly the kind of person that would have no problem ruining others if he faced ruin himself. He possessed a selfish streak a mile wide and Larry knew it.

He thanked Freeman for the drink and left to visit Winnie, but he was anxious about the Judge's plan. He thought he should warn William of the potential danger. He looked in the direction of Winnie's room, but instead walked in the opposite direction toward the library, and William Bird's office.

* * *

Betty knocked on the door and waited. It was a long wait, and she was about to give up when the door opened and she faced Dennis Elliot. She smiled. "Is Janice okay? Can I see her?"

He frowned. "What is it to you if my wife is alright or not?" His voice was cold and bluff, and Betty realized she had to be careful. He may have no idea that Janice had been attacked.

She gave him a rueful look and shrugged. "Dennis, I'm sorry, Janice and I talked earlier and I upset her. Could I see her and apologize, do you think?"

Dennis chewed over her request for a moment but stepped back and left enough room for Betty to enter. She squeezed into the room and flashed him one of her best smiles, hoping her charm would melt his icy demeanor. If it worked, she couldn't tell. "She's still upset, don't make it worse."

Betty nodded and stepped quickly into Janice's bedroom, closing the door behind her to ensure privacy. The room was dim, there was only the soft gray light from outside, but Betty could see Janice on the bed, looking at her. "What do you want?" Her tone was cool, and Betty knew this was not going to be easy.

"You need to talk to William Bird. You need to tell him what happened to you."

"I already told you, no. I'm not saying a word to Bird or anyone else. I made a mistake. I was greedy, and I paid for it. I don't want William to know, and I'd prefer if you kept your business to yourself and left me to mine." Janice was angry, but it wasn't all directed at Betty, there was pent up fury at Junior too.

Betty thought about something Janice had said, something that made her think there was more to the story than she was telling. "What did you mean when you said you got greedy and paid for it? How did you come to be alone with Junior?"

Janice flashed a panicked look before she turned dark with anger, this time it was all for Betty. "Get out. Leave me alone and stop bothering me." She called for Dennis, who arrived quickly and ushered Betty out of their suite politely, but firmly. He closed the door after her and sighed. He tried to understand what his wife had meant about greed.

He had listened to their conversation through the bedroom door and had been pained to hear his wife's admission that she had done something to bring about the attack. She had not told him the truth, he was sure of it. He was also sure his wife had been dishonest about the bonus.

He heard Janice call, but he ignored her and went into the washroom and locked the door. He turned the shower on to drown out her voice and sat on the edge of the tub.

He watched his reflection disappear as the mirror fogged up, sure that his marriage was as dead as their employer.

Chapter Thirty-Five

William Bird worked on the spreadsheet on his laptop. It was a simple list of the ten names that would share Johnston Thurwell's fortune. They had agreed equal shares, which made the math easy. He waited for the Swiss bank to call with the exact value the fortune would be worth at midnight tonight. William wanted to be accurate to the penny.

He ran down the list. Every person on it had been changed by the experience of the last few days, and not just by money. These people, some of who had been close to Thurwell, and others who had been peripheral but pivotal, had all shared something of themselves, and few of them were better for the sharing.

He thought of the Thurwell brothers. Philip was disinherited and locked in the wine cellar. Junior was restricted to his room. He would take a tenth of his father's money, but his future was uncertain following his attack on his sister. Bethany and Camille had found a bond and grown closer as the week progressed. William thought there was little chance they would remain close. The final vote appeared to have split them permanently. It was a pity, but he had seen better families fall apart over less.

It had been part of the Old Man's design that the *Danse* would instigate conflict. He knew his children were spoiled and weak. It had been his intention for them to learn quickly to fight for something if they wanted it. Bird glanced up at the ceiling, as if to look toward his dead boss, and reflected that Thurwell had ignited more conflict than he could have anticipated.

The telephone rang and interrupted his thoughts. He picked it up and heard the clipped, efficient accent of the bank's representative. William wrote a number down and repeated it back to ensure it was correct. He thanked the man in Zurich and hung up. He looked at the number and whistled softly, the amount was far higher than he had imagined.

He reached for his calculator and punched the keys to find the amount the group would share. The forty percent they lost to penalties would enrich the Thurwell Foundation. The sixty percent remaining for the lucky ten was a large enough number to change their lives. Some would be disappointed when they saw it while others would hardly believe their eyes.

Bird didn't care what the beneficiaries thought. The numbers were what they were. The Thurwell Foundation would be grateful for the group's failure to agree until the third day, an outcome that would have pleased the Old Man. The lawyer knew that the only thing the Old Man really cared about was that the Foundation was his legacy.

Caroline Smith would not lead the Thurwell Foundation upon her return to the city. Bird had instructions to fire her if she failed to resign by the end of the *Danse*. The search for a new leader would rest with the Board. William had a seat and would help make that decision, but Junior and Bethany would be removed from their Board positions before any hiring decision was made.

Bethany and her brother were out of the family business. They didn't know it yet, but William would soon deliver papers to sever their employment with Thurwell Industries. The Old Man had seen no reason for the family that betrayed him to have any future role ruling his empire.

* * *

William realized his attention had wandered and returned to the papers in front of him. He divided the number by ten, wrote it once on the page and used his calculator to multiply it again by ten to make sure he was correct. Satisfied with his math, Bird took the spreadsheet and entered an identical number by each name. He checked his figures in the spreadsheet and smiled with quiet satisfaction when he saw his number matched the banks perfectly.

He opened the secure web page for the Zurich bank and punched his security code into his laptop. At the prompt, he placed his thumb on to a small black pad. He waited a few seconds while servers in Europe verified his password and thumbprint and issued authorization for him to continue. Bird called up the first name on the alphabetized list, Dennis Elliot, and transferred the first ten percent share into his account. He checked the number again and pressed the confirm button. He waited for computers in Switzerland to verify that Dennis was a rich man and then moved on to Janice's account.

Bird worked down the list, checking and rechecking every entry before he confirmed it. He reached the last name on the list, Johnston C. Thurwell III and tapped the keys to give Junior his inheritance. He validated the entries as a batch and sent them to the bank. He closed the laptop and waited for the telephone to ring.

The banker in Zurich called precisely one minute later, the voice on the telephone belonged to a full Vice-President though William thought of him as a clerk. William verified his identity with a personal sixteen-digit pass code and waited. The number and voiceprint were confirmed as matches. The banker thanked William for his business, wished him a good day and ended the call.

* * *

It was nearly over. Ten lives had been changed forever by a few minutes of tapping on a keyboard and a thirty-second international call. William felt a weight lift off his shoulders. He had wondered if he would ever get through this week, but now all he had left to do was deliver ten envelopes and host a dinner before he and his guests would part forever.

He still needed to figure out how to deal with Philip. He knew he was not able to be objective when the life Philip had tried to take was his own. He hoped now the *Danse* was almost over with, the Judge would agree to advise him. William wondered if pressing charges against Philip was even worth it. He had lost everything. Unless a sibling took pity on him, he would need to find an honest job to sustain himself, something for which he was in no way qualified.

William called Teterboro airport in New Jersey and spoke to Thurwell's private pilot. He instructed him to be at the local airstrip early the next morning, fuelled for a trans-Atlantic trip. The flight from New Jersey was less than an hour, and the pilot promised he'd leave as soon as the local airfield confirmed it was open. He would file a flight plan to Exeter in England to take Winnie Tremethick home. Ten or so hours after leaving the mansion, the old woman would be home.

William made a call to the City and ordered eleven cars to be at the mansion at ten the next morning. He considered ordering nine, but had no confidence the Elliots would leave together. It was better to have one too many cars than suffer the embarrassment of having too few.

The drivers were instructed to take their passengers wherever they wanted, no matter the distance. William guessed most would go back to their homes, but some might prefer to head to new destinations where they could get away from their old lives.

William leaned back in his chair and folded his hands behind his head. He wanted to smoke a cigar. The Old Man had left him one of his favorite Hoyo de Monterrey's to enjoy when the work was done. But it wasn't over yet. He would not be finished until the last guest left the mansion and only then would he enjoy his cigar.

It was time for him to finish processing the settlements. He reached into his desk drawer and pulled out twelve unsealed envelopes already labeled with the guest's names. He discarded the ones labeled Philip Thurwell and Winnie Tremethick. One would receive nothing and the other already had her money.

He wrote the amount of their share on each of ten letters that also instructed the recipient how to claim their money. He decided to deliver the letters personally rather than hand them out in a group. It would make for a quieter life. He didn't need the drama of some people gloating as others lamented.

Bird picked up the phone and called Jeremy. "The dinner will be tonight, in case you hadn't guessed already."

"Understood sir, I did take the liberty of beginning preparations. Are there any changes to the arrangements?" Bird smiled. If there was one thing he'd been sure of all week, it was that Jeremy was always one step ahead of him. "No Jeremy, we go ahead as instructed. Thank you."

Johnston Thurwell had chosen what his guests would eat and drink at their final meal together. His plan was so thorough he had even prepared a seating chart based on his assumptions of how the week would go.

Philip would be included in the dinner. The Old Man was clear that even people who had been eliminated would attend the dinner. William told Jeremy the two of them would talk to the youngest Thurwell before he was allowed to join the others. They agreed to visit Philip later that afternoon.

The lawyer tidied his office, replaced the unopened yellow envelopes in his safe and secured his laptop. He slipped the ten envelopes into his breast pocket and left his office to deliver them to the guests. He decided to see them in the same order he had enriched them, alphabetically.

* * *

Janice pleaded at the washroom door for Dennis to come out. She heard water running, but he would not acknowledge her, and she was frightened he had done something to himself. She swore at him through the door and rattled the doorknob to no avail. He would not, or could not, answer.

She lifted her hand to pound the washroom door again when she was stopped by a knock at the door. She opened it quickly and pulled the lawyer into the room. William listened to her breathless account of Dennis in the locked washroom and wondered what had occurred to make him take refuge there.

He calmed Janice and told her to wait in the bedroom while he tried to talk Dennis out. William tapped lightly on the bathroom door and announced himself to Dennis. The lock clicked, and Dennis looked out through a small crack. Once he was satisfied William was alone, he stepped out. "I'm sorry for your trouble, Mr. Bird. I was trying to think, and Jan won't let me have a moment's peace, so I locked her out."

William had a decent idea what the argument was about and wanted nothing to do with it. He reached into his pocket, selected Dennis's envelope and handed it to the manservant with a smile. "Perhaps this will help smooth things for you. It's your settlement and instructions for how to access it. There is also the number of an

353

investment advisor that might be of help. He's a good man, you can trust him."

Dennis took the envelope with a look that approached reverence. His hands shook as he held it, turning it over and over. But he did not open it. "Thank you, sir. I don't know what to say now it's over. Mr. Thurwell was good to his word, he promised he'd take care of me, but I never expected this."

William smiled. He knew the fondness Thurwell felt for Dennis and knew it would have pleased Thurwell that his loyal manservant was grateful. "I have to see Janice now. She has her own settlement here." William showed Dennis the other envelope and saw his face cloud over. "Would you like to step out, so I can deliver her envelope without you two getting into a fight?"

Dennis looked embarrassed but thanked Bird for his suggestion and left, tucking his envelope into his pocket. He'd look at it when he found a quiet place to himself. Janice stepped out of the bedroom as soon as she heard the outer door close. She had listened to everything the two men said.

She looked at the lawyer and held her hand out. "Give it to me, I want to see." He handed her the envelope, and she immediately tore it open. The number was written on the front page, she saw it right away and she gasped. "That much! I had no idea."

He turned to leave, but she stopped him with a light touch on his arm. "Wait. Wait just a minute. Please?" He looked at her with a curious expression and she hesitated. She had been about to tell him of Junior's treatment of her, but changed her mind. She had no need to dwell on the past now she was rich. "I'd like you to have Dennis' things moved out of my suite. I don't want him coming back."

William nodded and asked if there was anything else, but Janice said she wanted to be alone. With some relief, he granted her wish.

* * *

William used a house phone to call Jeremy and make arrangements for moving Dennis out of his wife's suite and asked the major-domo to tell Dennis of the new arrangements if he saw him. Then he walked quickly to Betty Freah's door and knocked lightly. Betty answered the door in a short robe, her hair wet and tied back. "I'm sorry, Bill, I took a shower, I must look a sight."

The lawyer thought she looked pretty good. Her legs were shapely, and she looked fresh and natural without make-up. "I've got your settlement, Betty." She took the envelope with a giggle and took a little jump in the air with excitement, a gesture he found utterly charming.

"Am I deliciously rich, Bill? Did we do well?" He shrugged and suggested she open the envelope to find out for herself. She looked at him and bit her lower lip nervously as she worked the seal open carefully with a fingernail.

Betty glanced up quickly before teasing out the papers inside. "Oh my God! Oh, Bill." She threw her arms around the lawyer's neck and hugged him tightly. "I can't believe it, thank you, thank you, thank you." She kissed him on the cheek before she released him. She trembled all over with excitement. She was flushed, and William thought he had never seen her look so attractive. He collected himself and told her how she could claim the money, but she wasn't listening. Betty danced from one foot to the other and her eyes sparkled with joy.

"I still miss him you know. Johnston meant something to me, but this sure makes grieving easier. Is that wrong?"

He smiled. "Not at all Betty. I think he'd be happy that you're happy. Don't forget we have the dinner later, okay?"

355

She agreed, and when he left her she was dancing in a circle and singing happily.

* * *

Ron Freeman was half asleep on his couch when he heard a knock on his door and William Bird's voice. He wondered what the lawyer wanted as he opened the door and invited him in. "Bird, I'm glad you're here. I've been thinking about Philip Thurwell and-"

He stopped when he was handed an envelope. Freeman listened to Bird explain what it contained. "I see. So this is what we've been fighting over. Well, let's find out what we've won at the cost of so much heartache." He tore open the envelope and looked at the number on the front page. He sat down heavily and rubbed a large hand over his head. It was a larger number than he had expected. He had been convinced the penalties had cost them dearly and had even wondered if he would have to continue to practice law. Now he saw that if he never raised a gavel again he would be just fine. Perhaps a political career might even be back on, if he could solve another problem.

William saw the man needed time to think. "I'll go. We can talk about Philip later. I have more of these to deliver." The Judge nodded but did not move from the couch. The letter slipped from his fingers and laid on the floor as he tried to comprehend the enormity of the change in his life.

Chapter Thirty-Six

William headed directly to Freddie Hagood's suite. The magnate, still dressed immaculately in a dark suit and tie, answered the door quickly. "Come in, Bill. What can I do for you?" William pulled out the envelope and handed it to Hagood. "Ah, so we come to the moment of truth. You work fast, Bill, thank you."

Freddie opened the envelope and looked at the number before folding the paper and placing it in his breast pocket. "Fair enough, I suppose. It wouldn't have been so bad if the others had agreed to agree sooner, but with Johnston's idiot sons, it was always going to be difficult. You've impressed me this week, William. If you want a job, call me."

Bird thanked Freddie for his consideration but knew he'd never work for anyone else again. Once he had collected his fee he and his wife would leave the city and retire to a small town not far from the mansion. He would be more than comfortable through a long retirement. The men shook hands, and the lawyer excused himself to visit the next beneficiary, Camille Jolivet.

* * *

Bethany opened the door to greet William and surprised him. He had been convinced the sisters had fallen out over her vote to keep Junior's inheritance. He realized he was dead wrong when he entered the room. Bethany took a seat next to Camille and they held hands, looking at him with trepidation. "Please, ladies, relax. I have your settlements."

He pulled out two envelopes, there was no point in making Bethany wait since she was already here. The sisters exchanged a look as he handed each of them their fortune. Bethany paused and looked at it. Her eyes filled with tears as she realized this would be the last thing she would ever receive from her father. Camille opened hers and looked quickly at the page, then at Bethany. "Mon Dieu. So much money, I had no idea."

Bethany smiled at her sister's quiet amazement and opened her own envelope. She looked at the number for a long time before looking up. "We wasted so much. Is this all that was left, Bill?"

The lawyer understood. She would have had a better idea than most of her father's material wealth. "There was only sixty per cent left, Beth. I'm sorry, but the penalties cost you."

She shook her head sadly as Camille looked at them in confusion. "How can you not be happy, sister? You're trés riches, we are both rich." Bethany smiled, and Bird saw genuine warmth between them. He was pleased to have been wrong in his prediction of their future.

Bethany's voice caught in her throat. "Yes. Yes, we are wealthy. But my father had so much more, and we lost it because we couldn't stop fighting. I feel ashamed."

She looked at William with a face full of worry. "Can we talk about the boys? What's going to happen to Phil and Junior?"

William stalled. "I can't talk about them right now. I have to deliver the settlements. I'll speak to the Judge later. I think he has some idea what to do."

She nodded. "Please, Bill. Let me speak for them when you see the Judge?"

He agreed. It was only fair for them to have an advocate present as their futures were decided. He noticed Camille dropped her eyes when Bethany raised the topic of her brothers and sensed there was still disagreement on that subject. He promised to call Bethany when he met the Judge and left them. Both were re-reading their letter, but with very different interpretations of what it meant.

* * *

Larry MacLean was shirtless when he opened the door. He had gone back to bed and looked like hell. He pulled on a plain white t-shirt and tried to smooth his tousled hair into some kind of respectable shape as William waited. He mumbled an explanation as he dressed. "I was trying to get some rest. I didn't sleep much last night, too much going on in my head."

William began to apologize, but MacLean dismissed it. "I said I was trying to sleep, I didn't say I was sleeping. I'll need to be out of this place before I can rest. This place is filled with Johnston, and my conscience is punishing me."

William saw deep lines around MacLean's eyes. Larry looked pale under his sailor's tan, and William almost felt sorry for him. "I've got your money, Larry and instructions how to claim it."

He handed it to MacLean, who took it quickly and tore it open. "Oh God, is that all? I thought it might be bad, but not this bad. What a mess." He slumped onto the nearest chair and shook his head. "I'll have to support my entire goddamned family with this... It'll be a big shock to them. They'll need to make cuts."

William was annoyed that MacLean had the nerve to complain about the money he was taking from the friend he betrayed. "It could have been a lot worse, Larry. Try to remember that." His voice was sharper than he intended, and it made MacLean start. He looked up and Bird saw shame in his eyes, and the sting his words left. "Make sure you're on time for dinner, I'll see you then."

William left the room before he said something else he might regret.

* * *

William closed MacLean's door behind him and leaned against it to take some deep breaths. He had to remain calm. He still had two envelopes to deliver and neither would be easy. He practiced breathing with his eyes closed until he felt his irritation recede.

When he opened his eyes, he was surprised to see Jeremy standing a few feet away, watching without appearing to watch. "Is everything alright, Mr. Bird? I've just moved Mr. Elliot's effects to another room. He's been informed of the change, and it seemed to suit him well enough. How about yourself sir? A cup of tea, perhaps?"

William shook his head. The major-domo amazed him with his tact. "Thank you, Jeremy, I'm fine. I have a couple more visits to make and then maybe I'll take a cup of your strongest coffee. I don't think tea would cut it for me right now."

Jeremy smiled and promised the best cup of coffee in the State anytime he wanted it and then was gone. He disappeared down the hallway in quick strides. William watched him go and took another deep breath. It was time to visit Caroline Smith.

She answered the door with her hair down. Her usual business suit had been replaced with sweatshirt and jeans. She stood in the doorway, blocking the entrance with her arm as she demanded to know what William wanted. He explained the reason for his visit and watched greed creep across her face. She suddenly became friendly and ushered him into her room with a theatrical flourish. Her eyes flashed with excitement as he reached into his pocket and drew out her envelope.

She snatched it from his fingers and ripped it open. She scanned the page until she found the number. She sneered in triumph as she read the letter that made her rich and William felt a wave of revulsion at her naked greed. She had harmed Thurwell's Foundation, his legacy, by accepting bribes. Yet now she was rewarded further. William wondered why the Old Man had included her in the group, she was unworthy.

She saw something in his eyes she didn't like and cocked her head to one side. "What, you don't approve? Well that's too bad. You can go, leave me alone." William suppressed anger at her imperious tone and left her. He shuddered at her ability to get under his skin.

* * *

William had one envelope left in his pocket and forced himself to walk to Junior's door to deliver it. He nodded at the burly guard who anticipated William's intent by rapping on the door for him. William could have wished for a moment to compose himself, but the door flew open, and he saw Junior. "What do you want, Bird? Are you checking I'm still here, that I haven't slipped past your dog?"

William remained impassive. He could not let Junior get to him. "I need to speak with you, may I come in?"

Junior snorted. "I don't see why you should be allowed in when I'm not allowed out. Why should I admit my jailer to my cell, are you going to search it for contraband?"

The lawyer pulled the final envelope from his pocket and showed it to Junior, who stopped talking. "Come in, then."

William glanced at the guard, who rolled his eyes dramatically. William almost laughed but managed to keep a straight face, the moment helped relax him as he followed Junior into the room.

"So it's done then? After all the fuss, those damned leeches get my father's money, and I get the crumbs from the table. Give it to me." William passed the envelope to Junior, who opened it and read the same number as the other nine people. "I knew it. This is a sick joke, Bird. This is a drop in the ocean. Those idiots stole my inheritance from me. If they had listened to reason, we'd all be richer, but look at this. I'm sure the whore and the help are thrilled to little bits, but you know this is a sick joke."

He threw the papers to the floor and turned his back on William, who dared not breathe a word for fear of telling Junior what he thought of him. He waited and watched Junior's back. Thurwell's oldest son was rocking on his heels, a sure sign he was agitated. Eventually he turned and looked at William. "Can I challenge this? I'm sure a court would look favorably on the family's claim that we have been robbed of what was rightfully ours."

"You signed an agreement, Junior, before you arrived. You all did. You all agreed the results of the week would be binding. My instructions are clear. If anyone challenges the settlement, they are stripped of everything. What you have now is the most you can ever hope for. You may not like it, but that's the reality. This week was your father's plan, his final wishes."

Junior glowered, but he knew the lawyer was right. He also knew if he challenged the settlement that news of his brutal assault on his sister would leak out. He was frustrated and angry. He hated to give up the fight almost as much as he hated to give up the last word on the matter. "So be it, then. A great fortune is wasted on leeches and sycophants. If that's how my ignorant father wanted it, fine. But I don't like it, Bird, not one bit. Now, when can I get out of here? I'm tired of this place."

"Tomorrow morning you will all leave. I have cars coming to take you wherever you want to go. You must attend tonight's dinner, but if you promise to behave, I'll have your guard stand down during the meal."

Junior nodded, something was on his mind, Bird knew, but what it was he could not tell. William picked up the papers from the floor, smoothed the creases from them and handed them once more to Junior, who took them and walked to the window. "Go, Bird. I'll see you for dinner."

William did not need to be asked twice, he left the room as fast as his dignity would permit. He nodded at the guard on his way out and went in search of Jeremy and the promised cup of coffee.

Chapter Thirty-Seven

The mansion hummed with activity as its working occupants busied themselves with preparations for the formal dinner. It was to be a grand affair that had been planned down to the last menu item by the philanthropist himself. The guests remained in their suites for the most part, either celebrating their new wealth, or lamenting a lost fortune, depending on their point of view and relative wealth prior to the settlement.

Snow continued to fall, and the wind raised white flurries that beat upon the windows as the storm gave a last defiant blast, like a wounded animal striking at its tormentor. The forecast for the next day was for clear skies, ideal for getting everyone away from the mansion.

William sat behind his desk and looked in turn from the serious expression on Judge Freeman's face to the worried look on Bethany Thurwell's. They had gathered to determine Philip's fate, and it was a personal matter for all three of them. The lawyer was thinking out loud. "I don't know if I should press charges. It would raise too many difficult questions about this week that I will not be able to answer because of privilege. Philip, however, will not be under the same restriction and could cause great harm. He has nothing to lose."

Freeman was more concerned that Philip would get away with another crime. He was determined to prevent that. "I understand what you say, William, but the fact is he tried to kill you. He has admitted to a prior murder. He cannot be allowed to get away with these crimes."

Bethany spoke in her brother's defense. "Judge, I understand you're angry with Phil about Georgia, but Bill is fine. Thank God, nothing happened that can't be forgiven. He was angry and lashed out, but I know him. If he's allowed to leave, the matter will be over. I promise. What he did in Georgia was also in the heat of the moment. He said so, didn't he? It's his temper. It's not his nature."

Freeman was unmoved. "Bethany, Philip is lucky to have a sister as loyal as you. The fact is he killed once, and he tried again." The Judge shook his head and looked at the lawyer. "William, there is no guarantee he will not break the secrecy of this meeting when we separate. He may feel aggrieved enough to go to the press, or start rumors. He is a very angry young man and will not give us a moment's peace. He must be charged. He must face his day in court and be held accountable."

Bethany had an idea. "What if you didn't charge him if he promised to stay quiet? I'm sure he'd agree to that, Bill."

William shook his head. "No Beth. If we did that, it gives him power. He'd know we need him to be quiet and that we want to avoid charges. I think he'd agree but would soon seek ways to profit from his power and reverse his disinheritance. No, that won't work."

She saw he was right. She could see how Philip would interpret her offer as a weakness to be exploited. Freeman spoke again. "William, you said you had instructions from the deceased Mr. Thurwell about many different circumstances. Was a physical attack not among them?"

William gave Freeman a rueful smile. "Unfortunately not. He left one marked *In Case of Murder*, but I think it was more gallows humor than anything serious. He spent so many hours putting the *Danse* together that sometimes he felt the need for some light relief. I'm sure it was no more than that."

The Judge shrugged. "I see, but why not open it and find out what he wanted you to do about a murder? Perhaps there will be enough to guide us through the current impasse."

Bethany nodded. "It might be worth a look, Bill. What's the harm?"

William leaned back in his seat and considered their plan. His instructions were to open an envelope only if conditions matched the descriptions on the label. He had to decide if he should open the *In Case of Murder* envelope for the actual crime of attempted murder. "I don't know. It seems like too much of a stretch."

364

The Judge and Bethany remonstrated at such length that he relented and agreed to see what the instructions were. He opened his safe and flipped through the yellow envelopes, found the one he needed and locked the safe again.

He looked at the others and tapped the envelope lightly against the desk, still in two minds about whether it was proper to open it. "You must agree that if I open this and share its contents, you will not allow the knowledge of what we find to leave this room."

Bethany and Freeman agreed, and each leaned forward in anticipation as the lawyer slit the envelope open.

The only sound in the room was the soft rustle of crisp paper and the hushed breathing of the three as William unfolded the letter. He read it aloud.

Bill,

I hope you never read this, for if you have cause to see these words then something terrible has happened. Let me be clear, if someone is dead, I bear responsibility for having thrown them together under the pressure of the Danse. I don't accept I could have avoided it. No man can tell for sure what another may or may not do when desperate.

If you're reading this, you've got a real problem. I can't change what happened, but I can fix it.

First, you are to carry out your instructions and see the Danse to its conclusion. Whoever did the killing must be stripped of any share in my money and isolated from the others. Once everything else is done, send them all home but keep the killer at the mansion. There is a sealed note with this letter. Leave it with Jeremy and return to the city. He knows what to do.

Never discuss the matter with Jeremy and tell any who ask that it was dealt with. Say no more and no less. I would say I'm sorry you have to perform this task, Bill, but considering the obscene fee I'm paying you, just get on with it.

    JCT2

No one breathed until after William finished reading. He held the sealed note in his hand, afraid to think what was inside. He saw the Judge, wide-eyed and rubbing his chin, while Bethany sat with a stunned look. "Does that mean what I think it does? Did my father just instruct you to have someone killed if they committed murder?"

The Judge answered. "We don't know that, with all due respect, Miss Bethany. We have no idea what the second note says. It might say any number of things that are more innocent than what you suggest." Freeman tried to rationalize it, but he sounded far from convinced. "William, you knew Mr. Thurwell, what do you think it means?"

William sighed. "I think it means the Old Man wanted an eye for an eye. This whole week was about settling scores, exacting revenge or delivering rewards. It's why Bethany and her siblings were made to fight to get a single penny of what he would normally have left them as a matter of course.

"It's why you were brought here Judge. To be given a chance to share in a great fortune for assisting Philip in Georgia. Each one of you either helped or hurt him, and he threw you all together to fight it out, trusting things would shake out to his satisfaction. Do I think he meant for a murderer to be left behind and disposed of? Yes, I think that is exactly what he meant."

Bethany sat in disbelief, and another question occurred to her. "What's the dance, Bill? He mentioned it twice, is that something that will happen at the dinner?"

"No, Beth, it's what he called this week. The *Danse*, spelled with an 's'.

He took it from the Danse Macabre, the dance of death. It was his notion that he would lead you into a state of chaos as you each would do anything to deal your way into the fortune."

"He figured you'd soon forget about the fact he was dead and that the money would seduce you into all manner of contortions to take what you could. He was right, too. The midnight deadline drove all of you to act in the basest manner. Take you for instance, Ron."

Freeman could not look up as William continued. "Can you imagine threatening blackmail before you arrived here? No. Yet that's what you did as soon as you thought you would be left out of the money. The Old Man had no illusions about the nature of his fellow man, even his family. He knew that within hours of learning of his passing, you would all cast aside grief, decency and honor to fight tooth and nail for a portion of a fortune you had no hand in building."

Bethany wiped a tear from her eye. Bird's words hurt, but not as badly as the wound her father had opened with his plan. She had acted badly too. She had made deals in bad faith, taken advantage of people with worse prospects than her but, who had treated her father better than his family. "I had no idea he was so bitter. He was so angry at us."

Judge Freeman was in discomfort as he reflected on his own actions. "I'm not proud of what I did. I can see how monstrous we have all been. Mr. Thurwell has exacted a price for his money. It's a heavier price than I would have thought possible. I've lost my self-respect." He stood and paced slowly up and down the office, his face a picture of internalized shame and pain.

"My God, he played us like puppets. We danced alright, he got what he wanted, I think."

William recalled the night he learned his beloved employer was dying. They had begun work to map out the

Danse that same night. As the sickness developed and his pain increased, the philanthropist's determination to make the *Danse* a tribute to the depravity of greed grew increasingly strong.

He had pleaded with Thurwell to construct a straightforward will, but he had been resolute in his purpose, and refused. He told his lawyer that a lesson had to be learned. A lesson he had learned too late, at considerable personal cost. The lawyer shook off the memory. His grief would have to wait. "We are no further ahead in our decision about what to do with Philip."

Bethany was firm. "Well we can't leave my brother here, not with the chance Jeremy might dispose of him. Please, Bill. Give him a chance, let him go. I'll share my money with him, Junior can too. He'll have no axe to grind if he has money. I beg you, Bill. You too, Judge, please spare my brother."

William looked at Freeman, who shook his head slowly. "I don't know. If we let him go he walks away from two serious crimes. If we charge him, we risk being exposed by a young man with nothing to lose and an opportunity to take revenge on his accusers. I don't see a way to win here. Perhaps we should let Mr. Thurwell's wishes prevail."

William shook his head. "We can't do that, Ron. These instructions were for a murder and fortunately, Philip failed to kill me."

Freeman was unmoved. "He succeeded in Georgia. We thought it was an accident, but he admitted it was deliberate. That's murder. It makes these instructions valid. There is nothing explicit that says anything untoward will happen to him if we leave him. Perhaps it only sounds ominous because that's how we interpret it. Let's leave Philip here and walk away, I can live with that."

The Judge sat back in his seat as if he had pronounced sentence over Philip, but Bethany shot to her feet, her eyes wide with panic. "No, you can't. I won't leave him. I'll stay here and make sure Phil is okay. My father would not want his son killed and dumped in the woods."

William decided. "I agree with Bethany. Sorry, Ron, but I can't do it. We either charge him, or we let him go. He assaulted me, so I think it's my prerogative to decide. I lean toward letting him go. I don't like it, but pressing charges makes life potentially too messy."

Freeman nodded. "I don't agree, but I see your point. I won't argue, for Miss Bethany's sake. As long as you agree he is released only after the rest of us are already clear of the mansion. I don't want to be looking over my shoulder for him on the way home."

William looked at Bethany. He sensed a resolution was near. "Do you agree, Beth? We can release him tomorrow after everyone else has left."

She breathed a deep sigh of relief. "Thank you, Bill. I'll make sure he behaves, I promise. Can I see him now, please?"

Bird nodded and called for Jeremy to come to the office. As the major-domo arrived, William walked Bethany to the door and instructed Jeremy to allow Bethany a visit with her brother. Ron Freeman stood by the desk and without anyone seeing, took the philanthropist's sealed note to Jeremy and slipped it into his pocket.

* * *

Philip heard the key rattle in the lock and stood ready to leap. He had been confined for too long and was prepared to try and escape his prison. He waited for the door to open and was prepared to charge whoever came through the door. But he was stopped by the sight of his sister. She stepped into the room, and the heavy door closed behind her. His chance of escape was gone, but he forgot about it as he and Bethany embraced.

She looked over the small decanting area he was in. His cot had been pushed to one side, so Philip could pace up and down without tripping over it. There was a large bottle of water and nothing else. The wine cellar was tantalizingly close, but Philip was only able to look through the heavy iron grille that separated him from his father's collection of fine wine. She looked through the grid and saw the light reflected from hundreds of bottles winking back at her like underground stars.

"Yeah. It's torture being able to look but not drink."

Philip sounded tired, and Bethany turned to him. "I've got good news for you, Phil. William has agreed not to press charges against you, and the Judge has agreed too. When everyone else has left in the morning, you'll be sent home too."

He smiled, but the look chilled her, there was a streak of malice in his eyes. She didn't like what she saw. "Listen to me Phil, this is your chance to walk away from this, don't screw it up."

He snorted in derision. "Sure, Beth, I'll go free, that's just great. Where am I supposed to go, do you suppose, with no fucking money?"

"I'll help you. Calm down, Phil, I'm on your side. I'll give you some of my money. I got a share, so did Junior. He might help out too, if you ask him."

Her brother shot a disgusted look at her. "So I'm to be supported by my sister and brother, if I beg just right. Is that it? I'm to get nothing of my own?"

Bethany felt anger rise, and she slapped her brother across the face, hard. He was stunned, and a red welt appeared on his cheek where her heavy ring had caught his cheek. "Shut up, Phil. So what if I give you money? Or Junior gives you some? So what? All you ever did was take father's allowance. You've never earned anything, never worked for a living, so what's the difference if your allowance comes from my pocket? What gives you the right to care about where your easy living comes from?

Pride? You never had any before, stop pretending you have any now.

"The only reason you have no money for yourself is because you're a spoiled jerk, brother. You admitted you killed a man, and you lost your inheritance because of it. You have no one to blame for your troubles but yourself. If you prefer, I'll stop helping. I'll go back to William and tell him to press charges, let you rot in jail somewhere. Is that what you want, Phil? Is it?"

She breathed hard as she finished and saw hurt in his eyes as he rubbed the cheek that had already been abused by Jeremy's blow. He dropped his eyes. He was ashamed that everything she had said was true. "Okay. I'm sorry. I need your help, and if Junior will help me out too, I'll be nice about asking for it. I have to get out of here, Beth. I can't stand being cooped up like this. Can you do anything to get me out of here before tomorrow?"

Before Bethany could answer, the heavy door swung open and William stepped into the room, followed by Jeremy. Philip took a step back involuntarily. He was afraid of the major-domo and did not like him too close. Bethany turned to the two men. "Phil was asking if he could get out of here."

William was happy to have Jeremy with him as he was haunted by the image of Philip standing over him, ready to stave his head in. "Yes, I can make that happen, at least for a few hours. Philip will join us for dinner tonight. Do you promise to behave, Philip? You will not be allowed any alcohol. Can you give me your word you will behave? If you can, I'll make arrangements for you to spend a more comfortable night in a guarded room instead of down here. You need not run. I'm sure Bethany told you that we're letting you go tomorrow."

Philip listened with his eyes fixed on the floor. His heart beat fast at the prospect of getting out of his cell. "I'll behave, you have my word."

371

The lawyer frowned, he would have liked a more sincere tone in Philip's voice, but it would have to do. "If you mess tonight up, Phil, my deal with your sister is off, and you'll leave tomorrow in the back of a cop car, got it?"

Philip bristled. "I gave my word, Bird. If you don't believe me, just say so."

The lawyer nodded. "Okay, I'll take you at your word. I'll have you taken to a room, so you can change. You'll be accompanied at all times. Not because I don't trust you, but because the others will feel safer knowing you are not roaming the mansion. Accept it as a consequence of trying to kill me and admitting to killing another man."

With that, the lawyer left and Jeremy followed, pulling the door shut behind them. Philip looked at his sister and saw her watching him closely. He struggled to suppress the anger he felt at being treated like a common criminal. He would wait, he would behave, he had to get out of here and forget this place. He realized he had been given a second chance and for once he decided to take it and not screw up.

He turned to his sister and took her into a hug and whispered. "It's alright Beth, I'll be good. I just want to go home."

He felt her draw closer, and she cried into his shoulder. "Thank you, Phil. We'll work it all out, just the family. You'll be okay."

After a few minutes, Jeremy opened the door and told Bethany it was time to go. He beckoned for Philip to follow. "It's time for you to get ready for dinner, follow me." Philip left the cellar without a backward glance and meekly followed the major-domo to his room. He kept his promise to his sister and behaved, but mostly because he was terrified of Jeremy.

Chapter Thirty-Eight

Jeremy checked to see that everything was ready for the formal dinner that would bring the *Danse* to a close. A vast table dominated the dining room. It was covered in a pristine white cloth with creases that looked sharp enough to cause injury. All the trappings of the philanthropist's immense wealth had been brought out for the occasion, and the table was laden with heavy silver candelabras and cutlery.

The meal would be five courses of the best cuisine, prepared on site by a New York celebrity chef who had been paid a handsome sum to be ready at short notice for the drive north. The guests would eat in style, and each course would be served on Thurwell's finest porcelain.

The major-domo was satisfied everything was perfect. He looked at the large chair at the head of the table wistfully. It would remain empty tonight, but each course would be served there. It was Johnston Thurwell's traditional place and where Jeremy had overseen many formal dinners. Some of the world's richest men had dined here, as had powerful politicians and leading thinkers of the time. The Old Man had been a consummate host, able to make everyone feel welcome at his country estate. Tonight there would be no gregarious host, only an empty chair.

Place cards printed on expensive card stock with an embossed Thurwell crest indicated the seat each guest would occupy. Jeremy had argued with William about changing Philip's position, so he could be controlled if things went awry, but Bird would tolerate no changes to the philanthropist's instructions. Jeremy had instead adjusted his staff to compensate and placed a burly waiter at the station nearest Philip. Not even the attentive lawyer would notice the subtle change, but Jeremy would feel more relaxed knowing he had the ability to control Philip quickly should the need arise.

He picked an invisible speck from the tablecloth and headed to the kitchen to let the chef know everything was on schedule. In thirty-five minutes, the first course would be served.

* * *

William cursed as he fumbled his bow tie for the third time. He looked at his reflection and tried to remember in which direction he was supposed to fold the black silk. He hated formal attire and thought he looked ridiculous in a tuxedo. The lawyer knew many clumsy men who could put on evening wear and be transformed into elegant creatures who moved with grace and confidence. He was not one of those men and knew it, he always looked a little unfinished.

Thurwell had threatened to haunt him from beyond the grave if William dared show up at the dinner wearing a clip-on, so the lawyer lifted his chin and tried to recall what to do with his hands. He watched his fingers fumble the fourth attempt and threw the tie on the bed in frustration. He would have Jeremy help him. There was nothing in the rules that forbade getting some assistance.

William's impatience was a symptom of his nervousness. He had tried to dissuade the Old Man from a formal dinner, but unsuccessfully. William had two tasks to perform at the dinner, he was its host, and he had to read a letter. His uneasiness came from the fact that he had no idea what the letter said. It was sealed in his safe and could only be opened in front of everyone. It had been the last thing the Old Man had written before he became too weak to continue. William remembered the moment his boss had grabbed his arm and handed it to him. His grip was a mere shadow of its former strength, but his eyes had been fierce with determination as he instructed Bird what to do with the letter.

William looked at his watch. Jeremy had found the valuable timepiece outside the boathouse and had returned it that afternoon. He was due to meet Jeremy in the dining room in a few moments. He took his tie and headed to his office to collect the letter before meeting the major-domo to throw himself upon the man's mercy for a decent knot.

* * *

Each guest was ready for the gathering. They had dressed in their best suits or dresses, and each sat or paced in their suite, waiting for an escort to the dining room. For most, the dinner was not a welcome event. Without exception, now the business was concluded, each person wanted to be as far from the mansion as possible.

William had been unrelenting in his insistence that everyone attend. In some cases, he'd threatened that nonattendance would cause the reversal of the guest's settlement. Most of his guests did not know the threat was a bluff and quickly acceded to Bird's demand. Only Freddie had called the bluff. He knew deposits to the Swiss bank were irreversible, but had agreed to attend anyway. His curiosity had gotten the better of him. He had to see what his old friend had in store for them at the finale of this extraordinary gathering.

William arrived in the dining room with Thurwell's last letter tucked safely in his pocket. Jeremy expertly fixed the lawyer's tie and walked him around the room to show him that they were ready. William nodded and gave the major-domo the word to bring his guests down.

Jeremy disappeared, and William took his prearranged place at the door to welcome each guest. He was not kept waiting for long. Camille Jolivet arrived first. She had tried to cover her injured face with thick make-up, but her right eye was still closed by the swelling. She greeted the lawyer with a grimace for a smile, and he waved her quickly to her seat, where her escort made her comfortable.

Camille's sister came next, keeping as much weight off her taped ankle as possible. She looked tired but was elegant in a classic black dress. A line formed behind Bethany and as each person filed in William thanked them for coming and encouraged them to find their place.

Philip Thurwell was the last to arrive, flanked by two men who stood close and kept a wary eye on the young man. Philip remained true to his word and greeted William politely. He was smart enough in a dark suit and crisp shirt, but he had been unable to resist the small rebellion of not wearing a tie.

William took his place and stood in front of his seat. He looked the length of the dining table at his guests. He faced Johnston Thurwell's empty chair and saw that many of the guests had taken note of the vacant place at the head of the table. He picked up a spoon and tapped lightly on the table to get their attention.

The air was expectant as twelve faces turned to him. "Ladies and gentlemen, thank you for coming tonight. This dinner will be last time we will be together as a group, perhaps it will be the last time some of you will see each other at all."

"We can only hope." Freddie's ad lib caused a ripple of laughter and William paused to let it fade. The lawyer shot a look at Hagood, who held his hands up and muttered an apology.

William took a breath and continued. "Our dinner tonight is the last wish of our friend, father and benefactor, Johnston Thurwell. You may have noticed his chair in its usual place, though he is sadly absent from our company."

They all looked at the empty chair, and Bird saw Bethany dab a tear from her eye. Tonight would be hard for those closest to the Old Man. He called their attention back with a soft clearing of his throat. "I ask only that you enjoy the meal and company, as a mark of respect for our host. Tomorrow morning you will be furnished with transportation to take you wherever you wish to go."

He nodded at Jeremy who in turn gave an imperceptible signal to his staff. Instantly they brought out the first course. A host of waiters unveiled carefully arranged dishes before each person, but instead of looking at their own dish, all eyes were on Jeremy. The major-domo placed a dish at the empty place and lifted the silver cover with a flourish as if the Old Man was sitting there to enjoy it.

Bethany felt her appetite fade to nothing as she thought of her father. She looked at her plate and felt empty. It was a feeling no amount of nourishment could fill. She put her salad fork down and bit her lip, fighting sudden tears.

Winnie watched Jeremy take his position at parade ground attention behind the great man's chair, his eyes fixed straight ahead. Yet she knew he saw everything. She felt a tug at her heart. Winnie had done little over the last lonely days but think about Charlie Wells. She only ever thought of the dead man as Charlie, the Thurwell name meant nothing to her.

William had explained that she was a wealthy woman, but what did it mean when she was alone? She would probably die alone on her farm. If she was lucky it wouldn't take many days for someone to find her body, but that was as much as she could hope for. Money meant little to her. She had rejected Charlie decades ago, and her grown children were not close. She looked at the empty chair and wondered how different her life would have been if she had accepted Charlie's proposal.

William ate slowly and watched those around him. Junior and Philip seemed unaffected by their father's empty chair and ate with enthusiasm, but the others hardly touched their plates. It was easy to imagine the great philanthropist sitting there, his trusted man at his back, as he held forth on the issues of the day. But there was no jolly raconteur to lead the festivities, only his shadow.

Larry pushed his untouched plate back and stood. He picked up a glass of wine and turned to face the head of the table. He raised the glass as the others watched. "I propose a toast to my friend. He was not my friend at the end of his days, but that was my fault. I earned his enmity. Rest in peace, Johnston, I'm sorry." He drank a deep gulp of his wine. A single tear rolled down his cheek as he sat.

The scene was too much for Junior. "Oh, please. Spare us the dramatic remorse Larry. You fucked my mother, broke up their marriage, wrecked my childhood and he ruined you for it. He was years too late, but he nailed you for what you did. So screw your remorse. You might as well have taken his money at the point of a gun this morning, the way you hijacked me. I'd puke, except this food is too damned good to waste."

MacLean looked at Junior with eyes full of hurt but said nothing. He looked once more at the empty chair and lowered his eyes. Junior snorted and stood. Mimicking Larry's gesture, he raised his glass and turned to the head of the table. "'Bye Dad, sorry your best friend turned out to be such a fucking loser."

Philip laughed. "You tell him, Bro. Mister goddamned high and mighty sure had no idea who his friends were. Jesus, just look around this table, the Old Man was getting screwed by more people than Betty could do in a good night."

Freddie growled. "You two shut up and have some respect. It's bad enough my friend had to tolerate you inadequates for his sons, I don't have to sit here and listen to you desecrate his memory and attack people who had genuine affection for him. Can it, both of you." His voice trembled with anger, and he looked at Betty, but she had already shrugged it off.

William put down his fork and looked at the brothers. He was disappointed in their behavior. "Please, let's just try and enjoy a civil dinner. There are no votes to be won tonight, no more negotiations. Let's eat and remember your father and have some respect for his wishes."

His appeal fell on deaf ears as Junior shot back. "Sorry, Bill, but fuck my father and his wishes. He screwed me out of my inheritance. What I got was a fucking insult and Phil took nothing. He could have treated us right. He could have been a big man about it, but no, he had to fuck with us. I hated him in life, but we're family, and that's what families do, they hate each other. That's still no goddamn reason to allow servants and losers to steal your fortune. I hate him more now than I did when I sold Freddie all those juicy secrets."

Freeman interrupted. His face was impassive, but Jeremy noticed that the big man's hands shook with rage. "You might remember your brother brought his fate on himself, it's got little to do with your father."

Junior chewed a mouthful of food while he contemplated the Judge's words. "Shut up, Ron. If my father had not thrown us into this stupid mess, Philip and Bill would have had no falling out. So it is Dad's fault, see? And don't pretend you're not glad Phil got tossed, you're still pissed he played you for a fool and you let him walk from your little hick town."

Freeman glowered and made to stand up. Jeremy stood ready, but William placed a hand on Freeman's arm and stopped him with a whispered word. Philip saw this and laughed. "Look, Bill's got a tame Judge. That's right, boy, sit."

Freeman's face darkened dangerously as he fought to control his temper at the racial slur, but William was on his feet. "Okay. That's enough. Junior, Philip, get a grip and act like civilized people. I know you're upset, but there is nothing you can do, nothing you can say that will change what has been decided. Start dealing with it. Philip, you need to apologize for your last remark, it was unfit for your father's table."

Philip sneered. "Really? Boy oh boy, I guess I really screwed up. Sorry, Ron." Bird shook his head and despaired that any pretence of civility had vanished. He whispered something in Freeman's ear. The Judge nodded, and a thin smile creased his mouth, but his posture relaxed, and so did Jeremy.

* * *

Dennis heard the brothers baiting William and the Judge and shook his head. He had heard Thurwell express disappointment in his sons on many occasions. Dennis saw Jeremy's position behind the Old Man's empty chair and felt a pang of jealousy. If the dinner had been at the New York home, it would be Dennis in that honored post. He thought about why he and Jan had been so favored when Thurwell had men like Jeremy, who had not been chosen for a rich reward. He admired the way the major-domo worked. Dennis was even prepared to admit the major-domo's capabilities exceeded his own.

The next hour passed in uncomfortable silence as each delicious course arrived. Few plates were more than barely touched. Caroline had tried to start a conversation by asking Betty what she intended to do with her new wealth, but Junior killed it with a flippant comment about a whore being worth the same as a family member.

William tried his best to maintain a cheerful countenance, but it was difficult when he was concerned with Junior's sour mood and the effect it had on his brother. Both men were bitter about the outcome of the week, and Philip did not seem at all grateful for being spared criminal charges.

A few conversations were held where guests were fortunate enough to be seated next to a well-matched partner. Camille and Bethany engaged in a whispered conversation though Bethany kept a wary eye on her brothers. Winnie Tremethick and Janice were chatting. The housekeeper appeared relaxed and to be enjoying herself. William wondered about Betty's claims of Janice being abused by Junior. He thought it could be true, but he also thought there was no chance she would say anything.

At length, dessert was served, to the relief of most guests. The morbid routine of serving the host's seat first no longer surprised them. The act of serving an entire meal to a dead man's chair had been uncomfortable but served the purpose of reminding them all they had been gathered together by a man who had the ability to influence them from beyond the grave.

Winnie Tremethick was the slowest eater of the assembled company, and as she placed her spoon on her plate, the dessert dishes were whisked away, and coffee and brandy was served.

Chapter Thirty-Nine

William waited until Jeremy and his staff left the room before he reached into his pocket and withdrew the letter. He walked to Johnston Thurwell's traditional place at the head of the table. He showed the sealed envelope to the group. "This is a letter from our host. It is a letter he wrote for this occasion at the end of your deliberations. He planned this dinner to the last detail. You ate what he decided you would eat, and you drank the wines he selected for tonight.

"Tomorrow, you will leave here and continue your lives as you choose. But it is my duty to read this letter to you. Once I conclude this final duty, you are free to do whatever you wish. Your cars will arrive at ten in the morning. Mrs. Tremethick will leave us earlier, as she has a plane to catch." He nodded at the old lady who forced a smile for those who looked at her. Janice patted her arm with an encouraging smile.

William made a show of opening the letter with a butter knife. "I received this letter from Mr. Thurwell personally, and it has been locked in my safe waiting for tonight. My instructions are to read it to you once and then destroy it. I cannot answer any questions about its contents, and I ask you to respect Mr. Thurwell's memory by not interrupting."

Philip uttered a loud sigh. "Couldn't he have just made a video and saved us the drama?"

He was surprised by Junior's angry retort. "Shut up little brother. Let's see what the Old Man has to say." Philip shrugged and fell quiet, embarrassed.

William unfolded the pages of the letter and began to read.

"If my lawyer has arranged everything correctly then I am addressing twelve people who shared an opportunity to enrich themselves from the fruits of a lifetime of my labor. I have no way of knowing who got the most, or who got nothing and frankly as I sit here with tubes coming out of my chest, I don't care. I have a few words for each of you, words you might not want to hear, but you're going to anyway, because the advantage of being dead is that I have no concern for your discomfort.

"To my children, John, Bethany, Philip and Camille, I hope you got what you deserved. I'm quite sure John is upset I didn't just bequeath my fortune to the family, and he's right to be upset. In normal circumstances, a man should ensure his sons and daughters are taken care of after he's gone. Unfortunately, I was not blessed with a deserving family, which is why you might have had to

382

fight like dogs this week to get a single dollar of your inheritance.

"Let me start with my youngest. Philip, I don't have enough life left in me to express all the ways you disappointed me, son, but let me tell you that it pains me to know such an indigent loser rose from my loins. My one regret is that I could not tell you this to your face. Once, in my haste to protect what reputation remains in my family name, I involved a good man in a scheme that might have ruined him. Philip, enjoy your life, son, you will never amount to anything. You might as well have fun rather than contemplate what a total waste of time you are."

William read as calmly as he could, but the words he read were stinging. Philip's eyes burned with fury before the weight of his father's condemnation overtook him, and he lowered his head. The others were keenly aware this was going to be extremely difficult to listen to as William turned a page and continued.

"Camille, my newly discovered daughter. I did not know you well. I hardly knew your mother. I'm told DNA never lies, so I accepted that you were mine. I consider myself blessed that I found out about you so late in my life, I am not certain how much longer I could have put up with your shit. I don't know if you're angrier with your mother or me, but your naked greed shines like a beacon. I've seen it too many times before not to recognize gold fever in a woman. Remember the pact we made, my dear, you were included in the family and may share in my wealth, but you are never to take my name as your own. You are unworthy.

"Bethany, my beautiful daughter and greatest disappointment."

William heard a sob and his heart wavered but he dared not pause. He steeled his resolve and plowed on.

383

"You were the family jewel for so long my dear. You were my solace that at least one of my children would amount to something. But you broke my heart, Beth. You know what you did, but you don't know that I found out about it. I will never understand why you did it, but I took it personally and I hope you take my disapproval to your grave. No forgiveness, Beth, not in this lifetime or a hundred more.

"The hardest thing about dying is that I long for good company. Bill is too depressing to be any comfort. I would have liked you by my side at the end, Beth, but I will die without you beside me because I can't stand the thought of you lying to me as I fade away. In the end, this will hurt you more than me. Now you know it cost me something to exclude you and I hope it tears you up, so you understand what you did to me."

Bethany sobbed as her father's words destroyed her. She felt something break inside. Camille held her hand and tried to comfort her, but she was inconsolable. "Monsieur Bird, please. No more, we have heard enough."

Bird paused briefly but shook his head and returned to the letter without comment.

"To Johnston, my eldest son. What can I say? You were a brat as you grew up and never changed in adulthood. It's ridiculous that a grown man allows others call him Junior to his face. You're a dangerous little prick, son. Don't think I haven't heard the horror stories about you. You might wonder why you didn't get a straight inheritance, or you might have figured it out, depending how the Danse played out. I knew about your betrayal of me, I knew the moment you started. My biggest regret is that I continued the family tradition and gave you my name. I can prevent Camille from taking my name, but I willingly bestowed it on you, and that's an error I take to my grave with bitter regret. Never was a man so unworthy of my name than you, son."

384

"Fuck you too, Dad." Junior muttered and flipped his middle finger at the ceiling, a childish gesture of defiance that illustrated perfectly the man his father had described.

William took a breath. The letter was far worse than he had expected. It contained all the pent-up rage Thurwell had for those who had wronged him. He should not have been surprised, the Old Man had been ruthless in his determination to gather these twelve people together to variously reward or punish them. His letter was the coup de grace.

"Freddie, my friend. Perhaps the nature of our long history has been revealed and perhaps it has not, but I want to publicly acknowledge your friendship. You know what it meant to me, and I hope I was as true to you, as you were to me. If you got some of my money, good for you. It makes me happy to think some of it went to a person that earned it."

Freddie bowed his head and whispered a private goodbye to his old friend. He smiled because his friend had ensured he had the final word, even in death.

Betty Freah looked up as she heard her name and trembled at what she might hear.

"Betty, my dear, thank you for your years of tenderness. You entered my life as a practical solution to a problem, but came to mean so much more to me. I understand it was difficult for you, tolerating how the other women in my life looked down at you. But you gave me more understanding and showed more respect and kindness than my own children. You will see that you meant more to me at the end than any of them. Take whatever money you got and enjoy a long retirement, you earned it in noble fashion."

Betty smiled at the last sentence. It had been a long time since the philanthropist had touched her. He had been impotent for years. At first, he kept her appointments to maintain appearances, but soon they were friends, and she became his confidant. She looked at Janice and Bethany, two women that had always hated her and wondered what they would have made of the fact she and JT had played cribbage more often than they had played around.

William tensed as he came to the next page, the pleasantries were over.

"Larry MacLean, what can I say about you? You claimed to be my best friend, yet stole my first wife from under me, only to abandon her. You may know already what I did Larry, but in case it has not been told, I ruined you. I bought your brother and drained your trust fund. I owe you more, but I'm out of time and must be satisfied that you will be left with a fraction of what you were worth, even if you do get some of my money.

"I trusted you so much that when I discovered what you did I couldn't believe it for a long time. I even argued you were so honorable that even if you had done it, you would have confessed. I was wrong, you have no honor, and I regret we ever met. My life would have been better without you in it."

MacLean wore a stoic expression. He did not look at William but at a point on the opposite wall. He deserved it. He had enough respect for his friend to know he had earned his scorn. If Larry regretted anything, it was that he had never admitted his guilt and apologized. The barb about his lack of honor stung because once Larry had been honorable. Now his friend, his reputation and his family fortune were gone, and he had only his settlement to live out the rest of his life. By the time he had taken care of his family, Larry would be living a shadow of his former profligate lifestyle. He breathed a sigh of relief when he heard the lawyer move on and looked at his neighbor to watch her reaction.

"Caroline Smith, I don't have much to say to you. I know what you were doing at the Foundation, and you

will soon know how angry I was when I found out. You're fired, of course.

"It's possible you might have gotten your clammy hands on some of my money. Enjoy it while you can, because when you return to New York, the FBI will be waiting. I worked hard all my life and the Foundation is my legacy. If you thought you could corrupt it, you were wrong.

"Your personal greed will not sully my Foundation's reputation and so you must be publicly punished to restore confidence in the good that my legacy can do. It's possible you have learned of some indiscretions by your fellow participants this week. Let me caution you against using anything you know to plead a deal. I have enough dirt on your husband to put him in jail too, stuff I doubt even you know about. Breathe a word of what you might have heard this week and your children will grow up with two parents in jail."

Smith turned as white as the silk scarf she wore over her evening dress and had trouble catching her breath. She reeled, she had thought she had finally achieved wealth but now understood she had lost everything.

William's hands shook as he finished reading Caroline's section. He suddenly understood what one of the yellow envelopes in his safe was for. It was labeled *The Professor* and had puzzled the lawyer from the moment he saw it. There was no professor among the guests, but Caroline's husband held tenure.

William took a drink of water, his throat was dry.

"Dennis and Janice, two of my trusted and loyal people. You helped make my house a home and took care of everything for many years, thank you. I hope you are taking away some of my money, you deserve it. Thank you for the services you provided that went far beyond your normal duties. You know what I speak of, and that is all I will say.

387

"I have a gift for you, Dennis. As the longest serving person on my staff, I hereby instruct William to sign over my New York apartment to you. Call it insurance, in case the others managed to short change you and your wife out of my money. You'll find the place is worth quite a tidy sum. Do what you want with the place. Sell it or live in it, but if you sell, you must share the proceeds equally with Janice. Bill, take care of that business as soon as you get back to the city."

The Elliots exchanged shocked looks. Thurwell's home in New York was a two-story 12,000 square foot penthouse apartment with Central Park views. Dennis had no idea what such a property would be worth, but Janice immediately estimated its worth and a wide grin broke out on her face.

Bethany and Junior stared open mouthed at the servants. Junior had figured his father's properties would be returned to the family, but now the most valuable asset had been given away to his manservant. Junior wanted to protest, but no words came and he sat in furious silence.

William continued to read, but made a mental note about another yellow envelope labeled *NYC Apartment*. His hands shook. The philanthropist had even managed to surprise the man that had been by his side for the entire preparation of the *Danse*.

"Judge Freeman, we never met in person, and I owe you an apology. Had I been less invested in the reputation of my family name, you would not have been dragged into this sorry mess. I know now that what I asked of you was too much and what I did to secure your assistance was regrettable. I should have looked into you before I acted, not after, because I see I compromised a man of honor and integrity."

Junior and Philip grunted, and some of the others rolled their eyes as they recalled the Judge had ruined their first settlement with a blackmail attempt. William ignored the interruption, and the Judge listened carefully.

"I hope you are taking away some of my fortune and that any difficulties I landed you in can be relieved. I believe you had designs on a political future, and I wish you well with your future endeavors."

"Is that it? An apology and he hopes I got some money?" Freeman was surprised and felt slighted. His anger grew as he recalled the methods used to drag him into the plot to free the philanthropist's no-good son. He looked at Philip, and made a decision. He apologized for the interruption as William moved to the last person in the letter.

As she heard her name, Winnie Tremethick bit her lip nervously.

"So I come to Winnie, my lost love. You might have received a letter by now that explains what you meant to me. If not, you will very soon. I wish you had accepted my proposal all those years ago, but it was not to be. Our lives took a different path, one that sent us in very different directions.

"I regret never seeing you again, Winnie. I wish I had tried to contact you sooner, but when I returned to America, I had to let Charlie Wells go. I had a wife and soon we had a son, too. Time escaped me, and now, when I have no time left, I find my mind returns to our one perfect summer. You saved my life and stole my heart, Winnie.

"I would trade it all in, everything I have now, everything I've built and bought in my lifetime. I'd give it all up if I could return to that cliff top and hear a different answer from your lips. I'm sentimental these days. It's a new trait I find increases with every passing day. Knowing that I'm counting down my remaining time makes me nostalgic.

"I've made arrangements that you will be financially well off for the rest of your days. It's the only thing I have left to give these days, money. I married twice in my life and fathered children that turned out to be nothing but trouble. As I look back, I know my marriages failed because I was never as in love with my wives as I was with you. The rest of what I have to say is in another letter and is for you alone."

The old woman's cheeks were streaked with tears as she heard the words from her old love. Had she paid attention, she would have seen that others, too, had moist eyes. Bethany and Janice were moved, even though in Bethany's case it had been tainted with a vicious barb. Janice held Winnie's hand and felt her grip tighten as she wept and regretted her answer of forty years ago.

William saw the old woman's reaction and Janice's kind gesture. Even the hardened lawyer had a lump in his throat as he read Thurwell's last words to Winnie. He coughed to clear his throat and gain the groups attention. He had one final paragraph to read.

"My time is almost over. It's taken me three days to write this letter, and I get less done each day. The drugs dull my thoughts. I brought each of you here to either reward you or punish you, depending on what you deserved.

"I called this week the Danse, after my favorite piece of music. I head off to my death, but I've trailed you saints, sinners, leeches, loyalists and lovers along with me. Bill referred to this event as a meeting, but the label was inadequate. I have chosen to die without my family close by. I have my doctor and lawyer here to see me die. You twelve have been my puppets, but now the Danse is over. I release you back to your lives. Enjoy them, for now I know our time is too short."

William folded the letter and looked up to see a wide variety of emotions on the faces before him. "Ladies and gentleman, this concludes the Danse. I wish you good night and will see you in the morning, before you depart."

He turned on his heel and left the room. He had more work to do. He had discovered the meaning of two more of his yellow envelopes as he read the letter and needed to open them before he destroyed the Old Man's letter. He also realized the conditions to open third envelope had been revealed and hurried to his office.

Chapter Forty

No one moved or spoke after William left. The words he had read replayed in twelve minds, some stinging with rebukes, some glowing with praise. Caroline Smith left first, dabbing at her eyes with a tissue, her face deathly pale. She was shaken to learn of a pending criminal investigation. She had not been careful enough to survive a scrutiny of her deals to approve endowments. Once out of the view of the others she ran to her room, locked the door behind her and sat on the floor in the dark and sobbed at the prospect of jail.

She would have to spend a sizeable portion of her new wealth on her legal defense, and her chances of working again in any senior position would be over forever once the investigation made the news. She was ruined, and she sat on the floor and felt hate toward the vindictive philanthropist rise in her gut.

* * *

Bethany and Camille left together, each leaning on the other for physical and emotional support. Bethany was devastated by her father's harsh words. She had expected something of a rebuke, and regretted he had shared his contempt publicly. Her guilt was overwhelming. What upset her most was that her father had denied himself the comfort of her company at the end of his life. It was the cruelest cut of all and left a wound she knew would never heal.

Camille was relaxed, she had gotten away with nearly no mention at all, but then she and her father had exchanged most of their unpleasantness face to face when she arrived to make her claim as part of his family. Her face was sore, and she needed more painkillers, but she would console her sister first. Camille had been surprised to find she actually cared for Bethany and had decided she would like to maintain their relationship. Nurturing the nascent sisterhood meant Camille had to put Bethany's needs ahead of her own, so she popped a couple of pills and held her distraught sister's hand into the early hours of the morning.

* * *

Freddie offered Betty Freah his arm, which she took with a wide smile and a flirty look. Both of them were happy in the knowledge that they had been true to their friend and had been recognized for it. Freddie suggested a glass of champagne and was pleased when Betty agreed, but it was a short-lived triumph when she immediately invited Dennis and Janice to join them.

Dennis agreed, but Janice declined. She wanted to chat with Winnie Tremethick and said she might join them later. Freddie caught the Judge's eye to see if he wanted to celebrate with them and after a moment's thought the Judge agreed. "Sure, I'd love to. Why don't you three go and find a cozy spot in the library and I'll ask Jeremy to deliver the champagne?"

Freddie thanked him and led Betty and Dennis to the library.

* * *

Janice smiled at the old lady, whose eyes were still moist. "You meant the world to him, didn't you Mrs.

Tremethick? Yet none of us knew you even existed. He carried your memory as a private thing all these years."

Winnie nodded and dabbed at her tears with a tissue. "I feel so guilty. I should never have rejected him. I was too worried about what other people would think and that silly notion cost a wonderful man his happiness. I managed to forget him for a long time. I didn't even know it was Charlie when I got here. I'll never forgive myself for first rejecting him and then forgetting him. Not when he never stopped loving me."

She smiled at Janice's concern. "You're a dear for keeping me company, but I think I'll go to bed. I have to be up early tomorrow to fly home, and you should be celebrating with that husband of yours."

Winnie saw a flicker of something ugly flash across Janice's face and knew there was trouble in her marriage. But she kept her own counsel. The two women embraced, and Winnie went to her room, her heart filled with a warm glow from Charlie's last words.

* * *

Philip looked across the table at his brother, who sat with a brooding expression. "Well, I guess Dad didn't like either one of us much. Although, I think you might have gotten the worst of it."

Junior nodded, he had been wounded by the hard words from his father, but at the same time the knowledge the Old Man had his final say was empowering. "He's done now, though, for good. We'll never have to look at his sour face again, brother. He's humiliated me for the last time, and I don't know about you but I feel better just knowing he can't get in my way anymore."

Philip waved his hand and snorted. "You always did let him get to you, Junior. You needed to care less about what he thought. I never worried and look what he did for me. I treated him like a cash machine, and he gave me what I

393

wanted. Hell he even got me out of my jam. He was a pussycat. You just never had the balls to push it."

Junior regarded his younger sibling with envy. It was true. Philip had always had it easier than him. He narrowed his eyes and decided to jab his reckless young brother out of his self-satisfaction. "So I suppose you'll be asking me for money now? Can I expect the same gratitude?"

He was rewarded with a visible flinch from Philip, who instantly regretted his boast. "No. No way, Junior, not like that. Beth said she'd help. If you help out too, I'll never have to bother anyone. Hell, I'll ask the French bitch too, share the pain around the family, you know."

Junior nodded, he knew he would have to give up something to his brother, just to keep him off his back, but he could make him squirm. "I'll talk to Beth and see if she'll talk to the other one. I don't think she'd agree if I ask her."

He chuckled as he saw a cruel smile form on Philip's face. "Good idea. If she refuses, maybe it's my turn to mess her up a bit."

Jeremy interrupted the brother's dark conversation when he arrived with two men at his side. "These men will see you to your rooms. You may visit with one another if you wish, but I cannot allow you free roam around the mansion. These men will stay with you until you leave in the morning. Good night, gentlemen."

The Thurwell brothers did their best to ignore the men following them and went to Junior's room to share a bottle of expensive brandy.

* * *

Judge Freeman intercepted the major-domo as he headed across the lobby and pulled out the sealed note he had stolen from the lawyer's desk. "Jeremy, Mr. Bird asked that I give you this. It's from Mr. Thurwell and was to be handed to you directly. There was some mention you would know what to do, but with regard to what, I'm afraid we're in the dark."

Jeremy took the note and slipped it into his pocket without looking at it. "Perhaps that's for the best, sir." The Judge nodded and started to walk to the library when he remembered the champagne and called after Jeremy to have it delivered. Freeman's heart pounded as he joined the others in the library. He had set something potentially deadly in motion, but he smiled when the others greeted him happily. They had few cares now that the riches were shared, and the dinner was over.

The Judge had persuaded himself that the philanthropist's instructions were ambiguous enough that he had deniability should something happen to Philip Thurwell. The champagne arrived, and the small group broke into spontaneous applause as Jeremy uncorked it expertly and poured each of them a glass.

* * *

William looked up at the sound of applause that drifted into his office. Some of the guests were in the mood for celebration, even after the dinner and explosive letter. Bird could not hear distinct voices, but he guessed Freddie would be the leader of the group, and that it was made up of the people identified for praise in the philanthropist's letter. He checked to make sure his door was locked and returned to the yellow envelopes, reading the labels with renewed interest now more had their meanings revealed.

He put aside two, one labeled *NYC Apartment*, and a second marked *The Professor*. He knew roughly what was in the first and only needed to keep the second safe as a method of controlling Caroline Smith. The lawyer continued to look through the envelopes one by one and then stopped to read the label of the last one again.

He reached into his pocket and pulled out the philanthropist's letter, looking for a phrase. He found it: *"Saints, sinners, leeches, loyalists and lovers."* He looked at the last yellow envelope and read the label, *For a Loyalist*. There was no doubt the cryptically labeled envelope had been referenced in the letter. He opened the envelope and read the single sheet of handwritten text.

Bill,

This note should be one of the last you open, you are almost finished. By now, unless I am extremely mistaken, you will have come to rely on the services of my major-domo, Jeremy. He has been invaluable to me in more ways than you can imagine. I want you to give him Litore, my mansion, along with enough cash to keep the bills paid for as long as he lives. You can calculate that with his help.

Litore has been Jeremy's home for a long time, and I know no one else will appreciate it like he will. Jeremy likes to be out of the way, country life suits him. Transfer the title to him free and clear. If I'm wrong about him wanting to stay then he can sell it, no strings attached. Tell him before you leave and make it happen as soon as you can.

JCT2

Bird raised an eyebrow, *Litore* was a valuable property, the land alone was worth a small fortune. The Old Man had given his New York home to Dennis and his wife, now he had given his mansion to another servant. It was generosity the lawyer had not expected, but if Thurwell decreed it, so be it. The other major assets, like the landmark buildings, were all to be rolled into the Foundation. The full dismantling of the estate would take months of work now the personal fortune had been divided. All of it was destined either for charitable causes or the Thurwell Foundation. The family had received all they were ever going to get.

William looked at the four yellow envelopes that remained. He had no reason to open them because the required conditions had not been met. He thought about taking a look regardless, but hesitated. He had already opened the *In Case of Murder* envelope without proper cause. He decided they would remain unopened.

The lawyer locked the envelopes he still needed in his safe and carried the rest from his desk to the fireplace. He took the time to read the Old Man's final letter one more time and fed each page to the fire as he finished it. He threw the unopened envelopes onto the fire and watched the yellow packages darken around the edges and then catch alight and burn into curled black ash. He looked into the flames for several minutes. The firelight flickered over his face and revealed a somber man, deep in thought.

Another burst of laughter from the library broke the spell the dancing flames had cast over him. He called for Jeremy and unlocked his door and sat at his desk. As he waited for the major-domo, he contemplated the events of the week and wondered if the Old Man would have been happy with how the *Danse* turned out.

He heard a knock and Jeremy entered his office. William invited him to sit. "I have some good news for you, Jeremy. Mr. Thurwell has left you a generous gift, and I didn't want to wait to tell you." The major-domo wore a guarded expression, but his eyes were interested.

"I'm happy to tell you the mansion is yours. Mr. Thurwell thought you would enjoy it. It will come with enough cash so that you can afford to keep it, we'll figure out the amount together later. I'd like to add my own observation that if this week is representative of how you usually work, you have more than earned what is a most generous gift. Congratulations, Jeremy."

He stood and offered his hand over the desk, which Jeremy took with a look of bemusement. "Are you certain, sir? *Litore*? All of it?" The lawyer nodded and watched as the realization sank in. "I never expected to be so favored, sir. I am grateful and will keep the place as I know Mr. Thurwell would have wanted it. He loved it here. It was a pleasure to see him relax when he got out of the city."

Bird smiled, he had shared the same observation how the mansion affected Thurwell's mood. Jeremy saw a melancholy look come over the lawyer and took his leave. "I better get back to work for now, sir. Thank you for sharing the news, but until we have dispatched our guests I'm still just an employee."

The major-domo walked to the door and turned as he left the room. "Don't worry about that other matter, sir. I'll take care of it."

The lawyer nodded absently, paying only slight attention as his thoughts went to the Old Man's last days. Bird and the doctor had pleaded with him to return to the city and a proper hospital, but he had insisted he wanted to die here, in his retreat. He said it was the only place in the world he wanted to be.

* * *

Dennis was with the celebrating guests in the library and could see William's office door from his seat. He watched Jeremy enter the room and decided to intercept him when he left. When Jeremy emerged again, Dennis excused himself from the merry group and hurried after the major-domo.

He caught up with his target and begged a moment with him. Jeremy seemed distracted but remembered his manners and invited Dennis into the back where they could chat. Dennis faced the other servant and opened his mouth to speak, only to find he had no idea how to start the conversation. Jeremy looked puzzled and prodded the manservant. "You did ask to speak to me, sir. Perhaps just saying whatever is on your mind would be a good start?"

Dennis laughed. "I'm not used to being called 'Sir', that's usually my line."

He was rewarded with a polite smile from Jeremy who patiently waited to hear what he had assumed to be an urgent matter. Dennis stammered and felt awkward now he was face to face with the capable major-domo. "I wanted to tell that I admire your work. I served Mr. Thurwell in New York for many years and heard your name on a few occasions. I don't know why Jan and I were invited to this meeting and you weren't. I can only hope he has found a way to thank you. I just wanted to say that I see how much he meant to you, and I feel the same way. I would have been as proud as you were to stand behind his chair at dinner tonight. I was jealous, if I'm honest."

Jeremy relaxed when he saw Dennis was sincere. The effort of saying anything had not been easy, and he shook the offered hand warmly. "I have been given this property, just now, in fact. I had no idea Mr. Thurwell was going to do that, but he has and I consider myself richly rewarded. Thank you for your words, they mean something coming from a man I know Mr. Thurwell valued highly. I heard your name on many occasions and was always curious about who it was in the city that did everything right, all the time. I actually found myself competing with you, though we never met."

Jeremy stole a quick glance at his watch, an action Dennis took as a cue to leave. The men shook hands warmly, and Dennis invited the major-domo to visit the city apartment he had inherited, an invitation Jeremy readily accepted.

Dennis returned to the library with a warm glow in his heart at finding the major-domo was a like-minded man that understood duty and loyalty. He had felt awkward approaching Jeremy, but now it was done, he hoped they had sparked a friendship. Freddie and the others were enjoying themselves and welcomed Dennis back into the group, where they stayed and drank until Betty cried uncle and they staggered off to their rooms for the last time.

Chapter Forty-One

Jeremy and William were up early the last morning. The major-domo had arrived with hot coffee and toast at the lawyer's door before six. Everyone was to be served breakfast in their rooms, the lawyer did not want any opportunity for trouble in the last hours.

The sun shone weakly through a winter haze, but the snow had stopped, and the driveway had been plowed and sanded in preparation for the procession of cars already on their way from the city.

William looked at the report from the Swiss bank that had arrived overnight. It confirmed the transfers and balances of all the accounts. The guests could call the bank as soon as they left the mansion from the secure telephone in each vehicle. Once the formalities of account verification were over, the guests would be free to do whatever they wished with their fortunes.

The lawyer entered the confirmation numbers into his laptop and waited with a hot coffee for the first car to arrive.

* * *

Winnie Tremethick had not slept well, she was afraid of missing her flight and her head was too full of thoughts of her old lover. Her bag was packed and by the door. Winnie sat on the couch in her coat and gloves and waited for someone to tell her when it was time to leave. She had been in that position since five-thirty, even though she knew it would be around eight when the car came.

Eventually Jeremy appeared at her door with another man who picked up her bags and disappeared with them. She took Jeremy's offered arm, charmed as usual by his perfect manners as he escorted her to the lobby where William waited. "Mrs. Tremethick, I'm happy to report the aircraft is ready and your flight to Exeter is looking good. With no bad weather forecast, you should enjoy a comfortable trip."

She smiled, Winnie had forgotten in her excitement about returning home that she had actually spent a considerable amount of time of the first flight of her life being terrified. "I'm glad to be leaving, Mr. Bird. No disrespect to you or to Charlie, but this has been an uncomfortable week and I am glad to be out of it."

William smiled and shook her hand before handing her off to Jeremy, who led her to a waiting Lincoln Town Car. Moments later she was gone, the only trace of her car was lingering exhaust vapor that hung like a layer of fog on the driveway. Winnie Tremethick would be home in England in a little over nine hours.

William still had eleven more guests to see off. He looked at Jeremy and agreed that another cup of coffee was an excellent idea while they waited.

* * *

At nine forty-five, Jeremy's staff collected each guest's luggage and arranged it in neat rows in the lobby. The driveway filled with a convoy of black Lincolns. A few of the drivers had collected in the lead vehicle to share some company and coffee while they waited for the clock to reach ten.

At exactly ten, Jeremy and his staff collected the guests. Only Philip remained in his room with a man still at his door. William greeted each person as they arrived in the lobby and shook their hand before Jeremy escorted them to a vehicle and checked the correct bags were in the trunk.

Freddie Hagood left first. He shook Bird's hand warmly and waved to the others as he jumped into the back of his car with a sense of purpose. He wanted to get to the city and break the news of his old friend's death. The Hagood Business Network would own the breaking news and Freddie would make a lot of money from it.

* * *

There was an awkward moment when the Elliots arrived in the lobby. Janice refused to talk to her husband and insisted on a separate car. Dennis looked defeated, but had known this was likely. He even thought it might be for the best, but it still hurt. His wife had not been honest with him this week, a realization he had been slow to come to, but that he remembered as he watched her leave without him.

He shook hands with the lawyer and told him that he was going to the city and his new luxury home. There was also the matter of a gambling debt to take care of, but he didn't mention that. He reminded Jeremy of the standing invitation to visit the city before the car door closed, and the car pulled smoothly away.

One by one, the guests took their leave of the mansion, Camille shared Bethany's car as the sisters left holding hands, looking forward to a future together. Betty Freah gave Jeremy and William a kiss and a hug before she hopped into her car. She took a last look at the mansion, and a wistful look remained on her face the entire journey home.

Larry MacLean left without acknowledging anyone around him, he was anxious to get back to his boat. He needed to see sunlight sparkle on a bright blue sea and in the eyes of a meaningless young thing to forget the cold, painful days at the mansion.

Caroline Smith refused to shake William's hand. She had not slept knowing a criminal investigation would be her only welcome home. It even dampened her eagerness to see her family again. She thought about asking the driver to take her somewhere she would be hard to find, where she could send for her family. It was a vain hope. She knew she would return to the city, she had no choice.

* * *

Ron Freeman parted with warm words and a smile. He was going back to Georgia via New York and told Bird he was going to book a first-class seat on the first flight he could catch out of the city. William was polite as he saw the Judge off, but his thoughts were dark as he watched him go.

William had been fortunate this morning to recall the comment Jeremy had made the previous night and had questioned the major-domo about it when he delivered his breakfast. William had been shocked to learn the Judge had delivered the note to Jeremy.

Fortunately, the major-domo had not opened the envelope and returned it without protest. William watched the Judge's car disappear up the long curving driveway, happy to see the back of the vengeful man. He would need to find a way to make Freeman believe Philip had been dealt with, or the Judge might continue his quest for revenge.

* * *

Junior watched the others leave without acknowledging any of them, even his sisters. He stepped up to William, but kept as much distance as he could so he didn't appear too short when he stood next to the lawyer. "Well, Bill, I hope you're satisfied with what you've done here. You enabled my feeble minded father to steal vast portions of my inheritance and humiliate the family into the bargain. May you rot for it."

The lawyer swallowed a sharp retort. There was no point starting a fight. Junior needed the last word as a matter of course, and William conceded it. He watched as Jeremy walked the embittered son to the last but one limousine. Junior climbed in without so much as a glance at his father's mansion, and his car disappeared into the fog left by the other departing vehicles.

Jeremy returned to the lobby and stamped snow and sand off his boots and uttered a loud sigh as he looked at the lawyer. "Just young Mr. Philip left, sir. How long do we give the others before we let him leave?" William decided an hour was plenty of time to reduce the chance that Philip might encounter any of the others on the return journey. The major-domo nodded and set his staff about cleaning the lobby.

The lawyer went to his office to warm up. The lobby had chilled with the constant opening of doors for the guests to depart. Once behind his desk, he set about packing his documents into his briefcase and secured his laptop in its carry case. A car was booked to collect him at noon, he could expect to be in the city for dinner, a prospect he heartily anticipated. He had booked a table at his favorite midtown restaurant and had invited his wife to join him.

* * *

One hour after the others had departed, Philip was escorted to the lobby. He looked nervously over his shoulder at the major-domo as he realized there were no other guests to see if he got safely out of the mansion. He looked at William with a wary eye. "So, this is it Bill? I'm to just go and be forgotten, is that it?"

The lawyer nodded. "Yes, Phil, that is the plan. Your sister said she would help you, if you need it. You can leave here and start over with a clean slate, although I advise you against making any trips to Georgia. The Judge is less forgiving than I."

Philip had no intention of heading any further south than Atlantic City. "I blame you, Bird. I might have gone too far, I see that, but I blame you for disinheriting me. I'll never forgive you."

William could see the anger in the young man's eyes. "Are you going to be a problem, Phil? I hope I'm not going to have to look over my shoulder for you, because I'm not prepared to live like that." His eyes flicked over Philip's shoulder and caught Jeremy's.

The major-domo stepped forward a half pace, moving into Philip's peripheral vision. Philip saw the look and the motion behind him, and raised his hands to show he meant no harm. "No, wait a minute. I don't mean that I'd threaten you."

He looked over his shoulder and shuddered when he saw Jeremy's hard eyes. "Call off your dog, Bill. I just want to leave, okay? Let me get out of here, and you'll never hear from me again, I swear it."

The lawyer kept his expression grim. The plan he'd concocted with Jeremy to put a scare into Philip before setting him loose was working well, but he needed to sell the last act. "I want to believe you, Philip. I do. If I ever see you unexpectedly, or think you might have changed your mind about me or anyone else you might blame, Jeremy will come for you. Am I clear?"

He saw a look of terror on Philip's face and knew he had hit the target. "Okay, I get it. I'm not as dumb as you think, Bill. Here, let's shake on it, okay?" He offered his hand and the lawyer waited two beats before taking it and giving it a peremptory shake. "Get out of here, Philip, your car is waiting."

Jeremy escorted a shaken Philip to the waiting car and William saw a few words exchanged before the door was closed, and the car pulled away, taking with it the lawyer's last responsibility.

* * *

Jeremy returned to the lobby but did not disturb William, who was in his own world. He sent a man to collect the lawyer's luggage while he collected the briefcase and laptop. As usual, his timing was perfect as the last limousine appeared through the thin mist and approached the entrance. "This one is for you, sir. Here, slip your coat on, it's cold out there."

William let the major-domo help him put his heavy cashmere coat on and smiled. "I'll take those two bags in the back with me, please Jeremy. I can work on the journey." He saw his instructions carried out immediately as he stepped outside for the first time since the afternoon Philip had attacked him. The cold stung his face, and he drew a sharp breath as the wind blew. He lowered his head to avoid the worst of the icy day and hurried to where Jeremy held the door open. The two men shook hands warmly. "Thank you for everything, Jeremy."

The other man nodded, ushered his charge into the car and closed the door after him. The driver moved away from the curb at a sedate pace and William watched the mansion fade into the winter mist until it seemed like a dream instead of a real place.

The car pulled onto the road and turned south, heading for the city. William eyed his briefcase wearily and decided it could wait a few moments. He closed his eyes to the snow-covered trees as they whisked by outside the window and before he had traveled a mile from the main gate of the mansion, fell fast asleep.

Chapter Forty-Two

Winnie Tremethick was tired but excited as the driver turned at the village Church onto her lane for the last mile of her remarkable journey. Since leaving the mansion, she had thought about nothing but the extraordinary time she had spent in America and about how it would feel to see her farm again. The place hadn't changed much in the long years since her brief romance with the future philanthropist, so it was hardly likely to have changed in the last week.

She felt a thrill when she saw the moss-covered roof of the farmhouse appear in the headlights, and she asked the driver to pull into the yard. She stepped out of the car as soon as it stopped moving, not waiting for the driver to open the door. She took a deep breath of the fresh, damp air, infused with familiar scents of home she loved.

She frowned when she detected the smell of a wood-burning fire and looked more closely at her house. There was a light on in the kitchen, and someone had started a fire in her old range, but no one should be here. The driver stood with her bags as she fumbled in her pocket for her key, and she asked him to stay and see her into the house.

As she approached the door, it swung open, and she saw the silhouette of a tall man framed in the light. Winnie felt the breath leave her body as she watched him step out with his arms open wide. "Welcome home, we've been waiting for you."

She fell into her son's arms and saw a second figure appear over his shoulder, her daughter. The driver placed her bags inside the house and quietly took his leave, seeing the old lady embraced by her son and daughter in his headlights as he drove from the yard.

Winnie looked into her son's eyes with confusion on her face. He gave her the answers she needed as he led her into the warm, welcoming kitchen. "We got a call from

America a few days ago, telling us to get here as soon as possible. The caller was a Mr. Bird, and he said he was a lawyer. He sent a car for me and a fancy private plane for Joy, just to make sure we would be here. I don't know what you've been up to, mother, but he was insistent we be home when you returned."

Winnie quietly blessed the lawyer, now an ocean away. She moved around the small kitchen to hug and kiss her grown children. "Oh I've got so much to tell you, let me get my coat off." They helped her settle, and her daughter delivered her a steaming mug of tea, which she gratefully accepted. "Sit down, both of you. Let me look at you."

They were as bemused by recent events as she had been when she had been summoned to America. "I have to tell you a story, it's about a man I met and loved after your father died." The brother and sister shared a surprised look and leaned forward, each holding one of their mother's hands as she told her tale into the night.

The kitchen light spilled onto the worn cobbles of the farmyard until nearly three in the morning, when the family retired for the night with the surprising knowledge that their rich mother had been the undying love of a distant philanthropist.

The End